"I'm always fascinated when I read a debut novel that captivates me from start to finish. Where a novel is so well-written that I'm in awe of the author's writing as well as their ability to tell an amazing story. There are stories with great writing styles. Those that have amazing plots. Those that sustain your attention with every word. Ones that exceed your expectations of great lines, with a satisfying ending. Mr Dunn accomplished all of these aspects. I can only hope that the right person will come across *The Red Rider* and turn it into a movie that is sure to be a box-office hit."

Kym McNabney, Story Contributor, *Childhood Regained: Stories of Hope for Asian Child Workers* by Jodie Renner and Steve Hooley

"Action filled novel. Journey of a teenage girl. A story of love, courage, friendship and more. The author has got it all in this book."

Jay Deb, author of *The Assassin* and *Contrived*

Keep believing!
Randall Allen Dunn
-RAD-

THE RED RIDER

A PARANORMAL ACTION THRILLER

Little Red Riding Hood isn't little anymore.

RANDALL ALLEN DUNN

Copyright 2013 by Randall Allen Dunn

All rights reserved. Without limiting the rights under copyright reserved above, no part of this publication may be reproduced, stored in or introduced into a retrieval system, or transmitted, in any form, or by any means (electronic, mechanical, photocopying, recording, or otherwise) without the prior written permission of both the copyright owner and the above publisher of this book.

This is a work of fiction. Names, characters, places, brands, media, and incidents are either the product of the author's imagination or are used fictitiously. The author acknowledges the trademarked status and trademark owners of various products referenced in this work of fiction, which have been used without permission. The publication/use of these trademarks is not authorized, associated with, or sponsored by the trademark owners.

This book is licensed for your personal enjoyment only. This book may not be re-sold or given away to other people. If you would like to share this book with another person, please purchase an additional copy for each person you share it with. Thank you for respecting the author's work.

Randall Allen Dunn writes stories of action, adventure, and infinite possibility, as well as instructional books about writing. You can follow him on Facebook, Twitter, Pinterest, Goodreads and YouTube, and follow his Packing Action blog at www.RandallAllenDunn.com.

You can send comments or feedback to Randall@RandallAllenDunn.com

FICTION

High Adventure: The Solomon Ring of Kilimanjaro
The Red Rider
Den

NON-FICTION

Making Fiction Funny! How To Create Story Humor

The
RED RIDER

by

Randall Allen Dunn

MY SCARS

1.

"Hit her again, harder!"

Egged on by his friends, Jacque Denue smiled and rammed his fist into my gut. The jarring pain shook my prone body and made me want to vomit. I held back the bile, since the other four boys had me pinned and I didn't want to swallow it back down my throat. At least the early morning rain muddied the ground enough for me to sink into it, as it ruined my little dress and burlap cloak. When would Papa come back with the wagon?

I was too hoarse to scream any more. I could only raise an arm or a leg as much as they let me, curling into a weak ball to protect myself. The village boys laughed as they took turns trying to punch my stomach, chest, arms, groin and face. My horrible, scarred face that helped them justify their attack.

"You sick, ugly witch!" Jacque spat. "You stay out of *La Rue Sauvage*, you hear? Stay out of our village!"

His palm weaved around my arms and slapped me. Tiny lights swirled about my face as the sting settled into my cheek. I wanted to sleep. To sleep forever and make them go away.

"Monster!" one boy yelled.

"Disgusting hag!" shouted another.

I stopped trying to rise from beneath them. I shut my eyes, accepting blow after blow, my arms and legs burning with bruises. I no longer saw them, but I saw myself and the image they so hated. The eight-year old girl with blonde hair and blue eyes and three thick scars slashed across her face. They ran at a slant, like torn pink ribbons. The top one started above my left eye and ended below my right. The second ran below my left eye and scraped across my distorted nose. The last tore across my left cheek and my mouth, ending beneath the enlarged right portion of my lower lip. No wonder they called me a monster.

My mind pictured something else as they continued to hammer my stomach. I saw the wolf, large and leering and unstoppable, its jaws gaping wide to swallow me. The wolf that stood on its hind legs and loomed over me. The living nightmare that spoke to me through its grinning fangs: *Where are you going, little girl?*

I found my voice and screamed.

"Helena!"

"Run!" the boys shouted. The pain stopped – or at least, stopped mounting - replaced by a scuttling and sloshing of feet through mud and puddles.

"Helena! What have you boys *done?* Come back here, you!"

I kept my eyes closed and lay still, sobbing but relieved. Papa would stop them. He would chase them, punish them, make them apologize. He would catch every last one of them and make them sorry for hitting me.

Strong arms surrounded me. They snatched me up, then slowed to a gentle cradling motion.

"Helena." Papa's voice broke. "Helena."

"Papa," I rasped, too weak to embrace him. I kept my eyes shut against the pain, wincing out tears as he held me. Until I could breathe regularly again. I swiped tears from my eyes. "Did you get them?"

His chest sighed. "They ran away."

"All of them? You didn't catch *any?*" My voice sounded like a frog's croak.

"Helena, I'm taking you to Doctor Renoire." He rushed me to our wagon, which he had parked on the next street. I had wandered off to smell some flowers outside another shop, when the boys started hurling insults and chased me through the alley.

"I want to see Francois," I said.

Papa cradled me closer as he sloshed across the muddy path. My cloak scraped against my bare shoulders where my dress had been torn. "I'm taking you to the doctor."

"Am I dying?"

"No, Helena. You're not dying."

"After we're done ... I want to see him."

"I'll think on it. Lie still."

He laid me down on the hay in the bed of our wagon. I heard Papa's horse, Royale, snort his readiness from the front. Soon we were rolling and jostling along the dusty road, so much smoother than the hills outside our cottage. So smooth ...

And I was so scarred.

2.

I still felt stinging pain in my stomach and my face and between my legs as I lay on the cot in his visiting room. But Doctor Renoire cleaned me with soft cloths and lotion that took away most of the soreness. Soon I was able to sit up and eat some of the crackers he kept in his house.

They had left me alone to rest. I could hear Doctor Renoire out in the parlor talking with my father.

I slid down from the cot, wincing at new pains knifing into my thighs and lower back. My ripped, muddy dress had been thrown away. I now wore a pair of boy's trousers and a shirt, which Doctor Renoire said he borrowed from his son's upstairs wardrobe.

Only one item had been rescued, and lay on the table beside the cot. My burlap cloak. At least the dark bloodstain in the center gave it some color. I pulled it about my shoulders and hobbled to the door, the wooden floor chilling my bare feet. I peered through the crack and listened.

Papa leaned forward in a chair, burying his face in his hands.

Doctor Renoire kept a hand on his shoulder. "Relax, Henri," Doctor Renoire said. "Helena's going to be all right."

Papa sat up and wiped away tears. "This is why. This is why we don't come out any more. Why we can't."

"Because of her face?"

"No. Not exactly. I just don't want her to suffer any more harm."

My cloak scraped my bruised forearm as I pulled it tighter about myself. Doctor Renoire stared at the floorboards. "I understand. When you brought her in last summer ... I had never seen anything like it. At least, not anyone who survived. And certainly no child."

My breath grew quick and shallow. My skin bristled at the memories that still filled my nightmares. The wolf that spoke to me in the forest, that killed my Grand'Mere Marie and tried to kill me. The wolf that was anything but a wolf.

Doctor Renoire knelt before my father. "Perhaps it's distasteful to say, but you really should be so grateful, Henri. Just grateful to have her."

"I know. We are. That's why we can't let her go out. Not until we can know this won't happen again."

My foot shuffled against the floor. They both turned. I opened the door slowly as if I had just arrived.

Papa wiped his face. "Helena. How do you feel?"

"A little better."

"Come here, Helena," Doctor Renoire beckoned, still kneeling. I limped toward him, feeling some of my strength returning. "That's it. Good girl. You're walking fine. You just need to rest up for a few days. Your father agreed to let you skip some chores the next few weeks while you recover. But you should be up and around in no time. Nothing seems to be broken and you're already moving around much better."

They smiled. They seemed to be waiting for me to respond in kind, so I smiled back.

"You know, Helena," Doctor Renoire continued. "I've never seen a girl recover so quickly. You survived last year and again today. You're fortunate to be alive, both times. You're a true miracle."

My smile faded. "I don't feel like a miracle."

I clutched at my sore ribs as we trudged across the cobblestone street to find the village clothier. I was eager to barter for a new dress and return the trousers that felt so strange, clinging to my legs and exposing them in public.

We rarely visited the brick shops and stone houses of *La Rue Sauvage*. It seemed aptly named now: *"Wild Street"*. I had begged Papa to take me with him today, but he wouldn't allow it again. Not after this. Perhaps my parents were right to keep me close to home, never venturing too far outside. Where the wolf might be waiting. "I want to see Francois," I said.

Papa said nothing at first. "You could use some rest. We came to the village. That should be enough excitement for one day, don't you think?"

I heard laughter and flinched. A few men strolled by in front of us, chuckling. Not Jacque Denue or his friends. "I want to see Francois. Please, Papa."

He sighed. "I'll think on it. Let's focus on finding a new dress."

We arrived at the clothier and stepped up onto its stoop. The store sign suddenly flipped over to show it now closed as the front door slammed. Papa held my hand and stood in the empty street, staring at the shop door.

The sign above the door read: *Clothier de Denue*. I never knew Jacque's father sold clothes. He must have heard about what happened. Now he wouldn't speak to us, out of shame. Or fear.

Papa's hand tightened on mine. He clenched his jaw, then turned me away from the closed door. "Come on, Helena."

I glanced back at the shop. An eye peered out from a crack in the window shutter. Then it disappeared. "We're not getting a dress?"

"Your mother can make you a quick one, perhaps by tomorrow. We'll ask Doctor Renoire to let us keep these clothes another week. We're going to see Francois."

My heart soared. "Oh, thank you, Papa!" I nearly threw my arms around him. Then I slowed myself to hug him without upsetting the pain in my ribs. He knew I needed to visit Francois, especially today. Some days, Francois was the only person who could make me feel safe. Especially when I remembered the wolf.

Papa marched to the wagon without a word. He studied the noonday sun. He never let me travel all the way from *La Rue Sauvage* to Francois' cabin this late in the day, for fear of being out after dark. He never felt anything was worth that risk. We had to hurry.

I tightened my burlap cloak against a draft, scraping my bruises. I glanced back at the shop to see the eye staring at me again before it vanished. Jacque Denue's father was smart to stay hidden. Papa was no coward.

But why didn't he even knock on the door when we both knew Monsieur Denue was there? Why didn't he kick the door open and make him give me a new dress for the way his son treated me?

Why wouldn't anyone help me?

3.

As our wagon rolled up the muddy path to his cabin, I spotted Francois chopping wood outside and smiled. I loved watching his strong arms hammer down on a log with his silver ax. He was a burly man with a round belly and a scraggly beard that crinkled up in a grin whenever he saw me. A wave of warm sunshine bathed me from inside. For the first time since I saw him last month, I felt as though nothing could harm me.

Papa tugged Royale to a stop. I wanted to scramble down from the wagon without waiting for permission. But the pain in my side and my legs nearly slowed me to a halt. "Easy, Helena," Papa said.

I hobbled over to Francois as fast as I could, ready for him to scoop me up into his broad arms like always. He thumped his ax into the wood and hurried to me with a fat smile. "Well, well, Helena! What brings you all the way out here?" he boomed. He frowned upon seeing me limp and the pants I now wore. "What happened?"

I started to tell him, but I couldn't. I fell against him and wept, letting my itchy cloak fall to the mud.

He hoisted me into the air, but didn't swing me around in a big circle. Instead, he cradled me like a bear holding his tiny cub. I nuzzled against his warm chest, covered with wood splinters and dust.

He patted my back and hugged me. With his heavy arms, who needed a cloak? "It's all right, Mademoiselle. It's all right."

"Some boys in the village," I blubbered. "They chased me and hit me and wouldn't stop."

"Andre Denue's son and some of his friends," Papa said, striding up from behind. "He wouldn't even open his door to let us buy a new dress. These are from Doctor Renoire's son."

I sniffed and swiped a tear from my cheek, brushing one of my triple scars. "They called me a monster."

Francois' hands clenched against my back, then relaxed. "You're no monster. You just had some bad luck, that's all. Don't pay no attention to those morons. Sounds to me like a bunch of no-good bullies."

"I wish you'd been there. Papa let them get away."

Francois held me a moment longer. Then he gently set me down and knelt before me. His eyes looked worried. "Now listen, Helena. If I'd been there, I couldn't have done anything more than what your father did."

I glanced back to see Papa staring at the ground. I started to tremble. I never meant to dishonor him. I just wanted someone to protect me.

Francois' large finger turned my chin back toward him. "Your father took you straight to the doctor, didn't he? And you're here in one piece. Aren't you? I think he was more concerned about treating your wounds than getting revenge."

My face screwed up with tears again.

I fell against Francois and sobbed. Ashamed of the way I spoke about Papa. Angry at Jacque Denue and his friends for nearly beating me to death. And terrified of facing them – or anyone – again. Afraid of showing my horrid face.

"Helena. Your cloak," Papa said.

I turned. He held the burlap cloak out to me. I took it with a faint smile, then draped it back in place, careful to keep it from scraping my shoulders too much.

Francois patted my back. "Dry your tears now. I'm glad you came today. Been wanting to show you something, next time I saw you. Come on back."

He wiped my eyes with the tail of his thick tunic. I smeared away the rest with the back of my fist. He led me like a lamb, his large hand around my shoulder, toward the rear of his stable. I smiled, eager to see Francois' ebony horse, Lightning, named for the jagged stripe that covered her nose. I always felt better after petting her.

We came around the corner. Lightning lifted her head lazily.

A colt jerked its head from beneath her. It rose to face us, stamping its hooves in protest. Its flanks were red like flame.

I gaped. "What's that?"

"That," he said, "is our new colt."

Its blazing eyes locked on mine.

"She's *red!*" I squealed. My cloak fell off my shoulders again as I hobbled forward.

"Whoa! Stop!" Francois shouted as Papa also yelled behind him.

I limped to the gate as fast as I could. The fiery colt reared back, then ran at me.

"Helena!" Papa cried.

Francois tugged me back as the colt stamped and kicked at the gate. "Easy now, that colt's a wild one. Understand? Don't move too quick around it, you'll pay for it."

I stared into the colt's eyes. It did look dangerous, but that seemed all right somehow. It didn't seem mean, just frightened and ready to fight. The same way I felt, except I didn't have hooves to kick against a gate. "Let me give her some oats."

"Helena ..." Papa started.

"It's still a little fired up, Helena," Francois said. "I don't know."

"I can do it. I'll be careful."

After a silent moment, Papa nodded to Francois. "All right, if you walk up with her."

Francois led me to the feed bag hanging outside the stable. He dug out a handful of oats and emptied some into my hand. "Now you let me go first," he said. We stepped toward the colt, slow and steady. It watched our every move, looking curious, as I hobbled forward with a smile. Francois opened his hand and extended it beneath the colt's mouth. The colt snorted and tossed its head. Then it bent, sniffed, and nibbled like one of Papa's sheep.

"See, she's sweet," I said. I lifted my open palm with my oats, careful not to startle the colt. It stared at me for several seconds.

Then it nibbled from my hand. It tickled. When all the oats were gone, it buried his nose in my hand and nuzzled. I took a step closer, moving slow and gentle. It gave a low snort from somewhere in its belly, as a warning. I smiled and took another small step. It let me edge closer. Then I gently curved my hand around to stroke its jaw, and it relaxed. It took a half-step closer and bent its head to let me pet it. I laid my head against the colt and hugged it with both arms. "She likes me."

"Would you look at that?" Francois said, sounding surprised. "But 'she' is a 'he'."

"How do you know?"

"Just trust me, all right? So. Now you've got him settled, what do you think we should name him?"

My eyes lit up. "Crimson. His whole flank is crimson like fire." It was my favorite word for red.

Papa's face wrinkled at that as he held my burlap cloak he had retrieved once more from the mud. He looked more pained than offended.

"Then 'Crimson' it is," Francois said, petting the colt as he grew calmer. "And you can help me take care of him."

I looked up at him. "I can? You mean it?"

"You come out as often as you like, Helena. When you're older, I'll teach you to ride him."

My heart raced. Women rode in carriages, not on horses, and I had never heard of a girl learning how to ride. I leaned against him and threw my arms around his belly, squeezing him tight. "Thank you. Thank you, Francois."

He turned toward Papa, licking his lips. "If it's all right with your father, that is."

I looked back. "Can I, Papa?"

Papa looked pale. He wrung the burlap cloak in his hands. "We'll see. When you're a little older."

I hobbled to Papa and fell onto him in a tight hug. I limped back to Crimson, who continued to study my awkward movements, and petted him again. He leaned his head down and stared at me as though we could see into one another's souls.

4.

Crimson lifted his head and snorted. I released him as another horse whinnied in the distance. I hobbled toward Papa to peer around the corner of Francois' stable. A beautiful black coach was rolling across the muddy path to the cabin.

Papa's voice rose. "Were you expecting Duke Laurent?"

Francois arrived behind us. "Last person I'd be expecting out here. 'Course, I didn't expect to see you today, either."

Duke Laurent ruled the province, but he and Papa had become good friends. He always gave me the most delicious apples and pears whenever he visited Papa. He made me feel almost as safe as Francois.

As the adorned coach drew closer, I spotted a gray Palomino trotting behind it. I recognized the black cloak and hat of its rider and smiled.

"Or Father Vestille?" Papa asked.

Francois craned his neck forward and gaped. "Next to last person I'd expect. Unless he's short on confessions. I'm sure I could fill his plate, if he's feeling lonely."

Papa lowered his chin. "Show respect, Francois."

Francois raised his hands. "Sorry."

Father Vestille didn't always make me feel safe, but he always smiled and bent down to listen to me after the Sunday mass. When I was little, he let me sit on his lap whenever he came to visit us. Whenever I talked with him, I completely forgot about my scars.

The coach arrived first. I watched closely as the driver stepped down from his perch to open the rear door. I always felt proud knowing Papa was friends with the Duke of *La Rue Sauvage* himself. Duke Laurent jumped down and nodded his thanks to the driver. He gaped at us with wide eyes.

He ran to Papa, ignoring the mud that splattered on the fine wool-lined coat Papa made for him. "Henri, are you both all right? I heard there was some trouble in the village. Doctor Renoire said you had gone home, but we saw the tracks leading here."

Papa shook his hand. "She's all right. Doctor Renoire said she just needs to rest."

Duke Laurent regarded me with pitiful golden-brown eyes, which made him look even more handsome. He knelt before me, kissing both my hands like I was a princess. "Helena. I'm so glad you're all right."

"I'm all right. It still hurts, though."

"I'm sure it does. But you'll get well. Just get some rest, like your father says, and you'll be up and about in no time."

"That's what Doctor Renoire said."

"Monsieur," Papa said. "May I introduce Francois Revelier?"

The Duke stood as Papa and Francois bowed their heads. "The man who saved Helena last year?" He took a step back to view Francois' full height and size. "Such bravery should not go unnoticed. If I were back at the court in Versailles, you would receive a medal for protecting one of our precious citizens. I can't provide that, but I believe a banquet in your honor is long overdue."

My heart leaped as Francois gaped. "Well, uh … thank you. Your Majesty. Er, Your Grace."

The Duke smiled. "You may call me 'Monsieur'. Or 'Leopold', if you prefer."

Francois shook his hand. "Think it'll have to be 'Monsieur'. Wouldn't feel right using the first name of royalty."

"I'm not all that royal anymore," Duke Laurent joked.

"Any news from the King?" Papa asked.

The Duke's face fell. He glanced down at me, then back at Papa, spreading his hands. "He still refuses to answer my letters. I've tried, Henri. I can implore him to send some men, but --."

"I know," Papa said. "You have no authority to force them."

Duke Laurent shrugged and shook his head. "The perils of losing favor with the royal court. I'm fortunate to be given oversight here. I only wish I could provide better security for --." He glanced down at me and stopped himself. "… for our province."

Papa heaved a sigh. "We need soldiers here, Monsieur Laurent. There must be someone we can appeal to. Someone to make the King see reason."

"I'm afraid the only one who can change the mind of the King toward me and our province is the King. I've asked. I've pleaded. I've begged." His eyes burrowed into the ground. "I don't even know whether they open my appeals or if they immediately discard them upon seeing my name."

Papa whirled away with clenched fists. He unclenched them quickly as Father Vestille strode toward us, the sun glinting off of his bald head. "Abier. How are you?" he said, shaking hands. "You know Francois, of course."

Father Vestille nodded to Francois. "Of course."

Francois smiled, with less than his usual warmth. "Well, we're not on a first name basis."

"Perhaps we should be," Father Vestille said. "I haven't even spoken to you since --. Well, since last year." He glanced at me in the same way as Duke Laurent. As if I didn't remember what Francois did for me a year ago. He grinned at me with open arms.

I hugged him tight. "What are you doing here?"

25

"I heard there was a commotion in the village. I came to see you." He lowered his chin, his forehead creasing with worry. "Are you all right?"

I nodded, feeling better. Safer, even.

"I saw you weren't at home, so I followed the tracks here. I told Celeste I would find you both."

"Did you hear what happened?" I asked.

"Doctor Renoire found me. He told me what he knew. I'll have a talk with Andre Denue tomorrow, see if I can find out who the other boys were," he said, more to Papa than to me.

"Are you going to excommunicate him?" I asked, hopeful. "Or Jacque?"

Father Vestille blinked. "I don't think I'll need to do that, Helena. I would rather give them both a chance to make amends."

"But they beat me. And they wouldn't stop. You have to do *something.*"

"I will. I plan to talk to every one of them about what they've done. And help them understand the wrong of it."

I shook my head. "That won't help. You need to punish them, to make sure they can't do it again. You have to hurt them the way they hurt me. You should –!"

"Helena," Papa interrupted with a scowl. "That's enough."

"Yes, leave the punishments to me, Helena," Duke Laurent broke in. "After all, maintaining order is the role of government. Not the church."

Father Vestille looked sideways at the Duke and frowned. "Yes, that is true. Tell me, what *is* being done about these occasional … attacks?"

"All that the King will allow, which isn't much, I'm afraid. As far as France is concerned, we're on our own."

Father Vestille wrinkled his brow. "So the King plans to let *La Rue Sauvage* fend for itself? He refuses to lift a finger to help us?"

"Your words, not mine, Father," Duke Laurent replied.

Father Vestille stepped toward him, looking annoyed. Papa moved between them. I fidgeted, eager to avoid their argument. "I want to see Crimson again," I told Francois.

"Sure thing," Francois boomed. "Right this way. We'll let these gentlemen continue their civil conversation on their own."

He cast an amused glance over his shoulder, and I saw Papa make a sour face at him as we trudged to the rear of the stable.

Crimson stood by the gate and lifted his head as we returned, still focused on me. He looked as if he had been listening to everyone talking beyond the corner of the wall.

I limped back to the feed bag to give him some more oats. "It's all right, Crimson. Just Papa and Duke Laurent and Father Vestille talking. Nothing to be afraid of."

I watched the oats disappear from my hand as he nibbled. My sides still ached, but I felt numb inside. Numb and helpless, with no one to protect me from Jacque Denue and his friends.

Or from anything else.

"Francois? How often do you get scared?"

"I dunno. Now and then. Everybody gets scared sometimes."

I stroked Crimson's flank. "I feel like I'm scared all the time."

He didn't answer right away. "What're you scared of?"

"That the wolf might come back."

He shuffled his feet in the grass. "Hard to come back if he's dead."

I pictured its horrible image again. Its monstrous head. Its jagged ears. Its fanged smile. "I heard there were other attacks. Didn't the wolf kill some other people, too?"

Francois paced to one side, then back toward me. "That was before. Figure it was that same wolf. Sure, there have been other attacks, by wolves or some animal. But not like that wolf. He's dead now."

"Were you scared when you killed him?"

"'Course I was. But sometimes there are things more important than being scared. Things you've got to stand up and fight for."

"Like trying to save Grand'Mere?"

"Yeah. And looking after you. I mean, if I hadn't gone in after that wolf ... well, he would've gotten you, too. Can't let being scared stop you from doing what's right. If everybody stays scared, who's gonna protect us?"

I knew he was right. But the wolf was monstrous. And I was just a girl that older boys beat on. "Francois. Can you teach me to fight?"

His eyes bulged. "Uhhh, now why would you want to be taught that, Helena?"

I cocked my head at him. "You know why. So I can beat up Jacque Denue instead of him beating on me."

He frowned. "I'm not sure that's the answer to your problem, Helena. Certainly not the answer your father would give you."

"That's why I'm asking you. You know how to stand up and fight. You knew how to kill that wolf."

He scratched his beard. "Yeah. Funny thing, that whole business. I didn't actually strike it that hard, you know? I just got lucky. That big old wolf must have been tired or sick or something, because it just died as soon as I struck it. I barely grazed it."

I blinked. "I thought you chopped its head off."

"That was *after* he died. Didn't want to take any chances with a wolf that big. But ... well, anyway. Fighting's not the answer. Not for a young girl like you."

"So I just have to get beat up?"

He pressed his lips tight, then sighed heavily at the ground. He crouched beside me, his voice dropping to a low whisper. "All right, come here. Look. The thing about any fight is, not so much getting in your licks at the other guy, as making sure he doesn't get anything on you."

I squinted. "Huh?"

"I mean, don't tire yourself out. If he swings at you with his right, you step aside and let him miss. When he swings again, you step back or to the side again. Sooner or later, he'll tire himself out trying to hit you."

"And then you flatten him," I said, excited.

He half-smiled. "Well, yeah. But the same thing. Don't tire yourself out. Look, you're a girl. Boys are gonna be stronger than you most of the time, right? So don't just use your fists." He leaned toward the corner of the stable and listened to make sure the others were still talking. Then he leaned closer and spoke even softer. "Grab a stick. Or a brick. Or a rock. Or anything you can use to lay him flat."

My stomach churned at the thought of a brick smashing into Jacque Denue's face. "I don't want to kill him."

"Then don't hit him where you'll kill him. Just hit him hard enough in the knee or the gut that he won't think of bothering you again. All right?"

I nodded, satisfied. "All right."

"And, uh …" He glanced back to the side again. "Don't tell your father we had this talk. Think it's better that way."

I smiled. "Me, too."

He nodded, pressing his hands on his knees to rise. Then he bent back down. "Listen, Helena. If you ever run into trouble – real trouble – and I'm not around, I want you to look up a friend of mine in the village. Name's Gerard Touraine. He'll look after you."

I nodded. "Gerard Touraine. All right."

He glanced back at the corner of the stable. We could still hear Papa talking with the others. "All right, let me show you how to look after yourself." He stood a little, his hands on his knees as he bent over me. He made a fist. "If someone comes at you like this, see, you step sideways out of the way. That's it. Hey, even hobbling around, it's easier to move without a dress, ain't it? Now while he's swinging hard and hitting air, he's off-balance. See that? See how I'm ready to fall forward? So you knuckle both your fists together and swing hard on his back to carry him the rest of the way. He'll plant his face in the mud. Or he'll double over and you can bring your knee up hard to his jaw. Got me? But you gotta know how to keep from getting hit first, so you can use his own strength against him. Then you just knock him over or punch him in his ribs, hard. That'll take the wind out of him. Strike hard and fast. The faster you finish it, the less likely he'll be to mess with you again." He glanced up as Papa returned, and straightened to his full height. "… and *that's why* you should *never* fight with boys. That's what I say. So just stay away from those bullies." He gave a firm nod.

Papa smiled at him. "Duke Laurent and Father Vestille have gone home, now that they've seen you're safe. Don't think they see eye-to-eye on many subjects. Helena, it'll be dark in a few hours. Are you ready to go home?"

I smiled at Francois, feeling a new sense of confidence. "Yes. I'm ready."

Francois Revelier had taught me how to fight.

I had new hope.

5.

It was near dark when we pulled up to our cottage. Only a couple of the sheep lay awake bleating in their pen while the rest of them slept. Papa had driven Royale faster up the path when the sun dipped toward the horizon and the air grew chilly. The mud had dried, making the ride faster if not smoother.

Mama came out onto the front porch to greet us, her hands twisting around a cloth towel as if it needed to be wrung. She looked pale and her eyes were larger than usual. "Henri. You're so late. What on earth happened?"

"Everything's all right, Celeste," he promised. "Had an incident in town. Then we went to see Francois."

She squinted through the darkness to see me. To see my face.

Her eyes bulged. *"Dear –!* Come inside. What happened? Did *something –?* ... Come inside and let me clean you up. Henri, tell me what happened."

I hobbled over the hard ground to Mama. She held me against her as we moved indoors, leading me straight through the front kitchen and off to my room at the back of the house. She helped me lay down on my bed. It felt good to finally rest. Though I dreaded sleep, especially after today.

She unlaced my shoes, caked with dry mud, and pulled them off as Papa came in.

"Some boys in the village beat her. I took her to Doctor Renoire. He loaned us his son's clothes for a while, 'til next time we return to the village."

"Well, she's not going back to that village. You'll go alone next time." Her voice and face grew tight.

"I know. Never should've agreed to take her in the first place."

"Yes, you should," I said. "I can't stay inside forever, Papa. Sooner or later, I've got to stand up."

"Hush now," Mama said, stroking my forehead. "Henri, get a basin of water."

Papa left without a word.

"I have to stand up, Mama," I repeated.

"You need to lie down."

"No. I have to stand up to them. I have to fight."

"Hush. You just need to stay away from those boys."

I stared at her, marveling at her perfect appearance and poise. Her auburn hair up in a beautiful bun with ringlets dangling about her ears. Her homespun dress – she was an amazing seamstress – rising from her shoulders in shapely curves, its intricate pattern decorating her slim arms and wrists. Her face peaceful and soft, even when she flushed with anger. "Mama? Am I a monster?"

Her eyes flared. "What on earth would make you think that?"

"That's what those boys said. That's why they beat me. Because I'm so ugly."

She gaped at me as if I had burned down our cottage. "If *that's* why they beat you, it's those *boys* who are ugly."

A tear slid around my cheek as I admired her features. "I wish I were pretty like you."

She nearly lunged at me, scooping me into her tight embrace. Papa hurried in with the water basin, but when he saw us, he slowed and set it down gently.

"Helena, you *are* pretty. You're a beautiful girl. And you have a beautiful heart. Someday you'll meet a boy who sees that."

Papa glanced sharply at us. Then he focused on soaking a rag in the water. He didn't like for me to talk about boys at all, even with Mama.

"The boys in town think I'm a monster. Except Pierre."

Mama trembled against me. "Well, he's a nice boy, at least. You can just forget about the others. Now let's get you cleaned up."

Papa slid the basin closer and Mama helped me remove the boy's tunic and trousers. She cleaned every bruise and cut, put fresh bandages over a few of them, then dried me off and helped me dress in my nightgown. "Say your prayers," she said.

I knelt carefully beside my bed as they stood watch. My back and side and one knee still ached horribly. I made the sign of the cross over myself and folded my blistered hands. "Dear Lord, please bless and secure our home. Protect us and lead us. Bless our province. Bless Francois and Father Vestille and Duke Laurent, and help the King see that we need help. Heal me and help me sleep through the night. Amen."

I rose slowly, pulled back the covers and climbed into bed. Papa hung his head and tightened his fists. Mama kissed my forehead. "I love you, Helena," she said, her voice strained. "Sweet dreams."

They stepped out and shut the door, encasing me in blackness.

Nightmares, nightmares, nightmares.

I wandered through the meadow outside our home and on through the woods. My little basket swung at my side. I smiled at the red hooded cloak surrounding me, the one Grand'Mere made, warding off the early morning chill. My cheeks were rosy and free of scars.

I listened close, shuddering. Within the whistling wind, I could hear its voice.

Where are you going, little girl?

I started to run. Through the woods, past shrubs and pine trees and scurrying animals. The forest grew denser, until I felt it might close in on me. I scoured every direction for the source of the growling voice but saw nothing.

So nice to see you again, little girl.

My heart pounded. I ran faster. I stumbled, but rose to my feet and raced on. The voice grew louder.

I can see you, Helena. I'm coming after you ...

I emerged from the woods, from the heavy strangle of trees, into the meadow outside Grand'Mere Marie's cottage. I had to warn her. I ran to her door and pounded on it, stealing glances over my shoulder. The woods remained still and quiet, but the voice persisted from somewhere.

Helena. I'm coming for you ...

I heard snoring. I glanced to the neighboring cottage. The window shutter was open. I could see Francois' large frame, asleep on his cot.

Ah, there you are, Helena.

I spun around. The black wolf stood in a stream of fog at the edge of the dark forest. Its blue-gray eyes shone.

I twisted the doorknob and ran inside.

I slammed the door shut with both hands, then swung the bolt down to lock it. I turned to find Grand'Mere.

There on her bed, something shuffled in the sheets. The black wolf was inside, circling among Grand'Mere's nightgown and cap, now soaked in blood.

I gasped and fell against the door. The beast fixed its ghostly eyes on me.

Its voice rasped low and cruel. "Come in, little girl. Come see your Grand'Mere."

The same wolf that padded close to me in the woods, keeping its distance but calling out until I answered. Until I told it I was going to my Grand'Mere's house, and to leave me alone.

Instead, it raced ahead to devour her.

The wolf jumped down from her bloody bed and padded over to me. It stood – *stood* – on its hind legs, grinning. I hurled my basket at its face.

It scraped the beast's nose and bounced off. The wolf raised its eyebrows at me, its blue-gray eyes widening. It raised its paw, extending sharp claws. It swiped at me and I screamed.

Everything turned black. My skin felt clammy, my nightgown drenched with sweat. I sat straight up in bed, feeling the soreness in my back as I stared into the pitch darkness.

I heard banging along the floorboards. Then a faint light peeked beneath my door. Mama came in. Papa followed her, bearing a lantern.

Mama rushed to my side and cradled me. "Helena, you're all right. It's just a bad dream."

I clung to her, feeling numb. I stared at Papa's lantern, the only source of light. "It spoke again."

"Hush, Helena," she said. "It was just a bad dream. Wolves can't speak."

I let her rock me back and forth, back and forth. They never believed me, any more than Father Vestille or Francois did when they brought me to Doctor Renoire. They assumed I was hysterical and babbling in my delirium. They would never believe the wolf spoke. How could they?

I closed my eyes to shut out the nightmare. But my mind saw the wolf's leering grin. Heard its guttural voice. "Where's my cloak?" I asked.

They said nothing.

I opened my eyes.

Papa's posture turned rigid. "It's put away."

"Grand'Mere Marie made it for me. It's mine."

In the pale light of his high lantern, Papa's dark moustache formed a thick frown. "Your burlap cloak will keep you warm enough. And it won't attract attention."

A wolf howled in the distance. My body tensed in a spasm as Mama tightened her hold. Papa rushed to the shuttered window. He stood there, his broad back to me. For a moment, I thought he would throw open the shutter, to see if the wolf was lurking right outside. I expected him to leap through the window in one bound, race into the forest, find the wolf, and strangle it with his bare hands.

He only stood there, listening. The wolf's howls rose, rattling my nerves as though it lived inside me.

Papa stared at the closed shutter. "You can sleep in our bed again tonight," he said.

6.

The sun broke through the clouds and shone down on our lost sheep. It had wandered close to the cliff's edge.

"There she is!" Papa tugged on Royale's reins as he held up a hand to the rest of us. Our border collie, Valiant, barked beneath him.

Pierre pulled his horse, Diamond, to a jarring halt. His arm snaked around my back to keep me from falling off, pressing me closer against him. His father, Monsieur Leóne, followed suit and stopped Ruby, who shifted awkwardly beneath his weight. The four of us paused at the crest of the hilltop, at the edge of the forest. I clung to Pierre's warm back, the best protection against the biting cold. The broad grassland below was bathed in sunshine, lush and green and deadly. We saw where our sheep broke through some taller grass and nibbled its way near the cliff. Beyond its rim, the distant mountains stood guard in a hazy mist. I could barely make out the well-girded wooden bridge that connected them and disappeared in the fog halfway across.

"Careful now," Papa said, his breath a white vapor. "Don't scare it."

He started down first, leading Royale step by step, careful not to stumble. Valiant padded obediently beside him. I peered around Pierre at a huge hole in the ground, like some giant had taken a bite out of the hill. I hoped Papa and Valiant wouldn't fall into it.

I pressed myself closer, giving Pierre a gentle hug. "Thank you," I said.

"No problem, Red," he whispered back.

I smiled. "You know I can't wear my cloak anymore, Pierre." I didn't count the burlap shawl as a cloak, as I pulled it closer about my shoulders.

"Doesn't matter. You'll always be 'Red' to me."

Pierre was the only one who still called me 'Red'. I had worn that scarlet hooded cloak everywhere, even indoors, for two straight years. I swept into every room, beaming as the cape fanned out behind me. Wrapped inside it, I always felt as if nothing could harm me. No degree of cold, no sad news, no fears. I felt the same way whenever Pierre called me 'Red'.

Papa and Valiant drew closer and closer to the sheep. It seemed to take forever. I wanted to jump down from Diamond's back, rush down the hill and scoop it up myself. But, as Papa often reminded me, I needed to learn patience. My foot shook back and forth against Diamond's flank with anticipation. Diamond whinnied, annoyed.

"Helena, stop!" Pierre whispered.

"Sorry."

The sheep jerked its head up at the sound. Papa stopped Royale and waited, neither he or Valiant moving. The sheep finally returned to its grazing. Papa turned slowly to look up the hill at us. I swallowed, feeling my cheeks burn.

He continued down, one hoof at a time, as the sheep nibbled.

I stared again at the giant hole. "What's that?" I whispered.

Pierre leaned back to my ear. "Probably left over from the war, when everyone started invading. People had to find all sorts of places to hide away. This must be one somebody dug out."

I pressed against his back, pulling him tight. "Papa told me we had to hide when I was an infant. I remember looking up and seeing a wide door open above me. There was a big ramp with steps leading out into the sun. I think I was only three years old." Diamond shuffled his feet and whinnied again. Papa turned sharply and looked right at me. I shrank back behind Pierre.

Papa continued down the slope and pulled Royale to a stop, about fifteen feet from the sheep. He clicked his tongue at Valiant, who moved around the sheep, standing between it and the cliff's edge. He barked and the sheep jolted upright, bleating. Valiant barked louder, moving toward it. The sheep shuffled toward Papa, who led Royale behind the sheep to guide it up the hill. We would have no trouble leading it home now. "Come on down," he called to us. "Let's take a rest."

He climbed down and took some jerky from his saddle pouch. We descended slowly with Monsieur Leóne and the horses. "What's that bridge near the mountains?" I asked.

"Leads out of the province," Pierre said. "Across the gorge, then through the mountains. Eventually, if you keep going, you get to the royal palace in Versailles."

"That would be exciting, to see the palace."

Pierre shrugged. "I hear the King's corrupt."

"Who says that?"

"My father. He won't talk to Duke Laurent at all. We get no support from the court. He keeps asking them to send soldiers here, but the King won't even answer his letters."

"I heard Papa talking about that with the Duke a couple of months ago, when he told Francois about the banquet. I wish you could come."

He shrugged again. "Only rich people there, besides you and your parents. Heard they invited a couple of people Francois knows, but it's mostly the Duke's friends. Think he's trying to impress everyone with a show."

"You think so?" I asked, concerned.

"It's what royal people do. They don't necessarily do anything to help, just make it *look* like they're doing something. I think the party's more for the Duke to look good than to honor Francois."

I considered that, then waved it off. "That may be. But the Duke's not like other royal people."

"True," Pierre said. "If everyone at court were like him, we'd probably have those extra soldiers by now."

"Why do we need more soldiers?"

He stopped Diamond and turned in his seat, narrowing his eyes at me. They were brown and beautiful beneath his shaggy dirt-blond hair. He could have told me anything right then and I would have sat on his horse and listened for hours.

"Because of the wolf," he said.

A lump gathered in my throat. Riding with Pierre through the mountains and rolling hills after being penned up at our cottage these last two months, I had forgotten about the wolf today. "Oh," I said.

"You and your Grand'Mere weren't the only one attacked, Red. Other people have been killed over the last few years. But no one's seen this other wolf in time to stop it. We need soldiers to find it and kill it, so it'll be safe again."

Safe again. The idea sounded so strange to me. I couldn't imagine any number of soldiers making me feel safe in *La Rue Sauvage*. "Do you miss your mother?" I asked. I wanted to change the subject. It was easier to talk about Pierre's grief than my own.

He swiped at his thick hair, showing his forehead for an instant. "Sure. 'Course I do." He bit his lip. "But we've been pretty busy. Papa's teaching me all there is to know about smelting and making tools and pots. He tells me I've got the skill for it, as much as he did when he was my age. Thinks I'll make a great blacksmith some day."

Diamond shifted to one side as Pierre maneuvered him past some holes in the side of the grassy hill. I leaned forward and clung tighter to Pierre. "I think so, too."

"Easy there," Monsieur Leóne called to both of us, his belly shifting from side to side as he led Ruby down the foothill. "It's steep. Don't want to tumble off the edge."

"Yes, Papa," Pierre said.

Below him, Papa stood chewing his jerky. "Everyone all right? Frayne, thanks for spotting her." Valiant barked as if in agreement. Papa gave him a biscuit from his pouch.

"Thought it looked like yours," Monsieur Leóne said, struggling to climb down. "Next moment, it was gone. Can't believe it wandered this far so quickly."

Papa squatted and brushed some brambles off the sheep's wool. "Looks like it fell down a hill or two. Good thing it found plenty of grass to nibble on here, before it rolled into the ravine. Sit down. We'll head back in a minute."

We sat in the grass, chewing on jerky and biscuits and enjoying the fresh air and billowing clouds. I spotted a distant path around the left side of the mountain, far ahead. I stood and walked toward it as Valiant scampered after me, yapping.

Papa stood and almost choked on his biscuit. "Helena! Come back from the cliff!"

"I'm not near the edge. Look, there's a road down here." Someone had built a path around the side of the mountain. It sloped down and gradually worked its way back up to join the broad dirt path leading to the bridge and out of the province.

"I said, come back," Papa repeated. He finished chewing and climbed back onto Royale. "We've stayed too long already. Let's head home before it gets dark."

My heart sank. I knelt to scratch Valiant behind the ears. "Papa, it's a beautiful day. Can't we ride a little farther?"

"I let you come along because you wanted to help and you wanted to see Pierre, and I figured it's just as well to know where you are. We've had a nice rest, but it's time to get back home. Come along." He nudged Royale's flanks and started a quick trot up the hill. Monsieur Leóne followed suit with Ruby.

"Sorry, Red," Pierre said.

"It's so pretty here." I stared out at the endless mountain range beyond the bridge, shrouded in fog and mystery. I didn't mind the moist chill on my shoulders, if it meant being free to roam outside, beyond our meadow, even for a little while. I found myself staring through the haze at the bridge leading out of *La Rue Sauvage*. It lay just beyond the wide green plateau that stretched away on both sides and ended in two points, resembling a large sleeping crocodile.

Pierre climbed back onto Diamond and bent to offer his hand. I took it and climbed up behind him. We turned slowly from the inviting scene. Pierre took his time leaving, knowing how much I wanted to stay. He was giving me every second he could.

"Come on, Pierre," Papa called from the crest of the hill. "I thought you said that horse was fast." There was humor in his voice. I couldn't remember the last time he sounded happy.

"The fastest," Pierre called back.

"Well, prove it! We need to get the sheep settled so we can make it to the banquet."

"Hey, look at that," Pierre said, inspired.

"What?"

"There's a hole down on this end, too."

I looked where he was pointing, as Valiant started barking and growling at it. Behind a boulder at our far right, close to the edge, another enormous hole had been dug through the side of the hill, nearly big enough to fit a wagon. "It's a tunnel."

"Yeah. Leading straight up to the top."

I smiled. "You're so smart, Pierre."

"Hang on."

He spurred Diamond toward the hole as Valiant barked and chased after us. Diamond snorted and kicked up dirt as he sprang forward. I clung tighter to Pierre, glancing at Papa and Monsieur Leóne as they gaped. Papa's eyes bulged as they broke into a gallop after us. It must have looked like we were headed over the cliff. Valiant stopped short near the dark passage and fell back, to race up the hill instead.

We curved around the boulder and Papa's frantic image vanished as we descended into the tunnel's black mouth. The swallowing darkness frightened me for a moment, but I felt all right, holding close to Pierre. My eyes adjusted quickly, as light bled in from the other end of the tunnel. Diamond's thundering hooves echoed in the hollow tunnel, which had been perfectly dug and rounded out on both sides. It felt even safer, amid the damp air, knowing this had been built by someone, with several logs buried in the ground to create a stairway.

Something stirred in the dark. Up ahead, a large animal turned its eyes toward us.

Its blue-gray eyes.

The wolf growled from somewhere deep in its belly as we passed, its breath a white shroud.

"Hurry!" I cried.

Pierre leaned forward in the saddle and urged Diamond up the dark slope.

Behind us, the black wolf watched us go. I heard his mouth smacking on something he was eating. Something he must have dragged down here to finish off.

He started after us.

"Go, Pierre! *Faster!"*

Pierre kicked Diamond's flanks and we lunged forward. The large wolf took greater strides. It would lay hold of us in seconds.

"GO!"

Light filled the end of the tunnel as it formed a steeper angle, where extra logs had been laid. I sensed the sun's warmth as we neared the opening. The wolf slowed and skidded to a halt, letting us flee.

We burst out of the upper end, my heart pounding as I gasped for breath.

"Helena!" Papa thundered, his angry voice bringing a strange sense of calm. "What did you think you were doing?" Valiant barked and growled at the hole behind us.

Monsieur León trotted up to us, his eyes wide beneath his wild, unkempt hair. "Do you realize what might have happened? Who knows what might be in there?" I had never seen him so agitated.

Pierre was flustered. "Papa, there was something! There was –!"

"Let's go home!" I interrupted. "We're really sorry, Papa. Monsieur León. We won't do it again. Let's just h-hurry home so we can get to the banquet."

"But –!" Pierre burst.

"Pierre, we made a mistake. We shouldn't have gone in there. Let's just go home, all right? Let's just go home."

He breathed deeply in and out, staring at me in fright.

"Helena. What happened?" Papa asked.

"We ... We almost tripped. On a tree root. Almost fell over. We got scared. That's all. Let's just all go home now and forget about it, all right? Please?"

Pierre looked from me to Papa to his father and back again. He slowed his frantic breathing. Valiant watched the tunnel with a murmuring growl.

"All right," Papa said. "Just don't try anything so foolish again. You might both have been killed."

Pierre looked at me again, then back at the quiet hole. "All right. Let's forget about it. For now."

He led Diamond away. I looked back over my shoulder and squinted.

From deep within the darkness, the blue-gray eyes shone as if studying our every move.

7.

Papa parked our wagon near the front of the tavern. The sign above its hitching post said *La Maison de Touraine*. We sat for a moment as Papa regarded Mama.

She sat rigid, drawing her shawl closer against the evening air, her chin angled up. "I simply can't understand why it had to be here, of all places. I thought we were supposed to be honoring someone. What's honorable about being surrounded by a lot of drinking?"

They had been silent for most of the ride. I thought for a while that Papa was still angry at me for riding through the tunnel with Pierre. Then I remembered how Mama felt about alcohol and the place Duke Laurent chose for the banquet to honor Francois.

Besides, I already promised Papa I would never do it again. I meant it.

I could still see those blue-gray eyes, shining as they watched me. As they chased me and Pierre. Entering that tunnel again would be like jumping into the wolf's mouth.

Two men guffawed, one slapping the other on the back. I flinched. Their boots clomped up onto the porch beside the hitching post and I sighed.

Mama put an arm around me, tugging me close. She frowned at Papa. "Helena doesn't need to be around men like these. Especially after all that's happened."

Papa studied me, weighing his decision. "It's for Francois," he said. "We won't stay long."

Mama gave me another strong squeeze, then waited for Papa to hitch up Royale and help her down. He brought me down next. He never swung me in the air anymore, the way Francois did, though I was light enough and my wounds had all mended. Instead, he set me down like I was a porcelain doll.

Mama put her hand on my shoulder and we went through the large oak double doors.

Inside, men roared with laughter and shouts. Some waved their fists in the air as they spoke. I backed into Mama, then clutched her hand with both of mine. This place looked like it could get out of control in seconds.

Duke Laurent spotted us from across the room. He strode toward us with open arms, which gave me some assurance. No one could harm us with the Duke standing close by. "Henri! Celeste! So good to see you!" He shook Papa's hand and kissed Mama's, then smiled at me. "And how are you today, Helena?"

"A bit nervous," Mama answered for me. "I'm afraid this isn't the most suitable environment for an eight-year old girl."

Papa put a hand on Mama's shoulder, too late to quiet her.

The Duke's face fell. "I am so sorry," he said. "I know Francois frequents this place and I know some men who come here. I thought it would be ideal to recognize his actions. I'm afraid I did not consider what a difficult position it would put you in." He gave a little laugh. "Perhaps that is why the royal family puts so little faith in me."

"It's all right, Your Grace," Papa said. "We're sure you planned this out as best you could."

Mama's face softened as she met my eyes. I held her hand more loosely now, feeling safer with the Duke standing between us and the rest of the crowd. "Yes, we're here for Francois, after all," she said.

The Duke kissed Mama's hand again, bowing lower. "The grace of a Queen. Henri is fortunate to have you, and I'm fortunate to have your forgiveness. Now, please, come in and we'll find Francois. Ah, Simonet! You have not met Henri's family. Madame Basque, may I present my chief advisor, Siegfried Simonet. Monsieur Simonet, this is Henri's wife, Madame Celeste Basque, and their daughter, Helena Basque."

The Duke's advisor loomed over me, tall, thin and frowning, with stringy black hair that rode down his back like the Duke's. He regarded me with lazy eyes and gave a disinterested nod. I resisted the urge to flinch again.

Thankfully, Monsieur Simonet turned from me to shake hands with Papa and nod at Mama. He seemed just as unconcerned with them, and quickly turned to Duke Laurent. "How many more guests do you anticipate?" he asked. "Our guest of honor wants to make certain you are providing enough wine and ale."

The Duke laughed. He turned to spread his arms wide as Francois came thundering toward him. "For our hero, all the wine and ale he wants!"

"That'sss what I like to hearrr!" Francois said, stumbling a little as he approached. 'Most grateful for your hossspitality, Your Highnesss."

I prepared to run toward him, to let him swing me through the air. But Mama's hand pressed on my shoulder and held me back.

Papa stepped forward. "Francois. Good to see you."

"Heyyy," Francois said, blinking at Papa as if he didn't recognize him. "Henri. And Celeste." He turned to me and crouched, pressing his hands over his knees. One fist held a dark half-empty bottle. "And there's little Helena. How'rrre you, little Mademoissselle?"

"Fine," I said. "Are you all right, Francois?"

He waved me off and stood, like an old woman trying to rise from her rocking chair. " 'Courssse. 'Course I am. Just enjoying this wonderful party the Duke's giving me, that's all."

The Duke winked at me. "He's fine, Helena." He smiled at Simonet. "I don't suppose you'll indulge yourself with any wine tonight, Simonet?"

Simonet maintained his frown. "I prefer to keep myself alert."

Duke Laurent leaned toward Papa. "Simonet is extremely self-disciplined. He's the closest thing I have to a priest."

I looked about, hopeful to see our actual priest. "Is Father Vestille here?"

"I invited him," Duke Laurent said. "But he declined."

Francois barked out a laugh. "He's afraid of the beer!"

Papa leaned close to the Duke, as Francois continued his raucous laughter. "He's visiting one of the other provinces. Dijon. There's a large church there –."

"Ah, of course," the Duke said. "Can't expect him to remain satisfied with a tiny province like *La Rue Sauvage* forever. I wish him success."

Papa knit his brow. "He's not seeking a better position. Just visiting."

"Oh, he has friends there?"

"Yes. Well ... friends he's made there. On previous visits."

"Ah. I see," the Duke said, smiling.

I looked from one face to the other, trying to understand. "What are you saying, Monsieur Laurent?"

"Nothing at all, Helena. For any man, even a priest, there comes a time to think about the future. I came here from Versailles myself and I'm quite proud of our accomplishments. But I wouldn't blame anyone for seeking out opportunities in one of the larger provinces. Somewhere more comfortable or safe. A man like Father Vestille could become very influential if he found the right church."

I felt as if he had ripped my heart out and left a gaping hole in my chest. "You think he wants to leave?"

He shrugged. "I couldn't tell you what he's planning. But I find it hard to imagine him remaining content with a small church when he could do so much more, and be well-rewarded for his service."

Mama bowed her head and spoke in the firm voice she usually reserved for scolding me. "We've known Abier Vestille for years. We invited him here from Burgundy, after we settled. He's not an opportunistic man and never has been. He only wants to serve others."

"I certainly understand that," the Duke said. "But … well, it doesn't matter. I'm sure if you know him that well, you know the true purpose of his trip to Dijon."

Papa shifted his foot as Mama fell silent. "He didn't say. Exactly."

The Duke looked from Papa to Mama and back again, still offering a friendly smile. He cleared his throat, sounding uncomfortable. "No matter, Henri. Whatever the reason, I'm certain his trips take precedence. Come. Enjoy the party. We have a wonderful feast." He strode toward a table filled with rich food and we moved to follow him.

My throat felt dry. Father Vestille had always been like part of our family. Before last year, he visited our house every Sunday after mass. We ate lamb or stew and talked about the Scripture lessons and the events in the village and the new dress Mama was making. He sat me on his lap to tell him everything the sheep and Valiant were doing, everything I saw in the field that day, every cloud and flower and insect.

Before last year, that is.

Before the wolf.

"Hey, Helena," Francois said, bending down to take my arm. "Hey, let me introduce you to a friennnd of mine." He waved a heavy hand toward the bar, as though he were trying to fish something out of the air.

Mama started toward me, but Papa held her back with an arm around her shoulder. "She'll be all right. It's their party. We're safe in here, at least." Mama relented and they stepped away with the Duke.

A man wearing an apron stepped out from behind the bar and marched toward us. He had strong arms and a broad, crooked smile beneath a mop of reddish-brown hair.

Francois waved his arm toward the man and thumped him in the chest. "This's my bessst friend in all of France. Gerard Touraine. He owns the place."

"This is the one you told me about, right?" I asked.

Monsieur Touraine put his hands on his knees and bent toward me. "So you're the little girl my overbearing friend here rescued. May I say, Mademoiselle, how pleased I am that he did."

I felt myself blush. "Thank you, Monsieur."

"Like I said. If you ever need anything, if you ever need real help, Gerard's your man. He'll take care of you, whateverrr you need. I promisssse."

Monsieur Touraine slid a sideways glance at Francois, then smiled back at me. "Well, for now, how about this?" He reached into the front pocket of his apron and pulled out a peppermint stick.

"My favorite!" I gasped.

"Is it?" Monsieur Touraine asked, grinning at Francois. "Isn't that a coincidence? I had no idea."

"See what I mean? Anything you need, just come to Gerard. He'll always take care of you."

Monsieur Touraine put a hand on Francois's shoulder. "Such as taking care of seeing you home tonight, friend."

Francois sputtered and waved him off. "The Duke's servants're seeing me home tonight. You hear that? The Duke's!"

"A hero's wages," Monsieur Touraine laughed. He bent toward me and kissed my hand. "Pleasure to meet you, Mademoiselle." He turned and moved back to the bar, where he poured a drink for one of the men sitting there.

"He's nice," I said.

"The nicccest."

"I'm glad everyone knows you're a hero now."

"Awww." Francois blinked, his face turning serious. "You know what a hero is, Helena? A hero doesn't have to be big or strong or sssmart. He just has to stand up to do what's got to be done. People might not understand what you're doin' or why you're doin' it. But it's still got to be done, whether they understand it or not. A hero's somebody who stands up to do it when nobody else will. That'sss all. You gotta stand up and do something, or nobody's ever gonna get helped. All I did was stand up."

I smiled. "Well, you're *my* hero."

He grinned at me. "Yeah? Well, you're *mine!*" He lifted his bottle toward me. "Cheersss, Mademoiselle."

I clinked my peppermint stick against it. "Cheers, Monsieur."

He took a deep swig from his ale while I sucked on my candy.

8.

"That was the best party last night," I beamed, no longer focusing on the needle in my hands. Mama wanted me to practice sewing straight lines on an old patch.

She sat at the table beside me, creating a new dress. "It was interesting," she said, her voice subdued as she stared at the linen and lace spread over her lap.

I glanced at my needle to keep from pricking myself. "I met Monsieur Touraine. He owns the tavern and he's Francois' best friend. He gave me three peppermints. And we ate peanuts and pretzels and ginger beer, and Francois showed me how to blow bubbles in it."

Mama gave a small smile. "I'm glad you enjoyed yourself."

I fixed my attention on the needle and thread. "Once I learn how to sew this patch, I can start sewing dresses. And then you can teach me to use the spinning wheel."

"That's right, dear. But keep working on that patch first. Careful you don't get another snarl."

"I'm gonna be a great seamstress, just like you and Grand'Mere Marie."

Her gaze dropped into her lap. "... She made some beautiful things."

I squinted at the needle and thread. I stopped again. "When I'm older, maybe I can serve at a fancy party. I could make dresses for everyone."

"That would be nice," Mama said. "Or someone might invite you."

I shook my head. "No. But no one needs to invite me. I just want to make something beautiful for someone to wear. Something bright red. If I can't have a pretty face, I can still make pretty dresses like you."

Mama stared at the material in her lap, saying nothing.

I frowned. "Too bad Father Vestille couldn't come."

"Yes. We missed seeing him."

I pretended to study my needle. "Mama? Do you think it's true, what Monsieur Laurent said? That Father Vestille wants to leave?"

Her face screwed up. "Not a word. With all respect, our Duke doesn't know what he's talking about."

"How do you know for sure? What if Father Vestille wants to move somewhere else, like back to Burgundy?"

She put down her sewing. "Father Vestille came here when we learned there had been no priest in *La Rue Sauvage* for eight years. He's been here ever since. He has no intention of leaving."

"But that was before."

Her eyebrows rose. "Before what?"

I stiffened. "Before the wolf."

She leaned forward. "You imagine he's running away?"

I shrugged. "We never see him anymore. He's always traveling, always visiting other people. Ever since last year."

She lowered her chin. "Listen to me, Helena. Your father and I trust Father Vestille with our lives. He would not leave without telling us first, if he ever actually considered leaving. And he won't abandon us."

"But that was before. Maybe he's changed. How can you know? He's not like Francois or Duke Laurent. He's just an ordinary man. Maybe he's worried there's another wolf out there."

Mama sighed. "Helena. Father Vestille has always helped us whenever we needed it. He always will. I don't know what his trips involve. He never wants to discuss it. But I trust him. You don't have to know all of a person's activities to know you can depend on them. And you don't have to be strong or influential to be brave."

I hoped she was right. That Father Vestille would never leave us. But I couldn't stop wondering. "All right. If you're sure."

"There are many things I'm not sure about," she said. "But I'm sure of Father Vestille."

I didn't dare argue with her further.

I heard Papa's boots clomp onto the porch, then stop. We both turned. The front door creaked open, letting in the early morning chill.

Papa entered as though he had seen a ghost.

"Papa, what's wrong?" I asked. We left the banquet early last night and made it home well before nightfall, but Mama and Papa let me sleep as late as I wanted. My head was still filled with memories of the roast duck and caviar and raspberry tarts, and meeting Monsieur Touraine and the Duke's friends. What could possibly spoil Papa's mood after such a thrilling party?

"Celeste. I need … I need to speak with you."

"Papa?"

His eyes warned me to keep still. "Stay inside."

Mama dropped her sewing and swept toward the front door. She hurried outside without a word and Papa shut the door behind her.

I stayed inside as I was told and continued working on the practice patch, determined to sew a straight line. My thread snarled into another knot and I growled. How could I concentrate when Papa was on the front stoop sharing some dreadful secret? But I kept to my place. I tried to loosen the tiny knot and start over with my line. I didn't even creep closer to listen.

Until Mama wailed.

I ran to the door and threw it open. Mama covered her face with both hands, sobbing. Papa held her by the shoulders. She looked as though she might crumple to the ground if he let go.

"What happened? What is it?"

"Back inside!" Papa barked.

I stepped away from his glare of rage. I slammed the door and marched back to the table. I snatched up my patch, with its needle and tangled thread, and slapped it down on the tabletop. Stupid patch! Why couldn't I at least *make* something that wasn't ugly?

They were keeping something from me. Something terrible. Like they kept everything else. I couldn't venture outside. I couldn't be left alone. I couldn't go anywhere, even with them, if it got too late in the day. They meant to keep me cooped up in our cottage forever.

I slumped back into my chair. I was still seething when the door opened, an inch at a time. Papa trudged in with a wary look, like he was afraid of me. Or of something else.

"Helena …"

He moved like a sleepwalker to the chair beside me. Mama followed him like a dutiful soldier, head down. Her face red, her eyes squinting and sore. "Helena," Papa started again. "Something happened to Francois."

"What?" I glanced from one solemn face to the other. "Is Crimson all right?"

Papa seemed to stare through me at someone else or someplace else. "I believe so. But Lightning is gone."

"Gone where?"

Mama turned aside. The candlelight made the tears glint on her cheeks. "Perhaps we should talk about all this another time …"

"No, Celeste. She's going to hear it from someone, over the next few days. It's just as well that she hear it from us."

Mama fixed her gaze on me and stiffened. I felt like as though they were waiting for something to happen to me.

"What's wrong? Tell me."

Papa swiped his large hands over his face. As if trying to wipe something away. "Helena. … Francois is dead. So is his mare."

I stared at Papa, trying to understand. Stared at his mouth that had just spoken those words. Saw him speak them again, in my mind. He said Francois was dead, just like Grand'Mere Marie was dead. Just like Pierre's mother.

Dead.

"…What happened?" My throat felt strangled.

Papa licked his lips. Glanced from side to side. Sat back a little in his chair. "Some wolves attacked him. In his house."

I pictured the blue-gray eyes shining out of the black tunnel. Shining out of the dark forest. Watching me. Waiting. I breathed deeper. Felt my heart beat faster. "How did they steal inside?"

Papa scratched at his beard. "His door ... somehow came off its hinges. And they all went in."

My temples throbbed, my lip quivering. "How many?"

He shook his head. "I don't know. Looked like four of them, at the least."

"How do you know?"

"Henri," Mama interrupted.

"She's going to hear it," he repeated.

Mama bit her lip.

Papa swallowed. He stared straight into my eyes. "What happened to Francois ... was very sad. When they found him, he ... he was not in one piece. They tore him asunder. Lieutenant-General Sharrad figures it took at least four of them to do it."

My insides felt hollow as a log. "And the mare?"

"Henri ..."

Papa's eyes continued to burrow into me. "She was the same. All over the stable. They found the foal tied up in its stall. Seemed to be struggling to get out."

"We've got to go get him!"

Papa paled. "We can't care for an extra horse, Helena. He needs to go someplace where he can –."

"We've got to get him, Papa! We've got to bring him home before the wolves come back!"

Mama took a step forward. "Francois may have relatives nearby, dear. They might want the foal for –."

"Crimson is mine. Francois promised him to me."

Papa's eyebrows knit together. "He didn't so much as promise to –."

"He promised I could ride him. How can I ride him if someone takes him away? How can I take care of him? The wolves came back for Francois. They'll come for Crimson next."

They exchanged puzzled looks. Mama bent over me. "Darling, what do you mean, 'the wolves came back'?"

"Because Francois saved me. Because he killed one of them, and they wanted revenge."

Papa lowered his head and met my eyes. "Helena. Wolves don't take revenge."

My eyes narrowed back. "They're not *wolves.*"

They gaped at me in silence as I remembered the wolf looming over me on its hind legs, grinning with its sharp fangs. Those same eyes would always be there, shining in my memory and my nightmares. Mocking me. Terrifying me. Killing me inside. "Where is my cloak?"

Their eyes bulged.

Mama wrung her hands. "Dear. Why do you ask?"

"I want it. Where is it?"

"It's put away," Papa said, straightening in his chair.

"It's mine. Grand'Mere Marie made it for me. Give it to me."

Mama lowered her chin. "Helena, that is no way to speak to your father."

"Where's my cloak?" I demanded. I no longer cared what they would do to me for being so brash.

Papa's moustache formed a dark frown. "Helena. You're never to wear that cloak again."

I turned from them and marched through the cottage. I knocked over books and cleared away half-sewn dresses from Mama's table.

Papa stood. "Calm yourself this instant, young lady."

I rummaged through baskets and pots and wooden boxes. "Where is it? I want to wear it. It's mine! I want to wear it right now!"

"Helena, stop," Mama begged.

I ran to their room at the rear of the cottage. I opened boxes of their personal items, boxes I was never allowed to touch. "It's my cloak!"

"Stop it, Helena," Papa growled. "Stop now!"

I kept digging, past Mama's leather-bound journal and her flasks of perfume. Past Papa's snuff pouches and spare cartridges and his old crossbow from the war.

"Helena!"

Papa's massive fist closed around my wrist and yanked me away. He held me against his chest as I thrashed about. I didn't care if he dragged me outside and flogged me with a switch for acting like a spoiled infant. What did it matter if he beat me? What did anything matter anymore?

He held me. Held me tight and refused to let me go. I wriggled against him, pounding my small fists on his chest. I shut my eyes, ground my teeth, beat my head against his heart. Then I collapsed onto him and bawled. "I want to wear my cloak," I cried, gushing tears. "I want to wear my red cloak."

Papa's breath rustled in and out of his lungs like a bear, as Mama's gentle hands stroked my hair. "I'll ask about the horse," Papa said at last. "We can build another stall for the stable."

9.

"Ashes to ashes, dust to dust …"

We sat quiet and still in the pew at *la Chapelle de Saint Matthieu*, listening as Father Vestille gave the sermon and then prayed over the body of Francois Revelier. Incense filled the air, within the dim candlelight that cast dismal shadows on the stone walls and stained glass windows.

The casket was closed.

Father Vestille examined it, as if he could see the body beneath the heavy lid. "I did not know Francois Revelier well," he said. "I wish I did. What I do know is that he was a brave man. An honorable man. A man whom others could depend on. As a foreman in his woodcutting business. As a neighbor. And as a friend. Francois Revelier risked his life in an attempt to save his own neighbor, Marie Justine. He heard her cries too late to rescue her, but because of his bravery, his compassion, and his willingness to act, he rescued her granddaughter, Helena Basque, who sits here among us today."

He extended an open hand toward me. Several heads turned. Staring at me and my scars.

"Because of his swift and courageous action, the Basque family – and all of us as well – were spared sorrow upon sorrow. They lost a beloved mother that day, a kind woman I knew back in Burgundy, who moved here to be with her daughter and their family."

Mama withdrew a lace handkerchief, one she had embroidered herself, and wiped at her eyes, sniffing.

"Francois was a good neighbor to her, to the very end," Father Vestille continued. "If he could have given his life for hers, I believe he would have. Because that is what he was willing to do for Helena."

Mama wrapped her arm around me and squeezed me closer.

"It is ironic – and tragic – that he should suffer the same fate as Marie Justine, a year after destroying the wolf that claimed her life." Father Vestille paused, as though thinking of something else. Something important. Then he went on. "We can't fully understand these events, any more than we can understand any such tragedy. But I hope we can all agree on one thing. Whether we knew Francois as a close friend or neighbor, or only heard of his actions in saving young Helena, Francois Revelier was a hero."

I felt hollow inside. Father Vestille was right. Francois was a hero. But he was gone now. And the wolves were still out there. Who else would stand up to them?

The mass ended. Papa and Monsieur Leóne joined four other men to carry the casket outside. They secured thick ropes under it and lowered it down into a dark rectangular pit.

Then they pulled the ropes out and left Francois there in the dirt forever.

"I don't understand," Pierre said, suddenly beside me.

"Don't understand what," I said. My throat felt like sandpaper.

"Those wolves. Four of them, maybe more. Just breaking into Francois' house and attacking him, all at once. Like they meant to do it."

I said nothing. I just stared into the dark hole.

"Red. That animal we saw, in the tunnel near the bridge. You think that might have been one of them?"

"... yes."

"We should have said something. Somebody could've stopped it."

I kept staring into the emptiness. Wondering if Pierre was right. But who could we have told? Who would have stopped that wolf, let alone the others?

"We gotta be careful," Pierre went on. "Things like that running around, attacking out of nowhere. Now I understand why your parents don't go out at night."

"Pierre!"

I glanced to see Monsieur Leóne beckoning Pierre away. He was speaking to a couple of people I didn't recognize.

"I think Papa's gathering some new clients. Probably wants me to talk to them, too, to discuss what we can make for them." He touched my shoulder. "Red. You all right?"

I stood stiff and unmoving. Then I nodded, for Pierre's sake.

"Just take care, all right? Those wolves make me nervous." He hurried away to join his father.

"They're *not wolves,*" I muttered to no one.

At the back of the crowd, I saw Francois' friend, Monsieur Touraine. He stared sadly at the hole where Francois was laid, but his gaze soon turned blank. I wanted to speak to him, but he turned suddenly and disappeared.

"I'll write to the court again," Duke Laurent was saying, as Papa and Mama approached from behind me. "I'll send Simonet there in person if I have to. Maybe the guards will let him through. Or at least recognize the urgency. They have to see we need soldiers and hunters here, to help Lieutenant-General Sharrad's police kill these things."

"I would appreciate that, Monsieur," Papa said, sounding numb. Almost as numb as I felt. "Helena. Are you ready to go? Did you get to speak to Father Vestille?"

I turned about, spotting Father Vestille shaking hands with a couple of guests across the graveyard. "No," I said, my senses burning. "Not yet."

I strode straight past Papa and Mama and Duke Laurent toward Father Vestille, as he smiled and nodded and showed his concern for the couple talking to him. A couple of people I had never seen before. People he must have visited all of last week, when he disappeared on another of his frequent journeys.

Father Vestille lowered his head and spoke quietly with them, a man and a woman in a plain cloak and shawl, which the woman curled about her shoulders as she listened. Seeing me, Father Vestille stopped speaking abruptly. He managed a small smile. "Helena. I want you to meet some friends of mine. This is Monsieur and Madame Serrone, from DeSarte. They came to –."

"Where were you? Where did you go?" I glared up at him, fists clenched. I knew his friends were gaping at me in shock but I didn't bother looking. I couldn't care less about them.

"I was … visiting some friends." Father Vestille tugged at his collar with two fingers, looking uncomfortable. "I went to DeSarte, to visit the Serrones here, and some others at their parish."

"That's why you couldn't come to Francois' party?"

His Adam's apple shifted as he swallowed, like a minstrel performer who had forgotten his next line. Did he assume no one would question him? Where he went, what he did? And why?

"I wanted to come. I simply – There were other matters I had to attend to, Helena. I'm sorry I couldn't be with you."

"That doesn't help anyone now. Does it?"

"Helena!" Papa barked. "Mind how you speak to Father Vestille."

He bent down behind me, his harsh breath on my neck, but I didn't turn. I kept staring into Father Vestille's pleading eyes.

"I'm … sorry, Helena," Father Vestille said. "I would have come if I could."

"But you couldn't," I finished. "Because you had to visit your other friends."

"Helena, that is *enough,*" Papa growled.

As I held Father Vestille's gaze, his lip quivered. I didn't care. He should have been sorry. So should Duke Laurent, for not making the King listen and send soldiers. So should Papa and Monsieur Leóne, for doing so little to stop the wolves themselves, and Mama for pretending everything would be all right. Why wouldn't anyone do something? Francois was the only one willing to act, and now he was gone.

"Helena, we're going home," Papa said.

I didn't turn to him. I just kept staring into Father Vestille's sunken eyes. Then I whirled and marched straight toward our wagon. "We don't have a home."

"Helena!" Papa shouted. His voice broke off as he started to call me again, and I knew Mama's calming hand was on his arm.

I heard her speak gently to Father Vestille. "Please forgive her, Father. She's angry."

I marched to the wagon, ready to knock aside anyone who stood in my way. *Yes,* I thought. *I'm angry.*

10.

Crimson thundered across the grass, kicking up dirt as I pulled back on his reins for an abrupt halt. Over the last year, Crimson and I spent so much time riding about the tiny meadow in front of our cottage, I felt as though we could read each other's minds. I barely needed to pull the reins anymore, in any direction, to tell him what I wanted him to do. "Watch this, Mama!"

Mama sat on the front stoop. She looked up from her sewing.

"Turn!" I called, kicking Crimson's flanks and tugging the reins left. Crimson spun in a dizzying circle. Once, twice, a third time. Then he stomped his front hooves to stop as I pulled back on the reins.

"Be careful, dear," Mama said.

"I'm always careful. Watch this!" I kicked Crimson's sides again and we charged at the sheep pen, stopping right at the edge of the gate. The sheep bleated in terror and nearly fell all over themselves. "Did you see that, Mama? They're hilarious!"

"Helena. Don't scare the sheep."

I frowned. What else was there for me to do? The horses and sheep were all fed and watered. And I had long since given up on learning how to sew. I didn't have Mama's patience and I never would.

"Mama!" I called again as I climbed down from the saddle.

She looked up.

I moved around to Crimson's right side and stuck my left foot in the stirrup. I grabbed the horn of the saddle and shouted, "Hah!" Crimson trotted toward the stoop as I hung alongside him, one foot in the stirrup, the other dangling in the air.

Mama dropped her sewing. "Helena!"

"It's all right, Mama. I've been practicing."

She was still standing with her small fists clenched as we trotted up to her and I jumped down. Her eyes bulged.

"See, Mama? I'm fine."

She said nothing. Just stared at me with empty hands, her breathing shallow against the lace of her dress.

Crimson snorted and turned toward the forest. I glanced back to see Papa approaching on Royale. A thin animal carcass scraped across the grass behind them, tied to the rear of the saddle. "Papa!" I called.

He waved toward us and continued plodding closer. He always seemed to ride home slowly after a hunt.

I turned to Mama. "Can I ride over the hill? Just to the other end of the meadow?"

"You know you can't."

"Papa goes out."

"Papa hunts."

Royale trudged closer. I climbed back onto the saddle and kicked at Crimson to race toward him. "Papa! I learned a new trick today!"

"Helena, wait!" He held up a hand, looking alarmed.

"It's all right, I can do it!" I called as we drew near them. "What did you –?"

The carcass behind them was a black wolf.

Crimson whinnied. I tugged back on his reins and gasped, as his hooves kicked up dirt. Crimson snorted and stomped again. I patted his head and tried to calm him. "Papa! What –? Why did you –?"

"I was chasing a rabbit. So was this thing. I missed the rabbit but shot him." His face turned to stone. "It's meat."

I settled Crimson down with some effort. Then I spurred him to canter forward at an easy pace. We paused behind Royale and I stared at the silent animal. Its claws were open, as if they could still strike. The twisted jaws and fangs looked ready to devour. The open, unseeing eyes stared mindlessly at the sky.

They were not blue-gray.

I steadied my breathing as I examined the wolf. The wolf Papa brought to our home.

"It was all I could find," he said in a softer tone.

I focused on breathing in and out. In and out. "I understand," I said. I turned Crimson away and urged him back to the cottage. Crimson tossed his head once and snorted. He seemed just as agitated, seeing the creature that took his own mother from him last year. Though this animal was different. This was an actual wolf.

Mama gasped as Papa arrived at the front stoop. "Henri! What on earth –?"

"All I could find," he repeated. "Couldn't let good meat go to waste."

The sun had started to sink toward the horizon. It would be dark in another few hours and we would shut ourselves inside. I half-turned. "It's dead?"

"Of course," Papa said. "I shot it."

I looked back at the horizon, feeling chilled, though the sun still shone down on us. "It's all right," I said.

I heard Papa climb down from the saddle. Heard him untie the animal. The animal I didn't want to see, though I already saw it in my every nightmare.

I set my jaw. "Turn," I ordered Crimson, tugging his reins.

We turned about to face it. The long black animal that could no longer harm anyone or anything, because Papa had shot it. It could no longer attack me, except in my dreams. It was dead.

Papa carried it to the carving table next to the sheep pen, as Crimson and I watched. Mama wrung her hands and followed him.

I climbed down from Crimson's back and hitched him up to a pillar, then strode toward them.

Mama stared at the furry beast stretched across the flat surface. I heard Papa mutter, "It was the best I could do, my dear."

"I know," she murmured back. She heaved a slow sigh, then held out her hand.

Papa tugged the cleaver up from the wooden tabletop where he had buried it that morning. He handed it to Mama, then walked back toward the house.

Mama stared at the dead beast another moment before she swung the cleaver down to hack off its head. Blood spurted up and dirtied her lace dress. She didn't bother trying to clean it off.

I followed Papa into the house. He grabbed his pipe from the mantle and lit it, then sat in his rocking chair, puffing away. I stood by him but he would not look at me, as he kept puffing and rocking. Back and forth. Back and forth.

Back and forth.

"Papa, teach me to hunt."

He gagged and coughed a couple of times, his muddy boots stamping the floor as he bent forward. I feared he might choke on his tobacco. "... What did you say?"

"Teach me to hunt," I repeated.

He continued to stare at me. Then he looked away, returning to his rocking and smoking. "You don't need to hunt anything," he said with a dismissive air.

I relaxed my shoulders and stood taller. "You won't always be around. I can't stay indoors forever. Someday I'll have to go out. And I'll have to be prepared, if I ever meet one of them."

He waved me off. "No," he said in a harsher tone, his smoke permeating the room. "You don't need to worry about those wolves. It's not your concern. Duke Laurent will have the King send soldiers to handle them."

I took a step forward. "Papa. No soldiers are coming. We're the only soldiers we have."

He puffed in silence, staring at nothing. He leaned forward and swiped his hand over his forehead. As if he wanted to wipe away everything that had happened. Grand'Mere's death. My scars. Francois' death. All the terror we lived with for the last two years. But nothing could wipe it away and he knew it. I could tell, as he hung his head and shut his eyes.

"I know you want to protect me. But I can't stay here forever. Even if I do, what's to stop them from breaking in the windows, like they did at Francois' house?"

His eyes flashed at me in a sudden rage. As if he had never considered that possibility. Or as if he had considered it for many nights since Francois' death, but knew he could do nothing about it.

"Papa, I need you to really protect me. Protect me by showing me how to protect myself."

He stared at the far wall, as if I was no longer in the room. He puffed at his pipe, the smoke rising in gray wisps. "I'll think on it," he said. "Go settle the horses."

I walked out front, leaving him to smoke, his head in his hands.

I stepped outside and unhitched Crimson. Then I gathered Royale by the reins and led him past Mama to the stable, settling him in his stall and giving him some water. I stepped outside the stable to catch Crimson's eye and whistled for him. He sprang from his place and charged at me in a gallop. He knew how fast to come by how shrill and sharp I whistled. He glanced once at the wolf carcass and snorted at it as he passed, then thundered to a stop beside me. I patted his head and hugged his neck. "Good boy, Crimson. That was fast. Someday you might even beat Diamond."

Crimson tossed his head and snorted again, as if he knew I was daring to compare him with Pierre's horse. I led him back to his stall with my hand on his back, as he shook twice and snorted again.

"I know," I said, petting him. "I know you're angry about the wolf. But it's not the thing that attacked your mother. It's just a wolf, and it's dead. And someday we'll figure out how to get rid of those things, whatever they are. All right? We'll make sure they never hurt anyone again."

I drew his water and petted him some more, wishing I could ease his mind. He remained agitated, glancing back at the stable entrance twice. As if the wolf could rise from Mama's work table and attack us. I kept petting him. "It's all right. You're safe.

You're with me now. And I won't let anything hurt you, ever again."

I continued to smooth his mane and his neck, and he breathed easier. Then he perked up and glanced at the entrance.

Papa stood there, his hands at his sides. The pipe smoldered silently from his hip. His bearded face was in shadow and I couldn't see his features.

"If you wish to hunt, you must do exactly as I say, without question. You will step where I tell you to step. You will keep silent when I tell you to keep silent. You will shoot when I tell you to shoot. Whatever I tell you to do, you cannot hesitate. Understood?"

I shuddered. "Yes, Papa."

He stood there, a husky shadow, as if we stood in someone's tomb. "You'll rise early tomorrow. As soon as you finish your chores, we'll head into the woods."

The woods. Where the black wolf spoke to me. Where it watched and waited for me as I hurried to Grand'Mere's house.

"... yes, Papa."

His shadow nodded, then turned and brought the smoldering pipe back to his bearded lips, and strode back to the house.

I stood there, frozen. I petted Crimson again, my fingers shaking against him. "You see? I told you. There's nothing to worry about at all. We're going to learn how to hunt, and then we won't have to be afraid of anything anymore."

I laid my head against his, wondering how I would make myself sleep tonight. "Everything's going to be all right, Crimson," I said. "Tomorrow morning, we're going back into the woods."

MY RISE

11.

I smiled and patted Crimson's neck as Papa and Royale led us out of the dark forest. The large buck I had shot scraped the ground behind Royale, tied to his saddle. It was my twelfth deer since we started hunting over a year ago. Papa said this one was bigger than any animal he ever killed. He kept glancing back at it and smiling. Before we saddled up to head home, he actually chuckled and clapped me on the back.

Sunlight glinted through the trees, now in full bloom, their leaves still wet with mist and mountain fog. I closed my eyes a moment. I no longer minded feeling the sun on my triple-scarred face. The long days of summer were just a month away, when we could stay outside longer, riding and hunting. I unfastened the side holster of Crimson's saddle, which held Papa's crossbow. He had given me his old weapon from the war to use for hunting, until I was ready to borrow his musket. I never felt the need to switch.

I loaded a bolt and hung the crossbow's front end down over my right shoe. I looped its front strap over my toe and yanked up tight, feeling my firm bicep muscle twitch as I locked the bolt into place.

"What are you doing back there, Helena?" Papa asked without glancing back.

"Keeping myself ready."

I could hear the smile in his voice, as he relaxed in the saddle and took in the view of the fir and pine trees. He had trained me to stay prepared, to watch for signs of danger, to survive against predators in the forest. He hardly asked me questions anymore while we hunted, but whenever he did, I answered correctly. "Ready for what?" he asked.

"Anything."

He chuckled again. "Exactly, sweetheart. Exactly."

I sat taller in the saddle, enjoying the easy ride home, enjoying the gentle breeze on my face and the sounds of the waking forest. When we first started hunting, every rustling leaf or calling bird made me flinch. I tripped over my dress several times trying to cross a stream or climb over large rocks. I lost three slippers in the mud before Papa built me a pair of wooden shoes. I wanted boots like his, but we could hardly afford a second pair, just to train a girl how to hunt.

The first few months, I didn't have the strength to even arm the crossbow, let alone shoot straight. When I did shoot, I was terrified. Afraid of missing and afraid of killing.

"Shove your fear aside," Papa had told me. "Shove it aside and shoot."

I followed all of his instructions, as I had promised. No matter how pointless or exhausting it seemed. No matter how many bruises and cuts and open blistering sores my mother had to clean off of me later. Until I learned to clean them myself.

Over the last fifteen months, I grew stronger, faster and stealthier in the woods. I learned to measure the landscape before entering it, to keep from snapping twigs or slipping on a patch of muddy ground. A few months ago, I finally developed the strength to arm my crossbow from the saddle, something even a boy my age would struggle to do.

I enjoyed my new strength, to help Papa lift a deer carcass from the ground. To chase Valiant through the meadow for several minutes before I started breathing heavily. And to carry two large buckets of water from the nearby well, though Papa still watched me travel the whole distance, resting on the porch with his musket ready.

But he allowed me more and more freedom and asked me to help with more chores. I turned eleven last month, and I had developed strength and skills to rival most boys my age. Strength to survive.

As we broke through the trees to enter our meadow, Valiant barked from his place beside the sheep pen and came running to meet us. Mama watched from the stoop as we approached. She didn't stand like she usually did, but kept sewing.

My kill today would catch her attention. I led Crimson to trot over to her, beaming as Papa and I climbed down and untied the enormous deer. Together, we carried it to the carving table and hoisted it up. The buck's antlers cracked as it struck the oak surface in a heap. Mama's nose wrinkled as if a skunk had sprayed us. "A good hunt?" she asked.

I spread my hands toward the enormous deer and smiled, saying nothing more. Valiant barked, as if voicing his agreement.

"Come inside and wash up," Mama said. "Your father can clean the deer."

"It's a large one," he said. "I would like some help to –."

"I want a few moments to speak with Helena."

Papa gaped. Mama rarely dared to interrupt him. He bent to retrieve the cleaver that the deer had knocked to the ground, wiped it on his tunic, and set to work. They must have agreed beforehand on whatever Mama wished to discuss. I couldn't tell if it might be good or bad news, but I didn't care. I wasn't afraid anymore.

Of anything.

Mama clutched her side and winced as she stepped into the house. I followed her inside and shut the door behind us. I secured it with the heavy oak latch as we always did, even though Papa was still outside with Valiant and the horses. We would let him in later after he knocked and gave us his name.

Mama sat on the cushion of her wooden rocking chair, slower than I ever saw Grand'Mere Marie move. She motioned me to sit beside her with a tired smile. I pulled up a stool from our table.

"What is it, Mama? Is something wrong?"

Her eyes clouded over. "I'm concerned for you, dear. All this hunting. All these visits to the woods. Aren't there any other things you wish to do?"

"I still finish all of my chores. I've helped you more than ever, with the washing and cooking."

"Yes, I know. You're doing more than enough to help." Her hands fidgeted in her lap. "But don't you wish to spend time with other children in the village? Other girls your age?"

I felt an angry pang in my stomach. "So they can stare at my face?"

She swallowed, forcing herself to hold my gaze. "They don't all stare, do they, dear?"

I said nothing, but I felt myself shudder. I no longer felt afraid, even of the boys in the village. But I didn't want to talk about this. I didn't want to think about Jacque Denue and his brainless friends, or anyone else. "I don't know. We hardly visit the village anymore."

She gave a half-nod. "True. Though we've gone more often this year than last year. Now that your father feels you're ... better able to protect yourself." She pursed her lips.

I searched her face. "Mama, what's wrong?"

"I met the Verdantes in town, while we were there last month. Their daughter seems nice. Perhaps you could spend some time with her, now that –."

I laughed out loud. *"Celia Verdante?* That vain, empty-headed –?"

Mama was not laughing. I lowered my gaze and folded my hands. "I mean – I'm not sure what we would have in common."

Mama considered that. "Perhaps you haven't given her a chance. You might have more in common than you think."

"Mama. She's the most beautiful girl in the entire village. Her family's well-off. Every boy in town wants to ogle her. And they want to beat me. What could we possibly have in common?"

Mama wrinkled her brow, looking defeated. "Well ... there must be other girls you could spend time with. Or perhaps boys."

"I just told you, the boys in town want to beat me." I heard my voice rising, felt myself stand to my feet. "But the next time they try it, I'll knock them flat."

She gaped up at me. "Helena. I'm so frightened for your future."

I blew out angry breaths. "Why? What are you so worried about?"

She looked on me with a strange mixture of pity and fear. "I'm worried about what you are becoming."

"I'm becoming strong. I'm becoming brave, and able to handle myself. That's all."

She shook her head. "But that's not all there is. There's more for you, Helena. So much more. We've ... We've had very hard times, I know. I didn't want you to go hunting with your father, but you were so insistent. And I understand. I understand you needed to do this. But there's so much you don't know. About all that you can have and all that you can be. I want you to be happy."

"Then why are you worried about my hunting? I'm happier than I've ever been. I don't have to be scared anymore. I can fight. I can hunt. I can protect myself. That's all that matters."

"There's more to life than protecting yourself, Helena. Life is not a war. There are times of peace and joy and simply enjoying time together."

"Not for me," I shot back. I felt as though my gut would explode with rage.

"Why do you think that? Why do you need to do all this?"

"Because I'm searching for heroes and finding none!" I burst. "No soldiers are coming, Mama. Duke Laurent can't get anyone to listen. The King doesn't care about our little province. It's up to us. To fight, or die."

"Helena, you're not a soldier. You're a young girl. You should be enjoying your life. Attending parties, meeting young men – ."

"I've *met* young men."

"Not everyone is cruel, Helena. You know that. And a girl who can help around the house, who can cook and sew –."

"I *can't* sew!" I stomped to the nearby table, grabbing up the patchwork from my last attempt – the patch with snarls that Mama kept there among her own lace handkerchiefs and exquisite dresses she designed. I shook it at her face. "I've *tried* to sew! *You* can sew. But I'm not *you*. I never *will* be!" I threw the snarled thread and patch at her feet. "I can hunt. I'm good at hunting, like Papa. But I'll never be the person you want me to be. I'll never be pretty like you." Her image started to blur from the tears that welled up. "And no young man will ever be kind to me or come to my home and sit with me, because he would have to look at my ugly *face!*"

Mama stood to her feet, her eyes pleading. I turned away to escape, but she cradled me from behind. The next moment, I was in her lap as she sat back in her cushioned chair and rocked me gently while I sobbed like a child waking from nightmares. I cried and cried while she tugged me close and stroked my hair and pressed her cheek against my head. It was a full minute before I regained control. But she continued to rock me, back and forth, as I sniffed and ground my teeth together behind my misshapen lip.

"Helena, you have to give people a chance. You have to give your life a chance. You're changing now. Becoming a woman. You need to prepare yourself for the life you'll have when you marry."

I felt like I had a gaping wound inside. "I can never marry, Mama. Look at me."

She said nothing at first. She just kept cradling and rocking me, so warm I wanted to crawl inside her embrace and hide there forever. She seemed calmer now. More peaceful. "Someday you'll meet a boy who will see you for who you are," she said, quiet and close to my ear. "We all have scars, Helena. We all have shame. A boy who truly loves you will love you in spite of your scars. And even because of them."

I grunted. "Mama. No one will ever love my scars."

"Yes, they will. Your scars are part of you. They make you who you are. They're not ugly. And neither are you. You were a brave, beautiful girl before, and you still are. You just don't know it yet."

I stared at my mother's embroidered dress, so elegant and fine, as I lay against her. So demure in her cushioned rocking chair. So different from the person I was. From the person I was, in fact, becoming. "Will you always think that? Even if I ... even if I'm not the woman you want me to be?"

"Of course I will," she said immediately, lifting me upright to meet her eyes. "I don't want you to stop hunting. I don't. I only want you to have a life you can enjoy. To have a home and a family of your own. You'll have those things one day, Helena. Trust me."

I wiped my cheeks and puffy eyes. "All right."

She smiled. Then she slumped a little in the chair, as if something had sapped her strength. She took a deep breath and let it out. "Helena. I have something to tell you."

"Yes, Mama?"

She beamed. "I'm going to have a child."

I stared, thinking I misheard her. "You're ... You're having a baby?"

She nodded. I never saw her so happy. Not since I was little, before the wolf attacked. I threw my arms around her and hugged her tight.

She clutched me deep into her bosom. "I want this for you, Helena. I want you to know this joy. Believe me, you'll find a man who sees you for who you are inside, not just ..."

She stopped herself, wisely. With equal wisdom, I made no reply. We broke the embrace and I met her eyes. "I'm so happy for you, Mama."

She still smiled, but some of the sparkle left her eyes. "And are you happy, Helena? To be a big sister?"

Something stirred inside me. As if I was the one giving birth. As if it was my own child. "Yes," I said. "Yes. ... We're going to have a baby."

Mama clutched me to herself again. "You'll make a wonderful sister, Helena. And someday, a wonderful mother. I know it."

I wrapped my arms around her, feeling her heart beat. Wondering if I could sense the baby growing inside her. "Thank you, Mama."

12.

"Can't catch me!" Suzette giggled, dodging this way and that through the meadow. Her wooly blanket trailed behind, clutched in her tiny fist.

"Oh, I'll catch you!" I laughed back, stepping sideways to block her escape.

"Or I will!" Pierre said, rushing to the other side of her.

Suzette squealed as Valiant ran around us all, barking. We pretended my four-year old sister was too fast and agile for two fifteen-year olds to grab. We reached for her, missing each time, which made her laugh harder. "Come here, you!" I demanded in a playful tone.

"No!" she called, her short legs turning awkwardly to hurry away.

Pierre was better at pretending. He kept jumping right next to Suzette, while Valiant ran around his ankles, barking to keep him from harming her. Then he would nearly snatch the back of her cotton dress before his fingers closed on empty air. "Missed *again!* I can't *believe* it!"

"Too bad for you!" Suzette called.

I leaped to block her. She shrieked and turned away as Pierre barred her escape in the other direction. Then I landed behind her and seized the trailing end of her blanket.

"My fuzzy woolie!" She grunted, grinning as she tugged and refused to let go. I dragged her closer, then scooped her up from the ground and whisked her into the air.

"We got her!" Pierre called. He knelt down to pet Valiant, who started to growl at us.

"Got you by your woolie!" I said. I knew she wouldn't release it. Mama made it for her last year and she held tight to it ever since, the way I used to keep my red cloak.

Suzette struggled to pull free. "Lemme go! And gimme my fuzzy woolie or I'll beat your head! Nngh!" Her tiny fingers tried to pry my arm loose. Until I turned her around and held her against my chest. Then she threw her blanket over my shoulder, flung her arms around my neck and held on tight. "Take me for a big ride."

"All right, hang on!" I trotted like a horse, running in small circles around the meadow, while Pierre ruffled Valiant's fur. Suzette giggled as I bounced her up and down. Crimson snorted at us from the sheep pen, where he had been trotting. I trained him to stay close by, even when not hitched up, to show Papa how well we could take care of ourselves. Crimson appreciated the freedom, but now he seemed eager to join us.

"No, no!" Suzette said, laughing. "Take me for a big ride on *Crimson!*"

I whirled her around in the air and plopped her down on her feet. Crimson paced in front of the pen like a guard dog, stealing glances at us. I bent toward Suzette and lowered my voice. "You know we can't ride very long."

"I know, I know," she said with a frown. She rolled her eyes and bobbed her head, making a stern face like Papa's. "'It's almost dark, girls. We don't wanna be caught out after dark.'"

"That's right," I said, stifling a smile. "But we can run twice around the meadow if you want."

She shook her head and leaned toward me with a wicked grin. I bent closer. "Let's go scare all the sheeps," she said.

I glanced sideways at our empty porch. "... I don't know."

"Aw, come *on!* Papa won't hear us. They've been talking in there for *days!*"

"More like an hour."

"Don't know about what?" Pierre asked.

I curled my lip. "Suzette wants to scare the sheep."

Pierre raised an eyebrow. "You told me what he said last time you did that."

"They probably won't even hear us from the house," I suggested.

"Probably not," he agreed. "Mama could probably keep your mother talking all night, if she wanted."

"I like Madame Lisette," Suzette said, curling her arms around her blanket. "She plays with me."

"I like her, too," I said. I cocked my head at Pierre. "You call her 'Mama'?"

He shrugged. "Sure. She's been my stepmother over three years now."

"But you still miss your mother?"

"Yeah. But she's my mother now."

"I suppose."

"Will you guys stop talking about *mothers* and start scaring the *sheeps?*" Suzette demanded, jamming her fists on her hips.

We laughed. "Sorry, Suzette."

"What were we thinking?" Pierre said. He glanced sideways at the porch for any sign of movement. "Just be careful, Red."

"How come you always call Helena 'Red'?" Suzette asked. "Is it 'cause of her scratches on her face? 'Cause that's not nice."

Pierre shuddered. "Uh, no. It's because, uh ..."

I put up a hand. "She's just curious. It's because I used to wear a red cloak all the time, Suzette. When I was around your age."

"But you don't now. So how come he calls you that still?"

I smiled. "Some things just stick with you."

Suzette waved me off. "All right, then. You can be 'Red', fine. Let's just scare the sheeps."

"All right, Silly." I whistled for Crimson. He galloped straight at us.

I peered around Crimson to eye the porch once more. Pierre looked over his shoulder from the grass, as he held Valiant calm and still. I loved it when the Leónes came over to visit. Pierre was good with the animals, and wonderful for Suzette. He always made her smile.

I lifted her up onto Crimson's back and placed her in front of the saddle. She sucked on her blanket and smiled as I hoisted myself up behind her. "All right, hold on tight."

I wrapped my arm around Suzette and her blanket as she coiled her tiny arms around mine. Then I kicked Crimson's flanks and we charged at the sheep pen. Suzette squealed with glee.

The sheep heard us thundering toward them and paused, looking around for the source of the tremors. Spotting us, a few of them panicked and nearly stumbled sideways over one another, while the others kept chewing on their straw.

"Run! Run, sheeps!" Suzette cried. "We're gonna get you, sheeps!"

"HELENA NICOLETTE!"

I pulled back on the reins. Crimson skidded to a halt and I clutched Suzette so tight I feared I might cut off her air. But I leaned forward to keep us planted in the saddle.

Instead of wheezing, Suzette laughed. I sat up and turned toward Papa's booming voice. Pierre made a nervous face, clenching his teeth at me. Papa stood on the porch, his face flushed.

"Yes, Papa?" I asked in a quiet voice.

"What do you think you're doing? You want to give them a heart attack?"

"Papa, the sheeps are so really funny!" Suzette shouted, giggling.

"They won't be so really funny if they're dead."

"But, Papa! You should've seen how the sheeps –!"

I nudged her. "Hush, Suzette. He knows, trust me."

Papa still glowered at us, until even Crimson looked away. "Helena, I suggest you show more care around our flock, if you want to join me on the hunt tomorrow."

"When can I go on a hunt?" Suzette asked. "I wanna go on a hunt tomorrow, too."

Papa blinked. "When you're much older."

"I'm much older now. I'm as old as Helena was when it was the first time *she* hunted."

"I was nine," I told her.

"So? I'm almost nine, too."

I smiled. "Four is not almost nine. Or even close."

She soured and looked away. "Well, it is to *me.*"

"All right, girls, get inside," Papa said, waving us into the house. "It's almost dark. We don't want to be caught out after dark."

I tightened my lips to hold in a laugh.

"Papa!" Suzette called, laughing out loud. "We were just saying –!"

"Hush, Suzette!" I told her. "Let's get Crimson bedded and go inside."

I climbed down from the saddle and lifted Suzette down, then led Crimson to the stable. It was one of the few times I had to take his reins. He didn't like being cooped up in the stable, and I hated leaving him there, out in the open air. At least we had a lock on the door.

Pierre joined us with a guilty smile. "Sorry, Red. I was watching you and Suzette ride and suddenly he was right there." Valiant barked at Pierre's heels, as if supporting his claim.

"He has a way of doing that. It's all right. I'm sure Papa will calm down later."

He entered the dusty stable with us. I stroked Crimson's neck, like always, and tried to calm him. Crimson fidgeted and kept checking Royale's stall, as if to make certain the horse was still there.

"Is he always this agitated at night?" Pierre asked.

I kept stroking Crimson, speaking in soft tones. "I don't think he ever got over being trapped in Francois' stall when the wolves came. He couldn't do anything to stop it. Just had to stay there and watch, while they --." I glanced down at Suzette. "Well, Francois' mare, Lightning, was his mother."

"Helena, how come I can't hunt? I'll be good. I wanna be like you."

"Oh, you do?" Pierre bent down beside her. "You wanna shoot rabbits from fifty feet away like Red?"

I blushed. "Pierre. That was only one time."

He ignored me and dropped to one knee, spreading his hands to make it more dramatic. "Your papa told me about it," he said as Suzette sucked on her blanket. "He and Red – Helena – were out early one morning and they spied this rabbit way up ahead, moving behind an oak tree. They didn't want to move any further or the horses would've scared it off. So they stood there, drawing their weapons. Your papa's musket and Red's crossbow."

"It's actually Papa's crossbow, from the war, actually," Suzette told him. She learned the word "actually" last month and now used it whenever she could.

"Sure, I know. Anyway, they were gonna creep up closer, 'cause they were about fifty feet away, too far to get a good shot. Your Papa moved forward one step, real quiet. But something spooked the rabbit. Maybe he sensed they were there, I don't know. But he took off running and your papa figured they had lost it. But while he was thinking that, Red had her crossbow out and ready in a flash. She fired one shot, straight at the rabbit, and sent it flying into a tree behind it. One shot. Fifty feet away. It was amazing. Your papa came bragging about it the same day at my papa's shop, kept telling it to everybody who would listen. Some folks didn't believe him, but I've heard plenty of other stories about Red's hunting, so I know it's true. She's a better hunter than any of the men in town, but nobody wants to admit it."

"All right, Pierre, that's enough," I said, my cheeks burning. "Don't fill her head with stories."

"Well, it's true."

I sighed, not wanting to discuss the details with both of them together. "It wasn't exactly fifty feet."

"No?"

"No," I said firmly. I turned away, keeping my smile to myself. By Papa's measure from the trees where we stood, it was fifty-eight. Actually.

"Well, it's still an impressive shot, Red. One of many." His eyes lit up and he turned back to Suzette. "Your papa told me about another time when they –!"

"Pierre, no more hunting stories. It's time to settle down for the night."

"I like Pierre's hunting stories!" Suzette complained. "How come I can't go hunt with you and Papa, just one time?"

I stroked Crimson's neck, as his eyes darted back and forth at the stable's confining walls. *Yes, how come?* I wondered. We all needed to be prepared, like Papa said. Prepared for anything. According to Pierre, I could handle myself well enough. But what about Suzette? Who would protect her when the wolves came?

I leaned against Crimson and hugged his neck, my fingers brushing back his mane as he settled. "I'll talk to Papa," I said. "No promises."

Suzette's whole face brightened. "Yay! I'm gonna be like you!"

Pierre stood, looking pleased with himself. I hoisted Suzette into my arms. "Well, I want to be like *you*," I said.

She started one of her silly songs. "I wanna be like you, and you wanna be like me. And we wanna be like Crimson. And Crimson wants to be a tree."

I closed the stall door and locked it. "I doubt Crimson wants to be a tree."

"He has to. 'Cuz that's what rhymes."

"Why don't we let Crimson be whatever he wants."

She ignored me and started up again, scattering straw as she danced in a circle. "And Crimson wants to be a tree. Or a butterfly. Or a frog. And Pierre likes to call you 'Red'. 'Cuz you blush when he's around – !"

"Shush!" I scolded her.

"Well, you do. Go see your face. It's all –."

"Quiet, I said. It's almost time for bed."

"No, it's not, either. I can –!"

"Shush." Suzette grunted and sucked on her blanket. Pierre tightened his lips, looking amused. I forced an awkward smile. "… She's four."

He nodded with a grin.

We stepped outside and heard a horse approaching. In the waning daylight, Father Vestille trotted toward our stoop on his gray Palomino. My gut went hollow.

"Hello, Helena! Pierre! Suzette!"

"Father Vestille!" Suzette squirmed like a fish until I set her down. She ran at Father Vestille, waving her blanket. He climbed down from the saddle and scooped her up.

"Oh, you're so heavy!" he joked. "How much candy have you eaten today?"

She giggled. "I'm not heavy, neither, Father Vestille."

He held her over his head and twirled her about. The same way he did with me, when I was only a child. "I can barely lift you!" he said.

Suzette squealed, Pierre laughed, and Valiant barked. I stood rigid, watching.

"Time to get inside, Suzette," I said at last.

"Awww."

Father Vestille stopped, surprised. He managed a smile and set her down. "Your sister's right. Sorry I'm visiting so late in the day."

"Abier! How are you?" Papa appeared on the porch, with Mama and the Leónes behind him. He marched at Father Vestille and gave him a strong embrace.

"How have you been, Henri?"

They broke apart, looking a bit awkward. "We didn't know when you'd be back," Papa said.

"Neither did I. I wanted to let you know I'll be here this Sunday."

"We still gather." Henri nodded toward the smiling group on the porch. "I've been leading prayers. Last weekend we discussed showing honor to the King, in spite of any rumors and misgivings." He smiled sheepishly. "It was a humbling experience."

Father Vestille laughed and clapped him on the back. "You're a good man, Henri. There's no one else I would rather have leading prayers when I'm away."

"Come inside. Have some wine." They started walking toward the house.

"Only a little. I want to be up early tomorrow, visit some people in the village. I just got back and came here first."

"Why are *we* so special?" I asked.

Papa and Father Vestille stopped where they stood. Everyone gaped at me.

Father Vestille gave me his kindest eyes, the ones I remembered from years ago. "Because there's no one I care more about than you and your family, Helena."

I said nothing. Just stared back at him.

Mama stepped down from the porch and extended a hand toward him. "Come on in. Lisette brought over some fresh bread. She's trying to convince me to start a clothing business together."

Father Vestille smiled. "You should. Between the two of you, you already supply nearly half the dresses of the village."

Mama laughed.

Madame Leóne stuck her hands on her hips with a clever grin. "Well, Father Vestille, most women won't buy *half* a dress."

Everyone laughed, including Pierre, making Valiant bark again. I stiffened and waited for everyone to go inside.

"Madame Lisette!" Suzette called, running to her.

"Madame *Suzette!*" Madame Leóne squatted down. "How may I be of service?"

Madame Leóne was beautiful like Mama, but in a different way. Although several years older, she always looked radiant, her eyes always crinkling at the corners.

"I want you and Mama to make a special hunting dress 'cuz I'm gonna go hunting with Helena!"

Papa glared at me. So much for easing into the conversation. But he didn't scold me. He only wrinkled his brow as he continued past Mama, who gaped at me from the porch.

"Oh, a special hunting dress," Lisette said, playing along. "How about a little more blueberry pie instead?"

"No! I wanna have my special hunting dress!"

"Well, we'll have to see about that with your Mama and Papa, I think. Come on inside."

Yes, we will, I thought as the adults meandered into the house. Pierre lingered outside a moment with me. Madame Leóne gave me a sly wink before ushering Suzette in with a hand at her back. Mama threw a smiling glance at me before following them inside. I shook my head at their overactive imaginations.

Pierre shoved his hands in his trouser pockets. "How come you're mad at Father Vestille?"

I turned and started walking away, past the bleating sheep. "Who said I'm mad?"

"You did, with everything you're doing. Figured you'd start throwing rocks at him next."

I didn't want to talk about it. "We used to be close, when I was little. Then I grew up. That's it."

"Red." He stopped walking and faced me. "You act like he stole your horse. What did he do that's so horrible?"

I stiffened, wanting to turn away but wanting to answer him. I knew I could still talk to Pierre about anything. Even this.

"Nothing," I said in a feeble voice, feeling myself tremble. "He didn't do anything. When the wolf attacked, Francois came and killed it. Father Vestille came and helped get me to Doctor Renoire. After that ... he stopped coming around."

Pierre wrinkled his brow. "He's at your house all the time."

I shook my head. "He used to visit us every Sunday for lunch and stay until dark. Some weeks he visited us a couple more times. Then the wolf killed Grand'Mere Marie and left me like this, and he started disappearing, making long trips to other provinces. Refusing to tell us where he was or what he was doing or why he had to go. He's looking for a better church to lead, in a province that's not plagued by wolves."

Pierre dug his hands in his pockets and resumed our aimless stroll through the meadow. The sun dipped low, and I expected Papa's voice to thunder from the front stoop at any moment. *Don't be caught out after dark, Helena.*

"Doesn't fit," Pierre said. "The way he preaches, the way he helps people. He's been close to your parents since he moved here. Can't see him moving on to another group of people."

I bit my lip. "Shows how wrong you can be about someone. You think he'll be there when you really need him. Then when there's trouble, he's nowhere around."

"Hmm," Pierre said. "Well. Glad you're not mad."

"Look, I just don't –."

"Easy, Red. I'm teasing you. Will I still see you at mass Sunday? I can find you a good spot at the back to throw rocks."

"I'll be there. I can't tell Mama and Papa I refuse to go. But don't expect me to listen to anything he says."

Pierre fell silent. "You still pray?"

"Of course," I said. "Every morning and every night. But I haven't gotten any answers yet."

"You've got Suzette, right? I never thought you'd love anything more than that crazy horse of yours. That's an answer to prayer, isn't it, having a sister?"

I smiled. "Yes. It is. But those things are still out there."

"You mean the wolves?"

"They're not wolves. I heard another lady was attacked a few months ago."

"Yeah, Madame Genault, the miller's wife. We went to the funeral."

"Was Father Vestille there?"

"Uh, no. He was away. Another priest, Monsieur Genault's cousin, came from Dijon to lead the service."

"Hm. Surprising. The one thing Father Vestille rarely misses is a funeral."

"You are *really* angry at him. Don't you think you should give him another chance?"

I considered this for all of two seconds. "He used to be there for our family. Now he's not. And I've moved on. I needed him back then. I don't need him now."

Pierre sighed deeply, dropping the subject. "All right. What're you doing tomorrow?"

"Helena!" We turned toward the sound of Papa's voice, about fifty yards away. I barely noticed how far we had strayed. "Come on back. Pierre's parents are about to head home and you don't want to be caught out after dark. And you and I need to talk to your mother about Suzette joining us early tomorrow."

My pulse raced. "Yes, Papa!" I called back.

He wanted the two of us to talk to Mama, not for them to talk to Suzette. "Sounds like I'm going hunting," I told Pierre.

13.

We slowed to a trot and listened for movements. The forest was cool and quiet, hardly a bird whistling among the pine branches. Papa rode ahead on Royale while Suzette sat in front of me on Crimson, clutching her blanket – her "fuzzy woolie". Still as she was, I kept imagining that her racing heartbeat would frighten off every animal we approached. She practically bounced up and down when we left the cottage this morning. But Papa instructed her – as he had instructed me – to obey his every command and keep silent in the forest.

He put up a hand. I jerked Crimson's reins back for an abrupt stop. Papa rode Royale a few steps closer, one hoof at a time, his hand still raised to us. Suzette's pulse thumped against me through her back but she kept still, sucking on her blanket. She would make an excellent hunter one day. Once she lost her fuzzy woolie.

My eyes narrowed on the area Papa faced. Then I spotted it: a large white-tailed buck, bending to nibble some grass. I might never have noticed it through the dense fog without frightening it away, but Papa had a keen sense for subtle movements.

He raised his musket and took aim between the spread antlers.

The deer's head jerked up as something leaped on top of it.

Something large.

The enormous shadow spread over the deer, making Suzette scream. I clamped my hand over her mouth as the beast stopped and lifted its head.

I gasped.

It was the wolf, black as night. Its blue-gray eyes stabbed into us as its head rose, nearly as tall as the deer's. The buck staggered to its feet and fled, with the monster chasing it.

Papa drove Royale after them.

"Papa, stop!"

I kicked at Crimson. We galloped after them, my crossbow raised. Suzette squealed and gathered her blanket close to her chest. She grasped Crimson's mane as I goaded him faster. The trees blurred past as I fixed my eyes on Papa and Royale. Ahead of them, I caught shadowy glimpses of the escaping wolf.

"Come on, Crimson. Go!"

Suzette screamed. "Stop, Helena! Stop!"

I ignored her and drove Crimson harder. Royale began to pull away. I barely caught sight of the wolf's whipping tail.

As Crimson leaped over a thick tree root, Suzette slid sideways. She hung from the saddle as we sailed through the air. I yanked on the reins and we toppled over. I clutched her to my chest as Crimson fell on my leg like a pile of stones. I screamed. He rose off me instantly, as my heels slid and fell limply from the stirrups. I lay there and cradled Suzette as she squirmed. I bit my lip and waited for feeling to return to my leg.

After a few minutes, I managed to calm her down, assuring her I could still walk. My crossbow lay on the ground near my hand. It had fired its bolt when we fell. There was no time to search for it. "Bring me another bolt," I groaned.

Suzette got up quickly, smearing away tears with her blanket. She ran to the pouch hanging from Crimson's saddle. She returned with a new bolt as I grabbed the crossbow. I sat on the ground and loaded it. Then I put my left foot in the loop and leaned back to pull it taut, thankful to have one strong leg.

I crawled to a nearby tree for support and stood to my feet. I limped to Crimson and he nuzzled me with his neck, as I lifted my long skirt to examine my injury. The purpling bruise on my thigh and knee would spread over the next few days, but it would heal.

A gunshot echoed through the trees. We glanced toward the sound and froze.

I set Suzette in front of the saddle, planted my foot in the stirrup and hoisted myself up, swinging my dead leg over his back. I urged him on, prodding weakly with my left heel. But Crimson understood me and tore after Papa with all speed.

We came to a clearing and found the deer. Or rather, its head, ripped from its neck and lying in a pool of blood. There was no body.

Near the head, Papa's musket lay in the dirt, spattered with blood.

I held Crimson in position as I studied the weapon. Unwilling – unable – to move.

We finally started a slow canter, as I turned Crimson about to shield Suzette from the sight.

"Wait here."

"Helena. Wasn't that Papa's –?"

"Wait here, I said!"

Suzette sniffed. "Don't yell."

I cradled her carefully. "I'm sorry, Suzette. I don't mean to yell. But do as I say. Sit here and keep still."

She sniffed and buried her face in the blanket. "I *hate* this forest."

I hugged her tight, then swung my leg over the saddle and jumped down. The jarring pain rang all the way from my leg to my neck. I limped over to Papa's musket. It was still warm in my hands, and I could smell the gunpowder from its recent shot. He missed shooting whatever attacked him. Or his bullet failed to stop it.

Something rustled through the bushes at my left. I dropped the musket and aimed my crossbow at the approaching footsteps.

Father Vestille strode from the forest on his Palomino, right into my sight. He flinched as his horse started a little. I lowered the crossbow.

"Helena? What –?"

"Papa's missing." My words came out half-choked.

His eyes widened at the bloody musket I had dropped. He scanned the area. "Which way?"

I shook my head. "I don't know. I didn't see. Somewhere back that direction."

His face turned to iron. "Take Suzette home and round up some men. Go."

"I'm coming with you."

"Take your sister *home!*"

I bit my lip. I knew he was right. She had already seen too much. But I couldn't lose the chance to find Papa.

I had to trust Father Vestille to find him.

I hobbled quickly back to Crimson as Father Vestille galloped off. We raced home, faster than ever. It felt like forever.

When we finally reached the cottage, Mama sat waiting on the front stoop, as always. Suzette screamed for her and Mama came running. I left Suzette with her.

Suzette babbled, waving her blanket wildly as Mama hugged her tightly. She turned to me with frantic eyes. "What happened? Where's your father?"

"I don't know. Father Vestille's searching for him. I'm going back."

"Helena, wait!"

I sped away. I had no time to find more men in the village. Who would I find? Who would listen to me, other than the Leónes? Every moment spent asking for help was another moment lost.

We pounded back into the darkness of the forest. A few minutes later, we reached the spot where Father Vestille had met me. I yanked the reins, jarring Crimson to a halt, and listened. Crimson followed my lead and kept still, while my heart beat like a drum.

Something wailed.

We charged off toward it, darting around tree trunks. I ground my teeth, the crossbow in my fist. A dark figure knelt on the ground ahead. Crimson skidded to a halt as I aimed at the man in black.

It was Father Vestille, bent over on the ground. Sobbing as he clutched a scarlet cloth to his chest.

It was Papa's tunic.

Covered in blood.

I smelled the drying puddles of blood scattered throughout the area. I saw pieces of Papa. A scarlet finger. A boot with part of the torn leg still inside. Some piece of indistinguishable flesh lying mangled against a tree trunk.

Bile rose at the back of my throat but I stilled it. Crimson snorted and stamped his feet, sharing my shock and rage.

Father Vestille simply wept, doubled over my father's tunic, rocking back and forth.

I searched in all directions, listening, smelling the air. Nothing but pine and decay from my father's blood.

Father Vestille finally rose, still clutching Papa's shirt. His robe was covered with Papa's blood as he trudged to his horse. He didn't lift his head. "We must tell your mother," he rasped.

I kept scanning the trees, kept listening for movement. My grip ached on the crossbow.

Something started in the bushes. I fired as a reflex and pinned a small rabbit to the dirt. It let out a pitiful squeal as my arrow pierced its belly. I stared at it, then bent to grab another bolt from the pouch, loaded it with my left boot, and waited.

No more sounds. Only the bunny's plaintive cries.

No sounds at all. No more of Papa's booming voice, ordering me inside. No more of his smile or his pride in my latest kill. No more of his horsey-rides with Suzette bouncing on his shoulders. No more of his quiet kisses to Mama when he thought we weren't looking.

The forest was still.

I climbed down and limped to the rabbit, gritting through the pain. I jammed the bolt deeper and worked it back and forth until the rabbit stopped struggling. I picked it up and tied it to the saddle. "Dinner," I said as I hoisted myself up onto Crimson. I kicked at his flanks with my good leg. My other leg remained numb.

I rode back to the clearing with Father Vestille. I pulled Crimson to a halt and climbed down to gather up Papa's musket. I wiped off some of the blood – Papa's blood – on my burlap cloak. I cleaned it slowly, thinking about how well Papa used his gun. How fast he was to fire, how careful he was in the forest.

He must have shot the wolf. But it still killed him. And it still lived, somewhere in the black forest.

I secured the musket to Crimson's saddle beside the hanging rabbit. I climbed back up, allowing no more tears to start, no time to think. Only to act. I turned at a sudden sound and stared at Father Vestille. "Did you hear that?"

Father Vestille looked about. I had jarred him out of his grief. "I ... I don't know. What did you hear?"

I glared at him and wondered if I was going mad. "Perhaps nothing. We should go." I stared at the path leading out of the forest. "Don't want to get caught out after dark."

We turned the horses back to the cottage. But I still felt an unsettling tremor in my shoulders and spine. I could not possibly have heard what I imagined. Still, I glanced over my shoulder again as we rode toward home.

From the dark recesses of the forest, I could have sworn I heard some wild animal laughing.

14.

"Ashes to ashes, dust to dust ..."

We sat quiet and still in the pew at *la Chapelle de Saint Matthieu*, listening as Father Vestille gave the sermon and then prayed over Papa's body. Incense filled the air, within the dim candlelight that cast dismal shadows on the stone walls and stained glass windows.

The casket was closed.

Father Vestille examined it, as though he could see Papa's face beneath the heavy lid. "Henri Basque ... was my dearest friend. He was a kind man who always looked out for others. Always wanted to provide for others. Protect others. Shelter others. Even in his death, he died protecting his daughters from a dangerous animal as he ... as he chased after it."

I sensed people staring at me. I was thankful to have Mama and Suzette beside me, with Pierre and his parents sitting nearby.

"Henri and Celeste invited me here after they came, when they saw there had been no priest for several years. They allowed me to stay with them, until I was able to purchase my own hovel. They supported the new church here, attending regularly and helping draw others in. Henri wanted to provide for people's spiritual needs as well as their material needs. He lived his life providing for others, and he died protecting his daughters."

Mama withdrew one of her embroidered handkerchiefs and dabbed at her bloodshot eyes. She looked too tired to weep anymore.

I felt hollow inside as Father Vestille concluded his sermon.

The mass ended and the casket was carried outside by Monsieur Leóne, Duke Laurent, and four other men. They put thick ropes under the casket and lowered it down into the giant pit. Then they pulled the ropes out and left Papa's body there.

Pierre stood beside me. "Weird."

I said nothing, but waited for him to continue.

"I mean, you're certain your father wouldn't have missed. But if he hit the wolf, why couldn't they find it? It couldn't have gotten far."

I said nothing. I just stared into the dark hole.

He cleared his throat. "Sorry, Red. I shouldn't keep talking about the wolves."

He stepped away to join his parents.

I stood stiff and unmoving, saying nothing at all.

"I'm so sorry, Madame," Duke Laurent was saying to Mama as he led her gently by the hand. "Henri was a good man, one of the best I've known." He had a slight catch in his throat. "If there's anything I can do for your family, please let me know and it will be done."

"That is very kind of you, Monsieur," Mama said, sounding frail and numb. She turned tired eyes on me. "Helena. Are you ready to go home?"

I nodded, wrapped my burlap cloak around my shoulders, and put an arm around Suzette as she clutched her blanket. We returned home in silence.

The cottage seemed empty, even with the Leónes there. Mama sat in her rocking chair, holding Suzette in her lap, while Lisette sat beside her and held her hand. She spoke so softly I could only hear gentle murmurs from their corner of the front room. Suzette lay there, still and unmoving, staring across the room as she held the blanket in her limp hands. Monsieur León busied himself with cleaning, doing all the tasks that Mama was too distracted to do. Pierre sat with me at the sewing table, where Mama's latest projects lay in disarray. We said nothing.

I glanced over my shoulder at Pierre's father, scrubbing pots and pans in the kitchen. Something Papa never would have done. "It's so strange to see a man washing pots," I said in a monotone.

Pierre glanced at him, too. "We do what needs to be done. When Mama died, he had to take over doing a few things. He's used to it."

"Does Lisette clean?"

"Of course. But Papa still helps, now and then." We fell silent again. "He stays pretty busy. Always doing something to fix up the house or meet with clients or tell me what needs to be made."

"Doesn't he still forge his own tools?"

"Some. He does the more complicated projects. All the regular jobs – making fireplace pokers or pots or ammunition and so on – he leaves to me." He smiled, looking a little smug. "It turns out faster that way. I can do a lot of little jobs quick. And he lets me help on some of the more ornate work, sometimes."

I nodded, wishing I could care more. Or even pretend to care. Wishing I could show Pierre some of the kindness and patience he always showed me. Wishing I could care about anything at all.

A knock came on the door. Mama murmured something and Lisette called, "Come in."

Monsieur León moved to the door, a rag in his hand, as Father Vestille stepped inside.

I felt the blood surge to my temples.

"Father Vestille," Mama croaked. "Please. Come in."

"Thank you, Celeste. I can't tell you how sorry I am. What can I do?"

Mama thought for a moment, then shook her head, unable to think of anything. Suzette remained silent in her lap, her lips barely touching the blanket.

Monsieur Leóne offered the rag. "If it's not too irreverent, you can help me in the kitchen."

"Of course," Father Vestille said, taking the rag and rolling up his sleeves. He started after Monsieur Leóne.

"Abier," Mama said.

Father Vestille turned.

"What we spoke about before … still stands." She glanced sideways at Madame Leóne.

Father Vestille looked awkward. "If you're certain, Celeste. Just remember my position. It might be wiser –."

"No. Henri and I talked about it many times. There's no one else."

"All right. In any case, I'll be looking in on you all from time to time."

"Between your visits to other provinces?" I asked.

Mama frowned at me. As if she wanted to scold me but lacked the strength.

Father Vestille swallowed and met my glare. "No. I'll be staying closer to home from now on." He waited another moment, then moved into the kitchen to join Monsieur Leóne.

"Red. He's trying to help," Pierre whispered with irritation.

"We don't need his help. We'll be fine."

The day went on, minute by minute and hour by hour, until all the pots were scrubbed and the cupboards dusted and the sewing put away and Lisette had hugged Mama while she went through half a dozen handkerchiefs. Then everyone went home and the house grew even quieter. Papa would be glad they left before it got dark. Dark and quiet.

"I need to put Suzette to bed," Mama said. "Then you and I can talk."

"I don't want to talk. I'm tired."

She stood, tottering slightly as she struggled to keep Suzette aloft. Suzette turned and laid against Mama and her blanket. "Helena. There's something we need to –."

"I'm going to bed. I'll see you in the morning."

I went into my room, shut the door and latched it. My dark empty room. I lit a candle on my reading table. Then I fell to my knees, laid my forehead on the cot and prayed. I prayed and prayed and shook and cried until I couldn't cry anymore.

15.

I rode alongside Mama's wagon as Royale pulled her and Suzette through the pine forest. The noonday breeze brought a slight chill as the sun hid behind drifting clouds, which threatened to storm later in the day. Birds chirped warnings of the shift in weather, while squirrels and rabbits scattered out of our way. I kept Papa's crossbow ready and watched the forest for signs of trouble. I no longer flinched at the sounds of smaller animals, as I listened for other sudden movements or odd noises.

"How come you don't never come with us, Helena?" Suzette asked from the bumping wagon. She took the blanket from her mouth just long enough to speak. She rarely spoke to me anymore, especially when we traveled through the woods.

I continued to study the surrounding forest. "I need to hunt."

"Haven't you hunted enough?" Mama asked. "You hunt every morning. And whenever we go out for a visit."

My eyes kept searching the trees, the bushes, the dark patches where something might hide. "I need to hunt more, to make sure we have enough."

"We have plenty," Mama said, clearly annoyed. "We don't need any more wild game. We just need you with us."

"I'm with you now."

Mama turned aside in her seat, focusing on the path. "You didn't even come for your birthday."

"Yeah," Suzette said. "Father Vestille made you a cake. I had to eat it all up by myself."

There was no humor in her voice. Even when she tried to tell a joke, there was no joy in it. Not for several months.

"It's just another birthday," I said.

"It's not," Mama burst. "You're sixteen now. In another year, you'll be old enough to marry. Doesn't that mean anything to you?"

"Don't worry, Mama. I'm not planning to marry."

"I do worry. And you should marry. But when you do, I wonder if I'll ever see you again. I hardly see you anymore now."

We emerged from the suffocating forest into the tiny clearing where Father Vestille's hovel sat. "This is as far as I go," I said. "I'll see you both when you're done."

Mama tugged on Royale's reins and he rested there. She heaved a sigh and stared straight ahead as Father Vestille emerged and waved to us from his front door. "Good afternoon," he said. "I trust you all still like ham and potatoes."

"Sounds wonderful, Father," Mama said. "We'll be with you in a moment." She grew solemn again as she turned to me. "I wish you'd join us. When did you last spend an afternoon with Father Vestille?"

I shrugged. "Do I need to?"

"Helena. I want us to be a family again."

"We are a family."

"There are so many things we need to talk about. Life is different now. We know that. But we can still have a wonderful life together, the three of us. And Father Vestille is helping us."

"He might have helped us before."

"Will it hurt you to visit him for one hour? We won't be here long today. He's meeting with the Duke later on and we'll be heading home."

"Is he meeting with the Dukes of other provinces after that?"

"He was away for a while. We don't know why. Can't you forgive him for that? He wants to be part of our lives again."

Suzette took the blanket from her mouth again. "Helena. How come you so mad at me?"

I whirled in alarm. "What?"

"You don't never talk to me or play with me anymore. Is it 'cuz I went on the hunt and made Papa die?"

I coaxed Crimson to sidestep to the wagon, to stand beside them as Mama drew Suzette close. I took her hand. "Suzette, no. I could never be mad at you."

She stared out at nothing. "But I made Papa die."

Mama squeezed her tighter. "No, you didn't, dear. You did nothing wrong."

I glanced over my shoulder, conscious again of the dark forest, then looked back in my sister's sorrowful eyes. "Suzette, Papa died because … something bad out there attacked him."

Suzette nodded, sucking on her blanket. "The wolf. The one that scratched you."

I forced down the rage that rose inside me. I didn't want to frighten either of them any further. Either with the horror of those monsters, or with my plans to tear them limb from limb. "It's not a wolf," I seethed.

Father Vestille still waited outside, watching us with concern. I turned Crimson about. "I'll see you later tonight. Make sure he sees you home safe."

I rode back into the forest to search for game. For signs of the wolves. I had to know what they were, where they came from and how they could be stopped. Before another innocent was killed. Before another woodcutter or another father was taken.

As usual, I found nothing. A few times before, I found a wolf's paw prints – much larger than a normal size. But rain showers always washed away the evidence before I could follow it or show the prints to anyone else, had I ever wished to do so. At first, Mama urged me to take someone with me on my hunts, even if it was only Pierre. But I insisted that Crimson gave me all the protection I needed. Eventually she stopped pressing me about it.

I didn't want anyone else with me. I didn't want to lose anyone else. Not one more person.

16.

I entered *L'atelier de Forgeron de Leóne* – Monsieur Leóne's blacksmith shop – carrying a string of dead birds and a rabbit. I got lucky on my hunt. "Hello, Pierre."

Pierre grinned from beneath his mess of brown hair. "Afternoon, Red. Need that crossbow oiled?"

"Just some new bolts."

He held out his hand for the crossbow. I handed it to him. "I'll oil it for you, anyway. No charge. How many bolts?"

"Two dozen."

His eyebrows rose. "I'm not sure I have that many."

I shrugged. "As many as you have, then. I need to prepare myself better. The more bolts I have on hand, the fewer trips I need to make to your shop."

His face fell. He moved to the rear shelf quietly. "You can come as often as you want. What do you need to be so prepared for?"

I said nothing.

He turned back, concerned. "You still hunting for those wolves? You need to be careful, Red."

"I am. I haven't found anything, anyway. It's like they're holding back for a while, waiting for things to settle down before they strike again."

Pierre laughed. "You think they're planning everything out like soldiers?" He frowned as soon as he saw my expression.

"Maybe. Maybe not," I said. "But if I'm going to kill those things, I need to start thinking like them."

"Just watch yourself. You were lucky to survive the way you did, both times. You might be able to think like a wolf, but you can't fight like one. They've got teeth and claws, and you've got a crossbow that loads one bolt at a time."

I swallowed, having considered the same problem. "That's why I have to be better prepared."

He sighed, sounding annoyed. He turned to dig through the raised bin and produced a pile of iron crossbow bolts. "This is all I have made. Eighteen. I can make the rest for you, if you want to collect them tomorrow."

"Can you have them today?"

"It'll take a couple of hours."

I gathered the bolts from his palm. "All right. This will do for now. I'll be back for the rest later. Will you take these for them?" I held up the fat rabbit and the three fowl I had shot. A small turkey, a pigeon and a hawk.

Pierre took the string of carcasses and whistled. "This is incredible, Red. How did you manage to bag a hawk?"

"I caught a field mouse in the forest with my cloak, then set it loose in an open field. The hawk came after it, right into my view."

"Still. Impressive shot."

"What's all this?" Monsieur Leóne entered and stepped up to the counter from behind Pierre. "Afternoon, Helena."

"Monsieur Leóne."

"Red shot three birds this morning, one of them a *hawk,*" Pierre boasted.

Monsieur Leóne took the string from his son and eyed them. "Look at that. Ought to make for some fine dinner. What do you want for them?"

"As many bolts as you can spare."

"We've eighteen now, I believe. Will you take that?"

"She needs more," Pierre said. "I told her I could make another six today, if that's all right."

Monsieur Leóne nodded decisively. "Done. Anything we can do for this mighty hunter. How are your mother and sister doing?"

"They're well," I said. In truth, I had no idea. Escorting them through the woods to Father Vestille's hovel today was the longest I had seen them in weeks. I rose early each morning to hunt, brought food to Mama at the break of dawn, then mended fences and washed clothes and groomed the horses or whatever else I found to do until nightfall. My family was provided for, so they were well, as far as I knew. I didn't want to know anything more. I didn't want to be drawn into further conversations about Papa or Father Vestille or the wolves.

Monsieur Leóne squinted at me. "Let us know if you need anything else. Though if you keep bringing spoils such as these, you should want for nothing."

"She's hoping to bag a wolf next," Pierre said.

Monsieur Leóne paled. "... what do you mean by that?"

Pierre and I stiffened. We stared at Monsieur Leóne, whose expression hardened. "You're hunting the wolves? The ones that attacked your father?"

I stared up at him, unable to speak.

"Stay away from them, do you understand? Just stay away. Isn't it enough they killed your Grand'Mere and Francois and your father? You want them to kill you, too?"

The room felt cold as his eyes cut into me.

He glanced away, his face reddening. The gentility finally returned to his face, though he still seemed troubled. "I'm sorry. I don't mean to be harsh. Your father was a good man. A good friend. I don't want to see anything happen to you. Just keep away from those things. Care for your mother and your sister and keep them safe. That's the best way to honor your father."

Pierre and I held our place, saying nothing. Monsieur Leóne lifted the string of dead animals. "I'll set to cleaning these. Pierre can make record of the transaction, to finish up later when the other bolts are ready. You take care, Helena. Take care."

Monsieur Leóne retreated through the linen curtain to the back room. Pierre and I stared at one another.

"What was all that about?" I asked.

Pierre shook his head. "I don't know. He doesn't like talking about the wolves. Any time we mention them at dinner, he says it's not our business. He figures we should focus on our chores for home and the shop, instead of bothering with things out there that don't affect us. He says it's foolish to go looking for trouble because it only brings trouble to our doorstep." He gave me a sheepish glance. "Sorry, Red."

I twisted my lip, ignoring it. "I've been called worse things than 'foolish'."

"I could help you on one of your hunts some morning. Just let me know where you'll be and I'll find you."

I gave a weak smile. "I never know where I'll be next. I find different parts of the forest to start in, to vary my routine."

"Well, where do you expect to start tomorrow?"

I had an idea, but I didn't want to tell him. I knew he would meet me if I let him. "Pierre, you're a good friend. And a nice boy. Why would you want to hunt with me when there are plenty of pretty girls in the village to spend your day with?"

He shrugged. "No girl's prettier than you."

I squinted at him. "I know I'm ugly, Pierre. You don't need to pretend."

He narrowed his eyes back at me and smiled, as if I told a joke. "You're beautiful, Red."

He seemed so sure, so intense, he almost made me believe it. "I'm scarred."

He shook his head, still grinning, and turned to the metal figurines on his own small shelf, above the rows of pots and iron tools. "See this statue?" He brought down a silver statuette of a woman holding a bow and arrow. "This is Diana, Goddess of the Hunt. It's my favorite, of all the ones I've made. Her head is dented in a little. I couldn't form it quite right. But it's unique, nothing like the others I've made. It stands out."

He handed it to me. I turned it over, admiring the delicate curves of the face and body, the sweep of the tunic's folds, the sharp points of the arrow and the shafts inside the quiver. As well as the marred feature Pierre mentioned – an obvious dent on the left side of the head. The one imperfection that made it clear this was a statuette and not a human person made of silver. It marked Pierre as an amateur, while the rest of the figure could have been sculpted by Michelangelo.

I saw what he meant. The obvious flaw only drew attention to the immaculate beauty of the rest of the piece, and made any criticism of the flaw seem petty and foolish. In a sense, the imperfection made its sculptor seem more human. Made even the invincible goddess Diana more human, more fallible. More like one of us. And yes, more attractive.

"See, some scars make us more beautiful."

He stood before me and reached for my face. His fingers ready to gently brush my ravaged cheek. I seized his wrist in a panic. He held it there, waiting for me to let him continue.

My anger cooled, and I released him. He reached for me. His calloused fingers traced each of my scars, as gently as if he were stroking my hair. From the top of my forehead, then over the one that crossed my nose, and finally the lower one that stretched across my left cheek to below my lower lip. I trembled, enjoying his touch but feeling awkward. I didn't know whether I feared he would touch me more or that he would suddenly pull back in revulsion.

He held my gaze. "You're the most beautiful girl I've ever met."

I gathered in my breath. "You're a good friend, Pierre. You have always been." I set the figurine back on his shelf, gathered my belongings and moved to the door. "But you deserve far better than me. I'll return later for the other bolts."

"… I'll have them ready," he said.

I didn't look back but I saw his pained reflection against one of the metal pans hanging by the door. I hung my head as I stepped outside. I hated to hurt him. But as much as I wanted to embrace the idea, I knew we could never be together. He would outgrow his interest in me once he realized how attractive he would be to the other girls in the village.

Still, I felt my cheek, where Pierre had touched me – touched my scars – and I couldn't help smiling.

"The beast has returned!"

I looked up to see Jacque Denue and his four buddies standing between me and Crimson.

"Told you this was her horse," Denue said. He jutted his chin at me. "We told you not to come here anymore, you ugly witch. You deaf or just stupid?"

"I'll leave the stupidity to you, Jacque. Step away from my horse."

"What did you say, you hag? Come here and I'll beat some sense into you."

"Leave me alone. For your own well-being."

Denue snorted at a fat boy with food stains on his shirt. "Grab her, Port. I'm gonna give this witch a spanking."

The slob snatched at my arm. I dodged him easily and spun toward him, to hammer my locked fists into his face. He went down hard, but the folds of my skirt bunched around my legs. As I stepped to one side to move more freely, a taller boy seized my wrist like a vise and jerked me toward Denue.

Denue snarled at me. His breath smelled of chewing tobacco. "I dunno how you did that, freak, but you'll be sorry you did."

I tried to yank myself free but I was off-balance and my dress remained twisted.

"I'm gonna beat you so bad you'll never show your face outside again!"

He raised his fist. Then something knocked his friend into him and Jacque grunted as they both sailed to the ground. I tugged myself free of Muscles and stepped aside.

Crimson snorted down at the freckle-faced boy, who massaged his side as he lay sprawled on top of Denue. I felt a wave of relief as Crimson tried to kick at the rest of them. But they backed away from the post where I tied him. I couldn't get past them to set him loose.

Then Slob picked up a rock and hurled it past my head.

"Grab her!" Denue growled.

Muscles lunged for me. I dodged, still struggling in my long dress. The others bent to pick up rocks, standing between me and Pierre's door. If I called for help, they would only attack Pierre, too.

I hiked up my skirt and sprinted away. I could outrun them, but I had no place to escape between the closely-packed shops and houses. I hurried down an alley, their feet pounding after me. I crossed the next street and nearly fell beneath the wheels of an approaching carriage. The driver spotted me and jerked on the reins. Behind me, Denue and the others were closing in. I stood and ran to knock on the carriage door, seeing a young family inside. The woman saw my face and screamed.

"Please! Help me!"

The man blinked and gaped as the woman pulled a small boy close. I turned to glimpse Jacque Denue and his buddies rushing toward me. I ran past the coach and down the next alley. A rock sailed past me, missing my head and striking a wine barrel.

"Hey, now, stop that, you boys!" the driver called from behind. But he remained in his high seat as the boys' feet skittered across the cobbled path.

I hurried down the next busy street. "Help! Help me, they're chasing me!"

Everyone backed away, startled by my manner. Startled by my appearance. Men, women, children, all dressed well, all strong and healthy, stepped clear of me. Clearing a path for me to run and for the boys to chase after me as they shouted their threats.

"We're coming for you, Scars!" Jacque sang.

"We're gonna kill you!" one of his friends shouted.

I ducked into another alley and glanced over my shoulder. The boys grinned like demons, sprinting after me with rocks in their fists.

Ahead of me, the alley was bricked in.

I gasped and turned, searching for a way out. I grabbed onto an upper ledge and tried to scale the wall. But my skirt made it impossible.

"Trapped like a rat," Denue said.

His gang filled the mouth of the alley.

"More like a scar-faced pig, I'd say," Slob chimed in.

Denue tossed a rock up and down in his palm. "Keep your ugly face out of our village, Scars. This'll help you remember."

He hurled it at me. I ducked and it struck the brick wall. Muscles threw another one. I dodged and jumped behind a wine barrel. I sat with my back to it, like a child hiding in a cellar.

"Come on out, Scars," Denue demanded. "Come get your punishment."

Their footsteps strolled closer, taking their time. They threw another rock at the wall to frighten me. Which meant they gathered enough of them to waste a few.

My breath came in rapid gasps. I suddenly remembered the black wolf looming over me, mocking me. Knowing I could do nothing to stop it.

Until Francois charged in with his ax and struck it dead.

Shove your fear aside, Papa's voice reminded me, the day I made my first kill. *Shove it aside and shoot.* I tried not to imagine the boys' rocks striking my gut. My head. My face.

I remembered the voice of my other hero, Francois Revelier. *You gotta stand up and do something, or nobody's ever gonna get helped.*

Stand up and do something.

I looked around the empty alley, at the shrapnel of rocks and bricks scattered nearby. A broken wood plank lay among them. I seized it with both fists.

I rose.

The boys stared with surprise and delight. Denue hurled his rock at my eyes. I slapped it away with the plank and marched at them. Marched at Denue. The others fell silent and stopped. Muscles threw another stone. I smacked it against the wall and it shattered in half. Freckles hurled another one. I slammed it to the ground.

"Throw it!" Denue ordered the others. "Gimme the rock, then!"

Slob surrendered his stone to Denue as I closed in. He tried to throw it but I smacked his wrist with the plank. He yelped as I jammed the end of the board into his chest and drove him back out of the alley with his friends.

We emerged on the open street and I whacked him across the shoulder. He fell to the ground and rolled onto his back. I dropped to my knees in front of him, releasing the plank. The others gaped as I pummeled Denue with my fists. I continued with single-handed blows, one after the other. Until he lay on the ground, bloody and crying.

I stopped. He cringed and whimpered beneath me, his open palms shielding his face. I could have beaten him into a helpless mass, the way he beat me two years ago. But what would be the point?

I stood to my feet. "You're not the one I want. Just keep out of my way."

I stepped over him and walked back toward Monsieur Leóne's shop.

Denue called after me, half-threatening, half-sobbing. "You freak! You'll regret this, you scar-faced witch! You'll regret this!"

I ignored him. He was flesh and blood, like me. Beneath his savage surface, he was as frightened as the rest of us.

I wanted the wolves.

I returned to *L'atelier de Forgeron de Leóne* and the post where I left Crimson. He snorted and stamped his feet until I released him and stroked his neck. The fire in his eye matched my own. If he had been free to fight, those boys could never have chased me.

"I don't think I'll tie you up again, friend."

Crimson snorted. I think he understood.

17.

Something disturbed my senses as I rode through the woods near our cottage. Something in the air.

It was only when we emerged from the forest and I saw all the sheep lying on their sides that I understood. A breeze from our meadow carried the stench of drying blood.

I kicked Crimson and he charged toward the house. The front door was open. The sheep pen was silent, a few of them missing. The remaining sheep lay in puddles of blood. Valiant lay beside them in his own scarlet stream.

My crossbow was already out and loaded for our trip through the woods. I held it high as I leaped down from Crimson. In my hurry, my foot caught in the stirrup and I stumbled to the ground beside the carving table. I scrambled to my feet and ran inside.

Pots and pans, clothing and half-cooked food, were strewn everywhere and spattered with blood. Mama's rocking chair lay in splintered fragments on the floor to my left. I smelled Mama's stew bubbling in its pot on the cast-iron stove. I let it boil. Wind whistled through the house from the open rear door. Against the doorframe, a thick smear of blood was spread like tar. My throat went dry. On the floor beneath lay a large shred of Mama's dress.

I ran to it, clutched the fabric to my chest. I raised the crossbow high and kicked the back door open.

More blood formed a trail from the rear stoop out across the grass behind the cottage and on toward the stable. Crimson cantered around the cottage to meet me, drawn by the sound at the back door. He noted my intensity and looked to one side, perhaps wondering what I was tracking. He sniffed at the blood and snorted, sounding more angry than alarmed. I followed it to the stable entrance and hurried inside.

It was everywhere. The walls, the posts, the hay, the troughs. All matted with thick blood. Most of it had collected in Royale's stall. I moved toward it slowly, trembling. Within the stall, Royale's saddle lay on its side. Strands of hay stuck to the blood that coated it.

Beyond the stall, the rest of my mother's dress lay in a sickening pile of straw and dark blood. Crimson stood back and stamped his hooves. My legs felt like melting wax as I stepped closer. I found nothing else but her jewelry and one of her shoes. She had been taken naked, along with Papa's horse. They had taken everything from us. Everything.

Beside Mama's abandoned dress lay a hand. A tiny skeletal hand.

I fell to my knees before it. My crossbow fell to the hay. It landed on something soft and red. It didn't sink through it like straw. I reached down into the inky blood that coated the fabric and lifted it slowly. The blood clung to it and wouldn't let go.

It was her blanket. Her fuzzy woolie.

I felt the moan gathering in my gut before it reached my throat and became a wail.

Suzette.

"Celeste! Suzette!" It was Father Vestille's voice, calling from somewhere near the front of the cottage.

I considered calling out to him from the stable. To come find my family's remains.

My mouth would only whimper.

Father Vestille's feet kicked up a flurry of dust as he skidded into the stable. He gaped at me as I knelt beside Royale's stall, next to the dress and my sister's hand, holding her bloody blanket.

He stood at the entrance beside Crimson, his chest heaving. "Helena. What ... happened?"

I didn't answer. He knew what happened. Anyone seeing this would know. But just like Father Vestille, no one would admit to knowing.

A wolf howled nearby.

Dark rage surged through me and lifted me to my feet. I snatched up Papa's crossbow and ran past Father Vestille.

"Helena, wait!"

He ran after me with Crimson trotting along behind. At the edge of the forest, barely hidden among the trees, a wolf stood.

Stood.

I had not imagined it. The monster stood on its hind legs, even now, and grinned. Mocking me from the woods.

I lunged toward it. Father Vestille tackled me and pinned me to the ground. "Helena, no!"

He held me down with his full weight, pressing me into the dirt. I strained to rise. To strike at the beast. To fire a bolt into its belly and turn that smile into a grimace of agony.

I finally pushed Father Vestille off and rolled aside. I ran at the wolf as it turned to sprint away. I heard it laugh, actually laugh in a sort of whooping cackle as it left.

I charged at the spot where it had stood. I squinted for a sign of its vanishing tail while Father Vestille chased after me.

"Stop, Helena, stop!"

Crimson galloped from behind me and clomped to a halt, blocking my path. Doing what Father Vestille could not do. Stopping me from rushing straight to my own death.

Father Vestille soon reached us. Crimson snorted at me and I stood there, trying to control my rage. To focus it.

Father Vestille wheezed and bent over, his hands on his knees. He wasn't used to sprinting. "Helena, please," he gasped. "There's nothing ... you can do."

I stared through tree after dark tree, tracing the wolf's likely path. "Not yet."

Father Vestille swallowed and straightened, gathering his breath. "Helena. We'll ... We can clean up ... your cottage. I'll help restore it." He sounded as if he meant to convince himself as much as to console me.

"There's nothing to restore. They took my home. They've taken everything."

His eyes narrowed. "Who has taken everything?"

"The wolves."

He said nothing at first. He simply stood there, slowing his breathing, studying me. "Helena. You have a home. With me. I'll stay here if you wish. Or you can come to my hovel. I'll see to all your needs."

My breath came evenly as I watched the empty woods. The dark forest of wolves that had swallowed up Mama and Suzette. I had to stay angry to keep from screaming. "That's very kind of you. But I'll see to my own needs."

The wind whistled between us.

"I know you can fend for yourself, Helena. But we all have needs besides food and shelter. Your father and ... your mother ... they were my closest friends, since before you were born. And you and Suzette ..." His voice caught in his throat. "Helena, your family meant everything to me. I will not abandon you. Nor will I let you abandon yourself."

I stood like a statue before the woods. As a child, I always saw Father Vestille as a source of assurance and comfort. But there was no comfort here at the forest's edge. I scanned its endless blackness for signs of movement. Any signs of the wolf or its companions.

Nothing.

I turned from it and strode to Crimson, climbing onto his back. I snapped at the reins and galloped past Father Vestille without a word.

I returned to the village and rode straight to *L'atelier de Forgeron de Leóne*. When I threw the door open, Pierre seemed delighted to see me twice in the same day. Then his face fell.

"Red? What's wrong?"

"Can I sleep here tonight?"

"Of course, Red. We'll make some room for you in the loft. What happened?"

I tried to speak clearly. My voice rattled. "There was an attack. On ... our cottage. Mama and Suzette ... They're gone."

The color drained from his face. "Suzette? How --? What happened?"

"The wolves. The wolves took ... The wolves took them. They're gone. Can I sleep here tonight?"

"Yes. Sure, I said you could. Just ... sit over here. Did anyone else see it?"

I walked to the stool he offered, brushed sawdust from it and sat. Like a horse being led to its stable, without thought or will or emotion. "Father Vestille was there. He's ... He's been helping out, looking in on us more often, since Papa died. He wants me to stay with him."

Pierre waited for more. "But you don't want to. Why not?"

I pressed my lips tight, feeling my blood boil again.

"Red, what is it? Why are you so mad at him?"

"Because he did *nothing!*" I burst. "Grand'Mere died and he did nothing. Francois died and he did nothing. Papa died and he couldn't stop the wolf, couldn't even find it. And now ...!" I couldn't speak their names again. Couldn't say again that I had lost everyone. Even Suzette.

"But ... he's trying to –."

"Please, Pierre. Don't tell me what he's trying to do. Please don't tell me that people are trying to help, or that the King will send soldiers, or that everything will be all right, because it won't. Nothing is going to be all right, ever again."

"Red ..."

I fell into his arms and clung to him. I needed someone who could understand and let me lean against them and cry. Someone who wouldn't look down on me for my weakness or my irresponsibility or my ugliness. Someone who would let me cry, and never reveal it to anyone if I asked him. I buried my wet cheeks against his chest and sobbed in gulps, craving his comfort. He held me until I finished, then gently released me as I pulled away. He gave me a crooked smile and offered me a rag, beating some sawdust from it.

I took it gratefully and wiped my eyes and nose. "This never happened."

He wrinkled his brow. "The hug?"

"No. The crying."

"… Why?"

"I don't want anyone to know. And I don't want to remember."

"Everyone cries, Red."

"I've cried enough. I'm through crying."

He narrowed his eyes, not sure what to make of me. "Listen, Red. I'll let my father know you're here and tell him what happened. You're welcome to stay. I'll make up the cot for you upstairs and get some blankets so you can rest."

I nodded obediently, feeling numb. As if all the emotion had been drained from my soul. At least, all the emotion I could reveal. The rage, the fear, the storm building inside me – these had to stay hidden, lest they be unleashed.

Pierre lit a lantern and moved to the ladder at the rear of the shop. I followed him up to the loft.

We emerged through the square opening. Pierre's lantern lit the long-forgotten room in a dusty haze. Cobwebs connected the looming wardrobe on the far wall to a standing mirror, filmed over with dirt. Near the shuttered window stood a cot. I longed to collapse onto it and sleep for hours, as Pierre suggested. My mind and strength were spent.

He set the lantern on the nightstand and clomped to the wardrobe, his boots leaving footprints in the floorboard dust. He opened the double doors, peeling cobweb strings apart, and bent to lift two thick blankets from a bottom shelf.

Among the coats and dresses that hung above the blankets, something flashed a brilliant red.

I moved to the wardrobe and pushed aside the other garments. Behind coats, nightshirts and tunics, covered with dust and age, hung a long red hooded cloak. Just like the one Grand'Mere Marie made for me when I was little. The cloak I was forbidden to wear after the attack.

I pulled it out.

"That was Mama's," Pierre said.

I kept staring at it. "Sorry," I mumbled.

"No, it's all right. It's beautiful, I know. Like the one you used to – uh, here. You should be warm enough with these."

The hood and cloak looked roomy, slightly too large for me. But they would fit. "I want this."

Pierre turned to me. "Huh? Oh. Sure, I'll ask Papa. No one's using it, so it shouldn't be –."

"I want this," I repeated. "I'll give you anything you want for it."

"Red, you can have it. But you should get some rest."

I couldn't take my eyes off the cloak. The red hooded cloak. I had not worn anything red since before I started hunting. Since the wolves took all peace and happiness from our lives. Now they had taken our lives, too. Grand'Mere and Francois and my parents. Even Suzette. For the first time, I knew some of the joy my mother wanted for me. To feel like a mother, or at least a big sister. And they took it away.

I clutched the cloak to my chest. Then I moved to the cot. "I'll use this as well. To keep warm."

"All right," Pierre allowed.

I sat on the cot. "Father Vestille will plan a service for my mother and … my sister. Can you find out the time and have someone wake me?"

"Of course."

I clutched the cloak in my fist and viewed it once more. "I'll wear this to the service."

Pierre frowned. "We might have a black veil you can use. I don't think you can wear red for a funeral."

I flashed on him. "Don't *tell* me what to *wear.*"

He studied me, then shrugged: "… Red it is. Get some sleep."

I lay down, wrapped the red cloak around myself and pulled the blankets up as Pierre returned to the ladder. I sat up. "Pierre?"

His head poked up through the square opening.

"Thank you," I said.

He smiled and gave a nod, then descended through the hole. I blew out the candle and the room sank into darkness.

18.

Where are you going, little girl?

I saw myself walking through the woods and tensed. The same woods I traveled as a child. I was on my way to Grand'Mere Marie's house again, carrying a basket of bread and cheese. But I was myself, sixteen years old.

I knew I was having a nightmare, but I couldn't wake up.

"Where are you going, little girl?" a gruff voice repeated from the forest.

I peered through black trees, thick as a fortress gate. A pair of low eyes studied me. The creature came slowly between the trunks, a thick shadow of black fur and pointed ears. Eyes shone out from the shadow, a pale bluish-gray. The large wolf came into view, still lingering behind a few trees. I stepped backward, my heart racing.

"Don't be afraid," it said.

"… You're a wolf."

The shadow nodded. It seemed to grin.

"Wolves don't talk." I clutched the basket to my chest and took another step back. As if I could disappear within the folds of my cloak.

"*I* do," it said. "Where are you going, little girl?"

A chilling breeze tickled my cheeks. My voice was barely a breath. "To my Grand'Mere's house."

"And where does she live?"

"... just over the hill, past the three oaks." My eyes locked on the furry shadow as my fingers locked around the basket's handle. "I've never seen a wolf like you."

"No?" Its voice was sheer mockery.

I shook my head. I wanted to run, to scream. But my legs stiffened in place like a terrified fawn. The wolf stood taller than me, as it had appeared when I was only eight. Its head was half the size of my body. "You have ... such big eyes. And ears. And such big teeth."

His fangs spread with pleasure. "The better to see and hear you with, Mademoiselle."

I heard my breath moving in and out. In and out. "... And your teeth?"

It leaned toward me. It kept leaning in as it padded closer, closer. "The better to *eat* you!"

I clutched the basket and raised it to protect my face. To hide my eyes from its open, dripping mouth.

A sharp crack sounded over the hill. It was Grand'Mere's neighbor, Francois, splitting wood with his ax. He would hear us if I screamed.

The wolf regarded me casually. "We'll meet again, Mademoiselle. Soon. But keep silent about our first meeting." It raised its paw to its pursed lips, as if signaling me to be quiet. The way a human would. "Now run to your Grand'Mere's. Before she starts to worry."

The wolf turned and loped away. Beyond it, the eyes of six other wolves shone in the distance. Watching and waiting. I backed away carefully as they remained in their positions like sentinels.

I hurried off through the trees. As I ran, I noticed the first wolf nearby, keeping pace with me. Its enormous black figure loped gently at first. Then it bounded through the woods, leaving me far behind.

It was headed to Grand'Mere's. I gasped and ran harder.

I reached her cottage and threw open the door. Inside, on Grand'Mere's bed, the wolf circled about her sheets and nightgown, smeared with her blood. It turned and recognized me.

It smiled.

I had rushed too far into the cottage to retreat in time. I ran behind Grand'Mere's rocking chair to shield myself as the wolf jumped from the bed. It stood on its hind legs and knocked the chair aside like a toy. The black creature loomed over me, gloating, its eyes shining. It spread its claws.

I jumped back from it. Its claws still connected, cutting into the tender flesh of my forehead and cheeks. I spun and fell back. My own blood flew about my head. Then it dripped into a scarlet pool on Grand'Mere's wooden floor where I fell. The open wound burned like fire. I screamed but I couldn't hear myself. Couldn't think of anything but the wolf as it dropped to all fours. The monster prowled closer, its open mouth salivating.

Something kicked open the front door. Francois Revelier burst in, carrying his ax in two fists like a hammer of judgment. He rushed at the giant wolf and raised the ax. Its silver edge caught the sunlight from the door and flashed in the air. He brought the heavy blade down as the beast charged. He struck its shoulder, knocking it to the floor. The wound trickled blood as the wolf struggled to rise.

Then it stumbled, confused, and fell. Fell to the floor and didn't move. Francois squinted at it, looking perplexed. The wolf's vacant eyes no longer blinked.

Francois set his jaw and stomped forward. He lopped off the monster's head with one clean stroke. The wolf lay there in its own blood, still and horrible and harmless, while Francois stood over it like David over the head of the slain Goliath.

In that instant, I learned that heroes existed. People who would risk their own lives to save mine. People like Francois.

Something growled from outside. At each window, the head of another large wolf eyed us. The same wolves that studied me from the forest.

Francois turned as they burst through the glass. They leaped on top of him and bit into his back, his shoulders, his arms.

Francois dropped his ax and screamed as he sank to his knees beneath the bloodthirsty pile.

Then the head of the first wolf – the one Francois has slain – turned again to smile at me. Then – impossibly – its head slid back to its body to rejoin its neck, re-forming itself. It stood on its hind legs again and grinned at me in triumph.

Then it joined the others feeding on Francois as he flailed his arms and shrieked.

I jerked upright in bed. I whirled about in the blackness, trying to focus.

I relaxed my neck and shoulders in the dark room. On the cot in the loft above the blacksmith's shop, where Pierre let me sleep. I was alone. No beasts or monsters. Only me and my scars.

I lay back down and drew the red cloak back around myself. The cloak that belonged to Pierre's mother, before she died.

I pulled the blankets up to my shoulders and lay there on the warm cot, wide-eyed and shivering.

19.

"Red?"

Pierre's head popped up through the hole in the loft floor. I pulled the dress up in front of my bare shoulders and gasped.

He spotted me standing in nothing but my linen chemise, before I covered myself with his mother's cream-white gown. He immediately lowered his gaze. "Uh, sorry, Red. I just ... I noticed you lit the candle and you were up, so ... Just wanted to let you know Father Vestille's preparing for burial. People are already heading to the church."

"All right," I said, still clutching the dress. "My clothes were covered in blood. I hope you don't mind me borrowing one of your mother's gowns."

He cleared his throat. "Yeah. Sure. No problem."

I waited. "I'm just dressing now."

"Right. Yeah. Of course. I'll just, uh ... wait down in the shop."

"Yes, you will."

"Yes, I will," he repeated, and was gone.

I waited to hear him descend the last step of the wooden ladder before I lowered my hands. I resumed dressing in his mother's satin gown. It was the only suitable outfit that wasn't tattered with age.

A full-length mirror stood beside the wardrobe. The dress would work, though it seemed more suited for a ball than a funeral.

I donned her red cloak and tied it about my neck.

"Let me know when you're ready, all right, Red?" Pierre called from below.

I stared at my reflection. At the red cloak around my head and shoulders. The bright color I had been forbidden to wear for eight years. Ever since the wolves began to rule my life and the lives of everyone around me. Wearing this cloak gave me a surge of energy inside, a sense of strength I had never known, even when hunting.

"Yes, Pierre," I called back. "I'm ready now."

"Ashes to ashes, dust to dust ..."

I sat quiet and still in the pew beside Pierre at *la Chapelle de Saint Matthieu*, watching Father Vestille prepare to give the sermon and then pray over the bodies of Mama and Suzette. Incense filled the air, within the dim candlelight that cast dismal shadows on the stone walls and stained glass windows.

The caskets were closed.

Nearly thirty people had assembled to pay honor to my family's memory. As always, Duke Laurent's presence in the second row gave the service a significant prestige. His advisor, Monsieur Simonet, sat beside him, his usual frown seeming appropriate now.

Father Vestille hung his head, slow to begin. Finally, he lifted his eyes, grimaced, and spoke in a hoarse voice. "My friends ..." He cleared his throat and started again. "My friends. Thank you for coming. We are here to lay to rest ... the bodies of Celeste Basque and ... her youngest daughter, Suzette Basque. Both brutally attacked by beasts earlier this morning." He paused, closing his eyes. Gathering his breath. "Our hearts cannot be heavier. *My* heart cannot be heavier. To lose such a wonderful woman and her innocent child. The Basque family has been like my own family. They welcomed me into this community and into their home. Their kindness, their openness and hospitality, inspired me to be more open to others. To find ways to reach out and welcome neighbors and strangers, the way they welcomed me."

Father Vestille observed the silent coffins. He looked so sad, so defeated, as if he might struggle to lift his head. His voice choked. "Celeste and Suzette Basque have become ... even closer to me these last few months, since ... since Henri Basque died. He was also ... He was also cruelly taken by a wolf. Their eldest daughter, Helena, is still with us. And I urge all of you to do whatever you can, anything you can, to show her support and comfort in this time of great loss. It's more than anyone, especially a young girl like Helena, should be forced to bear."

I felt the eyes of others staring at me. Even Pierre glanced at me. To see my reaction.

I ignored all of them, staring back at Father Vestille in stony silence. Memorizing each hollow word.

He stood a little taller, finding more of his voice. "But we must encourage ourselves, not only in the face of death, but in life. In all that we face, even in the midst of the most horrible tragedy, we must seek the face of the Lord and draw strength from him to continue with every task of daily life. With every disappointment, every grief, every threat –."

I rose from my seat.

Father Vestille stopped.

I still wore the red cloak over the cream dress, which had drawn several curious stares from the guests when we arrived at the church. But no one said anything against what I chose to wear for the burial of my remaining family. And no one would interfere with me now as I stepped toward the caskets. I stopped in front of the smaller one and stared down at it. I turned to Father Vestille.

"Open it."

He gaped at me. His skin paled like a phantom. "Helena. I ... I know how horrible this is for you, but --."

"Open it."

He stood frozen behind the pulpit, with no idea how to respond. The rest of the crowd kept silent in their seats.

I walked around behind the wooden coffin. I peeled back my hood and lifted the lid.

Inside, a few pieces of Suzette's body were carefully laid. Each one stripped clean of most decaying flesh and dried blood. I marveled at how quickly Father Vestille had gathered and prepared them. All had been neatly arranged, the hand and partial skull and ribcage exactly where they should be. Except that the lower part of the ribcage was a pile of fractured sticks.

This was not my sister. Only her bones. My sister's soul had ascended and I would not see her again until my own death. All that remained of her was this pile of lifeless flesh, which would never smile again, never run again, never laugh again.

I faced the spectators. Neighbors, cousins, and friends I had not seen for months. I couldn't even remember some of their names. Pierre and his parents, Duke Laurent and even Simonet, stared at me in shock, almost fear.

I lifted Suzette's skeletal hand up high to show everyone it was no longer connected to her tiny wrist. Women squealed and nestled against their husbands, while mothers shielded their children's eyes.

I no longer cared. I met their stares, glaring back at them. I held the hand higher. "This ... will end."

I laid the hand gently back in its place with the rest of my sister's useless parts.

Then I slammed the coffin lid down, letting it echo through the sanctuary. I secured my hood once more and marched past the stunned crowd toward the rear oak doors. Ignoring Father Vestille as he gaped from the front. Past Duke Laurent, Papa's old friend, who seemed ready to stand and comfort or dissuade me, but wisely held his place. Past Pierre, wrinkling his brow with worry, as his parents looked on with fright.

I pushed the double doors open and strode to Crimson, who snorted eagerly beside Pierre's horse. I climbed onto his back and he lifted his hooves, as if sensing my urgency. We galloped off into the darkening afternoon as a storm threatened on the horizon.

20.

I rode back to *L'atelier de Forgeron de Leóne* and found the spare key beneath the stone near the front stoop, where I knew Monsieur Leóne kept it. I unlocked the shop's front door and went inside, wondering if I might ruin the late Madame Leóne's satin gown just by walking through the warm oily air.

I didn't climb up to the loft to rest or gather my thoughts. Instead, I lit a few candles and started rummaging through the shop. I had already decided on my next course of action. I just needed to work out the details.

I was still gathering bolts and knives when I heard hooves approaching quickly. I continued working as Diamond snorted from out front and Pierre came through the door.

"Red! Red, what are you doing?"

"Preparing for a hunt." I continued to pace the tables and shelves, selecting weapons. "I need your help, Pierre. I need a pair of boots."

"Boots?" Pierre wrinkled his brow. "What for? If you need slippers or sandals …"

"No. I need boots. I'm going hunting and I need boots to get through the mud."

He remained confused. "I know you can hunt, but … boots? I mean …" He shook his head, as if unable to speak.

"What?"

"Well … You're a girl."

We stared at one another in silence.

"I am aware of that. I need the boots, nevertheless."

"We don't even sell boots."

"I know." I bit my lip. "I was hoping you might have an extra pair I could borrow."

"Yeah. Sure. I guess. I have some old boots I meant to pass on to someone. They might fit you, if you really need them."

"Thank you."

He remained confused. "Still seems awfully odd for a girl."

I took another deep breath. "I also need a pair of trousers."

He stared blankly at me.

"I realize I'm still a girl," I said.

He studied the cold stone floor. "You're going after those wolves, aren't you?"

I said nothing. The wind outside gave a shrill whistle.

"I don't like it, Red. Those things could kill you. We can get some men together and –."

"No, we can't. Because none of them will go."

Pierre swallowed. "Then I'll go with you."

"No, you won't."

"Why not?"

"Because." I struggled for an answer. I would welcome anyone's help to hunt those beasts.

Anyone but Pierre.

"Because if anything happens to me, I need you to tell the others what I've done. Apart from that, I'm binding you to secrecy."

"What? But, Red –!"

"Promise me. Promise you won't tell anyone. If they know, they'll try to stop me, the same way you are. If they stop me, no one else will go, either. Then more people will be killed and it will never stop. Promise me."

All the color drained from his face, leaving him a helpless phantom. "… all right. I promise."

"Thank you, Pierre."

He looked about the shop. "If you won't change your mind, at least let me supply you with some good weapons."

"I've already started."

He studied my pile of knives and ammunition. "That's a good start, but you'll need more than that. If you're right, these are no ordinary wolves. You'll need extraordinary weapons. Too bad you can't have your own set of claws, to even it up."

I lifted my father's crossbow. "This should help, at least."

"Yeah," Pierre said, studying the crossbow with a curious look. He continued to eye it carefully as he spoke. "I've actually been working on something for you. I meant to surprise you with it, but … guess I'd better give it to you now. I also designed some tools people could use to guard their homes, with all these attacks." He shook his head. "Never thought I'd be giving them all to you, but … Let me find those boots, and, uh … a pair of extra trousers."

"Where are you getting those?"

"… from my wardrobe."

I swallowed, sharing his discomfort. "… thank you."

He nodded and stepped away. "Let me get you some gloves, too. Should come in handy out there, give you some extra protection. I'll be right back."

He dimmed the candles, lit a lantern and headed toward his room at the rear of the store. For a moment, I felt warmer inside, knowing Pierre would give me all the protection he could.

In the upper room, I untied my red hood and let it fall to the bed, then removed my cream dress. I donned Pierre's ivory tunic and deerskin trousers, feeling perverse. I had not worn pants since the week I had to borrow clothes from Doctor Renoire's son.

I wondered what my parents would think if they could see me tonight. Mama would grieve and abandon all hope that I might ever become a sophisticated woman. Papa might share her concern, but feel a sense of pride that I was doing what I had to do. What someone had to do.

I stifled a half-choking sob as I thought of them. But I had vowed to stop crying, to focus on the task at hand.

It felt strange, preparing to go out in public with folds of cloth surrounding my legs. At the same time, I felt freedom to move, back and forth, twisting and turning, with no skirt getting in the way. I tied the cloak about my neck and stood, moving my toes about in the boots, getting used to the feel of them. I stepped back a few quick paces, then forth again, then spun about. My cloak twirled after me, threatening to catch against me the way my skirt used to. But there was little comparison. I had to be careful how I moved, to avoid wrapping my shoulders tightly into the cloak, but I wouldn't fall over myself or tangle my legs together the way I might in a dress. And I needed the cloak to feel less exposed.

I smiled. In this outfit, I could run and leap without holding back. I could climb or descend a hill fast, or position myself to launch a bolt. Most important, I could fight. I could dodge or strike someone without fear of stumbling or appearing unladylike.

I caught my reflection in the mirror and my heart sank.

I looked like a man. Not even a handsome man, but a pretentious dandy with blonde locks. Scarred and disfigured by some accident, now trying to compensate for it by dressing in a flowing silk shirt, cuffed leather boots and an oversized red cloak. I looked horrendous.

I took a deep breath and released it. What did it matter how I looked? I had lived with my ugly scars for nine years. What did it matter if I looked even worse?

I kept staring at myself – at the strange person in the mirror – and wondered what would become of me, if I even survived this night. Would anyone mourn the strange scarred girl from the sheep farm outside the village?

But if I didn't go, who would be left to even consider mourning me? Those beasts would return, again and again. Picking us off one by one until they had eaten their fill. They had to be stopped. They had to be killed.

I donned the hood. It darkened my eyes and made me look fearsome. Otherwise, I felt naked with my legs uncovered. But there was nothing I could do about it. I left the dress in the wardrobe, my legs exposed for all the world to see. I prepared myself to head into the forest, looking like an animal myself.

I descended the ladder.

I heard Pierre scraping metal against metal, sharpening something, as I clomped onto the wood floor and turned to face him.

He gasped. "Helena. You look …"

"Even less attractive, I know."

"Uh, no. Just, uh … just different."

"How I look doesn't matter. What matters is how well I can move, and I can move more freely in this."

"Uh … All right." He continued to stare at me. At my legs in particular. "Are you sure you want to … go out like that?"

"Are you sure you can't stop staring?" I was glad the long cloak covered me from the rear or he might have had fits.

"Sorry. It's just odd to see you … I mean … for you to wear trousers."

I drew the cloak around myself a little, knowing how bizarre I looked. "Why should it matter? You've seen other men in trousers."

"Well, that's a little different. I mean … they're *men.*"

He finally shook his head, like a dog shaking himself dry, and tore his eyes away from my legs. Then he returned his attention to the table, where he had arranged a couple of slim daggers he had sharpened, several bolts, and a rope and hook beside a pair of leather gloves. "I've been working on some things here that should give you some extra help." He demonstrated the various tools, including an impressive grappling hook for scaling a wall or a cliff face. Its prongs flicked out when he slid a metal catch open with his thumb. With each new device, I found myself more enchanted by his cleverness. Finally, he held up a crossbow, crowned with something that resembled a long snuff box.

"What's that?"

"Chinese repeating crossbow," he said with pride. "I read about it and figured out how to build one. You load the top slot here …" He dropped in ten bolts, one at a time. "Then you just keep pulling back on this top lever. Every time you pull back, it fires another bolt."

I almost yanked it from him. I stared at it in my hands like it was a priceless treasure. "Pierre. This is ... incredible. Thank you."

He shrugged. "Anything I can do to help. I figure, this way, you can fire again if you miss the first time."

I raised an eyebrow at him. "I won't miss."

"All right, but ... if you need to shoot again, you can fire right away."

I studied the crossbow up and down. It was pure genius. "This is perfect, Pierre. Two shots to make sure I kill it. With enough bolts to shoot down four more before I reload."

"Four ... four more?"

I squinted at him, wondering why he seemed surprised. "Wolves hunt in packs, Pierre. You know that. There were at least four that attacked Francois."

"Yeah, but I didn't think ... I mean, you can't hunt them all down at once."

"I can try." I tugged Pierre's thick leather gloves on, then gathered my father's crossbow and a handful of bolts. I slung Pierre's repeating crossbow over my shoulder and grabbed the handful of knives from the table.

I strode into the brisk evening with Pierre fast on my heels. Crimson turned sharply at the opening door, eager to be off but still waiting for me.

"Red, you'll be careful, right? Promise you'll watch yourself."

"I'll watch myself." I hooked the repeating crossbow onto Crimson's saddle, along with Papa's crossbow and the knives, then hoisted myself up.

"With that red hood, they'll see you coming a mile away."

I knew he was right. But I refused to live another day in fear. "I want them to see me coming."

He narrowed his eyes. "... What?"

My blood surged. Crimson stamped his hooves, perhaps feeling the same fire. "I want to make them afraid, the way they made *us* afraid. Whatever those things are, I want them to know one of us is fighting back."

Pierre gaped, uncertain what to think. "Red, what are you going to do?"

I set my jaw like stone. "Something."

I spurred Crimson forth. He snorted and charged ahead. Lightning stabbed at the horizon as Pierre called after me.

I saw Father Vestille on his Palomino, trotting toward *L'atelier de Forgeron de Leóne*. We met with surprised eyes. I fumbled with the reins, nearly making Crimson stumble before he galloped past. Father Vestille tugged his horse to a halt and struggled to turn about.

"Helena! Helena, come back!"

I can only imagine how he would react to the bare trousers beneath my flapping cloak. I might be cast out of the church. But it no longer mattered. I still had faith, but I was out of patience. If he put me out of the church for trying to save our province, so be it.

The cries of Pierre and Father Vestille echoed behind me, farther and farther away as I galloped through the darkening streets.

MY DISCOVERY

21.

Rain started to drizzle as I arrived at *La Maison de Touraine*, but it didn't dampen the raucous laughter within its walls. I could see why Mama often referred to taverns as "dens". The crowd inside rumbled like a pack of growling beasts. I had never set foot in this place except for the banquet to honor Francois, the night he died.

But *La Maison* was a center for local gossip. The perfect starting place to learn what anyone knew about the wolves. Someone must have heard rumors or witnessed recent attacks.

An alcoholic stench filled the misty air. I wished for a safer way to seek information. My parents would have liked me to forget this place altogether. But Francois told me to seek out his friend if I ever needed help.

As we trotted toward the hitching post, two men stopped their conversation and stared. At the red horse and its red-cloaked rider. The short man's mouth hung open. I wondered how much I resembled the Apocalyptic horseman that brought a plague of war.

Though I doubted this squat man or his liquor bottle spent much time listening to the Scriptures.

"Evening, Monsieur," he greeted.

I said nothing as I swung off Crimson's flank to the ground. I had no business with this man and his tone seemed more demanding than friendly.

"I said, 'Evening,'" Squat repeated. He and his slim mustached companion stepped in front of the entrance.

"Evening," I muttered.

The mustached man squinted at me. He grabbed at my shoulder and spun me to face him. I looked up in his astonished half-shaven face. "Why, she's a girl!" he sputtered.

"What sort of game do you think you're playing, Mademoiselle?" Squat demanded. "This ain't no place for someone like you."

I swallowed down fear and anger. I had no time for this. "I'll see for myself and let you know," I said.

I started forward. Mustache moved to block me. Crimson grumbled and shifted uneasily behind me, while Squat took another swig of his bottle.

"You should listen to your betters, Mademoiselle," Mustache said. "If you want some drinks, I'll show you where to find some. More private, away from all these gawkers."

Crimson snorted, ready to charge him.

"Step aside, Monsieurs," I warned.

Squat chuckled and glanced at Mustache, who laughed along. "Now, now, Mademoiselle. You didn't say, 'please'."

I pulled my crossbow from beneath my cloak and aimed its bolt-end directly beneath Squat's jowls. They stopped laughing abruptly. "Please."

Squat nodded, slow and careful, as he backed away to let me pass. I lowered the crossbow slowly, measuring their reactions. Satisfied that they would not bother me further, I hid it beneath my cloak once more. "Could you look after my horse while I'm inside? He sometimes gets agitated around strangers."

Squat and Mustache looked at Crimson, who looked back with eyes that seemed to spit flame.

"Yeah," Mustache said dully. "Sure."

He took a step forward and Crimson stamped his hoof. Both men spread their arms as they backed up to the wall. Crimson would have no trouble with them.

I moved to the oak doors and pushed inside. Into a room of noise and smoke and laughter. Where men dressed formally but acted foolishly, and a handful of women moved from table to table, dressed even less modestly than I was, serving drinks and letting men gawk at them from every angle.

At the bar counter, separated from the chaos surrounding him, a plump man with thinning auburn hair stood polishing a wooden mug as he talked with two men. The tavern owner, Gerard Touraine.

I strode toward the counter, noting the quiet that came in my wake. Like the ripples of a swan wading through a polluted stream. Everyone seemed dumbstruck at the sight of me. Including the men seated at the counter, watching me approach.

For a moment, none of them spoke.

"That's quite a cloak, Monsieur," said Touraine, wiping the mug in his hand. He turned to put it away and grab a new one from the pegs on the wall.

I didn't know if he meant it as a compliment. I assumed not. "Thank you."

Touraine stopped and turned on his heel, ignoring the mugs. He took a step toward me and crouched to peer at my mouth beneath the hood. "Eh ... you lost, Mademoiselle?" he asked with a chuckle. Then his face fell. "Wait. You're that little girl, from Francois' party. With the ..."

His hand rose to make a gesture at his face. He stopped himself before making reference to my scars. I appreciated that. "Francois saved my life," I said. "He was a good friend of mine."

"Yes," Touraine said. He cleared his throat. "Mine, too."

One of the other men laughed. "What's this, Gerard? Your niece paying you a visit? Or is it someone else, eh?" He nudged his friend on the next wooden stool and both men chuckled.

Touraine ignored them, focusing on me. "Uh ... I'm afraid women aren't allowed in here, Mademoiselle."

I glanced at the tall brunette leaning over a table of men with her hands on her hips. *"She* is a woman."

"Of course, but she's ... eh ..."

"She has a point, Gerard," the other man insisted. "That is definitely a woman over there. So if this mademoiselle wants to –."

"Enough," Touraine said, silencing him. "She's made a mistake. She came to the wrong place, nothing more."

I climbed up onto the stool across from him. I had never sat in such a high chair. But then, I never decided to start wearing trousers before today, either. "All I want is a drink."

Touraine shook his head, his brown eyes apologizing. "I couldn't serve you."

"Oh, come now, Gerard." The man fished out some coins to toss on the counter. "Here, Mademoiselle. I'll buy you one."

"Move on," Touraine ordered the men. "I'll handle this. Find yourselves a table. We'll talk later."

The second man held up his hands. "We're only teasing her, Gerard. Don't get excited."

Touraine leaned toward them, almost menacing. "Find a table," he repeated.

The men climbed awkwardly down from their stools and walked away, staring over their shoulders at Touraine as he watched them go.

"I only want water," I said. "Can you serve me that?"

Touraine paused to consider, then turned to grab a fresh mug.

"I am also curious," I said as he filled it.

"You're curious?" he asked, amused. "You enter a tavern with that huge cloak and you're curious. Very well. What are you curious about, Mademoiselle?"

"Wolves."

His wrist twitched, then continued to fill the mug. He set it on the counter before me, his head down. He looked up. "Wolves in general?"

"Wolves in particular. A large wolf that killed a little girl near here."

"Heard about that. Tragic."

"She was my sister."

Touraine buried his heavy gaze in the floor. "… Very sorry, Mademoiselle."

"I'm curious about that wolf. A lot of people pass through here. Have you heard anything about it?"

He narrowed his eyes, looking confused. "I don't know. But why should I tell you if I did?"

"Tell me tonight and you'll know why tomorrow."

He moved around the counter. "I think someone should see you home, Mademoiselle."

"I *have* no home," I said. The sudden rise in my voice stopped him cold. "The wolves took it from me."

"Well, what about your parents?"

My shoulders trembled as I thought of Mama and Papa and Suzette. I stiffened to hide it. "… The wolves took everything."

He swallowed. "I'm so sorry, Mademoiselle. I am. But I don't see how I can help you."

"You can't tell me what you know about the wolves that killed my mother and father and little sister? That keep killing off more and more people in the village? I only want to know what they are, what they might be doing."

"Look. I understand you're hurting. But whatever killed your parents and your sister is dangerous. Probably more dangerous than you can imagine. It's no business of mine and certainly no business of yours. And I don't think you want me to hear of *another* young girl's death tomorrow. *Do* you?"

"But you have heard things. *Haven't* you?"

He started to say something. Then chewed on his lip.

"I think they're the same wolves that killed Francois," I prodded.

"Francois was a good man," he said, sticking his lip out in a sideways pout. He heaved an inward sigh. "A very good man."

"He was too late to save my Grand'Mere from the wolf, but he saved me. If it weren't for him, I wouldn't be here. He was my hero. He still is. He's the one who sent me to you."

Touraine shot a look at me and narrowed his eyes. "How's that?"

"He said if I ever needed to know anything about anything in the village or beyond, you would be the one to ask."

This was not quite true. Francois had told me to seek Touraine out if I got in real trouble. But this qualified. I needed help and Touraine was the one who could give it.

I pressed on. "He also said people need to stand up and do something to help others. Or there would be more killings. More children suffering. He said we can't let fear stop us from doing what's right, because some things are worth fighting for."

Touraine lifted his chin. "Francois said that?"

I stiffened my jaw. "Yes."

He stared at me. Then he relaxed. "Yeah, that sounds like something Francois would say. Good man."

"But he's gone now," I said, leaning forward on the stool. "He's dead. A pack of wolves broke into his home and killed him."

Touraine nodded. "I know."

"You also know something about those wolves. I'm a good hunter. If you tell me, I can stop some of them, at least. If you don't, they'll keep killing."

He still hesitated, but seemed intrigued. Almost believing me.

"Please."

He studied me another moment. Then he resumed his position behind the counter and leaned over it. "If I don't tell you, you'll find out from someone else. Won't you?"

I nodded.

"All right, Mademoiselle. Don't ask anyone but me. Understand? You want to know anything, or if something is true, you come straight to me, no one else."

"I will," I promised.

I meant it. This was exactly what I wanted.

Touraine glanced from one side of the bar to the other. Then he started to polish a new mug as he spoke in a low murmur. "I don't know much, Mademoiselle. Some men come in here regularly, and they seem to know something about those wolves. Always eager for news about them, just like you. Always asking for details about recent attacks. It's odd. They seem delighted by it, like someone's telling a joke. Lately they've been asking about Monsieur Favreau's farm."

"Monsieur Favreau?"

"Pig farmer on the other side of the hill, west end of the forest. Not far from here. Lost four of his fattest pigs to a wolf over the last two weeks. He's worried he'll lose the rest, though he's got plenty to spare, if you ask me."

"When did he lose them?"

Touraine rubbed his stubbly chin. "One was two nights ago, the other two nights before that." He narrowed his eyes and blinked with sudden realization. "Seems it's been every two nights since it took the first one. Following a pattern."

"Which continues tonight," I said, finishing the thought that was surely brewing in his mind. I rose from the stool.

"Mademoiselle, your drink."

I turned back and retrieved the mug. "Thank you. I'll need it." I downed the water in one long swallow and returned the mug before heading to the door.

"Mademoiselle?"

I turned at the door.

He looked helpless as a child. "I trust … you have someone to look after you?"

"Yes," I said, stepping out into the storm. *"I am."*

I let the door thud behind me.

22.

Favreau's farm was easy enough to find. I just followed the smell. Even in the rain, the distinctive odor of pig manure spread for a mile.

Smoke rose from a thin chimney above the farmer's spacious cabin, set in a broad clearing surrounded by dense forest. A long narrow pigpen sat beside it, the large pigs kicking up mud and manure as the silvery moon rose above the trees. To the left of the pen sat a small and well-kept stable, housing perhaps two horses.

Monsieur Favreau would have his eyes and ears pricked for any intruders. He must have noticed the same pattern of attack by now, how the wolf seized one of his pigs every other night. Tonight he could expect to lose another one.

I climbed down from the saddle and led Crimson carefully around the perimeter. He moved so cautiously, I don't think he broke a single twig.

Hidden from the cabin windows by the horse stable, I crept toward the front with Crimson. Seeing me, Monsieur Favreau's horse started in alarm. I quickly found the feedbag, hanging from a hook on the wall, and grabbed a handful of oats. I held my hand open for the horse to see and sniff. He calmed immediately and let me approach so he could nibble from my hand. I shared some with his companion, who had just woken. I grabbed more oats and fed them again. Once they relaxed, I brought Crimson into the stable to stand between their twin stalls.

I scanned the clearing. Nothing moved in the dark woods around the farm, though the drizzle made it difficult to be certain. I hoped any wolves would have equal trouble spotting me.

Dim light issued from within the house. Monsieur Favreau must have lit a lantern to keep a late vigil over his property.

I grabbed more oats and prepared to lay the pile in my skirt. Then I remembered I was no longer wearing one. I stuffed them in my pants pockets instead, wishing I could store more. I reminded myself that the trousers still gave me the best advantage.

I crouched and crept toward the pen. A few pigs squealed upon seeing me approach in my sweeping cloak. I scattered a few oats at them, and they returned to their agitated pacing. Farmer Favreau wasn't the only one anxious about the wolves tonight.

I crawled carefully between the wooden bars of their pen. The pigs backed away and huddled against one another, but they no longer cried out. They gradually spread apart to move freely about the pen once more, though they kept an eye on me, snorting little warnings as they passed by.

I crouched in the filthy mud and slop and waited, forcing my senses to adapt to the intolerable smell. At least the rain would wash away some of the manure from my clothes, once I left the pen. But that would be a long time in coming. I would keep vigil until the wolf arrived.

I felt the crossbow at my hip. Not my father's, but Pierre's Chinese repeating crossbow. As brave as I made myself appear to everyone else, I couldn't afford to miss or waste time reloading.

I sat for over twenty minutes. By then, the pigs seemed to regard me as part of their pen – a piece of scenery to walk around as they continued their nervous pacing. Nearly half of them had fallen asleep. The others seemed as tense as I was.

I finally sat in the slop. My knees and thighs were tired, and I no longer cared how I looked or smelled, or what I had to scrub off the cloak later. In any case, this almost guaranteed that the Leóne family would not ask for it back. I leaned against the gate post, turning my head now and then to check for anything approaching from behind the farmhouse.

It felt good to finally rest. Nervous as I was, my shoulders and head felt heavy. I closed my eyes and thought of Suzette. Sweet, pure Suzette. Playing among the white daffodils in our meadow, running from me and laughing, her golden hair streaming in the biting wind.

She ran toward the dark forest. Beyond the first line of trees, the woods were black as coal.

Except for the eyes. More than a dozen pairs of eyes, shining from the darkness.

"Suzette, stop!" Papa called from behind me. "Come back!"

"Suzette, no! *Suzette!*" Mama screamed.

Suzette continued to laugh and run in an irregular pattern, playing a game of escaping me, escaping us all, while the eyes watched from the forest.

"Suzette, turn around!" It was Francois Revelier shouting, beckoning her back.

Suzette wouldn't listen.

"Helena, go after her!" Papa told me. "Bring her back!"

I stood where I was. I watched Suzette, laughing and playing as she drew closer to the forest.

"Go, Helena!" Mama urged. "You can get her! Bring her back!"

"But the wolves …" I muttered. I felt a tremor through my skin, like a spider crawling up my spine.

"You can bring her back, Helena," Francois said. "You're the only one who can do it."

Suzette giggled and dodged back and forth, closer and closer to the forest. To the waiting eyes that had grown in number, nearly twenty of them now.

"But they'll kill me, too …"

"Helena," Mama said in a quiet voice. "Helena, please …"

"You can do it, Helena," Papa said. "Bring her back. Bring her back."

A tear flowed down my cheek. "I can't ..."

Suzette's laughter echoed from the forest's edge. "Can't catch me!"

Then she turned and ran straight into the dark abyss, where teeth flashed open beneath each pair of eyes.

"Papa?"

I started suddenly. Soft rain fell on my cheeks and I rankled at the damp odor of pig manure. The tiny voice came from the front porch.

A little freckled girl stood there in her nightgown, staring out into the dark clearing. I looked and saw a heavyset man standing between puddles, holding a musket. Farmer Favreau, no doubt, watching for the wolves.

I had dozed off. Never even noticed him leaving the house. As he surveyed the outer perimeter of trees, I craned my neck, letting the rain needle down on me. Moonlight shone between rolling clouds, directly overhead. I had slept nearly an hour.

I looked back at Favreau as his gun whirled in my direction. Its barrel aimed squarely at my hooded forehead.

I sat frozen in the mud and darkness.

The mustached Favreau stood rigid, squinting through rain at the pigpen. Watching for any movement, listening for any strange sounds. I made none.

He finally relented and turned slowly back to the trees, while rain pelted the surrounding leaves. I felt my heart start beating again.

"Lucille, go back to bed," he called over his shoulder, still watching the forest.

"I'm not sleepy, Papa," the girl complained, rubbing her eyes.

I estimated her to be four years old. A year younger than Suzette, but just as lively, just as playful. Just as innocent. "Get back inside," I muttered in a violent whisper.

"Into bed," he repeated. "Your mother wouldn't have wanted you out in this cold, God rest her soul. Now go on."

I swallowed. He was a widower, raising little Lucille on his own. Just the two of them.

"Papa, what're you doing? Did you hear the wolf?"

I felt my breath through my teeth. I alternated between my study of the trees and of the inside light shining on little Lucille's white gown. "Get back inside," I murmured again.

"I heard something," Favreau said over his shoulder. "Might be that wolf, so go on inside, like I told you."

"Yes, Papa," she said. The rising irritation in his voice finally convinced her.

My shoulders relaxed.

"Look, Papa! There it is!"

Blood flooded my temples as I sat higher.

Lucille was right. Striding forth from the forest was a gray wolf – taller and larger than a normal wolf. It grinned, showing no fear of the musket. Perhaps it had never seen one.

Or simply didn't fear it.

The rain fell harder as I raised Pierre's crossbow. If the wolf didn't fear a bullet, it certainly wouldn't fear a bolt. Until I sank enough of them into its belly.

At least, that's what I hoped.

It padded through the muddy field toward Favreau. As if daring him to shoot.

"Get inside, Lucille," Favreau ordered.

"Kill it, Papa. Kill it before it takes another pig!"

"Inside, I said!"

Favreau couldn't escort his daughter to safety and face down the wolf at the same time. He leaned his head to one side and sighted the animal patiently. Letting it draw closer into range, he waited for the right shot and pulled the trigger.

A beautiful shot, right to its face. It sent the beast spinning backward to the slippery ground, dead.

Favreau lifted his head as Lucille jumped up and down on the porch, her fists raised in victory.

"You did it, Papa, you did it!"

The clearing fell quiet. The creature was dead.

It was over. I was never even needed. I felt relieved and strangely cheated. But I couldn't help but feel grateful over the huge wolf carcass lying still on the soaked grass.

Then four more wolves padded into the clearing. They emerged at once, from four different positions, like an organized battalion. They marched at Monsieur Favreau like soldiers, as large and grinning as the first one.

23.

Favreau stood staring at the gathering wolves, his fingers loosening and tightening on his gun. They moved closer, ignoring their fallen companion as the mounting rain pelted his carcass.

"Papa, there's more of them!"

"... get back inside," he said quietly. He started to back away slowly.

The wolves picked up their pace.

Favreau continued to back up. He lifted his musket to a firing position, but abandoned the effort as the wolves kept coming, kept grinning.

They weren't rushing at the pigs, or even at Favreau. They focused their attention beyond him, at the porch.

At Lucille.

My head pounded with terror. They had planned this, waited for this opportunity. They stole a pig every couple of nights to draw the family out into the open, until they found an opportunity to attack Favreau's daughter. Then they all emerged at once, the same way they must have attacked Francois at his home.

Favreau would never get Lucille inside before the beasts devoured them both.

I flicked out one of Pierre's blades and sliced into the side of a pig standing in front of me. It squealed in pain and ran to the other side of the pen.

The wolves jerked their heads toward the commotion as the pigs started to rush back and forth, thumping and sliding against one another. I cut into another one, encouraging their panic. Two wolves sniffed the air, perhaps smelling the flow of animal blood.

I rose, my cloak billowing up from my shoulders as I raised the crossbow. The wolves gaped along with Favreau and his daughter, as I rushed between the pigs to the gate. I kicked up at the top bar, flinging rainwater from it as it flipped open. The pigs spilled out of the pen and darted back and forth across the clearing, slipping and stumbling in terror and confusion.

The wolves continued to stare as I marched out of the pen and fired my crossbow at the nearest brown beast. It fell to the ground hard.

The others snarled and charged, struggling for traction.

"Get inside," I ordered Favreau.

"Who are you?"

"Get inside!" I stepped sideways, angling to face the next approaching wolf. The others closed in, eyeing me warily. I pulled back twice on the crossbow's lever, firing one bolt into the first animal's gut, the other into its paw. My racing pulse had thrown off my aim, but at least I wounded it.

I moved in a curving path between the pigs as they skidded through the muddy grass. The other wolves circled around me, arching their necks to peer over the pigs as they tried to get at me. Between the misty haze and the wild flurry of pigs, I couldn't tell whether there were three wolves or two. My heart and the pigs were both racing too fast for me to tell. The wolves ignored Favreau and his daughter, focusing on me as he scuttled her into the house and shut the door. That was all that mattered.

The wolves bared their teeth, dripping with saliva. I registered three of them surrounding me, a gray one to my left, brown to my right, and black behind me. The rain had played tricks on my eyes. What seemed like a perfect hit on the second wolf must have only grazed him.

Two of them charged from either side. I whirled to fire a bolt into the gray one's stomach as it leaped at me. It spun and rolled aside, howling, while I dropped backward to the ground and planted my elbows in the mud. Then I kicked at a squealing pig as it scurried in front of me and thrust it at the attacking brown wolf.

The startled pig knocked it a short distance away, stopping him for a second. Long enough for me to roll to one side and fire a bolt behind me, into his companion. Then to fire two more into the brown wolf as it bore down on me, dropping it to the puddle-soaked field. I scrambled to my feet. Three bolts left.

The gray wolf struggled to its feet and turned to lunge. I fired once, keeping my final bolts in reserve. It spun to the ground as the black wolf struggled to rise and sprang at me. Another bolt finished it as the gray wolf reared back to lunge again. I tugged back on the lever, sinking my last bolt into its heart.

It fell in a heap and lay still.

I stood in the quiet. Chest heaving in the drizzling rain. Waiting for my pulse and heartbeat to slow, while the remaining pigs squealed and ran in circles through the clearing. My hands shook. I took deep breaths, ordering my arms and shoulders to relax. I reached into my pouch for another round of bolts and started loading them into the top slot, one by one, in case there were more of them.

More of them …

I turned back to the clearing, where the first gray wolf had fallen. The grass there was matted down a little, where the wolf had lain. But it was now gone.

The rain wasn't playing tricks on my eyes. Four wolves came from the forest, but after I struck down the first one, four wolves remained. Only one of the wolves was gray. The first wolf, the one Favreau shot with his musket. It had risen to join the others and attack me again.

The wolf nearest to me – the one I shot four times – groaned and rolled to its side. Then it rose and shook its head to recover. I watched, crossbow ready, as it studied its wounded paw, from which a bolt still protruded. Two similar bolts remained embedded in its stomach. It lifted the paw to its teeth, bit hard on the bolt, and tugged, nearly dislodging it.

Then the creature set its paw down and reached for the bolt with its other paw. I gaped as it wrapped its claws around the bolt to seize a firm hold, the way a human would – and pulled it out.

It dropped the bloody bolt to the ground and turned to me as I tried to comprehend its impossible feat.

Crimson whinnied from his hiding place in the stable behind me and burst into the clearing. He pounded toward me at full gallop. I grabbed onto his saddle as the wolf's jaws opened to chomp at my legs. Crimson whisked me away and raced into the woods, as I hung on with one foot in the stirrup. Behind me, three other wolves rose in similar fashion, grinning and showing little signs of the battle.

Crimson knew when to run.

24.

Crimson thundered through the rain over twigs and pine needles, leaving Favreau's drenched field behind as I hung alongside, one foot in the stirrup. I grabbed the saddle's horn and tugged myself onto his back, crouching low against him as he galloped through the black woods. My fingers ached from their grip around the repeating crossbow. But I refused to let go of it, despite how little it helped me. What were these creatures that looked like wolves, but grinned and withstood bullets and pulled metal bolts from their paws?

I hung onto Crimson's neck and glanced back at the monsters chasing us. Up ahead, more pairs of red and yellow eyes leered from the darkness. I tugged at the reins and Crimson skidded to a halt, twisting to one side. Three wolves strolled out from behind tree trunks, cutting off our exit while the others closed in from behind.

I tugged Crimson to the right. Two more pairs of eyes blazed in the distance. The wolves that owned them padded into the spreading moonlight. I continued circling. Another wolf loped toward us from the opposite direction.

We were dead.

I swallowed and drew Pierre's crossbow. If I sank enough bolts into one of them – just one of them – it might bring him down. It was the best I could do. I was about to die, like my family. Like Francois. I would never know love. Never have children. Never see Pierre or Father Vestille or Monsieur Laurent or anyone else again. And no one in the village would know that I died trying to save them.

But I could still honor Suzette, if I could just kill one of these monsters. Just one.

The wolves blocking our escape stood ready to attack yet restrained themselves. I turned about to face the wolves that chased us from the farm. Their gray leader strode toward me, his three companions following close behind.

I choked back a sob. Why did I have to die? A young girl, scarred and helpless and stupid enough to fight these creatures because I knew someone had to. Why should I die while these beasts lived to kill again?

I had six bolts. I fired the first one. It sank into the gray wolf's chest, throwing him backward in a tumble. The others waited as it lay on the ground. Then it rolled back to its feet, the bolt protruding from its shoulder. One of his companions padded over to him and yanked the bolt out with its teeth. Then they marched forward.

I fired another. I struck him in the same place, close to his shoulder wound, to weaken it. They were strong, but their blood couldn't flow fast enough to heal the same damaged spot.

The wolf rolled backward, grunting against the pain of the blow. Then it rose to its feet, letting another wolf tear the bolt out. They continued toward me like soldiers, grinning.

Tears streamed down my cheeks. I fired a third bolt. It gleamed in the moonlight as it flew, striking the wolf in the center of his skull.

The animal tipped backward and its eyes rolled in a look of surprise. It spun onto its back and lay on the ground.

It did not move.

The forest fell quiet.

The other wolves gaped at it. Not with anger or fear, but a look of actual shock.

They turned toward me and I shuddered. I raised the crossbow with its pitiful three bolts remaining. I wondered how it would feel to be torn apart and eaten.

Instead of attacking, the pack stared at me with wide eyes, as if frightened. Or awestruck.

They backed away. I turned Crimson to face the two wolves behind me, expecting them to pounce. At my sudden turn, they skittered backward. So did the wolves on either side.

I turned Crimson again to face them, measuring their reactions. They turned and ran off in all directions, howling and scrambling as if I had set them on fire. Every last one of them.

The leader's carcass lay on the ground. Rain dripped like a drum from the tree leaves, as I felt the wild pounding of my heart. Crimson shuffled his hooves in the mud, looking from one side of the dark forest to the other. He seemed to share my relief and confusion.

One bolt – one single bolt – had killed this beast, when every other one failed.

What sort of monsters were these?

I waited for a few seconds. A few seconds of quiet and calm and a cooling breeze from the rain as it dissipated. I climbed down from the saddle and stepped carefully to the ground, as though I expected it to swallow me up.

But nothing happened. No wolves returned. The gray wolf leader didn't rise to attack. Its open mouth made no breath, no movement. The beast was dead as a fallen log. As any wolf should be after being shot seven times.

But why didn't the first six bolts kill it? Why only the seventh? And why only this wolf?

I recalled the wolves from the clearing. This first one entered and was shot by Monsieur Favreau. Four more joined it, and this gray wolf rose up to attack alongside them. But only four of them followed us from the farm.

I grabbed the bolt in the wolf's forehead and pulled. I pressed my boot heel over its open eye and tugged, but it wouldn't budge. I flicked out one of Pierre's blades and cut into the forehead around the bolt, sawing until I made a wide bloody hole. The quieting rain turned the fresh blood even fouler. I swallowed back the bile rising in my throat and spat on the ground. I seized the bolt with both hands, pressed my boot against the wolf's face and yanked hard. The bolt came free all at once. I fell onto my rump holding the shaft, covered with the wolf's blood and bone and flesh.

I shut my eyes and quieted my soul a moment. Then I stared at the mess of animal flesh and fur matted with blood. What made this bolt so powerful? It looked the same as every other one.

I stood and shoved it into the pouch hanging from Crimson's saddle. He flinched slightly. His stomach seemed stronger than mine, but not much stronger.

I climbed onto his back and returned to the Favreau farm. I drove Crimson hard, but he needed little encouragement. We both wanted to escape the forest and find shelter before the wolves returned. Favreau's farm was the last place I wanted to be, but we had to go back.

We arrived at the clearing. A dim lantern still burned within the house. Favreau might be watching us from inside or rocking his daughter back to sleep, or both. Near the house, a single brown wolf lay still, unmoving.

Dead.

We trotted up to it. I shot and killed this wolf the same way I killed the gray wolf in the forest. But these wolves died, while their companions survived every attack.

I swung down from the saddle, landing on both feet. I ran to the carcass and rolled it over on its belly. Two bolts stuck out from it like nails. But blood surrounded only one bolt, in the animal's stomach. The other bolt yielded no blood, though it struck the wolf's heart. I pressed my boot against its pelt and tugged the bolt free. It pulled far more easily than the bolt from the gray wolf's skull.

I stared at the bloodstained bolt in the moonlight, turning it back and forth in my fist.

Something howled in the distance. Crimson and I whirled toward the forest.

I shoved the bolt into the pouch beside the other one and hurled myself onto Crimson's back. We fled, leaving the large wolf carcass for Favreau to clean up in the morning, if he ever chose to leave his house again. I had to find out how Pierre forged these two bolts. And I had to live long enough to do it.

25.

We charged through the forest, pounding over twigs and pine needles as the rain turned to mist. Back to the village and to *L'atelier de Forgeron de Leóne*, the only home I had now. How long it would remain a home, I couldn't know. But Pierre and his father had to let me stay at least one more night!

Another howl rang through the trees, closer than the first. The wolves had picked up our scent.

Crimson thundered ahead faster without any prodding. My sides ached from the jarring ride, but I refused to restrain him. Not with so much forest to cover.

More howling. From what sounded like two or more wolves. They could be organizing themselves, picking out a trail, searching for us. They would find us in minutes.

Well before we reached the village.

More wolves joined the howling.

We raced on, sweating in the fresh humidity. They would surround us again, in greater numbers. This time, they would not hold back.

"Helena? Helena!"

I gasped. It sounded like someone called me. I wished it was possible, this deep into the forest. I tugged on Crimson's reins for a moment.

"Helena! Helena, is that you?"

I froze in the saddle. Crimson stamped his hooves, eager to flee. I scanned the area, searching between black trees. A horse approached from the fog, its rider bearing a lantern. The trotting silhouette took on a dark shape, lightening as it drew closer. Beneath the wide-brimmed hat, Father Vestille's eyes held a look of horror.

"Helena! Helena, what's happened? Are you all right?"

I couldn't answer as he came toward us, appearing from nowhere. I was too exhausted to think.

"Helena, what's wrong? I've been searching everywhere for you."

The wolves howled again, less than half a mile away. I jerked at the sound.

Father Vestille studied the woods behind us. "You went after them, didn't you? The wolves."

I said nothing.

He turned sharply at another shrill howl. "They're closing in. Come. My hovel is nearby."

He turned and took Crimson's reins, leading us away at a fast trot. I said nothing, did nothing to resist. The battle and blood and terror left me numb and aching. I only wanted to sleep. To sleep without dreams or nightmares.

We continued through the woods at a steady pace. Father Vestille focused on the muddy path, seeming to ignore the wolves' rising howls.

We entered the little clearing where his house stood, a sturdy structure of clay and large stones, small but protected. For the first time since my childhood, the sight of Father Vestille's hovel warmed my heart. A place to lie down and rest, where the wolves could not break in. I was so intent on returning to Monsieur Leóne's shop that I never considered retreating to Father Vestille's home. But I wouldn't even have accepted his invitation tonight if I wasn't so desperate.

He led us to his stable behind the cottage and jumped down from his saddle. He looked about, then led his Palomino into its stall, closed the gate and moved to the pile of hay beside it.

I sat atop Crimson, heart pounding, chest heaving. The wolves would find this stable any moment. But I waited, my mind and body numb. Waited for Father Vestille to hurry!

Even if I escaped into the stone house, the wolves would pass by here soon and catch Crimson's scent. My throat went dry as I imagined them feeding on his flanks while I drifted off to sleep in the warm cottage. We couldn't stay here. We would have to race on to the village and take our slim chances.

Father Vestille set down his lantern and grabbed a pitchfork from the wall, then started to scrape and pitch hay in a mad rush. I gaped, exhausted and horrified at his sudden desire to clean. His own fear had driven him mad.

He cleared the hay in front of the stalls and set the pitchfork back in place. Two narrow wooden doors, over twelve feet across, had been built into the floor.

I blinked. "What is that?"

He glanced about once more, then pulled up on the ropes attached to each door handle. Hay and dust fell from them, making my nose twitch. I waved it away and squinted at the wooden ramp extending beneath them. It led deep into the earth below Father Vestille's hovel.

He retrieved his lantern and beckoned us forward. Crimson took a cautious step, then permitted Father Vestille to lead him by his reins down the broad ramp. I expected to duck my head as we descended, but found even Crimson could stand upright on the ramp and in the long musty room below. A dusty cot stood in a cobwebbed corner, opposite some wood crates of ammunition and gunpowder to the right.

"The man who sold me this property served in the war," Father Vestille said in an urgent hush. "He built this underground shelter to hide supplies and weapons. I've since used it to hide people, but not for many years."

Near the cot sat a sturdy, long forgotten rocking chair. In addition to soldiers, this place had housed families and mothers with small children. Who had Father Vestille hidden down here?

Crimson snorted at something on the far right. I wrinkled my nose at the molded hay strewn across the floor, next to a hitching post built into the wall. This secret cellar was designed to hide horses as well as their riders. A true shelter. Sheer genius.

"I'll clean that out of here and get some fresh hay in the morning," Father Vestille said, setting his lantern on a table. "I'm afraid you'll have to endure the odor for tonight. Come. Let's get you cleaned up so you can rest."

I climbed down, but ignored Father Vestille's offered hand. Instead, I led Crimson to the hitching post, letting Father Vestille hurry back up the ramp to pull both doors shut. He tramped back down as I removed Crimson's saddle and to let him bed down beside the old hay. He gave no argument, showing the same exhaustion I felt.

I turned back to Father Vestille. He paled. "Helena, what — what happened? Who *did* this to you?" He wasn't staring at the blood or pieces of wolf pelt or even the manure staining my clothes. Only the trousers that shamelessly exposed my legs to the world.

"I did," I said weakly.

"What?" He stared at me as though I had told him I stuck my hands into a fire.

"I can't explain right now. I just ... just want to rest."

He stared a moment longer, then recovered. "Of course, of course." He moved to the old cot and lit a candle on the table beside it. "Let me clean this off so you can lie down."

"There's no need," I said, dropping backward onto the mattress and sending up a cloud of old dust. I shut my eyes and shielded my nose. I couldn't get any filthier.

"Helena. We should clean you up ..."

"I just want ... to sleep ..."

The wolves howled from the forest above us, their cries now faint. I opened my eyes to see Father Vestille studying the ceiling. He listened intently for a moment, then turned back to me. "All right, Helena. I'll be back for you in the morning. Get some rest. And ... tomorrow, we can talk. All right?"

I didn't answer or make any promise. I just stared back at him, tired and weak. He nodded, as if we had agreed on something, and stepped away. He left the candle burning for me, to give off a dim light. Finally safe, finally free for a few hours, I shut my eyes and descended into heavy sleep.

26.

I awoke with a start as something pounded in the darkness. I sat up in bed and blinked, trying to distinguish shapes and remember where I was. Had I returned to Pierre's loft? My head ached as if something was hammering my skull.

The pounding continued from above. I squinted in the hazy light. The candle had burned down to a fuming spark, but dusty rays of light shone through cracks and holes in the ceiling.

"Helena, are you awake?" Father Vestille's voice was muffled.

"I'm –," I rasped. I cleared my throat and called louder. "I'm awake. You can come down."

One of the long shaft doors creaked open, shedding more light on the tiered ramp. Something surged inside me, a strange sense of hope and freedom that I couldn't understand. Then Father Vestille's boots descended the thin boards of the ramp, carrying a tray of food. He wore plain tan trousers and suspenders with a linen shirt. I wrinkled my brow, feeling even more like an intruder.

I had rarely seen him without his priestly robe, not since I was a child. He looked tired and worried.

"Good morning," he said. I sat up in bed as he moved past Crimson, who was rousing himself from the floor.

He set the tray on a small table beside the cot. Warm bread and cheese and smoked sausage. The welcome smells nearly overcame the cellar's musty odor. My stomach rumbled as I closed my dry mouth. Why did I suddenly feel so safe here? Not just in this secret hideaway, but under Father Vestille's care?

He pulled up a stool beside the bed, sliding it past the rocking chair. "Go ahead, Helena. I'm sure you must be famished."

I swallowed. "Thank you."

I started in, seizing the bread with a ferocity that startled me. I didn't realize how hungry I was. How tired and sore. I felt like a wounded stray puppy Father Vestille had rescued from the forest.

He watched me, saying nothing. As though he wanted to make certain I ate. "Do you mind if I join you?"

I chewed on one side of my mouth to answer. "Of course. It's your food."

He smiled. Then he closed his eyes and crossed himself, mouthing a silent prayer.

I stopped chewing, feeling ashamed. It never occurred to me to pray over the meal, as I normally would. I was too hungry.

He lifted his head and opened his eyes.

"I'm sorry I didn't pray."

He shrugged. "The Lord understands. I expect you've had quite an ordeal."

I chewed quietly on the bread.

He glanced at my legs, covered only by trousers, then looked away, embarrassed. He met my eyes. "Can you tell me what happened?"

I kept chewing. He waited for me to swallow. "… It's more than I can explain."

He frowned, studying my face. "Very well." He took a piece of bread and sliced off an end of sausage. "I'll bring down a wash basin for you to bathe, whenever you're ready. Or you can bathe upstairs and I'll wait outside."

I sat up at the thought of leaving the dingy cellar to clean up. "If ... you don't mind ... yes, I would rather go upstairs."

He gave a curt nod. "I'll show you where the sponges are. And I'll start cleaning down here. Or I can wait outside, if you wish, and watch for any uninvited guests."

I lowered my gaze, eyeing the plate of warm food. I never expected him to accommodate me so much after I ran off last night. Especially with the way I now looked. He had no idea what I had done or what monsters were chasing me. Yet he welcomed me into his home without demanding any explanation. "Thank you. But I don't think they'll be looking for me now."

His eyes looked kind but wounded. "Are you all right, Helena?"

I curled my lips shut. I wanted to tell someone what happened. What I discovered about the wolves, whatever that was, exactly. I needed to learn what made those two bolts kill the wolves when the others failed. But Father Vestille was the last person I wanted to confess my activities to, let alone boast about them. "I'm all right," I said. "Thank you for your hospitality. It's very kind of you."

He seemed ready to say something, then shook his head slightly. "You can stay here if you wish. I'll keep you hidden. It's your choice. My home will always be open to you, no matter where you go or what you do. I just want you to be safe."

"... Thank you. I'll consider that." I hardly knew what to say. He was offering me a home. His home. Or at least, the secret longhouse situated beneath it. After I had lost my parents and Suzette, and rejected every offer of hospitality from Father Vestille, he still offered me a place to stay for as long as I wanted. My own underground refuge. It seemed right to hide here somehow. So safe and familiar, so comfortable, in spite of its musty odor. As if I belonged here, where nothing could touch me.

As Father Vestille leaned forward on the awkward stool to tear off some bread, I studied the dusty rocking chair. "Who did you hide down here during the war?"

He blinked in surprise. "I hid you."

I coughed and nearly choked on my bread. He leaned forward anxiously, but I held up a hand as I chewed and swallowed. "What?"

"You and your parents, and your Grand'Mere. When foreigners started raiding the villages, they were hunting for soldiers. Like your father. This underground shelter was a secret that the former owner shared with me, for just such a purpose. We've all kept it secret ever since." He shook his head, recalling troubled times. "Your father came home frantic, not certain whether to fight the invaders or protect your mother, who was with child – you. He decided, wisely, to protect his family. You were born down here, with your Grand'Mere serving as midwife. You all lived here nearly two years, while the invaders tried to secure territory up above."

I stared back at the rocking chair, laden with years of dust. I tried to imagine Mama rocking an infant in it. Tried to imagine her wondering how long she would be confined to this underground prison, struggling to keep her child hidden. To keep *me* hidden.

Father Vestille folded his hands over his mouth. "They never bothered me. I was only a priest, submitting to their rule. So I could keep you all safe." He lowered his gaze. "That's all I've ever wanted to do. Your parents invited me here from Burgundy, and let me stay with them until I could find a place of my own. This place. I owe them a great deal."

I felt cobwebs lifting from my memories. "I remember a wide door opening in the ceiling," I said. "I remember sunlight pouring in."

He smiled. "We all celebrated when the King's soldiers arrived to secure order. We were free. Free to return to our separate homes. But we kept meeting every week at your home."

Until the wolf attacks, when you decided to spend your time visiting safer provinces, I thought. Still, it was clear my family owed him a great debt. *I* owed him a great debt. "I never knew that," I said.

He ate his bread and sausage while I broke off a chunk of cheese. We chewed in silence. When we finally finished, he gathered up the tray and moved to a far corner of the room, where a ladder stood upright near the wall. It ended at the dusty ceiling. "Let me show you where the basin and sponges are. Then I'll get some oats for your horse and start tidying up down here." He moved the tray to one arm and started up the ladder.

I stood, amazed. "This leads up to your home?"

"Of course," he said. He pounded with one fist against the ceiling and pushed open a door. Light poured in from above. I felt the same rush of memories from childhood, the feeling of instant safety and freedom.

Father Vestille slid the tray up onto the floor above, then brushed away clumps of dust from the opening. "It was designed well, to hide soldiers and refugees as well as weapons. If anyone attacked, there was another means of escape. You can eat meals with me or down here. Or you can stay somewhere else and come here if you need refuge. Whatever you choose."

He ascended the ladder into his home. I hesitated to follow him. He had invited me into his home many times, but I never looked or smelled so foul. With my strange and wanton appearance, I expected him to deny he even knew me.

I rose from the cot, feeling stiff pain throughout my body, especially my ankles and lower back. I didn't realize how much last night's ordeal took out of me until I tried to simply stand up. Crimson went back to sleep on the floor. He felt the same exhaustion I felt, perhaps more.

I climbed the ladder, stepping gingerly on bruises and blisters that stung the soles of my feet. I clutched the rung and grit my teeth. If I expected to continue this crusade, my body would have to adapt.

The door in the ceiling opened onto a corner of Father Vestille's front room, warm and free of dust. I breathed in clean air and felt my body relax. He had few furnishings, but they looked comfortable. Three cushioned chairs, a breakfast table, a reading table with a lantern and his Bible, a broad round rug, some portraits of the Christ and of some friends, and a stoop leading up to the front door. The outer porch was all I had ever seen of this place. Who could imagine it hid such a refreshing home?

I looked back at the wall of portraits, seeing one that looked familiar. I stepped forward and saw that it was my parents, with me as a child, only a few years old. Mama held me on her lap, unable to contain her smile. Papa sat beside her, strong and upright, lifting his stiff chin as if daring anyone to attack his family. I forced down emotions, refusing to let myself cry, especially here in Father Vestille's home.

Then I realized, he had no paintings of any of his other friends. He kept this portrait alone, alongside the portrait of the Christ. A picture of Mama and Papa and me from long ago, before I was scarred. I tightened my lips and stood taller.

Father Vestille noticed me staring at the portrait. "You were only four then," he said. "That was painted by a young man who came through the village, a couple of years after the war. Your father paid to have it made and insisted I have it. He could tell I wanted it badly, but I would never ask. I still feel it should have been hanging in your home all these years, but he insisted." He pointed at a large oval washtub against the wall. A bucket was set beside it with a rag slung over its rim. "The washbasin is here. I'll fetch some water to heat up and fill it for you. Should have it ready in less than an hour." He pointed at the rear door. "My room is in the back, if you need more rest while you're waiting."

"Father Vestille. My clothes are filthy. I can't lie down on your bed."

He didn't look at me. "I can wash the bedsheets later. Right now, I'm caring for you."

"Don't you need to know what happened? Where I went after the funeral?"

He grabbed the bucket and started toward the front door. "I'm sure you'll tell me when you're ready, if you wish to."

"Why did you ask if I went after the wolves last night?"

"I heard them howling. Obviously, they were chasing you."

"But why did you hide me underground? You don't mind me being here now. Why didn't you take us straight into the house last night?"

He stopped with the door half-open. He stared down at the stoop.

He closed the door and stepped down, setting the bucket on the floor. "Helena, sit down."

"I told you, I'm filthy. I can't sit on these nice –."

"Helena, please," he implored in a mournful tone. "I need to speak with you."

He sat in one cushioned chair. I sat in the one opposite him, struggling to ignore the mud and manure on my cloak that stained its cushion.

173

Father Vestille folded his hands and stared at the floorboards. "I hid you underground because ... I thought others might be chasing you. Along with the wolves."

I stared at his balding head. Wondering what secrets he held inside it. "You know something about these attacks."

He looked up, his eyes desperate and sad. "Helena. I don't know what happened to you as a child. I don't know what killed your parents and Suzette."

"Father Vestille, I think I –."

"— but I have my suspicions."

Blood surged through my cheeks like fire.

"I've heard many rumors over the years. Of attacks on women and children in this area and others I have visited. In Gevaudan and Dijon and several villages throughout France. Attacks by *wolves*."

My breath grew heavier. My heart beat harder.

"And not ordinary wolves. Witnesses describe them as something larger than a wolf, but similar in appearance. The largest wolves are about five feet long, but these are more than six feet long, standing over four feet high."

I stifled an inward gasp. He was describing the size of the wolves I fought last night. The size of the wolf that scarred me when I was seven.

"People also claim these wolves act strangely. Almost cunning in their approach, in the way they avoid men and their weapons. Almost stealthy in their patience and strategy, attacking victims when they're alone and most vulnerable. Some insist they have noticed these wolves waiting several nights for an opportunity to seize a small child, the moment she ventured outside her home."

In my mind, I saw Favreau's farmhouse and the thinning ivory nightgown of his young daughter. I felt a shiver in my skin. "What are these creatures?"

Father Vestille shook his head, looking helpless. "I don't know. I have no idea. But there have been other rumors of other activity in those same areas. Some people claim to have learned of a cult that is said to worship wolves. They revere them, believing them to be superior to men in power and cunning. They call themselves the Lycanthru." He held my locked gaze. "Many believe the Lycanthru are responsible for those attacks."

I could hear my breath now, feel my chest heaving up and down. "How?"

He shook his head again. "I don't know. Some say they capture wolves and practice witchcraft on them. They believe the Lycanthru have the power to transform these wolves into the creatures that attacked those women and children."

My mind, every nerve of my body was on fire. "How do I find them?"

"You *don't!*" he barked. He struggled to calm himself, shaking. "Helena. I'm telling you this so you can understand. These men are practicing witches. They're performing rituals on wolves to make them kill people."

I stifled my fear. "Like Mama and Papa? And Suzette and Francois?"

He frowned. "Yes. And like you, if you keep after them. Do you understand?"

I stood to my feet. "Someone has to stop them, whatever they're doing. Someone has to make this stop."

He rose with me. "But you are not that person, Helena."

"You don't think I can face them? You're wrong. You would know how wrong you are if you saw me last night. I killed two of them."

"Two of how many? There have been over a hundred attacks reported, just in the surrounding villages. Do you expect to hunt them all down?" He stopped himself and hung his head. He took me by the shoulders. "Helena. I know you've suffered. I've suffered, too, though not as greatly. I lost your father and mother and your sweet sister. I don't want to lose you, too."

I felt my cheek twitch, but I steadied my resolve. "I'll see to it that you don't."

"It's not that simple, Helena." He turned from me, wringing his hands. "What happens when they come after you? Were they chasing you when I found you?"

I said nothing, but shuddered.

"You're dealing with something far more dangerous than you realize."

I bit my lip. "Maybe I am. But someone has to."

He hung his head, defeated. "I cannot tell you what to do. I can only beg you to stay away from those people. These attacks have been occurring for decades, and no one has yet found a way to stop them."

I thought of the two crossbow bolts in my satchel bag, my senses on fire. "I might have found it."

He blinked and narrowed his eyes at me. "How, Helena?"

"I'll look into it further and let you know." I knew better than to tell him anything more. He had little faith in my abilities now. What would he think of my report that two bolts somehow killed the wolves when the others failed, and I just needed to figure out why.

"All right, Helena." His eyebrows lifted in a shrug of surrender. He stood to his feet as if carrying a heavy weight on his back. "Please consider what I said. And don't do anything foolish."

His warning had come far too late, but I said nothing.

"I'll fetch water and heat the bath. You can rest in my bed until you're ready. You can make this your home, if you wish." He frowned again. "You are … You're the only one left of your family. I'll do whatever I can to help you. Please stay safe."

I swallowed. "I will. I promise."

He nodded, accepting my assurance but knowing I wouldn't give up my plans. He retrieved the bucket and moved to the front door. He creaked it open just enough to scan the clearing for any intruders before stepping outside.

I felt a strange emptiness in the silent house as he left. Father Vestille was the last person I wanted in my life, especially now. But he might understand my loss better than anyone else. In an odd way, he was the closest thing to a family I had left.

I sighed, dismissing my grief. His cottage kept me warm and secure. That was all that mattered. If this Lycanthru cult was behind the attacks, they would never search for me in a priest's cottage, let alone his secret underground retreat.

I realized I could no longer sleep in the loft at *L'atelier de Forgeron de Leóne*. Not after attacking the wolves last night. Some villagers might suspect that I would seek help from Pierre. I would have to avoid meeting him too often, or I might endanger him and his parents.

After I returned there today, of course.

27.

By late afternoon, I had bathed and eaten a little more. I even slept another few hours in Father Vestille's underground retreat, which smelled much nicer after he finished his cleaning. After I woke, I cleaned and fed Crimson, who seemed to feel as fresh and alive as I did, eager to gallop again.

As we pounded toward the blacksmith shop, a few villagers cast odd glances at my bright hood and burnt umber horse. They would surely have gaped at my offending trousers as well, if they knew I was a girl.

The odor of burning iron filled the inside of *L'atelier de Forgeron de Leóne*. Pierre looked up from his smelting pot and quickly extinguished the flame, setting his tools aside. He met me with eyes full of panic. "Red! Where did you go? Where have you been all day? Father Vestille was searching for you for hours, and I've been –."

"He found me," I said. "I'm –." I stopped short, catching myself before I announced I was staying with Father Vestille.

Pierre was the one person I could confide in. But to protect him and myself, I had to keep that retreat secret. From everyone.

"What?"

"I'm not sure where I'll be staying now."

He looked wounded. "Red. You can stay here as long as you want."

"That's not entirely safe. I appreciate your offer, and I'll take advantage of it now and then. But your loft can't be a permanent home. It will draw too much attention."

"From who? I don't care what anyone in town thinks."

"Not from people in town."

"Red, what's happened?"

"I found them."

Color drained from his cheeks. "The wolves?"

"And I fought them. About twelve of them."

He glared at me, starting to tremble slightly. He looked me up and down, apparently checking for cuts or missing limbs. "Are you ... Are you all right? You ... You got through it."

"Yes," I said, sounding more annoyed than I should have. Pierre knew I was a better hunter than most men. But no one, man or woman, would likely survive an attack from a dozen wolves. If it weren't for Father Vestille, I would be dead. I softened, touching his hand. "I'm fine, Pierre. Thank you for your concern, and your help. Everything you gave me."

He released an anxious sigh. "The blades worked for you?"

"Yes. They work just fine."

"And the new crossbow?"

I lifted the repeating crossbow for him to see. "It worked perfectly. Twice. That's why I need your help."

He took the crossbow and studied it with a quizzical expression. "It only fired twice?"

"It fired perfectly, thirteen bolts."

He blinked at me, even more amazed. "You *missed?*"

Heat rose in my cheeks and I stuck my fists on my hips. "I sank every single bolt into those things."

"Oh," he said, satisfied with the answer to one puzzle but still confounded by the one that remained.

I calmed myself and realized he was complimenting me. He believed his own repeating crossbow was more likely to fail than I was likely to miss. "Most of my shots would have killed a normal wolf. But these things kept coming. The bolts had no effect on them. Except for these two." I held up the grimy bolts I had pulled from my satchel.

He took them from me and squinted closely. "What's so special about these two?"

"That's what I need you to find out. Do you make every bolt the same way?"

"Yes," he said. Then he seemed to recall something and looked a bit ashamed. "Although ... the process is the same, but ... we don't always use the same material. You asked me to make you extra bolts, so I used the metal we had in supply. I had to mix in some other metal for some of them, to give you a few more."

"How many bolts did you make that way?"

"Only two or three."

We stared at one another, astonished.

He moved to an empty smelting pot with the bolts. He cleaned most of the blood and grime from them with a hot wet rag. Then he started a high flame and held it beneath the bolts, melting them slowly. I watched a few drips fall into the pot, then stepped aside to sit on the bench. This would take some time.

Pierre's father entered from the back room. "Pierre, I need you to finish those stokers for Monsieur Denue by Friday."

Pierre extinguished the flame and turned on his heel to stand at attention. "Yes, sir."

Monsieur Leóne studied his son a moment, then noticed me sitting quietly in the corner. "Helena? What are you –?" He gaped at my legs and fell silent.

I broke the silence. "I came to ask Pierre for some help. Something's wrong with my bolts."

Frayne Leóne continued to stare at my legs. His whole face seemed to wrinkle in disgust, until I crossed my legs and tried to pull the outer edges of my cloak over them.

It didn't help. He seemed just as perplexed, just as offended. "Helena ..." He started to speak, wrinkled his brows some more, and shut his mouth. He tried again. "Helena, I ... I'm so sorry for your loss. Your mother and Suzette, they were wonderful people."

I stared back, feeling numb. "Thank you."

He couldn't tear his eyes away from my masculine garb. "Do you ... need anything? Food or ... clothes?"

"No, thank you. I'm well taken care of."

He said nothing. Then at last, he turned and walked away. He stopped to address his son. "Pierre, I need to pick up some more iron. The miners finally broke through and found a rich supply, so we won't run short again. I'll return in two hours." He glanced sideways at me once more, then looked back at Pierre. "Can you handle everything while I'm away?"

"Of course, Papa."

Monsieur Leóne gave a curt nod, glanced at me once more, then left through the back door.

Pierre looked irritated. "First time he's ever asked me if I can handle the shop by myself. I usually do when he's away."

"I don't think he approves of my wardrobe," I said flatly.

Pierre shrugged. "Well ... it's a little different."

I looked away, feeling even more isolated. But I no longer cared what Monsieur Leóne thought of me. Or what anyone else thought.

Pierre studied the falling drips of metal. "Nothing unusual so far. Regular iron, like we always use. Some lead, though, showing here. All right, so this one had some other metal mixed in. But I can't see how that would matter, when ... wait ... all right, some copper. Traces of silver ..."

Blood surged through my shoulders. As though I was meant to pay attention to that detail. As though I had been given the answer.

Silver.

Francois said his ax blade was made of silver. His blade that killed the wolf instantly, though he only grazed it.

"Try the other one," I said.

He narrowed his eyes at me, confused. "I haven't finished studying this one."

"It's enough. Melt the other one."

He frowned, but set his tools and the first bolt aside to start on the other one. Within a few minutes, he found what I expected him to find.

"... some lead in this one, too ... Some traces of silver. Must have just poured everything in at once. Nothing else yet, but –."

"It's silver," I said.

"What?"

"Silver. That's what kills them."

"Red, that makes no sense. A silver bolt couldn't hurt a wolf any more than an ordinary bolt."

"You should tell them that."

"But how's that possible?"

"I don't know. But these bolts killed them, and so did Francois Revelier's silver ax. Killed it easily, just like the two I shot last night. That must be the difference."

"Red, silver isn't any kind of poison."

"It might be to them."

He shrugged again. "All right. How can we know for sure?"

I sat rigid on the bench and stiffened my lip. "Only one way. I'll have to start using silver bolts."

"You're going after them *again?*"

"Yes. But this time, I'll be better armed."

"Red, if you're wrong, they'll kill you!"

"They'll kill us all, anyway," I said hotly. "That's what no one seems willing to grasp. They're not going to stop. They'll keep coming. They'll keep getting stronger and growing in number and killing whenever they feel like it. We can die trying to stop them or we can sit at home and wait for them to come. I'm not waiting."

"But ... silver? That's impossible, Red."

"So are these wolves, over six feet long and able to ..."

He waited for me to finish. "Able to what?"

I almost said they could talk and stand upright. Something I never shared with anyone outside my family, not even Pierre. At least, not after the day of the attack, after seeing the confused faces of Father Vestille and Francois when I told them what happened. I couldn't bear to receive that same look from Pierre. "... able to organize themselves to attack in large numbers. They staked out that pig farmer's house to get at his daughter."

"What makes you think that?"

"There were plenty of wolves on hand last night to attack. Yet for the last two weeks, they only took one pig at a time. They didn't care about the pigs. They only wanted to draw out the farmer and his little girl. Once she came outside, the wolves showed up in full force."

"But why would wolves attack a little girl when they could go after a whole herd of pigs?"

I thought of Father Vestille's story about the Lycanthru, practicing witchcraft on wolves. "They're not wolves. I'm going to need silver bolts. My blades and other weapons need to be silver, too. Even my grappling hook, just in case."

Pierre wrinkled his brow. "We don't have that much silver to spare, Red. How much does it take?"

I peered into the smelting pot at the sparse drops of melted silver. "How much was in the bolts?"

"Barely a trace."

"Then that's all I should need. Just a little on the tip of each bolt and the sharp edges of each blade."

Pierre rubbed the back of his neck. "Red, suppose you're right. Suppose this will kill them. They're not likely to show up at that farm again. How will you even find them?"

I thought of Touraine, telling me about the men who delighted in reports of wolf attacks.

Men who might belong to the Lycanthru.

"I have an idea where to start."

28.

A few hours later, after I ate some bread and pork prepared by Pierre and slept a little more in his loft, I rode toward *La Maison de Touraine*. Pierre had outfitted all of my weapons while I slept, gilding each new bolt and knife edge with silver. He said his father would be furious to learn he had melted down other customers' works to make new bolts for me, putting their orders further behind. But he planned to tell him he found some imperfections and needed extra time to finish. I thanked him for it.

It was near nightfall. Villagers started to tug their cloaks about their shoulders as they passed by in the street. Many of them stared at me with a fresh sense of surprise. Instead of wrinkling their noses at me, they stopped in their tracks and followed my movements, almost in a sense of wonder. As though it had suddenly become admirable to wear a giant red cloak.

I rode up to the hitching post at *La Maison* and left Crimson to stand beside it. I patted his neck. He had slept well at

Father Vestille's last night and gotten more water and oats from Pierre. He seemed fit and ready for whatever might come tonight.

I pushed through the thick doors of the tavern.

Raucous conversations stopped. I scanned the room. Every eye fell on me.

I stood at the door, uncertain what to do. Were they staring at my scars? At the red hood?

I stepped forward, listening to my own slow boot steps on the floorboards as I approached the bar counter. People began to murmur and resume their excited conversations, now strangely hushed. Were they talking about me?

At the bar, Touraine wiped the counter where a man had just spilled his beer. As I drew near, the gaping man slid off his stool, filling my face with his alcohol breath. He continued to stare as he turned in a circle and backed away, forgetting the rest of his drink on the counter.

"So," Touraine said quietly. "You've returned."

"I seem to be popular tonight."

His broad shoulders heaved and sighed. "Yes, you are. You went to Favreau's farm last night." It was not a question.

"I might have."

"You fought five or six large wolves there, killed two of them. They found the bodies this morning."

"There were about a dozen, actually. They chased me into the —."

"You're him, aren't you?" interrupted a well-dressed man. His large elbow came to rest on the far end of the counter. His voice was smooth, almost mocking. "You're that red rider. The one who fought all the wolves at that farmhouse."

I turned slowly to face him, saying nothing. It seemed prudent to let him think I was a man.

Even more prudent when I took a good look at him. Tall and strong, with a broad black moustache. He held his drink at his side, grinning as if he was somehow challenging me. Not doubting me, but wanting to test my abilities.

"Move along, Brocard," Touraine said. "Those are just rumors. How could one man take on a pack of wolves by himself?"

The man didn't budge or acknowledge Touraine. He sipped his drink, studying me. "Those wolves. They're dangerous, you know. You're lucky to be alive." His face lit up like the devil, or something worse. As if he was picturing the wolves tearing me apart. "I'm Jean Paul Brocard. I farm cattle and do some business in the village. I trade livestock, horses, weapons, tools. Anything a man might need." He raised his eyebrows with an unconvincing show of friendliness. "Perhaps I could outfit you some day, Monsieur. A man who fights off a whole pack of wolves will surely need help now and again. Extra food for your horse. Extra bolts for that crossbow."

Touraine cleared his throat, looking nervous. "I really don't think the man's interested, Brocard."

The smiling man edged closer along the bar counter. "You might discover I'm a good man to have on your side, Monsieur. You need someone you can count on, to help you survive. When the odds are overwhelming." He slid his drink along ahead of him, stopping it in front of me. He sat on the stool beside mine and leaned forward, folding his fists as he tried to look beneath my hood. "Because those wolves will eventually come looking for you, you know. All of them. And they'll find you. They'll find you and tear you into small pieces. Who will help you then?"

I stood and raised my crossbow to his face. Every conversation stopped again as Brocard lifted his chin. His Adam's apple swallowed hard. He smiled wider to cover his anxiety. I understood, since I had drawn my crossbow to keep him from seeing my shoulders tremble. I focused on steadying the weapon, the way Papa taught me to do when hunting, to push aside my fear.

Brocard lifted his palms in gracious surrender. I allowed him to take a step back. "I see it is a 'No' for now," he said. "We'll talk again another time, Monsieur."

He continued to back away, hands raised as he grinned. I turned toward the watching crowd. They all kept silent. A few of them turned away as I met their gaze.

"Yes, you're popular all right," Touraine said. "Be glad I'm not telling anyone you're a girl. A strange young girl at that, dressing like a man and fighting wolves in the dead of night. They'd never leave you alone."

I frowned. "Am I really that strange?"

He pursed his lips. "Have you seen a mirror lately?"

"But you meet all sorts of people here. Even women. Am I actually the strangest girl you've ever met?"

He considered for a moment. "Ever?"

I nodded.

"Yeah," he said. "Yeah, you are. Just watch yourself. Men like Brocard are charming enough, but he's part of a dangerous crowd."

I resumed my place on the stool. "Dangerous, how?"

"Excuse me, Monsieur." I flinched at the gruff voice. A tall man marched straight at me. He wore the broad blue cloak of the village police. "I hear you were involved in an incident at Monsieur Favreau's farm last night."

I kept my head down a little, hiding beneath the hood as best I could while I studied him. He looked strong and severe, with inky black hair beneath his broad-brimmed hat. He squinted at me with narrow eyes.

Eyes that were blue-gray.

I stiffened, feeling my blood race through my veins. The same blue-gray eyes of the wolf that killed Grand'Mere Marie and left me scarred. The same eyes of the wolf Pierre and I saw in the dark tunnel. What in God's name did it mean?

"I'm Lieutenant-General Vigo Sharrad," he said, his words coming to me in a fog. "It's my job to protect the people of *La Rue Sauvage*. And their farmland."

"I think someone's been spreading rumors, Monsieur Sharrad," Touraine said casually.

Sharrad jutted his broad chin at Touraine, as if threatening to stretch forth and bite him. "And who's spreading those rumors, do you think?"

Touraine shrugged. "I don't know. But I can't imagine anyone fighting off a pack of wolves on their own. Let alone this ... person, wearing a bright red cloak. Can you?"

"I can imagine a number of things." Sharrad glared back at me. "I expect you've got a wild imagination, too, don't you, Monsieur?"

"Monsieur," Touraine broke in again, leaning on the counter with a smile. "This gentleman's just here for a drink. Maybe some people don't like how he looks. Maybe they're jealous of his cloak. So they're making up stories about him. He hasn't really done anything, has he?"

Sharrad's eyes burned into me. I kept my head lowered, but kept watching him. Watching his eyes.

"Not yet," Sharrad said. "But I've heard reports, and I'll be watching you, Monsieur. If I hear of any more unprovoked attacks on wolves or other animals, you'll see me again."

"But, Monsieur," Touraine continued. "If someone's killed some of the wolves that have been attacking people, that would be good, wouldn't it?"

Sharrad faced him with his fists on his hips. "When I need a tavern keeper to help me keep order in the village, you'll be the first man I call on. Until then, why don't you keep quiet and bring me and my friends another round?"

"Of course. Sorry, Monsieur. Be there in a moment."

Sharrad cast another glare in my direction. "You keep that crossbow put away while you're indoors, understand?"

I gave a slow deliberate nod.

Sharrad regarded me another moment before striding away toward his table. I watched him go, feeling myself tremble. I tried to tell myself that I could not have seen what I did. But I couldn't deny it. I would have to watch Sharrad very closely until I could reason it out.

Touraine glanced in Sharrad's direction. "Do me a favor. Try not to get yourself arrested. Or killed. Seems you're making the wrong people angry. Of course, now that you've killed a couple of giant wolves, you probably think you can handle anything."

"Tell me about those men. The ones who enjoy hearing about wolf attacks."

He nodded back at Lieutenant-General Sharrad. "He's one of them. So is Brocard. They come in here with their friends every time there's an attack. In fact, someone from their group is usually the first to report it." He wrinkled his brow. "Matter of fact, I never knew you used a crossbow, 'til Brocard mentioned you might need more bolts for it."

"I thought Favreau told everyone that."

Touraine shook his head. "No one's seen Favreau. His brothers found his pigs and rounded up most of them. But Favreau wouldn't come out or let his daughter out, even when they beat on his door. Just kept telling them to go away."

I felt a shiver inside. "So how did anyone know about the wolf attack last night? How could anyone know I was there?"

Touraine shrugged. "Just be careful. Someone knows what you did, and they're spreading the word."

"Someone who was there," I said. "Someone like Sharrad and his friends."

"Likely."

"So am I some kind of pariah now?"

"Maybe. No one's sure what to make of it. Someone attacking wolves late at night on a farm and killing two of them. Some think you're a hero. Most didn't believe you existed." He surveyed the room of hushed murmurs. "Of course, they do *now.*"

I turned to view Sharrad and his table. The crowd's murmuring hushed as I faced their direction. Some of them watched my every move, perhaps fearing I might draw my crossbow again.

Sharrad's cold eyes continued to watch me. Beside him, Brocard raised his mug toward me with a smile. None of the other seven men at their table were smiling. They stared at me or looked over their shoulder, scowling and whispering at one another's ear. They were all dressed differently, representing different jobs, different ages, different tastes. Yet they shared the same vicious scowl. I wouldn't trust myself alone in a room with any of them.

"How often are those men in here?"

"Every night on the weekends," Touraine said. "Either that crowd or some of the others."

"There are more?"

"Plenty more. A few dozen, I'd expect. All different walks of life. Some farmers, some carpenters, merchants, woodcutters, coopers, blacksmiths. Some of them are very well off, some are barely managing. Not sure what they've all got in common. Except maybe a cruel sense of humor." He shook his head again. "I'd stay away from them, if I were you."

I studied the gang of rough-looking men as they eyed me with contempt. "Yes," I said. "That would be wise."

29.

It was near midnight before Sharrad and his associates left the tavern. I watched them from a darkened alley, feeling the evening's chill, as Crimson waited behind me in quiet obedience. They seemed in good spirits now, shoving playfully at one another and making threatening growls, like rough-spirited children. Like Jacque Denue and his companions. Hairs rose on my skin. I could see what Touraine meant about avoiding these men. I didn't want to follow them, but I had to know how they were connected with the wolves.

They mounted their horses and trotted off toward the woods. Brocard, still grinning to himself, led the way with a torch held aloft. I allowed them time to gain some distance, then climbed onto Crimson's saddle and rode after them.

I tugged gently on Crimson's reins, keeping us shrouded in the darkness of the forest. We kept still as Brocard and the others entered a clearing on the outer edge of a sprawling farm. Whoever owned it seemed well-off. A field of wheat spread for several acres beyond the grove of trees that hid the barn and silo. Yet there was no house connected with the barn, so the owner could afford to hire out farmers while he sat at home and raked in his profits.

Sharrad and the others dismounted to enter the barn. They glanced about, as if spying for intruders. Crimson kept perfectly still for me in the shadows.

When they were satisfied, Brocard raised his torch higher and led the way to the barn. He tugged open the front door. Within the barn, more torches blazed and several other men had gathered. I couldn't see any particular person, only a small crowd. They went inside, casting final glances over their shoulders, and shut the door.

Something felt wrong, like a snake burrowing under my skin. I prodded Crimson forward by cautious steps into the dark grove, and surveyed the grounds to make sure no one else approached. A noise rose from within the barn, like a unified cheer, or a collective moan from a herd of beasts.

Crimson slowed his pace. I couldn't blame him. Something about this place and the gathering disturbed us both. I felt a crawling chill in the air. Like something small and devilish laughing in the wind.

We edged forward and moved to a side of the barn. I dismounted and drew Crimson forward to stand close to the wall. The din inside grew louder and clearly human, almost musical in its unison. I crept to the front door and searched for a discreet way to enter.

Up above, beams of light broke through the wall, revealing the loading entrance for stockpiling hay. I withdrew Pierre's grappling hook and slid back the lever, letting its prongs spring out. I squinted, spotting a small triangular hole above the loading door where the wood had worn through. I swung the steel hook in circles, then let it fly straight up. It caught the hole above the door and I tugged on it, feeling it embed itself in the wood. I paused to listen for any sudden movement, then started up the wall. Thankfully, I had only a few steps to climb to the loft. I righted myself and stepped carefully along the slim ledge as the strange rhythm within grew louder. Even more so after I tugged the prongs free to return the hook to my belt and slowly opened the door.

Hay and dust trickled down from the pile that had been shoved against it. I wrinkled my nose at the moldy straw pushed to the outer edges by fresh hay. I spread the hay apart with caution, as if wading through weeds in a pond. The noise beyond the hay pile grew louder and stronger, the chant drumming through my entire body as I waded deeper in. Something within reeked of sulfur, permeating the inside of the barn.

Finally, I broke through part of the hay to peer through a giant square hole in the center of the loft. A large gathering of men stood on the floor below. They wore black hooded robes and stood in formation like soldiers, chanting in a strange language that sounded like Latin. Towering torches burned at either end of the ceremony. One robed man stood on a platform between two short pedestals, his arms raised to the assembly. Their hoods each held a picture of a grinning wolf, making every person look like a black wolf with the body of a robed man. Behind the leader, a large vat bubbled up something foul, the offensive odor I had detected.

The hypnotic chant continued as two men each brought an animal carcass toward the leader. They laid both corpses on a pedestal, bowed to the leader, and backed away to resume their positions.

They were two dead wolves.

I shuddered. I had found the Lycanthru.

Something shuffled nearby. I noticed four robed men standing on either side of me, looking down on the ceremony from separate corners of the loft. I steadied my breathing and tried to keep still.

The leader produced a curved dagger and cut away a section of one wolf's back. He held up the small rectangular pelt, showing it to the crowd as the chanting slowed. Then he wrapped it around the back of his neck, wearing it like a priest's collar. As he did so, the other men produced similar wolf pelts and placed them around the backs of their own necks. Then the leader pointed up at the ceiling.

Was he pointing at me? I held my breath.

When no one reacted to my presence, I noticed they craned their necks toward a skylight cut into the roof, which shed light on each of them.

Moonlight.

The leader lifted his arms, welcoming the moon's rays the way someone might welcome the sun on his face after a rainstorm. The others followed suit, raising their hands to the moon as if praising it.

Then they produced small flasks from within their robes. The leader took his to the bubbling vat behind him. He lifted a large iron ladle from the vat, filled it with the foul goldenrod liquid, and poured it into his vial with a doctor's precision. As he stirred the vat with his ladle, it bubbled a little more, refreshing the sulfur stench in the air. He extended his arm to the other hooded figures. They stepped forward, one by one, to have him fill their own flasks.

When everyone had taken from the vat, they returned to their positions to face the leader. Then each one drew back his hood.

I leaned forward and squinted at the leader who looked down on them all.

I gaped at the handsome features and piercing eyes of Duke Leopold Laurent.

Duke Laurent, Papa's influential friend.

The man who bent down to smile at me after Jacque Denue's friends attacked me, to ask if I was all right.

The one who held a banquet to honor Francois, for his bravery in killing the wolf that killed Grand'Mere Marie. A banquet from which Francois went home drunk and was devoured by a pack of wolves on that same night. As if by coincidence. Or by design.

Duke Laurent, who made an appearance at every funeral of every person killed by the wolves. Who railed against the King for ignoring his letters, in which he begged the court to send soldiers to protect us. Letters he never truly sent.

Laurent.

I clenched my jaw and tensed my shoulders to keep from shaking the straw that covered me.

Laurent spread his arms to the crowd. "My brothers. I know you have concerns about the men we lost last night, and the red-cloaked rider who killed them. I assure you, we will find him, whoever he is, and make him suffer. As to how he did it, I have sent word to the Prime, and I will let you know his conclusions once I receive them. You have my word."

I bit my lip, seething. His *word.*

"Meanwhile, I am pleased to announce that Her Majesty has accepted my invitation." This brought a cheerful murmur of approval and a few joyful shouts. Laurent waved down their excitement with his hands. "So do not be distracted by last night's incident. It is of little consequence, and in another month, will amount to nothing. So let us celebrate these fresh kills from our two newest initiates, and the strength they will soon share with us. Not to mention sharing in our glorious destiny. Soon all of our patience will be rewarded. Let us drink to that."

A few men laughed. Duke Laurent held up his flask with two hands as if it was a precious infant. The other men followed suit. Laurent tipped his head back and they all drank. He winced as if it tasted bitter, but then licked his lips to savor it, like a drunkard sucking down stale alcohol solely for its effect.

He stepped forward to stand directly beneath the skylight. The moon shone on his face as he closed his eyes with a look of rapture. He shed the black robe from his shoulders, revealing that he was completely naked. I nearly gasped, but kept quiet in spite of my shock.

Duke Laurent's face began to change. His strange grin pulled back at the corners of his mouth and somehow kept pulling, widening his lips. At the same time, his ears seemed to stretch away from his jaws, and moved impossibly up toward the top of his head. His nose grew in size and length, extending over his chest along with his jaws, lengthening like that of a dog. Gray hair sprouted from his cheeks, forehead and chest as he hunched forward. He fell to his hands and knees and I saw a bushy tail grow and lift from behind his back. His arms and legs narrowed while his hands and feet thickened and grew into paws. He crouched on the floor of the barn and opened his fiery eyes, grinning again to display canine fangs.

Laurent had become one of the six-foot wolves I fought at Favreau's farm.

The Lycanthru weren't simply worshiping wolves. They *were* the wolves!

30.

I inhaled with a sharp squeak, unable to stop myself. The four robed men standing in the hayloft turned sharp eyes toward me. The nearest one clawed through the hay and seized my wrist. Before I could think, he yanked me from my hiding place for all to see. Straw and dust fell from my cloak like a rainshower.

"It's him!" shouted my captor. "It's the red rider!"

He tugged me toward himself again as Laurent – in his horrid wolf-form – gaped up at us with bulging eyes. Others turned toward us as well, while the rest of the men in the hayloft ran at me.

I kicked at the man's shin and he groaned, clutching his knee. I grabbed a pitchfork set against the wall and turned it on the man rushing at me. I thrust the tines toward him a few times. He backed away and lost his balance, falling backward from the loft, screaming, onto the crowd below. The other two paused before continuing toward me. I couldn't fend them both off at once.

I turned back toward the hay pile I had hidden in. I shoved at it with the pitchfork, forcing the heavy pile out the loading door. I pushed myself out into the cool night air, in the midst of the thick hay.

I landed hard and rolled, my side aching from the impact on the grass. Thankfully, the previous night's rain left it soft enough to ease my fall. I whistled for Crimson as angry shouts grew within the barn, rushing toward the front door. Crimson galloped straight at me, as if the barn's rising chaos helped him sense my need. I stood and grabbed the horn of his saddle, letting his momentum propel me up onto him as the door flew open and the Lycanthru poured out.

I glanced back as we raced deep into the forest. The men stood outside the barn, gulping down liquid from their flasks and removing their black robes. I barely glimpsed them as they crouched low to the ground and their naked bodies changed, like Monsieur Laurent's, becoming an army of enormous wolves that bounded after me with nerve-rattling snarls.

I drove Crimson harder, pounding past dark pine trees. The welcome cover of branches and leaves gave little comfort, since the Lycanthru wolves would know the forest terrain well. They growled behind us. I turned to see three of them closing in. I drew my father's crossbow, already cocked. Slow and steady, keeping a sure grip as we galloped on.

I took aim at the tan wolf nearing Crimson's heels and fired, praying I was right about the silver.

The bolt struck his flank, behind his head. A clumsy shot.

Yet he fell to the ground with wide-eyed surprise. The next two wolves scrambled past him. One glanced twice over his shoulder at the dead wolf, seeming confused that the creature failed to rise.

So much for my doubts.

I just killed a man. A man who could transform himself into a wolf. My fist clenched the reins tighter.

The other two wolves quickened their pace. I leaned forward in the saddle to draw another bolt from my satchel pouch. I loaded it and carefully lowered the crossbow's strap to my right stirrup, my body in rhythm with Crimson's stride. After looping the strap under my boot, I yanked up on it to cock the bow. I turned in time to see one wolf opening its jaws to nip at Crimson's hind leg. I fired straight into its skull and it slumped to the ground.

The third wolf glanced back at it, his rushing gait faltering for a moment. I re-loaded and cocked the crossbow as I glimpsed more wolves, perhaps eight of them, approaching from the distant fog behind me. I shot the third wolf in his neck and he spun to the mud.

They would reach me in less than a minute. I could never hold them off with my few remaining bolts.

I clung to Crimson and kicked at his flanks. We surged forward, heading for who-knew-where. I had to find an escape, somewhere. Anywhere. Anywhere to hide from these beasts that were once *men!*

Father Vestille was right about the Lycanthru, just as Pierre was right about the hood, now a bright red flag drawing them straight toward me.

A sudden inspiration struck me. I bent to slide Papa's crossbow back into place and grabbed the repeating crossbow, slinging its strap over my shoulder. Then I untied my cloak with one hand. The wind blew the hood wide as I pulled it against Crimson's neck and tied it fast to the reins. I pushed the flapping cloak from my face and looped the crossbow strap over my neck, then gripped the reins in my left hand as I drew my grappling hook. I flicked its prongs open and let the hook dangle at my hip.

I spotted a thick tree limb, the kind I needed, and swung the hook toward its base. It looped under the branch and locked in place as I gave Crimson a final kick and a shout. Then I lifted my heels and clung to the rope, tugging myself out of the stirrups. I curved up under the limb as Crimson fled beneath me. He paused and glanced back, and I shouted at him again to continue. He obeyed, confused, but slowed to a trot, refusing to wander too far away as I scrambled up the rope. The wolves were still too far back to notice me climbing in the dark fog. At least, I hoped they were.

I grabbed hold of the limb and hoisted myself up, straining to wrap my leg around it. I straddled the branch in time to see the wolves approach. They stared straight ahead, focused on Crimson and the flapping cloak. I slid the repeating crossbow strap off my shoulder and aimed. Pierre had melted down enough material to fully load it with ten bolts, all tipped with silver.

I fired at the three nearest wolves as they rushed toward my tree, plugging each one.

They dropped to the ground and lay silent. The silver worked.

I fired at two more oncoming wolves, who broke their stride to glimpse their fallen companions. Once struck, they lay a few feet past them in a heap.

The other wolves slowed their rush. Some stopped altogether and hunched down, twisting their necks toward the surrounding trees. I fired at the two in front, dropping them where they stood.

The rear wolves backed up a few paces. Some turned and fled.

An auburn wolf growled back at them. "Cowards!" he shouted in a guttural voice.

My blood ran cold. It was true, what I heard as a child.

They could speak.

They were men who could turn into wolves, but still think and speak like men. And they had organized themselves into a small army to attack the people of *La Rue Sauvage*. To attack families and their children. Why?

I dismissed my questions for the moment. I had three bolts left. More than a dozen wolves remained below.

I had to frighten them off. If I took out their leader – the auburn wolf who shouted back at those who fled – then the others might back down. He still faced them while the other wolves paused in the clearing, shifting from side to side and looking uncertainly at one another. I took aim at his head, just below the pointed ear.

He charged back toward the other wolves as I fired. "Come bac–!" he growled as my bolt sank into the tree trunk behind him.

The wolves froze. I trembled, trying not to give away my position.

Two bolts left.

"There!" the auburn wolf snarled. "He's up there!"

The others padded a few steps back from me. Perhaps to get a better look. Perhaps out of genuine fear. I focused on the auburn wolf but he bounded away, toward the wolves that escaped.

I puzzled over that while the others shuffled back and forth in the muddy ground, disquieted.

I struggled to slow my breathing. Where did that auburn wolf go? To gather reinforcements from the barn? I couldn't last long against them all or wait them out until daybreak. I had to use every small advantage I had. Such as the fact that wolves could not climb trees.

Something snarled and rushed from behind the other wolves, who parted to make way for it. The auburn wolf charged between them, sprinting madly at the tree trunk where my bolt had embedded itself. He leapt at the tree and bounded off it to jump higher at another tree near me. He struck that trunk and sprang from it, launching himself at me like a flying nightmare, his jaws wide.

I noted that *normal* wolves can't climb trees, as I fired on a reflex, sinking my last two bolts into its mouth and gut. The wolf spun backward in mid-air and twirled to the ground. It hit the earth like a sack of potatoes and lay dead.

No bolts left.

The other wolves stared at the auburn wolf and glanced back at their companions, shifting their paws. But they didn't leave. Some kept their eyes fixed on the auburn wolf. Others backed away, ready to run.

A few growled up at me.

I turned toward a shuffling sound farther up the path. The other wolves also turned. Between the leaves, over the bushes, I could see Crimson's head as he trotted back and forth. He had insisted on staying close.

I whistled for him. Time to escape, if we could.

The wolves glanced in all directions. Crimson bounded through the trees, the red cloak wafting behind him like a soldier's flag.

The wolves backed away.

"There are two of them!" one snarled.

"Run!" growled another. Half the pack turned and sprinted away as I watched, amazed. It wasn't just Crimson that startled them. They withdrew at the sight of my hooded cloak.

The remaining wolves lost their courage and ran as Crimson charged at them. Ran from the sight of my red hood.

I swallowed, releasing a hard breath. I shimmied down the rope as Crimson drew near, then jumped onto his saddle and kicked at him, leaving the grappling hook behind. I could retrieve it tomorrow. Or Pierre could make me another one.

We galloped toward Father Vestille's hovel, kicking up mud and leaves, Crimson's hooves pounding with the rhythm of my heart. I steadied my breath and tried to gather my thoughts. Everything had suddenly become clear, in one horrifying night. One horrifying hour.

The wolves spoke. I had not imagined it. The wolf that killed Grand'Mere Marie spoke to unsettle me. He never expected me to survive and expose his strange ability. The Lycanthru were transforming themselves into wolves to attack people, led by Duke Laurent.

But I discovered their weakness. The slightest touch of silver killed them. They now feared me. Feared my red hood.

I thanked the Lord for revealing everything to me, my senses surging with relief and rage as we rushed through the frigid night. Everything became so clear. I could stop them.

I could kill them all.

MY WAR

31.

We emerged from the seclusion of the forest pines and trotted into the clearing where Father Vestille's hovel sat. Nestled deep in the woods, his home was easy to reach and easy to maneuver from. Riding all the way into the village was out of the question, now that I knew the Lycanthru's secrets. They would hunt me down. I could never use Pierre's loft again.

I tried to settle my racing heart. The Lycanthru. Duke Laurent. I still saw the image of his face beneath that monstrous wolf-hood, standing before the cult that was terrorizing the province. Still saw Laurent and the other men drink that foul sulfurous liquid and step into the moonlight to transform themselves into enormous wolves.

I shook off my fears. Silver would destroy them. *I* could destroy them. I had to keep my courage. More important, I had to keep myself hidden so I could rest. No one could know that I had anything to do with Father Vestille anymore. Or all of our lives would be forfeit.

I led Crimson to the stable behind the stone hovel and surveyed the area for any witnesses. Then I kicked aside straw and lifted the secret door to Father Vestille's underground sanctuary. I checked again for any sign of movement from the surrounding trees, then led Crimson down the ramp. He could fill up on oats and bed down for the night. I lit a candle and noted the underground room was much cleaner now. No more cobwebs or dust clouds, and only a faint lingering odor of mold. Father Vestille must have spent a good part of his day making this place into a home.

I swallowed. Could I ever again have a place to call home?

Yet Father Vestille did his best to provide one, without even knowing whether I would return. I stepped back up the ramp to pull the top door shut, then got Crimson settled. Once he lay on the straw pile – much larger and fresher than last night – and bowed his head to close his eyes, I climbed up the ladder and knocked on the trap door. I heard Father Vestille's muffled voice and some quick shuffling overhead. I was growing so accustomed to this night life, the life of a nocturnal beast, I forgot that normal people still retired to their beds after midnight.

"Helena?" Father Vestille called in a harsh whisper from above as he creaked across the floorboards.

I pushed the door up and climbed into the warm candlelight of his front room. He stood there in his nightshirt, holding the candle on its tray. His anxious eyes were bloodshot.

"I'm here," I said. "Crimson's settled for the night." I stepped up into the room and eased the door shut. He deserved far more explanation of my activities, but I acted as though I had said all that was necessary. I couldn't expect him to understand.

He accepted it, clearing his throat. "Do you … Have you had anything to eat?"

My pride urged me to lie and say I didn't need anything. But my more practical stomach growled.

"I'll get you some bread. I still have some cheese and lamb from tonight's supper. I hoped you might return."

He shuffled away to his table. I followed slowly as he unwrapped the remains of bread from a cloth in a round basket, unwrapped some cold lamb and hunks of cheese from another platter.

He looked at me, somewhat abashed. "I can light the fire again to heat this up."

I shook my head. I didn't want him to have to do anything more. Nor would it be wise to send up chimney smoke from his hovel after midnight. Not with the Lycanthru searching for me. I shuddered and clutched my shoulders. "It's fine. Thank you."

I grabbed the meat and tore off a chunk with my teeth. I had not eaten for hours and the excitement in the forest only made me more ravenous. I was well into my second bite when I noticed Father Vestille staring at me with concern.

I realized I had failed to give thanks again. I stopped chewing in mid-stride and bowed my head to thank the Lord for the food. For this place. For my life. Whatever might be left of it.

I opened my eyes to find him still staring. Perhaps he was less worried about my prayers than for my half-starved condition.

"Can I get you anything else? Do you need to bathe again? I can wait out here, or outside if you like."

I shook my head and chewed. I had to discuss tonight's events with someone, and quickly. Even if it had to be Father Vestille. Before it was too late.

"Father Vestille," I began, then finished chewing. "... Something happened tonight."

He stood listening. Then he turned and pulled up a stool to sit before me. I sat in the chair by his table. It felt good to sit. To do something normal and safe. To imagine I could be safe again someday.

I swallowed and lowered my eyes. "I saw them. The Lycanthru. I saw them all."

His voice rose in a panic as he gripped my shoulders. "Helena. Are you all right?"

I nodded. I didn't shake him off. It felt good to be held, the closest thing to an embrace that I would experience for some time. My entire life had changed in a few days. In one terrifying night. I could never be the same person again. I could never again enjoy a feeling of safety or home or family.

"There were several men, wearing robes. With images of wolves on them. They performed some sort of ritual. And … they changed into animals." I met his eyes, which held horror but no disbelief. "Father Vestille. They're the wolves that have been attacking everyone. They *become* wolves."

Father Vestille stared at me, then swallowed hard. "Are you all right?" he asked again.

I gave a small nod.

"Did they see you?"

I felt cold inside as I nodded again. "They chased me. I shot a few of them."

"You *shot* them?" He seemed equally horrified.

"Yes," I said, offended. "It was wise at the time."

He sighed with some irritation. "Go on."

"Never mind," I said, starting to rise.

He remained in his stool and put a hand on my shoulder. His eyes were repentant. "Please."

I fumed for a moment, then sat back down. "I saw their leader. He removed his hood to drink some potion that changed him into a wolf. It was Duke Leopold Laurent."

Father Vestille glared at me for several seconds. "The other day," he muttered.

I squinted at him. "What day?"

He looked off, grinding his teeth. "The day your … your mother and Suzette … were killed. Duke Laurent invited me to his chateau for a talk."

My nerves flared with rage. "About what?"

He set his jaw, narrowing his eyes. "To see how your family was faring. After the loss of your father."

I gasped and shook. Laurent had planned every attack. The banquet to make Francois drunk while Laurent's own friends surrounded him at the tavern, waiting to strike at his home later that night. Then luring Father Vestille away from Mama and Suzette so the Lycanthru could murder them in broad daylight.

Laurent.

"Helena. I'm glad you choose to confide in me, but … why, exactly, are you telling me all this now?"

I shivered. We both knew I had pushed him away, rejected his every offer of help or friendship. "Someone needs to know," I said. "I can't be the only one. Someone else needs to know, in case …" I broke off, uncertain how to finish.

He finished for me, his eyes wide. "In case anything should happen to you." He rose and turned away, frustrated. "I *told* you the Lycanthru were dangerous. And if the *Duke of La Rue Sauvage* is involved –."

I stood and leaned toward him. "He's not just involved. He's *leading* them!"

"Leading them against *you!*" he said. "Because you challenged them. Because you sought them out and found them."

"I can't change what I've already done."

"But what will you do now? Will you go on fighting them? Killing them? These are not animals, Helena. They're human beings."

"They're not animals, and they're *not* human beings. They left their humanity behind to become these things."

"You can tell yourself that if you wish. It's still murder."

"This is a *war!*"

"A war you started."

"No. A war *they* started. They're killing innocent people. Innocent *children!* And you want me to *let* them!"

"You know I don't want that."

"I don't know what you want. You want to help me. You want to shelter me and care for me. But you don't want me to fight the things that killed my family."

He strode at me. "Because I don't want them to kill *you, too!*"

We held one another's gaze for a moment. He was shaking.

"I don't want them to, either," I said quietly. "But I can't let them take any more children. Ever again."

He struggled to calm himself, unable to respond. He knew what I felt, having hidden my family away during the war. But perhaps he had forgotten how to take risks to protect innocent people.

"Helena. I appreciate what you're trying to do. But I'm worried about you. Not just for your physical well-being, but also for your soul. If you wage this war, I fear for what you might become."

My stomach churned. He was like a man with a musket who refused to fire at the predators on his doorstep. "If you're that concerned about what I'll become, I can find another place to stay, so you won't be burdened."

As I folded my arms and glared at him, I realized I felt something more than disgust at his cowardice. I feared he might be right. If I kept on fighting these monsters, could I become just as cold-hearted and bloodthirsty? Would I become the scar-faced monster that Jacque Denue and his cronies feared?

"You are no burden," Father Vestille insisted. "You can stay here for as long as you wish. I will gladly shelter you and feed you, and give you whatever you need to live a full and rewarding life. But I cannot help you kill."

I kept my back to him. I couldn't expect a priest to help me kill anyone, beast or not. It seemed he was doing everything for me that his faith would allow. Which made me question my own faith. Was I truly seeking justice or merely revenge? Yet how could I let them ravage our people, our world, while I retreated into a safe, warm house and pretended there were no monsters outside my door? When I could do something to stop it.

I turned back to face him. "Right now, what I need most is your confidence in me."

"I have every confidence in you, Helena. But I cannot help you take up a sword. I might as well be putting it to your throat. It will only end in death."

I swallowed, but kept my body rigid. I couldn't let him know the fear I felt, or let him put any of his own fear into me. I had no choice but to fight these beasts. Except to retreat, and wait to die.

I lifted my chin. "Then let's say we understand one another, and agree to disagree on what must be done."

He looked sad and distant, as if I were his own daughter leaving home, never to return. As though he was mourning the loss of my soul. I prayed he would be wrong.

"I will accept that, for now," he said. "I only want to help you, Helena. You're all the ... You are the only one left from your family now. I don't wish to lose you, too."

"I'll do everything I can to see that you don't. I promise."

He glanced aside, shuffled his foot, cleared his throat. "Come. Finish your supper and you can get some rest."

I followed him to the table without another word and did as he said, like a condemned man marching to the gallows.

Crimson woke before me. He stood in the darkness, where stripes of light shone through the cracks in Father Vestille's floorboards above us. I ignored both Crimson and the light and shut my eyes, drifting back into a swallowing sleep.

I woke perhaps an hour later, feeling refreshed and stronger. I sat up on the cot and had an odd feeling. A feeling of freedom and security. Of home. The underground cellar held little light or fresh air, but it was safer than any place where I could take refuge above ground. Where the wolves reigned.

For a few brief instants, it felt as if the wolves didn't even exist. Until I reminded myself of them.

I stood to my feet and stretched. I wore one of Father Vestille's old nightshirts, which hung down to my knees. But it kept me warm through the night, along with the blanket, and helped me feel human again for the few hours I slept.

I looked about for my clothes. Then I remembered Father Vestille had offered to scrub them clean for me, despite my protests. I smiled now at the thought of him with a basin of soapy water and a washboard, working away at the filth on my pants. The pants he was embarrassed for me to wear in public, as anyone would be. The pants I wore to move freely enough to kill the wolves. Yet he cleaned them for me, despite his discomfort with my new life.

It almost felt like having parents again. Someone to care for me. To accept and support me, even if he didn't agree with my choices.

I started toward the ladder to retrieve my clothes. Then I found them right in front of me, folded in a basket at the foot of the ladder, along with my cloak and boots. The basket had a rope tied to its handles, which lay in a heap beside it. He had finished the work and lowered the container to the floor, mindful of disturbing my modesty by not entering the room.

He was a good man. Better than I had thought, while he cared for Mama and Suzette over the past several months. Better than I treated him. Still, for all he had done to help us during the war and for all he did to shelter me now, he abandoned us when we needed him most. When *I* needed him most. After the wolf attacked, we needed courage and guidance, but he was away visiting other provinces, other churches. Seeking his own escape instead of facing them down, however he could. If he wanted to help me, I would gladly accept it, but I couldn't forget the past.

I sighed and grunted. I had no time to mourn his choices. From the look of the sunrays entering from upstairs and my well-rested state, it was already midday. Only a few hours left to report last night's events to Pierre before darkness set in again.

I reached for my clothes and carried them to the cot with my cloak and boots. Time to set to work.

32.

L'atelier de Forgeron de Leóne smelled of rich oil and fire from the day's work, nearly over now as dusk approached. Monsieur Leóne was away again, delivering special orders and securing more material.

Pierre could not stop gaping at me for the entire time I told my tale. The events of last night – the Lycanthru, their ability to speak, the clear effect of the silver bolts, their new fear of my hood – every detail enthralled him. I told him everything, except for two significant details.

"Where did you go then?" he asked.

I curled my lip. "I can't tell you that."

He blinked, wounded. "Why not?"

"Pierre, I trust you and I value your help. But I can't reveal everything that I'm doing. Just trust that I've found shelter."

"But why can't you stay here? You're welcome to sleep in the loft anytime you want."

I touched his hand to show my gratitude. "I know. But I can't let anyone find me here, or find you. Too many people know I've visited you before. That alone places you in danger. And I can't let anything ... I don't want to endanger you any further."

His brows curved up in hurt, but he nodded his understanding. "Did you see any of them?"

I blinked. "The wolves?"

"The Lycanthru. Did you see any of their faces? Recognize anyone?"

I stared blankly at him, imagining his obvious emotions on display as one of the Lycanthru – perhaps Duke Laurent himself – questioned him. I pictured them seeing through his attempts to protect me as he claimed to know nothing. I saw them seize Pierre by the throat and drag him deep into the woods where their mouths would transform into hungry jaws.

"No," I said. "I never saw their faces. I don't know who any of them are."

Pierre frowned. "Too bad." He locked his gaze on me. "Especially if they know who you are."

"They don't. Yet," I assured him. "But they will."

"Red, don't do anything dangerous."

I blinked at him. "I think it's too late for that."

"Anything *more* dangerous than you've already done," he clarified, sounding annoyed. "If you keep after them, they're going to come after you. And they'll find you."

"I don't think so," I said, thinking of the safety of Father Vestille's hideaway. Wondering how long it might remain safe. "In any event, they'll be searching for me already, don't you think?"

Pierre swallowed hard. "Of course. You saw them. Saw what they do. They won't let that pass."

I nodded. "Which means I've got to stop them first."

"Red, you can't! These people – these monsters, whatever they are –- how are you going to stop them? You don't even know who they are or where to look for them next."

"I know where to start."

"All right. Then I'm coming with you."

"No, you're not."

"Come on, Red. How do you expect to stop me from following you? You know I'm a faster rider."

"I know." I sighed and turned toward the other work table beside us, wishing I could take him along and lean on his help. But it would mean exposing him to the Lycanthru and marking him for death, the way I had been marked. "Forgive me later?" I asked.

He squinted, confused. "For what?"

I struck his jaw hard and he spun in a half-circle on his way to the ground. Thankfully, his head missed the edge of the oak table.

I dropped the heavy chunk of lead back on the work table, where I had just snatched it. I shook my stinging hand as I stared at Pierre's quiet body lying on the floor, hoping the lead punch wouldn't leave much of a bruise. I wanted to embrace him, stroke his head, thank him for his endless support and care. Instead, I had knocked him unconscious.

I kept staring at him, wishing I was a different person. Someone he could love and be happy with.

But I wasn't. The Lord had assigned me a strange destiny, however short-lived it might be. To stop as many of these murdering creatures as I could. Before they finally killed me, too.

I blew Pierre a silent kiss, hoping he truly would forgive me as I asked. For what I had done and for whatever I was becoming.

I stepped over him and headed out the door.

33.

The same hush fell over the crowd of swaying onlookers as I entered *La Maison* tavern, crossbow in hand. Before I pushed through the heavy doors, they were joking, shouting, jostling one another. Now they all fixed a silent gaze on me before quietly returning to their drinks and murmured discussions, stealing glances at me over their shoulders and cupped hands. No one risked speaking to me, perhaps fearing my wrath, or being otherwise drawn into my dangerous world.

Touraine eyed me from the bar as well, ending his conversations and shooing people away. He looked serious and uncomfortable as I approached. He turned his back to me as I took a seat on the stool. "Order a drink," he muttered.

I considered reminding him that his tavern refused to serve young girls, but this was no time to make sport. People were watching us. I laid my crossbow on the counter. "Monsieur," I said, acting as if I was seizing his attention. He turned. "A glass of your best wine, if you please."

He soured. "Buttermilk it is," he said, reaching below the counter.

I frowned. "Just put some water in a mug. And make it look dangerous."

He took a new mug and a pitcher and turned his back to me again. "You had another busy night."

"Very busy. You heard of it, then?"

"Heard there was a hunt. Heard some men found a pile of dead wolves out in the woods. Large ones. But no one knows who found them, and there's nothing there anymore."

I narrowed my eyes. "Nothing there? Then how do they know there were any wolves there in the first place?"

Touraine bowed his head, pretending he needed to polish a mug with his rag. "It's a rumor. Some claim they saw that red rider fighting wolves in the forest. They say he killed a few and left them there. But they're gone now. Others say that was just a rumor spread by some drunkards. What do you say?"

He handed me the mug and I drank, wondering how to pretend it was alcoholic. I decided to drink it slowly. "It's no rumor," I said, staring down at the counter as he turned his back to me again. "I suspect someone started talking about last night's events until someone else ordered them to keep silent. Have those men been back tonight? The ones who love hearing about wolf attacks?"

"Same place as always. They're calmer tonight, though, maybe because Duke Laurent joined them. He made a rare appearance."

I turned to see them, gathered around the same table as last night. Lieutenant-General Sharrad was there again, near the head, his blue-gray eyes shining. Beside him sat Leopold Laurent, like a spider at the center of its web. His advisor, Simonet, sat in the next chair, wearing his usual callous expression. They all studied me with violent disdain.

I grabbed my crossbow and rose from the stool.

"Mademoiselle?" Touraine asked, turning suddenly. "Mademoiselle, where are you going?" he demanded in a whisper.

The crossbow hung at my hip as I strode toward the table. The table where the Lycanthru gathered to celebrate their victories after attacking people in the village. After chewing on the flesh of innocent mothers and fathers and five-year old girls. My cloak rippled behind me as I marched at them, my boots clomping across the floorboards. They set down their drinks and sat taller, their backs rigid, their attention focused. Observers shrank back at the surrounding tables, eager to avoid us.

I stood before the Lycanthru's table and stared straight at Laurent. No one moved.

Duke Laurent squinted, confused. He blinked in surprise. "Helena?" A strange smile twisted across his lips. "Is that Helena Basque beneath that hood?"

He recognized my scars across the lower half of my face. I no longer cared.

I grabbed a nearby chair and slid it to the end of the table, opposite Laurent. I sat there with all eyes on me, as I lifted my hands to draw back the hood, revealing my face and blonde hair. Their eyes bulged in an odd mixture of horror and delight. They seemed outraged to discover their adversary was a mere girl. Yet they seemed all the more eager to take their revenge, now that they saw my face.

"So," Laurent said, breaking the thick silence. "I haven't seen you since ... oh, yes. Since your little sister's funeral."

Blood surged through my neck and temples. I wanted to stretch across the table and strangle him. But I could do nothing to him here, in front of so many witnesses. People who only knew him as I once did: as a generous benefactor to our tiny community, a man we were all blessed to have leading us. He was a true wolf in sheep's clothing.

He saw he had rattled me. He continued to study me with measured calm, watching my reactions. I couldn't let him unsettle me again.

"Well," he went on. "... What new things have you been up to lately?"

I stiffened my posture and steadied my breathing. "A lot of hunting. Late at night."

Scorn lined every face around the table. I could almost feel, almost smell, their hate for me. Even Simonet narrowed his eyes with bitterness. Though I was only a girl, they wanted to destroy me at least as much as I wanted to destroy them.

Laurent twisted his lip. "So I hear."

"So you witnessed," I said. "From your platform."

The men around the table drew a sharp intake of breath. Sharrad bared his teeth, looking so savage I thought he might spring for my throat.

Laurent fingered his mug, lifted it and drank. Then he continued to study me. "You seem to have learned a lot in one night."

"Not enough. I know what you are. What you become. But I don't know which of you attacked me, or which of you banded together to kill Francois Revelier. Or the rest of my family."

Laurent squinted at me, cockeyed. "You're accusing me of attacking you, Helena? And of killing your woodcutter friend? Forgive me, but I thought you were both attacked by a wolf. Isn't that the story you've been telling everyone? Weren't you attacked by a big, bad wolf?"

The men snickered.

Laurent continued, like the ringmaster of a traveling circus troupe. "If you change your story now and say you were attacked by a man ... well, I'm not sure how many people will believe you."

"There were witnesses."

"Oh?" Laurent asked in a mocking tone, as if this was new information. "Where are they now? Was that woodcutter one of them? Or your Grand'Mere? Or your Papa?"

Hot blood rose to my temples.

Laurent folded his hands, satisfied. "Seems you're the only one left to tell your tale, Helena. And people don't often listen to hysterical little girls who lose their temper at funerals and refuse to associate with anyone. Especially when they take to dressing in men's clothes and running through the woods late at night, hunting for witches and big bad wolves."

The others burst into laughter, except for Simonet. He continued to watch me with eyes that were angry but reserved.

I waited for the rest of them to finish their mindless chuckles. "I'm not interested in exposing your dirty secret activities."

"No? Then how can I help you, Mademoiselle?"

My cheek twitched, but I kept my body rigid. "I only want our province, once and for all, to be rid of you."

They stared at me in stunned silence. Then exploded into laughter. One man actually wiped tears from his eyes as he attempted to regain his composure.

Laurent looked over the heads of his comrades and smiled. Other raucous conversations had resumed behind us, drowning out whatever was said at our table. Laurent smiled at the group and leaned forward. "Mademoiselle, let us be honest. You've done very well. You struck at us and actually did some damage. I'm not so proud that I cannot admit you beat us down. Twice. So you have my respect and admiration, and I congratulate you." His grin hardened into stone. "And now it's over. You cannot seriously hope to 'rid' your little province of me. Or the rest of our order, which happens to hold eighty-eight members. All with the same abilities that my friends and I share."

I tensed my back and shoulders, keeping my lips impassive. I couldn't let him know he frightened me. "Eighty-eight? Still?"

He grinned, looking genuinely amused. "I apologize. You have reduced our ranks down to, what? Seventy-five? Yet as I see it ... seventy-five to one? I think we can still rely on our numbers."

"Rely on them while you have them."

Laurent leaned forward again, incredulous. "So you're serious, are you, Helena? You intend to take us all on?"

I said nothing.

He kept his eyes on me as he leaned toward Simonet. "Tell me what you see, Simonet."

I met Simonet's cold eyes, which seemed to pierce my soul.

"She's passionate in her position, Your Grace. Unfortunately for her, she has no real plan. She might continue to do damage, but she knows she won't last long."

I tried to steel myself against all fear. To keep him from seeing it.

Laurent turned to his right. "What do you think, Sharrad? Does she look serious?"

Sharrad locked his gaze on me. His thin lips spread in a cruel smile. "I think she looks delicious." His stare burned into me until I could actually feel his hunger.

"You don't frighten me," I told him, stiffening my shoulders to convince myself. "You killed my Grand'Mere and you scared me in the tunnel when I was a child. But you won't frighten me again."

Laurent squinted and exchanged looks of confusion with Simonet and Sharrad. "You think Lieutenant-General Sharrad killed your Grand'Mere?"

"I recognize his eyes."

Laurent seemed to understand, but acted as if I said something amusing, while Sharrad flared his nostrils. "Helena, dear. The wolf that killed your Grand'Mere is dead. Your friend, the woodcutter, killed him with an ax. That was not Vigo Sharrad, the head of our police force. Tell her who it was, Vigo."

Sharrad's blue-gray eyes blazed. "That was my brother, Gaston."

I shuddered, while Laurent grinned with malice. It was Sharrad's brother, with the same unsettling eyes.

"And tell her what you've wanted to do since that day, Vigo."

Sharrad twitched, as if he wanted to leap at me from his chair. "To devour the one who killed him. Which we did, a few years back. And to finish the job Gaston started."

"He means you, my dear," Laurent said with delight. "Helena, consider what you're getting yourself into. I'm willing to forget these recent incidents and we can part ways. I don't expect us to remain friends, but if you walk away now, I promise you'll live."

"No guarantee from me," Sharrad said.

Laurent put up a hand to quiet him. "I can keep our order in line, Helena. Including our respectable Lieutenant-General. I can ensure your survival. However, if you continue this reckless endeavor ..." He raised his hands in surrender. "There is little I can do to protect you. You can see how angry my friends are. I believe they want your blood."

"Blood, flesh and bone," another man snarled beside me, his hair and eyes wild.

"So as the last living member of your family," Laurent continued. "If you place any value on your life at all, you'll take this chance now to leave with your life. Otherwise, I cannot be certain what will happen to you."

He looked as though he expected me to believe his lies, the way Papa believed him. I felt myself trembling in my seat. I no longer bothered to hide it, even from Simonet. Despite my fear, I shook with something else now: rage. "Nothing is ever certain in *La Rue Sauvage*, Monsieur Laurent. Except death."

I pushed the chair away and stood. My cloak whirled behind me as I strode toward the door.

"Where are you going *now,* little girl?" Sharrad called across the room.

I spun back at them, the blood filing my cheeks as they laughed. Sharrad meant to unnerve me, using the same words the black wolf had used. His own brother, the Lycanthru with shining eyes who killed my Grand'Mere and left me scarred. They wanted to remind me that, after all these years, I would not find anyone to believe my reports about them. About men who changed into talking wolves and threatened to gobble up little girls in the night. To remind me I was completely alone in my fight against them.

But I already knew that.

I raised the repeating crossbow to my shoulder and they abruptly froze, falling dead silent. Two of them shrank back. Other conversations stopped abruptly around the large room.

"Hunting," I said flatly.

Everyone in the tavern watched me, with what might have been awe or revulsion. Either way, it was mixed with fear, which was what I needed. I had made the Lycanthru afraid. If the rest of the town feared me as well, so be it.

I stepped outside and climbed onto Crimson, anxious to ride off and get my shaking under control. They unnerved me, but I also unnerved them. I simply had to focus and quiet my fears, unleash my anger.

They would remain in the tavern, deliberating over how to deal with me. I would have to be even more cautious about my contact with Touraine and Pierre, to keep them from linking us to one another. Which left me even more alone.

I had no choice. I knew what I had to do. What I alone could do. I destroyed a handful of them. There were seventy-five Lycanthru left. I would start keeping count.

I rode hard into the open plain and galloped toward the forest.

34.

"Did you hear about Helena Basque?" asked a meek young man on the street below.

I turned and peered down from the rooftop edge at the two men on the street corner directly beneath me. I didn't recognize them from that angle, but I recognized the two young girls they spoke with. The raven-haired Celia Verdante and her friend, Marie Beauchamp. The four of them huddled together to ward off the night chill, and to keep from being overheard by others standing across the street outside *La Maison*. From my secret perch, I merely shrugged off the cold. I had spent many nights spying from rooftops like this one over the last two months. The frigid air no longer bothered me

"I've *heard* of her," Celia Verdante said with a charming lilt. "But I haven't had the misfortune of *seeing* her for quite some time."

Her friend and the other man laughed. His was hearty and rough. If only Mama were alive to hear the superficial girl she thought I should befriend.

The meek-sounding man looked at each of them, not laughing. "Yes, that's unfortunate, what happened to her. And to lose her entire family afterward. But have you heard, they say she's the one killing all those wolves for the last two months. She's the Red Rider!"

Celia grunted with disgust. "I suppose if I were that scarred and hideous, I might also wish to hide myself under a hood and sleep in the forest. Or I might become so desperate to attract a man that I would shamefully expose my legs to everyone. But I would hope not."

"Perhaps some wild animal will find her attractive," Marie chimed in. "Since no man ever will."

They laughed again. All but the first man. "I think you're being too harsh. That girl has suffered a great deal. All due to those wolf attacks. If she can now stop them, well, I'll be glad to have our town that much safer, won't you?"

"Safer?" Celia challenged with a mocking tone. "With a wild girl galloping around town firing that weapon of hers in every direction? We might as well all shoot cannons at each other."

"I close my shutters every time I hear her passing by," Marie said.

The man lifted his palms. "How do you know it's her?"

She laughed. "It's not hard, with everyone shouting, 'It's the Red Rider!' in the streets."

"Along with the screams of whatever poor creature she's just killed," Celia added.

"Screams?" The man sounded aghast. "Those 'poor creatures' have been devouring children in the village for years, from what I hear."

"Not the wolves," Celia corrected. "I'm talking about people."

"You think she's killed someone?"

"Several people, from what I hear," Marie said. "Haven't we noticed some men turn up missing from the village, since she went mad?"

"I don't believe she's mad," the man defended.

"Then you haven't seen how she dresses," Celia joked.

"And I don't see what those disappearances have to do with her," he went on. "If she's killed them, as you say, where are their bodies? Do you imagine she's dragged them off somewhere by herself?"

Thankfully, I had discovered that when the Lycanthru die, they remain in whatever form they had taken at the time. When I killed them, they died as wolves.

"There's no reason to imagine she killed any of those men," the man continued. "But large dead wolves have been found every week for the past two months. And several people now admit they were rescued from those wolves by the Red Rider. People feel free to speak up, now that the wolves are dying off. And the other day, someone remembered how Helena Basque wore that red cloak at her sister's funeral, before she disappeared."

"And good riddance," Celia said. "If that bizarre girl moved into the village, I think it would be safer for us all to sleep in the forest."

The others laughed again.

"How can you say that? Haven't you heard a word I said?"

The dark-haired man put a hand on the first man's shoulder. His voice was deep and smooth. "I must admit, I believe the ladies are correct."

I recognized his voice. It was Brocard, the mustached Lycanthru who approached me at *La Maison* the night after I fought them at Favreau's farm. My blood ran cold.

"I, too, have heard the rumors that Helena Basque is this 'Red Rider' character. That much I believe to be true. As to her making the village safer ... Well, it's hard to accept that a young deranged girl is responsible for killing all of those wolves. They must have been killed by other hunters or died of some disease. After all, how many of them have died over the last two months? Nearly a dozen of them? All by her hand?" He lifted his palms, doubtful.

It was fourteen. Actually.

I smiled. From this same perch, I had listened to hushed conversations of men leaving *La Maison de Touraine*, night after night. They gossiped about wolves attacking in various farms and isolated cottages. I later visited those places to confront the wolves when they attempted another strike. The silver bolts allowed me to dispose of each wolf with efficiency and precision, save for one frightful night when I lost my balance and my crossbow at once. Yet I managed to burn the approaching wolf with a nearby torch before he devoured me.

I spared several innocent lives, just as I spared Favreau's daughter that first night. And I kept count. In two months, I had eliminated another fourteen of them, leaving only sixty-one more wolves.

Brocard went on. "I find it far easier to believe that pitiful girl, deranged with grief, has lost all sense of control and gone on a mad killing spree. Even if she is killing a few of those wolves, as you imagine, what will she do after she's finished them all? Who will she want to kill next, to satisfy her bloodlust? No, I fear Celia is right. The streets of *La Rue Sauvage* are far more dangerous since Helena Basque started running wild."

There, Brocard, I agreed with you. The streets were far more dangerous. For you.

I learned nothing further from Brocard and the others. They quickly switched to other subjects, as Brocard invited Celia to a masquerade ball as his personal escort, and offered to arrange an escort for Marie as well. The girls were delighted at his invitation and quickly forgot their concerns about my activities.

Nor did I learn anything from the others gossiping in the streets below. It seemed the wolves were holding back now, striking less often over the last three weeks. Or perhaps they were planning some new strategy of attack.

It was just as well. Celia's callous remarks distracted me for the rest of the night. Though they shouldn't have. I was used to people drawing away from me. I simply had not heard anyone speak of it for a while.

When the first man walked away from them, I felt compelled to follow him. I foolishly wondered if he might defend me to someone else. I didn't realize how much I needed to hear those words until they were spoken. That a few people – even a handful – were grateful to have me here.

But I remained on the roof, where I needed to be, to hear if Brocard might meet another of the Lycanthru and reveal something I could use.

He didn't. I trudged back to retrieve Crimson from the public stable and rode home, ending a cold, wasted night.

I woke at midday to a banging noise overhead. I rose from the cot as Crimson stirred suddenly from the hay, looking up at me. Something banged again and I wondered if Father Vestille had fallen. I tossed my blanket aside and hurried to the ladder to listen.

I heard him walk across the floorboards to his front door and I breathed a sigh of relief. I heard him open the peephole, then unlatch the oak door and creak it open. "Monsieur Laurent," he greeted.

An icy chill raced up my spine. Laurent had found me.

"Please, come in," Father Vestille said.

A gap between two warped floorboards let in extra light from above and allowed me to hear more clearly. Which meant I couldn't retreat to my bed or risk any other sounds. I turned toward Crimson and held up an urgent hand. Either he understood my command for silence or my intense actions alerted him to danger. He kept still.

"Thank you, Father," Monsieur Laurent said as he entered the room. As he stepped across the wood that separated me and my dressing gown from him. I tried to slow my rapid heart beat.

"To what do I owe this pleasure?" Father Vestille asked. He sounded more cordial than pleased.

"No pleasure at all, I'm afraid," Laurent said. "I came to ask you for some direction on a troubling matter. It's about Helena Basque."

My shoulders tensed, my lip trembling. I glanced at my clothes beside the bed and my crossbows beside them. How quickly could I retrieve them if Laurent threw open the trap door?

"What about her?"

Laurent paced across the floor, walking away from Father Vestille. "You have no doubt heard of her recent activities.

Dressing strangely, keeping odd hours. They say she prowls the woods at night, looking for large wolves."

Laurent seemed to wait for a response.

"I have heard these rumors," Father Vestille answered. "I cannot tell you for certain whether they are true, in regard to the stories that she hunts for wolves at night."

"But you are familiar with the rest."

"Sadly, yes," Father Vestille said.

"I am quite concerned for her," Laurent went on. "You know they suspect her of causing the disappearances of several men in the village?"

"I have heard those rumors as well. Hard to believe that, of course."

"Of course," Laurent replied. I could almost see his patient, condescending smile. "I have always tried to help the Basques and she is the last surviving member of her family. I want to see to it she gets the help she needs, before she does any harm to herself or others."

Father Vestille took a while before he answered in a dull tone. "What sort of help do you wish to offer her?"

"Whatever is necessary. As of yet, she has broken no laws that I know of. So she is in no danger of being arrested, unless someone proves she had something to do with those disappearances. But her wanton and violent behavior, her rejection of everything feminine, her hysteria about hunting wolves in the night … Quite frankly, it's frightening. If she proves too disturbed for anyone to reason with, we may be forced to commit her to an asylum."

Tense nerves seized the back of my neck. My fingers ached from their grip on the ladder.

Laurent stepped a few paces closer. As if he sensed me hiding directly beneath his boots. "Have you seen her?" he asked, sounding coy. "Some people reported seeing her ride in this direction."

Father Vestille sighed deeply. He cleared his throat. "Like you, I have been a good friend to both Henri and Celeste Basque, and even their youngest, Suzette, God rest their souls." I could almost see Father Vestille crossing himself. "But their eldest daughter ... I am afraid she is a lost soul. I still pray for her, but I have not seen her."

Laurent waited, perhaps skeptical. "Not at all?"

"Monsieur Laurent. Why would I have anything to do with a girl who dresses like a harlot?"

I felt a new sort of chill, this one deep inside my heart. As if something had reached into my very being and hollowed everything out.

Laurent lingered a moment. Then he finally relented. "Very well, then. If you do hear anything, please notify me at once. You can send word to *Chateau de Laurent*, or find someone to report it to me."

"Of course. And you can always find me on Sunday mornings at St. Matthew's. Perhaps I can assist you there as well."

Laurent paused again, longer. Surely unnerved at the idea of entering Father Vestille's church. "Yes, perhaps. Thank you, Father."

"You're welcome, Monsieur. Take care."

Father Vestille saw him to the door, then closed and latched it. I stood, clutching the ladder, still trembling. It had grown cold in the cellar, and cold in my soul. What was I becoming?

I grabbed my robe – the robe Father Vestille had provided me – and pulled it on. I felt a sudden need to cover myself, in addition to warding off the chill. I drew the robe tight, as if it was hugging me. As if Mama was there to warm and comfort me.

I stepped up the ladder, pushed up the trap door and let it slam to the floor.

Father Vestille jumped. "Helena! You're awake."

I stared at him from the ladder steps, not knowing what to say, my head peeping out of the hole. I was like a protected rodent living beneath his home. He would care for me and keep me safe, but I would never be truly welcome.

"Did you mean what you said?"

Father Vestille blinked. Then he lifted his chin in recognition. "You heard just now?"

I waited. "Did you mean it?"

He lowered his chin. "I had to be convincing."

"None of it?"

"Helena. I don't agree with what you are doing. But you are always welcome here."

My heart swelled a little, but I couldn't fully believe it. He knew how to comfort people with his words, just as he knew how to persuade Laurent to leave. I stepped up into his home and closed the trap door gently. I folded my arms across my chest and walked toward the window, to make certain Duke Laurent was long gone. I peered through the gaps in the wooden shutters where strips of light broke through. "Even if I dress like a harlot?"

He had not moved. As if he knew that any attempt to approach me or give false comfort would be a wasted effort. Not after he confessed what he truly thought of me. "Helena, I had to be harsh. I had to make him believe I would never let you stay here. So that he won't come looking again."

"Because a harlot would never be allowed in a priest's home."

"You are no harlot."

"But I dress like one."

"You dress the way you must. I understand that. Frankly, your manner of dress is the least of my concerns."

I whirled at him. How else did he plan to insult me?

"Yes?" I asked.

He sighed and hung his head. He stepped closer to face me. "Helena, I *am* concerned for what you are becoming. You come from an innocent family, and they raised you to be innocent. Not a murderer."

I glared at him. In his eyes, I had become a murderer and a harlot, all in one day. Unless he had thought this about me all along.

He turned and sat at the breakfast table, wiping weary hands across his face. "I have long prayed for these killings to stop. For the Lycanthru to be destroyed. But this is not what I prayed for."

My blood brewed inside me. I would never have chosen this life, either, if I had a choice. No one asked for my consent before allowing my parents and Grand'Mere and Suzette and Francois to be devoured by these horrid beasts. I set my jaw. "While you pray, I act."

Father Vestille's face was serene as he looked back at me. "While you act, and kill, I pray and trust *God* to act."

"Can't we do both?" I pressed, taking a long step toward him. "Didn't David kill Goliath? Didn't he fight the armies of the Philistines?"

"There is a significant difference between you and King David."

"I know. He was a man."

"No. I mean, yes, he was, but I meant to say that David was anointed. He was commissioned by the prophet Samuel, chosen from among all his brothers, to serve the Lord's purpose. Is the Lord leading you to do this, or is it your own plan?"

"You believe God wants this to continue? You believe he wants more innocent children to suffer?"

"You know I don't. But it is not for us to become judge or executioner."

I spun away from him, trembling with anger the way I trembled with fear at Laurent's visit. "This is why I didn't want to stay with you. I knew you would do nothing, and encourage me to do the same."

He made no response. The moment the words came out, I realized how badly I had hurt him. He wanted to protect and care for me, the way my parents had, and I wanted none of it. But I was only returning his insults in kind. "Father Vestille, I'm sorry I haven't given you the answer to your prayers. We don't always get the answer we pray for. But we do receive an answer. We can challenge it and keep praying for something else, or we can be grateful we were heard. I don't know if this is what I'm meant to do. I feel it is. It's all I know to do. It's all I can do."

He kept silent for some time. Then he sighed. "Do what you must. I will continue to pray for you, to remain safe. And you are always welcome here, for as long, or as briefly, as you wish."

I kept my back to him, too angry to face him. I wanted to apologize, but when would he apologize to me? When would he accept me for what I was, whatever that might be? When would he stand up for me, rather than just hide me away to keep me alive? Some of the villagers despised me and I accepted that. But some of them applauded me for doing what no one else had. Why couldn't Father Vestille recognize that, even in part?

"I must go," I said, giving no further explanation as I marched to the trap door and hoisted it open. I descended down the ladder, never meeting his eyes.

"Stay safe, Helena," he said as I descended into the darkness and pulled the heavy door shut.

35.

I crouched behind the woodpile next to the Leóne family's shed, trying to avoid a pair of bees that hovered around it. Another few weeks and summer would begin. The time Papa would normally be finished shearing the sheep and ready to relax a little, letting Suzette and I play outside longer into the warm evening. I stifled the memory, swallowing it deep.

Just after two o'clock, Pierre came out the back door of *L'atelier de Forgeron de Leóne*, as usual, to gather extra wood for their stove. I watched him swipe at his unkempt hair as he approached, looking focused and diligent about his task. I let him collect a few heavy pieces while I made certain no one else was nearby. I also let myself admire his rugged features and the amount of weight his arms could carry. "Pierre," I whispered.

He nearly dropped the whole pile on his toes, stepping aside as three large pieces fell. He held the last thick stump by its branch as he stared down at me. "Red!" He glanced over his shoulder for any witnesses, then set the stump back on the woodpile and crouched beside me. He looked like he wanted to grab me by my shoulders but he rested his hands on his knees instead. "How are you? Do you need anything?"

"As many silver bolts as you can make."

"I've made plenty and set them aside. Papa doesn't know. I keep telling him I'm making mistakes and we need more smelting iron. How are the blades working?"

"Fine."

We knelt there a moment, staring into one another's eyes. I had to keep hidden, so I was hesitant to move. Yet Pierre hesitated, too.

"Uh ... come inside the shed," he said at last, glancing behind himself once more. "I'll bring them out to you."

"All right." I waited, watching him look this way and that as he returned to the shop. After he closed the door, I peered around the corner of the shed to survey the area, then hurried inside it.

Crimson snorted at me as I entered the dusty room, piled high with wood. I had already thought to use the shed as a hiding place, but I wanted to meet Pierre where I knew I could whisper. I held up a hand and shushed Crimson. He stamped an eager hoof once, then remained still.

A few moments later, Pierre entered the shed with a large satchel. He set it atop a woodpile and spread it partway open. There must have been at least fifty bolts piled within.

I gaped, astounded. "Pierre. That's incredible. Thank you."

He shrugged. "I do a few each day. I did some late at night, but Papa noticed the lamp and woke up, so I had to pretend I had gotten hungry and needed some food. He noticed me yawning the next day and seemed suspicious, so I haven't tried that again. But I still get enough done during the day. I also found about a dozen of these in the woods, where you said you shot them." He looked sheepish. "Sorry they're not fresh ones."

I smiled at him. As if I should care. But he was a master craftsman and took pride in all his work. "They're magnificent, Pierre. You found the ones I missed." I glanced down, feeling my cheeks flush. "You do so much for me."

He shrugged again. "I'd do more if I could, Red. It's the least you deserve." He swallowed and took a step closer in the dusty shadows. "I'd do anything for you."

We stood barely an inch apart, and I saw his face. His handsome boyish loving face. Like I just noticed it for the first time.

Then he seemed to notice me, too. He stopped and stared into my eyes, his own blue eyes revealing all the passion and nobility of his soul. He leaned toward me, his hand reaching up to stroke my face ...

I whirled and stepped away. "I can't stay. I have work to do."

I kept my back to him as I grabbed the satchel from atop the woodpile and tied it to Crimson's saddle. Pierre shuffled about suddenly to face the door. "Why do you pull away like that?"

I took extra time tying the satchel, as if I had difficulty securing the knot. I pretended to make one attempt after another, again and again. Finally I turned. "Why do you bother with me, Pierre? Why do you have such a low estimation of yourself? Plenty of girls would be happy to have your attention. Girls who don't wear pants."

He turned with an expression that was partly wounded, partly annoyed. "I don't want any other girls."

"Why not? Are you so afraid of them that you shun every pretty girl and choose an ugly one instead?"

He glared at me, not at all pleased. "You're not ugly."

"I'm scarred, and these scars won't go away. Ever."

"I don't care. You're the most ..." He broke off.

"The most what? The most unusual? Most disturbed? Most frightening?"

"... The most beautiful girl in the province."

I started to respond, then stopped. He couldn't truly believe that, could he?

I swallowed. "I'm not a fool, Pierre. And I'm not a child. You don't need to coddle me by lying."

"I'm not. You've always been beautiful." He straightened his shoulders to stand even taller, as if summoning his courage. "I've never wanted to be with anyone else. And I never will."

I fell silent. I was thankful the hood shrouded my misting eyes. This was the boy my mother told me about. The boy she promised would come. The one who would accept me, no matter how I looked or what I did.

But I couldn't let him make that choice, to ruin his own life on a romantic whim that could never be satisfied. I cleared my throat and steadied my voice. "Pierre. Don't waste your efforts on me. I'm not fit for that kind of life. Not anymore."

"But –."

"No. We could never be together. Not when I am what I am."

"What you are is who I love. Who I've always –."

I put my fingers to his lips. I stared at him, wishing things could be different. Wishing I could do more than silence him. Wishing I could hold him in my arms and let him hold me. "We'll never speak about this again."

He stared at me as though I had stabbed him. "Why not?"

I curled my lip, determined to bridle my emotions. "Because," I said. "Because I care for you, Pierre." I moved to the door, crossbow in hand, leading Crimson by the reins without looking back. "And that's something I cannot allow."

The door jerked open before I reached the handle. I raised the crossbow to the intruder's chest as a reflex.

Monsieur Leóne frowned down at me from the doorway. I lowered the weapon slowly. Neither of us spoke as he studied the large satchel hanging from Crimson's saddle, the lined bulges clearly showing the pile of bolts within.

Monsieur Leóne's focus shifted to his son, then back to me. "I thought as much," he grumbled. His eyes blazed at Pierre. "These are the 'mistakes' you've been making? Supplying her with weapons for her crusade? Didn't I tell you to keep away from her?"

I stood quietly, feeling the sting of Frayne Leóne's disdain.

Pierre hung his head. "Papa. She's keeping the village safe."

"Safe?" Monsieur Leóne demanded as he marched toward us and shut the door quietly behind him. "Is this safe? Hiding in the woodshed and hoping no one hears? Hoping no one followed her here to our home? To our shop? To our beds?"

Pierre struggled for words. I wanted to help him, but I felt even less equipped to answer. Pierre shoved his hands deep into his trouser pockets. "We've got to take some risks now and then. She's made a difference. She stopped some of them."

"Then *let* her, if that is what she wishes to do. It's nothing to do with us." He glared down at me, quaking with rage. "Helena. I loved your parents and your sister dearly. I'm sorry you've chosen this sort of life, but I won't have it anywhere near my home. You are never to visit my son again. Do you understand?"

"Papa!"

I met Monsieur Leóne's eyes. Behind the rage, I sensed something else. The fear and desperation of a man who knew that my very presence placed him and his son in danger. "I understand. I was just leaving."

I peered outside.

"Red, wait!"

I glanced back at Pierre, one final time. I wondered how long fifty bolts might last. I would need to take more care in retrieving my spent bolts from the forest. In any case, I couldn't let the Lycanthru find Pierre, or know we had anything to do with one another. "Goodbye, Pierre."

I scanned the outer yard once more, then led Crimson outside. Then I mounted him and spurred him to the cover of the forest.

36.

I found it more difficult to sneak into *La Maison*, an hour later. Crimson waited for me in a thicket of trees, keeping out of sight, while I stole through back alleys toward the rear of the tavern. After waiting for what felt like ages, I seized an opportunity to cross the street, using a passing carriage to hide from onlookers. Then I rushed to the cellar door, yanked it open and dropped inside, finding a basement corridor that led to the recessed storage area. I waited even longer in the wine cellar itself, though I felt far more secure within the quiet room, free of witnesses.

Finally, Gerard Touraine descended the steps to the corridor and entered the wine cellar with his lantern.

"Monsieur Touraine," I whispered.

He whirled about, wrinkling his brows as he held up the lantern. His face softened as he recognized my hood, hiding behind the wine shelves. "Mademoiselle? Is that you?"

"Are you alone?"

He glanced over his shoulder on instinct, but there were no other footsteps. "Yes. Where have you been? I haven't seen you in over a week."

"I know. I've been finding information elsewhere. It's safer that way."

He pursed his lips, understanding but looking disappointed. "So why are you here now?"

"To see what you know. What you've heard. It's not the safest, but it's still the best. I haven't heard much information lately, but I didn't want to endanger you any more than I had to. I'll understand if you wish me to leave." I swallowed at the biting memory of Monsieur Leóne's dismissal.

He set the lantern on a wall hook. "I don't wish that. But there's one thing I would like."

"What is it?"

"Your name. Unless you prefer to be called 'The Red Rider' now."

I smiled. "It's Helena."

He nodded, satisfied. "Helena Basque."

I squinted at him. "If you already knew who I was, why –?"

"I like to hear from the source directly," he said. "Now. A boy's been looking for you."

I frowned. I left that boy at *L'atelier de Forgeron de Leóne* to be chastised by his father. I hoped Touraine had something more to tell me than that. "I saw him this afternoon. For the last time."

Touraine wrinkled his brow. "He's upstairs now, asking for you again."

I blinked. "Who are you talking about?"

"Said his name's Jacque. Jacque Denue."

A flush of anger and fear surged within me. I wanted to confront him and start beating on him before he got the chance to hit me again, but I saw no point. "What did he want?"

"Wants to meet with you. In private. Said he knows something about the, eh, the 'Licannors', something like that."

I stiffened. "The Lycanthru."

"Yes, that's it. The Lycanthru. Something about the Lycanthru and Duke Laurent."

A dozen possibilities raced through my mind. Had Denue truly discovered something of their secret activities, and of mine?

Was he one of the Lycanthru himself, though all their other members were men? Was this another ploy, a petty attempt to ridicule and attack me again? But I had not seen him since before Suzette's funeral. Why seek me out now just to abuse me?

"You said he's upstairs?"

Touraine gave a curt nod. "In the bar."

Denue might have some information I could use against Laurent. He knew about the Lycanthru and perhaps Laurent's connection to them. Could he know something else that might help me stop them?

"Go about your business," I told Touraine. "Say nothing to him."

"You don't wish to meet him, then?"

"Perhaps. But I don't want him to connect me to you. Can you keep him in the bar until nightfall?"

"Most likely."

"Good. Can I keep my horse in your stable by the cellar?"

"Of course. It's for guests of *La Maison*."

I nodded, hoping no one would recognize Crimson. But I had nowhere closer to hide him. "Thank you. If you're willing, can you find an opportunity to stand there? My horse is just within the forest. I'll get to the stable and whistle for him when you're ready, so you can lead him across before anyone sees him."

He considered this, looking up and stroking his chin. Perhaps deciding how to maneuver so as to draw the least attention to himself and Crimson.

"Or I can try to lead him there myself. You don't need to risk anyone seeing you with my horse."

He shook his head, smiling. "My pleasure to help ... 'Red Rider'. Be back in ten minutes."

He left. I stood behind the shelves of wine that would so offend Father Vestille, and marveled at Gerard Touraine's bravery on my behalf. I now saw that Francois placed him in high regard for more than his knowledge of the town gossip.

37.

From the rooftop of *Focult le Tonnelier* – Focult's Cooper Shop across the street – I watched Jacque Denue stroll out of *La Maison*. The moonlight cast a dark, swaying shadow of his clumsy movements as he continued past the building where I perched.

I had stolen out of the cellar as night fell, while villagers poured into the front doors of *La Maison*. Those who wished to drink were focused only on the tavern entrance, while those who did not were focused on retiring to their own cottages. Giving me ample room to climb to the roof of *La Maison* with Pierre's grappling hook, then leap across to *Focult le Tonnelier* after most of the drinkers went inside. As I waited and listened, first on one roof and then the other, I heard a few people mention Jacque Denue searching for the Red Rider. Apparently he had confided his search with several others besides Touraine.

Now I descended from the roof of *Focult le Tonnelier* into the dark alley beside him to find out why.

"You've been asking for me."

Jacque Denue nearly fell over his own feet as he twisted about to meet me, peering at him through my large hood.

"You," he gasped. "Y-Yeah. You've been fighting them, haven't you? Killing them?"

I frowned, recalling Father Vestille's displeasure with my crusade. "Yes."

"You know what they are, right? That they're not ... not wolves. They're not even human."

He knew. He knew everything I had learned and perhaps more. "Yes. I know. But what do you know? About Duke Laurent?"

He looked about, nervous. Almost terrified. "I can't be seen with you. They'll kill me."

"They'll kill you, anyway, so talk."

He shook his head, looking hysterical. "They got people all over, you know? They could be watching us now." He looked around again, over his shoulder and down the street. "Look, I'll walk a block. Watch where I go and meet me there later. Don't let anybody see you."

He backed away, half-stumbling as he marveled at my cloaked appearance. I let him move away, then crept to the corner of the wall to see where he headed. He hurried across the street, still glancing in all directions. At the end of the block, he stopped in front of a large horse stable and examined it. Looking around to confirm no one was watching, he threw up the latch on the door and stepped inside.

I waited a few moments in the quiet, listening for any other movement. I studied the torch over the tavern door behind me. No one else would leave *La Maison* this early in the evening. I hurried from one alleyway to the next, moving down the street. Then I broke into a quick run for the stable doors and went inside.

The stable felt even larger within, with room for over twenty horses. A single lantern at the opposite end of the stable gave sparse light, where Denue stood waiting. He seemed calmer now, standing taller as I strode toward him, my cloak wafting behind me. Nevertheless, his face paled as I approached. "Now. Tell me what you know of Laurent."

"All right, I'll tell you." His voice turned menacing. "He's eager to meet you."

Hay shuffled behind me and strong arms coiled around my waist. I gasped as they squeezed harder, pinning my arms into my abdomen. I struggled to break free but my assailant was too strong. He hoisted me off my feet and I noticed a sign burned into the wall overhead: *Les écuries de Brocard* – these were Monsieur Brocard's Stables.

The Lycanthru used Denue to set me up.

Denue smirked as two of his cronies strode up from behind me. I recognized Slob and Freckles as they grinned in triumph. The one holding me had to be Muscles. Denue leaned into my face to gloat. "What you gonna do now, 'Red Rider'?"

His friends laughed. I kicked hard against Denue's chest with both heels, knocking him off his feet as he wheezed. My kick pushed me back against Muscles and we fell to the ground hard, though his bulk softened my blow. He released me and I rolled away, rising to my feet. The fifth boy from Denue's gang stood behind us with a toothy grin. They seemed to have forgotten how I beat them last time. Or they assumed they had me outnumbered.

I kicked Muscles' jaw as he tried to stand. I needed my strongest attacker to stay down. He grunted and moaned like a wounded animal, rolling in the dirt as he clutched at his face. Tooth kept smiling and spread his feet in a fighting stance, as the two beside Denue did the same. Then they all drew hunting knives and held them out, preparing to lunge.

"That's right, wench," Denue said from behind me. "This time, we brought better weapons than a club."

"Clever," I said. "Wish I'd thought of that." I raised my crossbow to Tooth's startled eyes. He dropped the knife and raised his hands, backing away as I circled behind him. I was out of patience.

He joined Slob and Freckles, who still gripped their knives, unsure. I cocked my head at them.

Both knives fell to the floor. I nodded toward the ground beside a horse stall. "Over there."

They raised their hands in surrender as they backed toward it. Muscles crawled after them, still rubbing his jaw. Freckles scowled at me. "We'll get you. You just wait," he said.

I fired a bolt between them. Freckles squealed as it struck the wood of the stall behind him. "Sit down and keep quiet," I said.

They dropped to the floor, hands still raised. I slung the crossbow over my shoulder and approached Denue.

He drew a knife from his rear pocket and lunged, the blade flashing in his fist. I kicked at his wrist and pinned it against a pillar. He whined in pain as the knife fell. I kept his hand there and backhanded him across the jaw. I punched him a second and third time to send him spinning to the dirt.

The other boys leaned forward, ready to stand. After I glared at them, they sat back on their hands. I grabbed Denue by his tunic and tugged him to my face.

His eyes bulged as he squirmed. "Lemme go, you witch! You wear pants and fight like a man. What kinda girl are you?"

"One with little patience." I shook him for emphasis. "Who told you to attack me? Was it Laurent?"

"Yeah," he grumbled. "Figured it'd be easy to nab a stupid girl."

"Capture? Not kill?"

He shook his head. "I ain't no killer! Just needed money. He's paying us plenty to bring you unharmed."

"He wants me unharmed so he can harm me himself. You know what he is. You told me yourself."

"That's what he told me to say, to make you come with us. I don't know nothing else. Those are just stories to scare little kids!"

"They're not stories and you know it. Even if Laurent was an ordinary man, why would he pay you to capture me? What do you think he'll do with me? And how long do you think he'll let you live, after you do what he asks? Another night? Another few weeks?"

Jacque shook his head. "He don't care about me, so long as I help him."

"Once you've outlived your usefulness, he'll make a meal of you. Like he does with the rest of *La Rue Sauvage*."

"Yeah, so what am I s'posed to do about it?"

"You know what sort of girl I am. What sort of boy are you? Sooner or later, he'll kill you, now that you know his secrets. You can help me stand up to him, or start numbering your days."

"You're crazy! I ain't fighting the Duke of the whole province!"

"You don't have to. Just do what he told you to do. Take me to him. Tell him you captured me, but leave me opportunity for escape. When he least suspects it, I can –."

Something shifted in his eyes as he glanced toward the horse stalls. I whirled toward his friends, still seated, in time to see a horseshoe flying at me.

It struck my forehead. The stable spun as I fell to the ground. I blinked at the dull pain as everything started to blur. Denue loomed over me, grinning. "Change of plans," he said.

I tried to clutch at him but I could barely sit up. His fist connected with my jaw and everything went black.

I woke to shouts.

"Imbecile! I told you to bring her last night!"

It was Laurent's voice. I shuddered, feeling cold and confused. I lay on my side, my jaw aching, my head throbbing. My throat tasted like dry manure, and there was a suffocating smell of dust from the surrounding hay. But not from Brocard's stable where Denue struck me. Somewhere less clean. Somewhere I had been before.

I blinked awake with terror. I was back in Brocard's barn in the forest, where I intruded on the Lycanthru's ceremony. Only now I lay on the ground floor, a few feet away from the raised platform, where the vat of sulfurous liquid filled the room with its foul odor.

Standing over me on the platform, just fifteen feet away, Laurent glowered at Denue in a rage.

"I fell asleep," Denue said. "She took a lot out of us. But I got her and she's here now. What difference does it make?"

Laurent backhanded him with a fist that sent Denue sprawling from the platform onto the dirt. *"That* is the difference, you impudent fool. From now on, do as you're told."

My shoulder ached where I had been lying on it. My head pounded like a drum. I squinted at the room as early morning light settled into it. How long had I slept?

Ten or more of Laurent's men stood around him. A few wore their black robes and hoods. Others wore their daytime clothes. His advisor, Simonet, stood close by, his hands folded behind his back.

Beneath their feet, I saw my repeating crossbow. If I could leap for it before they noticed me ...

My body pulsed as I prepared to rise, but I couldn't move my hands from behind my back. I tugged again. Then I fingered the thick hemp binding my wrists.

"Your Grace," Simonet said in a monotone. I glanced back to find him studying me.

"Look who's awake," Lieutenant-General Sharrad snorted.

Laurent regarded me and his entire posture relaxed. He strode toward me with a grin and knelt down. Then he gripped my cheeks hard and lifted my face to his. "Good morning, Mademoiselle. A pleasure to see you again."

I grunted and tried to pull away. The other Lycanthru grinned like hyenas.

"But a little too early, I think."

He released my head to fall painfully back to the ground. Then he raised his fist and brought it crashing down onto my jaw.

38.

I woke again more slowly, roused by the sulfur stench. Muscles ached in my shoulders and thighs and the back of my neck. My chin rested heavily against my chest. I had trouble opening my eyes and lifting my head. The rest of my body felt somewhat numb. *Wake up,* I ordered myself, inhaling the sulfur deeper, listening to the bubbling vat. *Wake up!*

The room was bright and full of noise. Or so it seemed, as my temples throbbed and I struggled to grasp my surroundings. With an effort, I lifted my head to meet the eyes of Leopold Laurent, flanked by Simonet, Sharrad and about twenty other men. He grinned as he held my crossbow.

I flinched and shuddered, which made them all laugh. I felt paralyzed, unable to move anything but my head and neck. I glanced to either side and discovered my arms were spread apart and bound. Thick ropes extended from my wrists to distant supporting pillars.

My breath caught in my throat. I tried to move my legs, to stretch my sore thighs. But they also stood apart on the dirt floor, my ankles secured to the same wooden pillars. I stared down at myself, helpless before the entire cult.

"Welcome, dear Helena," Laurent said in mock greeting. "Or should I call you, 'The Red Rider'?"

They exploded with hoots of triumph. All but the stone-faced Simonet, standing at Laurent's side. A few men wore their black robes, but most were ready to resume the day's normal work.

"I can't tell you how pleased I am that you chose to visit us," Laurent continued, like a gracious host. "A pity you can't stay long. Although you'll be with us much longer than we hoped. We meant to finish you last night. To … what is the word? Ah, yes. To 'rid' ourselves of you."

This drew another round of cruel chuckles as Laurent patted my crossbow. I tried to stay calm as I tugged at the ropes, testing them. They had no give whatsoever.

"Unfortunately, your incompetent friend, Jacque Denue, failed to bring you at the proper time, but waited until it was near dawn. We all lead busy lives during the day, which only leaves us the night for our private activities. The saddest part is I have significant business to tend to this evening, so our plans for you will be delayed even further. But don't fret, Mademoiselle. Come midnight, we'll all gather to bid you a fond farewell."

I pulled at the ropes again as a reflex, knowing it was pointless.

"You can't see behind you, Helena, but there's a long trough there. That's where we'll toss your bones when we've cleaned all the meat off them."

My breath came in rapid gasps, to each man's delight.

"I claim her belly," said a gruesome red-haired man.

"I want one of her thighs," Sharrad said with a smile, narrowing his blue-gray eyes.

Laurent stepped forward. "All I want is her face."

"Not much meat there, Lord Laurent," Sharrad said.

"No," Laurent admitted as he stood before me. He squeezed my cheeks together so hard I struggled to breathe for a moment. "But I want to see her eyes, wide and screaming, as she realizes her little adventure is over. Just before I devour her."

I shook in his grip. They were going to *eat me!*

His face hardened into stone. "You should have accepted my offer to walk away, Helena. Now you can die like the rest. Except that you've earned yourself a much slower, more painful demise. I'm sure you're quite impressed with yourself, for how well you've done. So consider it an honor, the agony we intend to put you through this evening."

I kept my body rigid and focused on taking tiny breaths through my nose and teeth. I turned to Simonet, the only one not joining in the others' celebration. His dull, fixed expression made me tremble even more.

"The only reason we're not feasting on you now is we need moonlight to transform," Laurent explained. "Once we assume our new shape, we can keep it as long as necessary. But someone in town might notice if fifty men didn't perform their duties today. And to be frank ... every one of us wants a piece of you."

He released my face and I gasped, hanging my head.

"Sharrad," Laurent called.

Sharrad stepped forward with a strip of cloth. He yanked it apart with his fists, showing its thickness as he marched toward me.

"Why are you doing this?" I asked Laurent quickly. "Why are you attacking everyone?"

Laurent held up a hand, stopping Sharrad in his tracks. "Why?" he repeated. He spread his hands like a showman before the other men. "Why not?" They roared with sadistic laughter, as though I said something hilarious.

Laurent paced, as if considering the question for the first time. "Power, Mademoiselle. Unlimited, eternal power. The age-old lure of immortality. All we need to do is kill a wolf for its pelt ..." He aimed my crossbow between my eyes, smiling as he played a hunter. "And keep it among our possessions. Then with a ray of moonlight, we can transform into the most fearsome creatures the world has ever known. Provided we also drink the Lycanum potion." He waved a hand toward the foul, bubbling vat. "Together, these things make us stronger. We age less rapidly. We remain powerful, even in our normal form, so long as we continue to feast now and then. Especially when we feast on the innocent."

Quick as lightning, he backhanded my left cheek. It stung like a block of wood. The room spun for a moment while I regained my breath.

"You see what I mean?"

He yanked off my hood, his force nearly choking me with it. Then he seized a clump of hair at my scalp and wrenched my head back. I gasped at the sharp pain and let him hold me there like a marionette. Resisting would only make it worse.

"The intriguing thing about power, Mademoiselle, is that once a man tastes it, he can't stop hungering for more. Tonight, when the moon is high, we shall assume our more powerful form." He leaned close to my cheek, enough for me to smell his last drink of red wine. "Then we'll feed on you, piece by piece, growing stronger as you die, screaming."

No, I thought. *Lord, don't let me die like this. Help me escape! Send them away and help me escape!*

He grinned, my hair trapped in his fist. "I should conclude my business and join the others here by eleven o'clock. Then we'll spend the night tending to you, for the last time, before we feast on the main course. That gives you a full day to consider your folly and form your apology to me, for your brash interference."

"What about the silver?" I gasped. "Why does it hurt you?"

He gave my hair another sharp jerk. "You're so persistent, Helena. You still hope to learn something to pass on to your friends, if you have any left. If you do, don't worry. We'll find them and finish them off. Just like you."

I thought of Pierre and tugged violently at the ropes, in spite of myself. Despite the pain that shot through my scalp as he yanked my head back in place. I considered Father Vestille and Gerard Touraine. Even Pierre's father, Monsieur Leóne, who refused to involve himself, but was involved nevertheless. A few anxious words from any one of them, wondering whatever happened to me, could be enough to rouse Laurent's suspicions and seal their deaths. Because of me.

His voice softened to a purr. "Of course, if your apology is humble enough, I might let you beg for your friends' lives. As for the silver ..." He rested the point of my crossbow's loaded bolt against my cheek and stroked me with it like I was his pet. "When your friend, Francois, killed Gaston with his silver ax, we were surprised that anything could harm us. But we consulted the Prime, who is far more experienced in these matters."

"The Prime?"

"Don't concern yourself with that, Helena. In *La Rue Sauvage*, *I* am the Prime." The bolt jabbed at me as he growled, but didn't draw blood. He smiled, regaining his composure. "In any event, he explained that different Lycanthru had come into contact with silver over the years and died without explanation. We simply learned to avoid it. I don't need to know the reason, any more than I need to know why we need the Lycanum or the pelt or the moonlight. I follow the rituals that were written down in prior centuries and reap the benefits. So long as there are unsuspecting villagers with children in our midst, I should live to be well over a hundred, with no one daring to challenge me." He whispered harshly at my ear. "While you won't even make it to age seventeen."

He yanked my hair again. I yelped at the sudden pain, which ended abruptly as he released me.

I lifted my head slowly, feeling dizzy as the barn and Laurent blurred before my eyes. I blinked and saw that he held a clump of my blonde hair. He regarded it with mild surprise, then smiled at me. "I'll just keep this as a souvenir."

He slid the hair into his waistcoat pocket as if it was a precious heirloom. I stared in horror and disgust. They were demented, every one of them, and Laurent was the most twisted of all.

"Any more questions, Helena? Or are you finished?"

I quivered in the ropes.

"What do you think, Simonet? Is she through?"

Simonet observed me without expression. He stepped down from the platform and stepped toward me, examining my face like I was an intriguing bug. "She's frightened, Your Grace," he said. "She knows it's over."

I stiffened to keep from losing control. Anything I did or said now would only confirm the truth. I had no plan. No way out.

Laurent's eyes and face relaxed even more. "That's what I wanted to hear. Now, Sharrad."

He stepped back as Sharrad marched at me with the cloth strip. He ducked under my bound arm and stood up close behind

251

me, his broad chest against my back. "Wait! Someone will find me. You can't –!"

The cloth came down past my eyes and was tugged between my lips. I struggled, my nerves flaring, as Sharrad secured the gag, turning the rest of my sentence into muffled gibberish. He knotted it tight against the back of my neck, catching strands of hair.

Laurent stepped forward, studying me with a satisfied smile. I could barely move. Now I could barely utter a sound.

He raised the crossbow to my face. "By the way. I believe this is yours." He tossed it to the dirt beneath me. I stared down at it, loaded and ready to pierce their hearts. I tugged my wrists hard, which only tensed my sore muscles and kept my captors entertained.

Laurent gingerly drew the hood back up over my head. "No one is likely to travel this way, but we can't risk some fool hearing you struggle. Not before we've had our fun with you." He stroked my cheek as if he were still the family friend I once trusted. "Think about how to apologize, Helena, to save a few of your friends. You'll have all day to consider it. Jacquard will be here to watch over you." He smiled over his shoulder at a tall unshaven man who nodded from his seat on the steps. "The rest of us would be missed, but Jacquard's position is …" He pretended confusion. "What is it you do again, Jacquard?"

Jacquard twisted his lip with annoyance. "Cooper's apprentice," he said.

"Oh, yes, that's it," Laurent said, as if he just remembered. "And a poor one at that. His master might be relieved to do without him today. But he can keep an eye on you here, to make sure you don't … wiggle too much." He grinned like the devil. "Until tonight, then."

He walked out. Each of the Lycanthru filed out after him, smiling at me as they passed. A few of them waved. One man grinned and made a chomping motion at me. I hung there between the pillars, a chill of horror surging through my nerves as they strode by, each one hungry for my blood. Each one eager to taste it when night fell.

Behind them, Jacquard squatted and poked at the logs beneath the base of the vat, reducing the flame. I imagined them boiling me for their dinner as I stared into each ravenous glare.

A shorter man marched at me, grinning with malice. "The party won't start 'til nightfall, Mademoiselle," he said through tobacco-stained teeth. "Why don't you get some sleep?"

The men behind him laughed as his fist struck me and my world went black.

39.

I awoke with a start. I breathed the sulfuric air rapidly through my nose. The gag had grown stale against my tongue. I lifted my head and blinked.

The man named Jacquard rose to a sitting position on the platform, where he had been sleeping. My sudden movement apparently woke him. He snorted, stretched, then regarded me with a scowl. "Up and ready for the day?" he said without humor.

It remained bright outside, but the shadows had shifted to the opposite angle. It was a little past noon. I had gotten a full but fitful sleep that I now felt in my sore limbs.

I looked back at each of my wrists, still bound to the thick pillars. I shook my numb arms as best I could and rotated my wrists to get the blood flowing back into them. My lower back and the calves of my legs ached, from standing suspended for so long. Below me, the crossbow still lay useless on the ground.

Jacquard yawned and stood to fully stretch. I heard his back crack as he twisted his torso. Then he faced me with his hands on his hips. "Go on. Struggle some more for me."

I breathed slow and even.

"No?" he asked. "Too tired? Get some rest, then. You'll need all your strength tonight for screaming."

He sat back down and leaned lazily against the long counter beside the bubbling vat. He glanced at it, wondering whether to adjust the fire again. Then he folded his arms and studied me. "You thought you were something, huh? You really thought you could beat us."

He continued to study me from head to toe, watching for any sign of resistance, satisfying himself that I could not escape. Then he rose slowly and walked behind the long counter. He bent behind it and I heard him open cabinet doors and slide heavy objects across shelves. He stood, producing a small flask and a large bottle of liquor. He poured himself a small sampling and sipped it. He eyed me again, looking disappointed that I had not moved a muscle. He lifted his flask toward me. "Your good health, witch." He emptied the flask and filled it again.

I steadied my breathing. Everything happened so fast, I barely had time to think. And I could do nothing with the entire cult watching me. Jacquard would be a different matter, I hoped.

I kept still, spread between the pillars like an animal carcass to be carved and eaten over a fire.

Or Samson, the Bible hero who lost his great strength and was captured by his enemies who mocked and jeered at him, thinking him helpless. Until he asked them to place him between the pillars that supported their stronghold, where he pushed the supports apart when God restored his strength, destroying them all.

I lifted my chin and tried to relax. I allowed Jacquard to study me again before he poured himself another drink.

I couldn't reach the crossbow, but I had a few advantages left. Reminding myself of that helped me calm down. First, they left only one man to watch me. More important, they imagined me helpless. Which I might be if not for Pierre. Sweet, ingenious Pierre, who suggested the crazy idea of helping me fight like a wolf, before my first night out at Favreau's farm. "I can't give you teeth," he had said, "but I've got something that might work for claws."

He was so proud of his brilliant invention, as he should be, always asking me how my "blades" were working. And I always assured him they worked just fine.

I fixed my gaze on Jacquard as he tilted back another drink. Then I flicked my wrists, causing the silver blades to slide out from the top pockets in my gloves. They locked in place and I spread my fingers to hide them. If I closed my fists, the broad knives could be seen, extending just beyond my knuckles. With my palms open, Jacquard would never notice me sawing slowly through the ropes behind them. I just had to keep my movements slow and careful.

Fine, Pierre, I thought. *They work just fine.*

Shadows fell across the window as the wind rustled the leaves of trees outside. I scraped away at the ropes, one fiber at a time. It maddened me to cut so slowly. But anything faster would draw Jacquard's notice before I could free myself. Even more maddening, the ropes' thickness ensured I would be scraping through them, one gentle stroke after another, for quite some time. Of course, once they frayed most of the way through, they should pull apart all at once. Then the crossbow would be back in my hands.

Jacquard jerked up suddenly, narrowing his eyes. I stood still, like a woodland deer sensing a hunter's presence. I locked eyes with Jacquard and held still.

"Not trying to wriggle free, are you, Mademoiselle?"

My heart stopped. I stood rigid, hoping he would not step closer.

Jacquard lifted the flask to his lips, still watching me, then drank.

I felt a wave of relief as he refilled his flask. I resumed my sawing motion, one slow cut at a time, barely moving my wrists. I wondered if I was even making progress, but I dared not glance at the ropes. I had to trust they were fraying through, a little at a time, until Jacquard lost interest in me once more.

I prayed silent thanks that Laurent's guard was so lazy. A more responsible man might have checked the ropes again to make certain they were secure. But Jacquard had no reason to imagine anything otherwise. He knew nothing of Pierre's cleverness.

Pierre. I had to free myself and warn him. Warn Father Vestille and Touraine.

In my rush, my right hand blade wedged between fibers and jerked the rope. Jacquard glanced up, seeing the rope shake. I froze.

He almost smiled. "Go on. Try to pull free."

I ignored him, but kept my whole body rigid. Waiting for him to ignore me as well.

"No?" he teased. "You're not even going to try?" He chuckled to himself and poured another drink.

I had to slow down. I couldn't save anyone if I let Jacquard discover my actions. I relaxed my breathing again and focused. The moment he drained another flask, I glanced to my right.

The rope had started to fray.

I sawed at it again, seeing new fibers sprout up. Given enough time, I could free myself. I just had to remain calm and patient.

An hour later – judging from the shadows outside – I had scraped halfway through each rope. A few more strokes and the remaining fibers would start to shred. So long as Jacquard kept his distance for the next hour, I could pounce on him before he knew what happened. The silent crossbow still waited on the ground for me. Just a little more time and steady work …

Jacquard now sat back on the platform, still sipping from the flask in his hand. Over the last several minutes, his study of me grew more intense. I eventually stopped worrying whether he could see my blades working. Though he watched my every movement, he could not see the silver shafts behind my palms, or the ropes slowly severing behind them.

Yet he focused on me more than ever, while his head bobbed a little from all his liquor. He spent several minutes observing my boots alone. And of course, my trousers, which barely covered my legs.

He took another swig of wine, eyeing me strangely. "You know ... I like the way you look there, writhing."

My throat went dry. I glanced back down at the crossbow.

He rose slowly to his feet and staggered once. I hoped he might fall over unconscious, but he wasn't drunk enough. "About this power, Mademoiselle. It increases everything. Not just our strength. It also increases our appetites. I need to eat more, smoke more. Drink more." He lifted the flask. Then his eyes narrowed and traveled the length of my body. "I need more of everything."

I stiffened. As he took another swig, I made broader strokes against each rope.

He returned his attention to me and I stopped. He smiled, as if recalling a private joke. "You know, I crave things now that I never wanted before. Never even thought of wanting. Strange things, like seeing a woman ... or a child ... suffer."

My whole body pulsed and quivered. Jacquard seemed to delight in it, as he approached me in small, measured steps. "Good thing is, brave Mademoiselle, that now I can satisfy all my cravings. No matter how wild they get."

He set his flask at his feet and stood directly before me, smiling and reeking of alcohol. He reached up and gently drew back my hood. Uncovering my eyes and hair and my scarred face.

He snorted. "Not too bad, for all that." He nodded at my triple wounds. "Almost pretty. Anyhow, you'll do."

I fought to stay calm. To keep from jerking away at his touch, as he stroked my hair below the gag.

He undid the knot and pulled the cloth free. I gasped, sucking air into my stale mouth. He seized my face, cutting off my deep breaths. I panicked and tried to pull away but his grip was too strong, squeezing my cheeks tight as Laurent had done. But Jacquard's fingers jabbed my skin and pressed against my teeth, determined to produce pain.

I shook in the ropes. I cut at them again with a single swipe, while he stood an inch from my face. Then I cut again. And again.

"I know, my sweet," Jacquard said, grinning at my discomfort. "I'm supposed to leave you unharmed for tonight. For the others. But I figure, when someone's already this damaged, who's gonna notice a few more cuts and bruises?"

I seethed, clenching my teeth to speak. "I couldn't agree more, Monsieur," I said as I sawed through the last fibers.

The ropes fell like logs to the ground as my wrists dropped. Jacquard blinked at me, trying to grasp what had happened. I tensed my numb arms and drove my bladed gloves into his sides. His eyes bulged. Then the pain pushed through his stupor and he screamed, a horrid animal cry. He knocked over the flask at his feet and shattered it as his knees buckled. He clutched at my waist to stay upright.

I tore the blades free and shoved them into him again. He cried out as the blood clung to my knives. I shook, wanting it to end. Wanting him to be a wolf, so I wouldn't feel like vomiting, as I stabbed him again. He sank slowly, as tears streamed down my cheeks and his fingers lost their hold.

He crumpled to the ground and collapsed on his broken flask.

I collapsed after him, exhausted.

I had just killed a man. Not a wolf, but a man. And I could do nothing to take it back.

What had I become?

Something banged from the rear of the barn, behind the platform. I started suddenly and lifted my head to listen. Had they left another guard behind? Something struck low against the wall again like thunder, much harder than a human could have.

Crimson.

I pushed myself back and stretched toward my bound ankles. I couldn't hope to return to a standing position with my feet so far apart, but I stretched enough to saw through the rope encircling the inside of my heel. Once I freed my other foot, I raced to the platform door and threw it open. Beyond it, I found a spacious stable with eight stalls, only two of them filled. One with a horse that must have belonged to Jacquard. The other with Crimson.

He whinnied in a fitful rage as he saw me, tossing his head in the stall. He must have put up a tremendous fight after they found him, because they bound him in a cat's cradle of ropes, much like they bound me, securing his legs, flanks and neck, so he could only shake helplessly until they returned.

He was the main course Laurent spoke of, that they would enjoy after finishing me.

I threw open the stall door and saw he had finally wriggled one hoof free to kick at the wall. I hugged his neck to calm him. It did little to still my own rage, which began to boil over. "It's all right, boy," I seethed. "It's all right. We're leaving this place."

Night fell like thick tar. The flame beneath the vat had nearly died out, but I could still smell the sulfur amidst the barn's choking dust.

At long last, I heard their horses approach and gallop around the barn to the rear stable. The door to the stalls creaked open and there was a murmur of confusion and rage. I smiled, imagining their faces as they discovered Crimson was no longer bound in their cruel trappings.

Then came quick footsteps and the sound of the connecting door flying open. The men rushed into the center of the barn with their lanterns, scanning the darkness for me and Jacquard.

They found Jacquard soon enough. His dead body now hung where the Lycanthru had hung me, between the two pillars. It had taken an hour, with Crimson's help, to string him up properly. It was monstrous, I knew. But far less cruel than the Lycanthru tying me there alive.

They held their lanterns up to his face to confirm he was dead. They wondered among themselves what happened, how I escaped, where I ran off to, where my horse went. More of them poured in, as I hoped they would. At first there were only a dozen or more. Then I counted eighteen, soon twenty-five, finally thirty-three. They flooded in so quickly I nearly lost count, but I kept them in my sights. I had to know how many there were. They huddled together in outrage, blaming Jacquard's carelessness, blaming one another, demanding answers.

They prepared to search the barn, raising their lanterns and looking about. Only one of them sniffed at the alcohol in the air and fingered a piece of the hay I had stuffed into Jacquard's shirt.

I smiled. They had each brought the weapons I needed with them.

I stood up suddenly from the overlooking hayloft and stared through the enormous square hole at the men searching below. Hay and dust fell from my shoulders and my spreading cloak as I raised the repeating crossbow. My first shot tore through the lantern of the man in front of Jacquard's corpse. It yanked the lantern from his grip and knocked it into Jacquard's back, which I had dressed with hay and doused in liquor. His body burst into flames, a human candle that lit the length of both thick ropes. The fire caught on the pillars, also sprinkled with alcohol.

Everyone gaped at the erupting blaze as I shot the lanterns of two other men. The first one struck the ground and started a small flame on one side of the barn. But the second hit its mark on the opposite corner where I had spilled more liquor, creating a blaze that roared to life against the wall. It followed the trail of alcohol that lined the interior, the fire scrambling along the wall to connect at each corner.

The Lycanthru's eyes bulged as the room heated up. Crimson whinnied and rose from the darkness beneath the hayloft. I whistled and he leaped into position. I dropped onto his saddle, ignoring the bruising in my groin and thighs, and drove him to kick open the front door. We rushed into the night air and I leaped off to secure the entrance.

The men recovered from their shock and charged at me as I shut the door and threw the locking bar down. Crimson trotted back to retrieve me while I drove three bolts into the bar for good measure. A sudden shuffling of dirt within told me the Lycanthru had halted upon seeing the protruding silver bolts.

I stepped into Crimson's right stirrup with one foot and held on as he whisked me to the rear stable. I jumped off as two men emerged from the rear door, one carrying a lantern. I shot them both where they stood. Crimson galloped at a third Lycanthru as he tried to escape, whirling to kick him back inside the barn. I shut the stable door and threw the bar down, then shot another three bolts into it. After grabbing the Lycanthru's discarded lantern, I climbed back onto Crimson to circle around the barn. Light and heat emitted from every wall.

Nevertheless, I took the lantern and hurled it against the front door, as the Lycanthru pounded against the inside of it. "Rider!" they raged. *"Rider!"*

The lantern burst into a spreading blaze that licked up the alcohol on either side of the door and raced along the outer wall. I had lined the walls with liquor from corner to corner, inside and out, and spread the hay out evenly within. Creating an inescapable tomb of flames. I watched the rest of Brocard's barn erupt in a rising inferno, climbing higher and higher into the black sky, like a sacrifice on an enormous altar.

So now I was a murderer. I killed thirty-three men in less than a minute. Thirty-three men who gave themselves over to black magic to prey on the people of *La Rue Sauvage*. On innocent children.

But no more.

Whether I was a warrior or a murderer, I could do nothing to change it. I didn't ask them to attack my family. That was their doing. And this was the result. For them, and for me.

So be it.

I turned Crimson away from the mounting inferno and the Lycanthru's raging screams as fire billowed up every high wall. My cloak flapped behind me as we rode hard into the forest. I spotted a few other Lycanthru with lanterns moving into the clearing, stunned by the sight of the blaze. One noticed me riding off but only gaped at me, too surprised to give chase.

I had enough moonlight to find my way through the well-traveled woods. I was glad I abandoned the lantern, giving them no way to track me.

My heart and pulse raced, my nerves hot with rage and fear. They meant to kill us, to devour me and Crimson for their own sadistic pleasure. They only received a portion of what they deserved. But I would serve up more to them before daybreak.

MY SALVATION

40.

I rode on through the moonlit night, through the cool forest, pounding over pine needles and snapping twigs. Sore and spent but alive. The Lycanthru tried to kill me. Strung me up like an animal to be eaten, along with Crimson.

Instead, I escaped and locked thirty-three of them in Brocard's barn, burning them alive. Father Vestille warned me I could become a murderer. I winced at the visions dancing in my head. He was right.

My mind and heart felt numb. Numb with cold and struggle and death. This morning when I stood suspended between the pillars, Duke Laurent said he had important business to conclude this evening. Before he joined the rest of his cult to feed on me.

I clenched my teeth and tensed my aching muscles, forcing energy back into my limbs. I was a murderer. There was no returning from it. I just needed enough strength to last another hour or so. Long enough to ride into the village, find Laurent, and end this, once and for all. And pray I would find forgiveness.

I passed by his palatial home, *Chateau de Laurent*, on the way to the village. Its castle spires looked menacing in silhouette as I galloped past the endless wrought-iron gate. Bright lanterns blazed from within the main hall.

"Halt! State your business!"

I tugged back on the reins. Crimson reared and snorted as I instinctively started for my crossbow. Two men stood at the main gate, their muskets aimed at my head.

I froze. They were musketeers, not Lycanthru. A short distance behind them, a royal coach was parked beside the Duke's.

"Who are you?" the nearest soldier demanded. He had a thick moustache that made him look like a Scottish terrier when he spoke. "Answer, in the name of the Queen."

I lifted my hands slowly. "My name is Helena. I'm just on my way home. The Queen is here?"

"Her royal ambassador," the other soldier growled, bringing his musket closer. "To meet with Duke Laurent. If you're heading home, then be on your way. You have no business here."

I bowed my head graciously, then took back the reins and trotted past them. They kept their muskets trained on me as I continued down the stone pathway. I glanced back over my shoulder a few times as they watched me go.

After I distanced myself down the darkening path and they could barely see or hear Crimson's clicking hooves, the soldiers finally lowered their weapons. Then I veered off the path onto Duke Laurent's yard. I found no other soldiers about the perimeter. I urged Crimson toward another section of the gate, keeping a wary eye toward the distant musketeers guarding the entrance, as well as the brilliantly lit windows of the chateau. I kept Crimson at a slow trot right up to the gate. I paused and listened, hearing nothing but crickets and a light wind.

The gate stood eight feet high. I slung my crossbow over my shoulder and stood on the saddle, then seized hold of its upper bar and climbed up. I swung my legs over the top and eased myself to the ground. No one spotted me.

I hurried across the lawn and pressed my back against the chateau wall. Still no noise from any observers.

I studied the upper window. I couldn't risk the noise of the grappling hook. Fortunately, the jagged stone walls were easy enough to climb. Despite my soreness and fatigue, I made it to the window in fifteen seconds and stole inside.

The inner corridor was empty but well-lit with numerous high lanterns. An echoing discussion issued from a large open room at the end of the hall. I crept toward it.

The voices grew clearer as I reached the door. Laurent was speaking.

"-- and I can assure you that everything will be done to ensure Her Majesty's safe transport in and out of our province."

"Rest assured, Her Majesty's courtiers will see to that," said an elder man, presumably the royal ambassador.

I reached the entrance and peered between the crack of the door. A short, silver-haired man sat before Duke Laurent, listening attentively with his legs crossed. Lieutenant-General Sharrad and Monsieur Brocard stood nearby with Laurent's advisor, Simonet. Laurent apparently wished to make a good impression by having them represent the police force and business community of *La Rue Sauvage*.

"Of course," Laurent agreed. "Please express my sincere gratitude to Her Majesty for this opportunity to show how well we have managed our little province for the last two decades. I am sure that once Her Majesty sees –."

I strode through the doors. "Sees what?" I trained my crossbow squarely between his eyes.

They all gaped with white faces. Sharrad recovered and grabbed for his pistol.

"Go on, try to shoot me before I kill your master!" I dared him.

He kept his hand on his pistol a moment. Then he slowly withdrew it.

"Raise your hands where I can see them, all of you!"

They complied, the ambassador looking bewildered. Laurent rose gingerly from his parlor seat, palms lifted, and took a graceful step backward. "Now just calm down, Helena."

"I'm perfectly calm, Monsieur. Though you look a bit shaken. I hope I'm not interrupting anything important. I doubt you were expecting me. Were you?"

Brocard and Simonet backed away further, spreading out. I aimed my crossbow in their direction. "No one moves!"

They froze, waiting for my next instruction. My heart pounded madly. I had no plan.

"What do you want, Mademoiselle?" Laurent asked carefully. His eyes shifted between me and his official guest.

I returned my crossbow to his head. "First, I wish to alert you. Monsieur Brocard's barn is in flames."

Brocard lunged toward me. "What? You burned my –!"

He stopped cold as I turned my crossbow toward his chest. "You're accusing me of burning your barn?" I asked. "Why would I do that? Why would anyone in *La Rue Sauvage* wish to burn your barn?"

They stood speechless. The ambassador looked from one face to the other, perplexed. Laurent and his men couldn't accuse me of attacking them without raising the suspicions of their royal guest.

"I spotted some wild animals in the barn," I told Laurent. "They might have caused the blaze. We'll never know. The barn appears to have been locked, and they were all trapped inside."

Laurent grimaced, his cheeks purpling with rage. "How many?"

I met his gaze. "I counted thirty-three."

He glanced quickly at Simonet, now standing close to the wall. Without a word, Simonet opened a side door and disappeared into the next room. I was too late to stop him. It didn't matter, as long as they entertained the ambassador.

"He's alerting my guards, Helena," Laurent said calmly. "You might wish to surrender now, before they come. It will go better for you, I promise."

"You promise? Like you promised my father you would ask for more soldiers to protect us from the wolves? Like you promised to honor Francois with your banquet, when you got him drunk and attacked him in his home?"

The ambassador's eyes slid toward Laurent.

"Go ahead and summon your guards," I challenged. "I'll still end your malicious life before they can stop me. If they send me to prison, even if they hang me for treason, it will be worth it to set our province free of you."

The ambassador relaxed, then narrowed his gaze on Laurent. "She is making rather bold accusations against you, Monsieur."

Laurent smiled and shook his head, waving me off. "She is unfortunately delusional, Monsieur. She lost her parents and her younger sister and blames me, or anyone else she can start a fight with."

"Liar!" I exploded. "You killed my parents and Suzette and Francois! But you won't kill anyone else! I'll ..." I felt a sudden dizziness. I blinked and shook my head. I was staring at the floor.

I lifted my head, tried to raise my crossbow. "... I'll ..." My head drooped heavily again.

Sharrad now stood over me and easily tugged the crossbow from my hands.

"Just relax, Helena. Let me help you to the door," Laurent was saying, sounding far away. His image blurred like a reflection in the water. He turned back to the ambassador as I struggled to focus on his face, his voice. Anything. "As I said, Monsieur, she is quite ill. I have tried to help her in every way I can, but she refuses to let anyone near her." He started toward me. "Calm down, Helena. We only want to help you."

I felt like a drunkard, hunched over, struggling to stand upright. Laurent took my arm and guided me to the door. "I'll only be a moment, Monsieur," he called over his shoulder.

"My musketeers can assist you at the gate, Monsieur," the ambassador replied. "Know that they will report back to me on everything they witness tonight."

"Of course, Monsieur. We've nothing to hide," Laurent said.

He led me through the broad doors with Sharrad and Brocard, who closed the double doors behind us. The doors made an odd reverberating thud. The light of the high lanterns stung my eyes.

Laurent continued down the hall toward the parlor entrance, leading me like a puppy on a leash. "You are trying my patience, Helena," he hissed in my ear, tightening his grip on my arm. My nerves grew numb, barely feeling the pain. "I don't know how you escaped, but in a week's time, it will no longer matter. I'll be able to dispose of you any way I see fit, or make you suffer any way I choose. In a dungeon, in an asylum, on the gallows for everyone to see. But tonight you are interrupting."

"What did ... What did you ... do to me?"

He chuckled. "What I hoped to do later tonight, before we fed on you. That will have to wait. I would love to lock you away here, to torment you through the night and feast afterward on what's left of you, but that might arouse the musketeers' suspicion."

He continued to speak, continued to dig his fingers into my arm, as we clomped quietly over a smooth path. I felt a cool breeze tickling my cheeks and I lifted my head. We stood at the iron gate, fifty feet from the chateau's doors. The royal ambassador's guards stared at us, astounded. How had we gotten here?

"It's all right, gentlemen," Laurent told them. "She's quite clever but otherwise harmless. She's leaving now. Sharrad. Her crossbow."

I blinked, struggling to focus. I saw my crossbow sail beyond the open gate to clang and skitter across the outer stone path. I heard a horse galloping from the distance. I turned left to see Crimson hurrying toward us as the guards raised their muskets. "Don't bother shooting it," Laurent told them. "It's her ride." Crimson came to a halt at the gate and stamped his hooves at Laurent, his eyes blazing.

"Now limp on home, Helena, wherever your home is in the woods."

Brocard's voice rose in alarm. "You're giving her back her weapon?"

"What can she do with it? The poor deluded girl. Look at her. By morning, she won't even be able to stand up."

He was right. My head felt like it was stuffed with wool. My legs felt like they were made of straw. My gut burned as I doubled over. "What did ... you do?"

Laurent walked in front of me to block the guards' view. He bent his leering face close to mine and seized the back of my neck, his fingers clamping hard. "Remember, Helena?" he whispered harshly. "I have something of yours. Something personal and precious. And I'll treasure it always." He patted the side pocket of his waistcoat. He forced my head up and I found

Sharrad and Brocard now smiling openly, reveling in some dark secret.

Laurent's own blurring smile hardened like a gargoyle's. "From now on, Mademoiselle, wherever you go, wherever you try to hide, I'll find you. And I'll hurt you. As much as I want. As badly as I want. And as long as I want." He flashed wolfish teeth. "And there's nothing you can do about it."

He moved his hand to my back and guided me out the front gate. Crimson charged at him in a rage, his motions distorted so that he looked like several horses at once. Laurent released me and I fell to my knees on the hard path.

They waited in silence as I crawled toward my crossbow. I drew it close, and it scraped across the stone path, like a mosquito buzzing in my ear. I clutched it to my chest, then slung it over my shoulder and struggled to my feet. Struggled to find Crimson's flank and saddle, to pull myself up and rest against him. I rested there for some time. I didn't know how long. Then I grabbed hold of the horn and hoisted myself up. I barely managed to throw my stomach on top of his back. I rested again for a moment, then forced myself to sit up in the saddle as the world of stone and grass and trees spun before me.

"Farewell, Helena," Laurent called.

I stared straight ahead. If I tried to look back at Laurent and his men, I feared I might fall off the saddle.

Crimson carried me at a slow trot back the way we came. Back to the forest, back to Father Vestille's hovel. As slow as he moved, it felt like I was lying belly-first on a storm-tossed raft. I leaned against his neck, trying to rest comfortably against his dark mane, and held on. We left the lights of *Chateau de Laurent* behind us as the night and the forest swallowed us up.

Somewhere up ahead of us, the Lycanthru were still searching for me, and I could barely lift my head.

41.

Crimson carried me through the cool night, past dark pine trees that loomed like monstrous shadows. Past unseen crickets and snapping twigs and croaking frogs that hammered my senses with a symphony of chaos. I had traveled back and forth through these woods since I was a child, but now every sound, every tickle of the wind, frightened and unnerved me as though they might destroy me from the inside out. I jerked and twisted at each new sensation, frightened at first, then remembering what it indicated. A harmless insect, a rustling leaf, a change in the wind. I gasped for breath and clutched Crimson's mane, hugging his neck. What had Laurent done to me?

A wolf howled. The sound rattled my jaw and my spine.

It sounded close.

They would find me soon.

Crimson froze. I waited, resting against him, feeling for the crossbow that hung from my shoulder. The wolf howled again, farther off. They were moving away from us. Crimson waited, giving them time. Then I nudged him gently and he trotted on.

We still heard the distant howls as we trudged to Father Vestille's hovel. The moon was full, the night half-gone. But they would search the woods until they found us.

I slid down from Crimson's saddle as quickly as I could, then leaned against him as he moved to the rear stable. I felt like collapsing in the fresh hay, but forced myself to remain standing. I still rested on his flank as I kicked hay off of the twin trap doors. Then I carefully bent down to grab one of the secret handles.

I could no longer lift it.

I tugged hard and lost my footing, dropping painfully to my knees. Crimson whinnied quietly with concern.

A wolf howled, closer now.

We would never make it.

My heart thumped. My temples pounded. One of the wolves would find us at any moment.

I struggled to my feet and rested against Crimson, gathering my strength. Then I led him by the reins, resting against him and walking sideways toward the front door.

I clomped onto the wooden porch, taking one steady step after another, and knocked. I pressed against the door, listening for movement inside. My strength drained like water from my legs and I sank to my knees. I knocked again. "Father Vestille," I whispered. "Father … Vestille …"

I started pounding steadily with the side of my fist.

I fell onto my face as the door gave way.

"Helena! Helena, what happened?"

I shut my eyes. He squatted and turned me over, cradling me.

"Helena! Helena!"

I forced myself to look at him. At his horrified eyes. "Father Vestille … I'm dying …"

"No," he said in a small voice. "No. You're going to be all right, Helena."

I shook my head, weak. "… can't stop them …"

Something growled at the edge of the forest. Crimson snorted and whirled at the mud-brown wolf watching us from the black trees. We were dead.

I looked about for my crossbow. It had fallen from my shoulder onto the porch. I grabbed it with a firm grip and tried to aim. The wolf padded closer, saliva dripping from its fangs.

I could barely lift my arm.

The wolf snarled and tensed its raging features.

I gasped, one hand on the lever, the other beneath my crossbow. Too weak to lift it.

"Helena?"

I swallowed. "… can't …"

"Helena!"

The wolf growled again and charged.

Father Vestille's palm slid under my elbow. The crossbow lifted to the wolf's eyes and I pulled the lever back. The bolt struck his forehead, making him jerk, his front paws dangling helplessly before he fell in a heap.

Twenty-seven left.

My head spun as my breathing grew shallow. "You just … helped me kill."

Father Vestille said nothing. "Come inside, Helena."

I tried to sit up.

Father Vestille put his knee behind my back for support. He put his arms beneath me, gathered his breath, and lifted me up, pushing the door open with his foot. He carried me through the front room, moving past black silhouettes of his table and chairs. The room smelled of ashes from his fireplace. He must have cooked something recently, to feed me whenever I returned.

He laid me gently down on his bed, with the crossbow still cradled in my lap. Then he ran out and shut the front door behind him. Crimson whinnied once, not used to Father Vestille taking his reins. He sounded still and obedient after that, though all outside noise was muffled. I listened intently, each new sound bringing a disorienting pain that set my nerves on fire. I thought I heard the secret doors creak open. Then I heard Crimson clomp down the ramp of the underground shelter. He pulled the secret doors shut and the sound echoed through the floorboards.

A door smashed open, followed by heavy footsteps. I started up in bed, staring into the black void, expecting another wolf.

It was only Father Vestille, coming up the ladder. He closed the trap door and I winced.

He came in with a candle that threw menacing shadows on the oak walls. "I've got your horse inside," he said. "I'll feed him in a moment and settle him for the night. You're safe now."

I shook my head. "I'm not. Not anymore ... no one's safe ..."

"Helena, calm down. It will be all right."

I shut my eyes, tired and nauseous, as he took the crossbow and set it aside somewhere. He lifted my head and peeled back the hood, then propped a cushion beneath my neck and laid me down gently. I felt his wrist against my forehead.

He kept it there for some time. I opened my eyes.

He squinted, perplexed. "Strange. You don't have a fever."

I blinked slowly.

"Lie still. I'll get you some water. Then you can tell me what happened."

He set the candle on his nightstand and marched out. I shuddered with a fresh sense of shame. Lying in his bed, immobilized, smelling the remnants of the last meal he cooked for me. If he knew what I had done tonight, would he be so eager to nurse me back to health? Or would he eject me from his peaceful hovel, freeing himself of the girl who dressed like a harlot and had slain nearly three dozen men in one night?

I turned toward the candle, studying its hypnotic flame. Imagining the Lycanthru, struggling to escape the barn's inferno. Then I imagined the atrocities Laurent meant to inflict on me tonight, at this very moment, if I remained captive there. Which made me wonder what torments their other victims suffered. Papa, Mama, Francois ... And Suzette. What had that monster done to her in her final moments?

My pulse quickened. I shoved my horrific thoughts aside. I needed to rest and calm myself, as Father Vestille said. To recover from this sickness, or whatever Laurent had done to me. I had to regain my strength, to prepare for another night of battle for the survival of *La Rue Sauvage*. Another night of fighting them all alone.

The candle's flame dimmed. I studied it, confused. The fire didn't shrink, but simply dimmed as if fading away. The room grew darker and darker until it became pitch black.

I blinked again but saw nothing. I reached out to find the candle. To squint at the knuckles of my gloved hand. I still saw nothing, but I felt the candle's intense heat just before I touched its wax base. Before I knocked its saucer off the nightstand and it clattered to the floor. I sat up in bed, the queasiness wrenching my stomach, and gaped at the hot flame. A flame I couldn't see!

"Father Vestille!"

I blinked again and again, spreading my open palms out in front of me. I could feel the heat beneath them, rising closer to my legs. I stamped blindly with my boots, ignoring the sickening twist of my stomach. I found some of the fire and squelched it, but I couldn't see how much of it remained. I couldn't *see!*

I heard Father Vestille rush into the room, clomping to a halt. "Helena!" Something sloshed against the floor, probably the cup of water he promised to pour me. I heard him whip something at the floor, some blanket or thick cloth perhaps. Something scraped back and forth against the floorboards. I imagined his heel swiveling against the cloth to smother any lingering sparks. But I had no way of knowing.

He stood somewhere above me, gasping. "Helena. What happened?" He took a half-step closer and leaned down to my face. I could smell the ham he had eaten for dinner. "What's wrong with your eyes?" he asked.

I stared straight ahead. Straight ahead into pure blackness. Like I was living out another one of my childhood nightmares. "I don't know. I was just watching the candle. And then it faded." I quivered and swallowed. "I can't see. Father, I'm blind."

The room fell silent. I saw nothing but darkness, heard nothing but the sounds of crickets outside.

"How? Did you fall? Or hit your head? Did they … Did they do something to you?"

I wanted to tell him everything. But I knew what he would think of me. Yet I needed his help. I needed him to lead me by the hand. "Father. … I killed them."

Silence.

"What do you mean, Helena?"

"Thirty-three men. I killed thirty-three men. I locked them in their barn, where they held their ceremonies. And I set the barn on fire."

"Helena …"

"They tried to kill me, Father. They were going to eat me! And Crimson, too. We escaped. And I burned them."

"*All* of them?"

"No. Laurent and twenty-six others remain." A hollow chill swept up through me. "And they want revenge."

I remembered Laurent's warning.

Wherever you go, wherever you try to hide, I'll find you and I'll hurt you. As much as I want, as badly as I want, and as long as I want. And there's nothing you can do about it.

"Laurent," I gasped. "He did this. He made me blind."

42.

A fresh wave of nausea churned my stomach as I reached out for Father Vestille. I tried to steady myself by leaning on him. Intending to grab hold of his shoulder, I barely managed to find his elbow.

He took my hand and moved to support me. "Helena, come out front and sit, and tell me everything that happened. I'll make some stew and we can figure this out."

I could hear the catch in his voice. He didn't believe we could solve this any more than I did. If Laurent could do this, attack me from anywhere, at any time, then perhaps Father Vestille was right. I should never have challenged the Lycanthru in the first place. But if they could do this, why did they wait until now? Did they only now consider me a genuine threat?

I stood and let him guide me toward the door. The door I could no longer see. "Don't warm ... any food," I said. "Can't risk sending up ... chimney smoke ... especially now."

I shuffled a few steps ... and my legs collapsed beneath me.

"Helena!"

I fell against Father Vestille so suddenly he couldn't keep me from hitting the floorboards. I grunted, feeling foolish and helpless.

I tried to rise, but couldn't. I twisted at the waist, feeling the wood and dust beneath my elbows, but my legs would not move. I felt my thigh. Pinched it. Struck it hard with my fist. I felt the pain in my knuckles but not in my legs. "Father. ... I can't walk. I can't see and I can't walk."

"What happened?" he demanded, seizing my shoulders. He scooped me up in his arms again and laid me back on his bed. He scraped a chair across the floor toward me and settled into it. "Helena, tell me everything that happened last night." He had never been so aggressive. I couldn't tell if he was angry or frightened or both.

"They ... They tied me to two poles." The memory of it shook me more now than it had at the time. At the thought of what *could* have happened. At what they *meant* to happen. "They gagged me. They beat me. They left me strung up there all day. They were going to eat me, Father. They couldn't wait for nightfall, to come back and devour me. One piece at a time."

He paused, perhaps wondering if this justified my destruction of them. "Did they take anything from you?"

I blinked, feeling nauseous again. "... What?"

"Did they take anything important? Like a necklace or one of your weapons. Anything personal."

I recalled how Laurent patted his waistcoat pocket in front of his chateau, while the other Lycanthru grinned at me. He did the same thing at the barn before leaving me with Jacquard.

You know, I still have something of yours. Something very personal and precious. And I'll treasure it always.

I felt the blood drain from my body. I stared into black nothingness, as I lay immobilized on the bed. "He took my hair ..."

"Laurent?"

I nodded, numb.

Father Vestille blew out an angry breath. "He's established a connection with you. He's using his magic to strike at you, wherever you are. He doesn't even need to search for you."

Wherever you go, wherever you try to hide ... as much as I want, as badly as I want, and as long as I want ...

Tears started to stream down my cheeks. I didn't bother wiping them away. How long before I lost all feeling throughout my body? Before I lost the ability to hear or touch? "Father, help me. I don't know how to fight this."

His anger radiated like heat. "But I do."

He pushed the chair away and stood.

"I'm going to pray over you. Just lie still."

The floor creaked as he knelt at my bedside and started to pray in Latin. Praying with an intensity I had never heard from him. Never heard from anyone. My heart beat with panic, but the mere sound of his prayers was strangely comforting. He didn't judge or accuse me. He only questioned me enough to know how to act. How to rescue me.

My body relaxed. I still couldn't see or feel my legs. But I felt a peace growing inside me, a sense of safety I had not felt since Papa taught me to hunt. Since Mama taught me how to care for Suzette. Since Francois let me ride Crimson and urged me to fight for others. This was the same feeling, but stronger. A feeling of safety and belonging. A feeling that I was home.

I rested – actually rested for the first time in months, perhaps years – and let him pray over me, while I did nothing. My fears drifted away as he continued, and I saw something take shape before my eyes. Large round objects that seemed familiar as they approached me.

Each shape grew long hair and wild eyes, taking the forms of the wolves. My body tensed as they opened their fanged jaws and lunged at me.

"Father Vestille! Father Vestille, help me!"

They bit at me, clawed me, leered at me. Then they reared their heads back to attack again.

As much as I want, as badly as I want, and as long as I want ...

"Help me!"

His hand settled onto my forehead. I couldn't see him but I could feel his hand there, steadying me, comforting me, as he continued to pray.

As the beasts continued to lunge at me, feeding on my flesh. I felt their fangs sinking into my arms, my shoulders, my stomach. Again and again.

"Father!"

I heard his voice, angry now, shouting in Latin at the monsters. They drew back, like dogs being scolded by their masters. A few moments later, the blackness returned. I lay there trembling, and saw nothing more.

"Th-They were h-here," I stammered.

"I know. I saw them. Are you all right?"

"You saw them? But how –?"

"This is a spiritual attack, Helena. The Lord allows me to see what they are doing as I pray against it. Are you all right?"

In truth, I was terrified. My shoulder stung and I reached under my tunic to press my palm against it. I pulled it away quickly from something that felt sticky.

Father Vestille took my hand, then wiped it with a cloth. Probably the white cloth that had sat beneath the candle.

"What is it?" I asked.

He said nothing at first, but continued to clean my hand. "It's blood. Hold still."

He reached beneath my tunic to press the cloth against my shoulder. I winced at the pain. As though I had been shot with an arrow.

He removed the cloth and felt the area. I felt his fingers settle into a few puncture marks in my shoulder.

He sighed slowly. "They bit you, Helena. I will do all I can to make sure they cannot bite you again."

"They can bite me? When they're not even here?"

"They've cursed you and they are trying to apply their curse. But the Scriptures say a curse that is without cause is like a flitting bird. It will not land on you, because you have done nothing wrong."

I turned toward him. Toward the sound of his gentle voice. "I've done nothing wrong?"

Father Vestille laid his hand back on my forehead, as if tending a feverish child. "You must be doing something right for them to do this, to fight so hard to stop you. You have done nothing wrong, Helena. You have only fought against their evil."

I swallowed. "Thank you, Father."

"Now lie still. I will pray over you for as long as it takes to break their hold. I will do whatever the Lord directs me to do, to set you free. Do you trust me to do that?"

I nodded.

He continued to pray while I stared into complete darkness, lying helpless in my comfortable prison. My exhaustion soon overtook me as I listened to his relentless prayers, and I fell fast asleep.

I woke several times, falling in and out of nightmares. I saw vivid images of the wolves attacking me, of fighting back at them. Sometimes winning. Sometimes being devoured. Most of the images were dreams, I knew, because I could see things more clearly. Other times when they attacked, their images were hazy and fleeting, but their bites felt all too real.

Father Vestille continued to pray in Latin, sometimes kneeling, sometimes pacing, sometimes shouting, sometimes near tears. Speaking words that were foreign and strange and beautiful, but with an unmistakable sense of passion and protectiveness. Like a warrior charging into battle with a drawn sword. Like Francois with his silver ax. Or Mama, watching over me whenever I fell ill. My family was gone, but Father Vestille had become father and mother and protector to me.

I could no longer see or walk or distinguish what was real. But I was home.

43.

Images came and went, along with pain and screams and terror. Wolf claws reached out for me, sliced at my face over and over again. Wolf fangs bit into my thighs, ankles, neck and back. Leopold Laurent loomed over me several times, smiling in sadistic triumph.

But later, Laurent's eyes often grew wide with astonished anger and his image quickly disappeared, like a candle being blown out. Until finally, he appeared once more, his features tensed as if he struggled to concentrate, to maintain his presence.

And then he was gone.

Everything turned gray. Then the shades of gray shifted and fluttered as I moved my head back and forth, searching for something I could see. The room smelled musty as a cave and I heard a faint mumbling close by. It sounded sad, almost pleading, while something scraped and stamped at the far wall.

I squinted at a tiny white dot at my left. It grew larger, expanding and changing to a pale yellow color. Then it became a bright yellow flower of some type, atop a tall straight stem. Beside it, a large boulder began to take more definite shape.

I blinked and the boulder became a large pinkish ball with cottony flowers gracing either side of it, while the flower trembled slightly and waved. I blinked again. The flower became a short candle, gently flickering. The pinkish rock became the bowed head of Father Vestille, his hands folded in prayer as he rested his face against my cot, murmuring in Latin. I recognized the words from a previous mass, when Father Vestille led us to ask the Lord for divine mercy and intervention. Shadows striped his figure, as the noonday sun peeked through the planks of the ceiling. We were in the underground shelter. Across the room, Crimson stamped his hooves and scraped the dirt floor, anxious.

I was alive.

I continued to stare, gasping with shock and relief.

Father Vestille's head jerked up. "Helena! You're ... Are you all right?"

Crimson snorted and pounded the floor, tossing his head. I tried to sit up to embrace Father Vestille, but I couldn't move my arms. I stared down to find my arms and legs tied down with ropes.

"Sorry for that," he said as he grabbed a knife from a tray of food. The bread and fruit had scarcely been picked at. He sliced through the ropes and I stretched my legs –my *legs!* I could bend my legs again!

"You were thrashing in your delirium," he explained as he blew out the candle, now almost burned to the wick. "I had to stop you from scratching at my face. At whatever you thought was in front of you at the time." He shook his head and wiped his tear-streaked face. "After the first few attacks, I knew they could no longer bite you. I sensed that power had been broken, and you bore only a few wounds. But they still attacked your mind, making you believe they were biting you. I had to bring you down here, to prevent anyone from hearing you."

"It's all right," I said, sitting up. I must have beamed, because he smiled, too. I had not seen him smile since he played with Suzette in front of his hovel, while I watched them from a distance. "Thank you, Father."

"I felt everything break a minute ago. I sensed they had lost their power over you. But then you lay so still, I feared ..." He didn't finish. The last wisp of smoke dissipated from the spent candle.

I touched his arm. "I'm all right," I assured him. "Thank you. You must have been praying over me all night."

His face paled. "Helena. You've been delirious and under attack for six days."

"Six days!" I jumped to my feet, instantly regretting it as my legs buckled. I stumbled but recovered quickly. My legs were numb and out of practice, but otherwise my reflexes felt fully restored. "Laurent might have done any number of things in the past week."

"I'm sure they have taken advantage of your condition. They meant to harm you. To make you suffer. However, they also meant to incapacitate you. But their hold over you is broken. I felt it in my spirit, and you can see it for yourself. They can't harm you anymore."

Crimson looked rested but anxious, stamping his hooves again. "Hopefully, we can still do some harm to them. Before they attack anyone else."

"Wait a moment," Father Vestille said, rising to stop me as I crossed the room.

I turned back to him. "Father, I know you don't believe what I'm doing is right, but I have no choice. I have to stop them, however I can. Just tell me what I must do when it's over."

He cocked his head. "What you must *do?*"

"To absolve myself. What must I do to make up for killing those men?"

He pursed his lips. "Nothing."

I waited for him to explain. "Father Vestille?"

"Helena. I have visited many churches over the last several years. People who share the same faith, but apply it in different ways. I see the Scriptures differently now. The Scriptures say it is by grace we have been forgiven and set free. Not by our own efforts. How can we do anything to make ourselves presentable to a holy God who knows no sin? He simply forgives us. And accepts us. Just as we are."

"But it's wrong to kill."

"There is a time to kill, just as there is time to heal. A time for war and a time for peace. Yes, you killed. You killed men who would have killed you, and who would have continued to kill other innocent people. You did something that others could not do. Something that *I* could not do. We must each perform the tasks that the Lord assigns us, even if they are distasteful. Even if they cost us our reputation, our friends, or our lives. You did what had to be done, because you knew someone had to do it. However it appeared to others or to me, you did what was right."

I swallowed. "Why now?"

He squinted at me.

"Why are you doing all this now? After you left us all to fend for ourselves? Where was all your courage and help then, when we needed you most?"

"Helena, I know you feel I abandoned you –."

"You *did* abandon us!" I burst. "They almost killed me. They *did* kill Grand'Mere Marie, and Francois a year later, a whole pack of them! I was a child. I was scarred and ugly and frightened and you were nowhere to be found! If ever a girl needed a priest, it was then. But you took one long journey after another, visiting other provinces while Mama and Papa defended you, saying your heart was still here with us. Maybe your heart was, but you weren't! Then Papa died and you thought you could just walk right back into our lives as if you never left. But you *did* leave. And I got used to surviving without you."

He hung his head.

"When you finally returned, I no longer needed you. I needed you before. I'm sorry, Father Vestille. I'm glad for your help, for everything you've done for me the last few months. But I find it hard to trust you after you ran off to meet with other people in other provinces, to find someplace safer to start a church. I know you're here fighting for me now, but I need to know if you'll always be here, or if you'll run off again, the next time the Lycanthru attack."

"That's not why I visited other provinces."

"Then tell me why. What was so urgent, after a wolf tried to kill me, that you had to separate yourself from us, from our insignificant little family? What were you looking for?"

He gave a heavy sigh. "I was looking for the Lycanthru."

All the air seeped from my spirit. "... what?"

He half-chuckled. "Naturally, I didn't … didn't know that's what I was looking for when I started. I just … I had to know more about the wolf. I had heard of other attacks in other villages. Just rumors. But after I saw the body of the wolf that killed Marie Justine, I had to know what was happening. Something about that creature … it wasn't natural. It wasn't simply a large wolf. There was something unusual about it. Something evil. It had the same shocked eyes I had seen on men and women who died suddenly. I never saw an animal with such animated features. Almost human. And the way you spoke about the attack, saying the wolf stood and spoke and swiped at you. The way a man would attack." He shook his head. "It unsettled me. I knew your parents would care for you. I wanted to be here for all of you as well. But I had to find out the cause of this. Who else but me could have done that? Who else would recognize true evil, lying there on the floor, and do something about it?"

I gaped at him. "You never told us."

"I never told anyone. How could I? How could I say these creatures were some sort of demons, until I learned more about them? I had to be certain. So I traveled to places where there had been other strange attacks from wolves. Gevaudan, Normandy, my former home in Burgundy. I spoke to people in churches, yes, and in villages, asking about their community and lifestyle. This allowed me to ask about safety in their province and any dangers they feared. Which helped me learn about the wolves. I met people who actually witnessed these creatures. Later I met with other priests and scholars who informed me of the Lycanthru cult. The more I inquired, the more I became convinced the Lycanthru were here in *La Rue Sauvage*. But I had no proof. Not until you saw them yourself, and survived."

My heart felt like it had dropped to the ground. "Father Vestille … You never told us. You did all that … let everyone believe you were pursuing other positions … You did all that for us."

He sat heavily on a stool, as if weighted down by his secret. "If I revealed my true purpose, no one in the other provinces would have spoken to me. And everyone here would have panicked. Over rumors. But after they killed Henri … your father … I realized I was wrong. I wanted to continue learning about them. What they were up to, who they were. But it cost me my best friend. I couldn't bear to lose any more of your family over it. I would gladly have remained ignorant of the Lycanthru and all their activities for just a few more months with your father."

I swallowed back shame. He had never abandoned us. He had been fighting for us all this time, unrecognized. "You did what you knew you had to do. Even though no one understood it. Just like me."

His eyes burrowed into the dirt floor. "That's one way of looking at it."

I moved to kneel beside him. "Father Vestille, I'm sorry for what I said. For everything. Can you forgive me?"

His entire face showed his brokenness. "If you can forgive me."

I threw my arms around him. He closed the embrace. Suddenly, it felt like I had my family back.

I finally pulled away, smearing tears from my face. "Father Vestille, when this is all over and I can return home, I'll come see you. Every week. Or you can visit me, whenever you want."

"I would like that, Helena." His face hardened. "But for now, we both have work to do. I'll trust the Lord to use you to do His work. Can you do the same?"

I nodded.

"Then kneel."

I stared at him, astonished. Did he mean what I thought he meant? After all his fears about the dangerous person I might become? Whatever he intended, there seemed little point in arguing with a priest. Especially one that had just saved my life. I knelt.

He stood and reached for a small flask on the table. It smelled of thick oil and incense as he poured it into his palm.

He spoke something in Latin as he smeared the oil on my forehead with two fingers, forming the sign of the cross. Then he said, "Thus I ordain and commission you to do the work for which Almighty God has anointed you, to protect our village and our people, our workers and our children, to preserve our present and future, and eradicate the demons that seek to devour us. In the name of the Father, the Son, and the Holy Spirit, I bless you and anoint you for this holy calling."

A strange sensation filled me like fire from inside. It surged through my nerves until I expected my hairs to stand up on end. I felt this power before, at times when I hunted and when I fought the wolves. I never considered it could be the Lord's power working through me. Especially when all of my actions seemed so bizarre, even to me.

The surging power diminished slowly, leaving me speechless. Father Vestille not only forgave me, but appointed me for divine service. His anointing empowered me with a new strength and confidence I never felt before. I stood shakily. He seized my arms and helped steady me.

"Thank you," I said, swiping away a tear.

"I have prayed every night for your safety, and for your soul," he said. "From now on, I will also pray for your success." He crossed himself and waved another blessing over me. "Whatever you need, tell me. I'll do whatever I can. Just be careful." He turned and grabbed my hooded cloak, holding it up with a smile. "Don't forget this."

44.

Crimson pounded through the cool forest, trampling over twigs and branches, seeming as anxious as I was to find Laurent. For six days, I lay paralyzed at Father Vestille's hovel, too delirious to focus or even wake from my living nightmares. But now, with Laurent's curse broken and with Father Vestille's anointing still tingling my senses, I felt stronger than ever. More than ready to handle Laurent and the Lycanthru, with plenty of bolts left from Pierre's last supply.

I needed that strength to regain lost ground. With me out of the way, the Lycanthru might have launched any number of attacks against the people.

As we neared the village, a picture posted to a tree caught my attention. It was a sketch drawing of *Chateau de Laurent*. The place I last saw Duke Laurent, as he entertained the royal ambassador. The night he cursed me, after his men failed to devour me. A seething rage rode up into my shoulders. I tugged Crimson's reins for a closer look.

The notice announced a formal masquerade ball being held by Laurent at eight o'clock tonight, to welcome the Queen of France to *La Rue Sauvage* for the first time in history.

By invitation only.

My eyes narrowed as I read the details. This was the important business Laurent had to tend to last week, when he hosted the ambassador. I was too enraged, too frightened, to think of it at the time, but everyone knew Duke Laurent had fallen from favor with the court at Versailles. He was banished here, assigned to oversee *La Rue Sauvage* as a merciful punishment for his offense, whatever it was. But he had no contact with the royal family since that time, since before I was born, apart from the letters he claimed to have sent them. Why would Her Majesty choose to visit him now?

What was Laurent planning?

I sat atop Crimson in the center of the cobblestone street and waited, ignoring the gasps and shrieks of onlookers. Duke Laurent's carriage approached, heading straight toward me. Its driver yanked back on the reins when he saw the point of my repeating crossbow aimed at his head.

"Stop," I said.

He stared at me, dumbfounded. His horses snorted and settled into place.

No one moved. Villagers murmured behind me. A woman told someone to fetch the police. I fixed my eyes on the driver and the carriage, and waited.

Just past Laurent's carriage, Jacque Denue and two of his friends started across the street, pausing as they saw me. Anger surged in my cheeks as Denue gaped at me in shock. He was probably heading back to meet the Lycanthru to run another errand for them, or to beg forgiveness for his failure. He watched me, not moving.

The rear door finally flew open. "Lafayette, is something wrong?"

Laurent's boot stepped down. I tugged Crimson around to meet him. Laurent halted halfway down the steps as he met my crossbow, aimed squarely between his eyes. "Good afternoon, Monsieur."

He recovered quickly, resting a hand against the carriage. "Well, well, Helena. Up and about in less than a week. I'm impressed."

"I don't care." I edged Crimson closer.

Jacque Denue cast an anxious glance up at Laurent, then moved to intercept me. "You better keep your place, witch, if you know what's good for –!"

In an instant, I was off of Crimson's back and hitting the ground with both feet. In the next, I kicked down hard on Denue's kneecap. He howled in pain as I shoved him aside with my boot and kept walking.

I trained my crossbow on Laurent. The surrounding crowd held its breath, no one daring to intervene. I wondered if any of the villagers anticipated this day. If they knew Laurent and his men tried to kill me. If they knew the Lycanthru feared me at least as much as I feared them.

Laurent licked his lips, clearly thinking. Scheming. "You look well, Helena. Except, of course, for the, ah …" He made a circular gesture about his face to indicate my triple scars. "But that can't be helped, can it?"

I offered him a grim smile. "Wars take a toll, Monsieur Laurent. I believe your losses bring you down to twenty-seven now."

He straightened and made a show of confusion. "I don't know what you're referring to, Helena."

"Of course you don't."

"You! Drop your weapon!"

Lieutenant-General Sharrad stood fifteen feet to my right, his pistol aimed at my head. I could see him well enough without turning from Laurent.

"You shoot me, I shoot him. No more Lord Laurent."

Silence.

"It's all right, Sharrad. Helena appears to be upset. But I'm sure we can resolve this peacefully. Put down your pistol."

"But, Monsieur –!"

"Down, I said!" he barked. Sharrad did as he was commanded, and Laurent settled into a tolerant smile. "Now, Helena. How are you feeling? I heard you were ill."

I circled around him, away from Sharrad. Securing a clear shot at his forehead. "I'm fully recovered. Thank you for asking."

He eyed me with distaste. "I'm curious. What did you do to recover so quickly?"

"I'm more interested in your party to welcome the Queen. I thought the King banished you."

He lifted his palms upward slowly. Carefully. "Sadly, the King is no more, as you are surely aware. His passing has left the country in a state of concern, with his sole heir being a child, far too young to rule in his place. Her Majesty has graciously accepted my invitation to put our differences aside, in the interest of building a unified France. After all, we have waged war with one country or another for centuries. We need strong leadership to protect our fragile borders. The invasions that occurred less than twenty years ago might threaten again at any time. But our enemies will reconsider such attacks when they see the power of our new throne."

A chill ran through me. Laurent recognized it and grinned. "You're still trying to steal the throne," I said quietly. "You invited the Queen here to kill her and take over, as the next in line."

He shrugged again. Standing close by, Sharrad could barely contain his devilish grin. "It is true, as the King's half-brother, it is my duty to assume the throne, should anything happen to Her Majesty, and of course, to her five-year old son. But, Helena, you accuse me of plotting to kill the Queen? That would be impossible to even attempt. Her Majesty is no fool. She knows a show of forgiveness toward me will help strengthen our country, but she's not about to ignore all the charges brought against me. No, she has consented to come and she's on her way. But she'll be surrounded at all times by armed guards. She'll be well-protected against *any* form of attack. As our ball runs late into the night."

I shuddered with horror at the thought of Laurent devouring the Queen and assuming control of the monarchy, along with the rest of the Lycanthru.

"Everyone's talking about this, Helena. It's going to be the premier event of the springtime. All young maidens are expected to attend, for the singular opportunity to mingle with royalty." He made a sympathetic pout. "However, although it is a masquerade ball, maidens who dress like men would present an oddity that might offend Her Majesty. I'm sorry to say ... you are not invited."

I seized the crossbow lever, ready to pull back. Sharrad grabbed at his pistol while Laurent put up a hand to him, smiling.

"Really, Helena. You have your whole life ahead of you. Do you wish to spend it rotting in the Bastille prison for murdering your Duke in the streets?"

I blew out an angry breath. "You'll never get the people to come to your sick massacre," I hissed. "I'll warn them all off."

"Ah. Let me assist you." He stepped down to the cobblestone path and turned, lifting his arms to the crowd. "Ladies and gentlemen. Everyone! Please, heed this warning. Our wolf-chasing young friend here, Helena Basque, insists that you refrain from attending my gala, as she fears that I might *eat* you all!"

The villagers roared, surrounding me with laughter. I bit my lip, keeping my weapon trained on Laurent. Knowing it was useless.

Laurent raised his eyebrows. "I don't think they believe you, Helena."

I whirled and marched back to climb onto Crimson. Sharrad pulled his pistol.

Laurent held up a hand again to stop him. "Let her go, Sharrad. She can do no harm."

My cheeks burned. Laurent was right. Who in *La Rue Sauvage* would believe me over him?

"So be on your way, Helena. I have a party to host in a few short hours, and you'll have to make other plans for how to spend the evening. We can talk again tomorrow, under far more favorable circumstances."

I swallowed. I had only a few hours to stop him from assuming control of all France. I tugged Crimson away from the mocking crowd.

"You cannot rid the province of me, Helena," Laurent called over the jeers of the relieved villagers. "I *am* the province!"

I leaned closer to Crimson, feeling as though he was the only one who had complete confidence in me.

Except for one other person, of course.

I kicked his flanks and we galloped off toward *L'atelier de Forgeron de Leóne*. Pierre's father had forbidden me to come near their place again, and I meant to stay away.

But I had no choice.

45.

The back door of *L'atelier de Forgeron de Leóne* creaked open. Frayne Leóne stepped out and scanned the area. I ducked deeper behind the woodpile before his eyes passed over me. Crimson kept quiet among the thick trees behind the shed. The sun was still high, the air warm. I had about six hours before the start of Laurent's masquerade ball.

Satisfied, Monsieur Leóne moved back inside and shut the door. A moment later, Pierre emerged and strode to the woodshed. Monsieur Leóne stood just inside the door, watching him. Taking no chances of Pierre holding another secret meeting with me.

After a few minutes, Pierre finished gathering the extra wood and brought it back. Monsieur Leóne glanced about once more before retreating inside. He had turned his shop into a fortress.

I bit my lip. I needed ideas for infiltrating Laurent's royal ball. I hoped Pierre could develop some tool to help me enter unnoticed.

I waited another few minutes to make sure Frayne Leóne would not peek back out. Then I crept back into the forest to retrieve Crimson. I led him slowly by the reins through thick fir trees, around to the side of the shop. I considered the upper window of the loft, where I first donned the red cloak. This side of the building held only one other small window. There was no movement behind it.

I crept forward, staying low and out of sight until I reached the wall. I pressed my back against it and listened for any movement or discussion inside. I heard only the continued hammering of hot metal being forged.

I withdrew the grappling hook and released its prongs. Stepping away from the wall, I studied the windowsill above, then swung the hook up to catch it. It dug into the wood ledge and held firm. I tested it with my weight, then started up. With a few quick steps up the wall, I reached the sill and hoisted myself up. Sitting on the ledge, I tugged my hook free and slid it closed. Then I used it like a chisel to poke through the center of the two wooden shutter doors and snap the latch between them. I edged to one side and opened a shutter door.

All was dark inside, save for the light issuing through the square opening from the shop below. I leaned into the window and tumbled inside to the floor, steadying myself with my hands. Thankfully, nothing had been re-arranged within, so I could ease myself the rest of the way to the floor without stumbling over anything. The heat was stifling now, rising from the fires below where the hammering continued, filling the atmosphere with smoke and oil. I took small breaths as my eyes adjusted to the blackness and shapes began to form. The cot I laid on. The table where I lit my lamp. The wardrobe where I found Madame Leóne's red cloak.

I listened at the loft opening and waited until Monsieur Leóne told Pierre he had an errand to run. He gave stern warnings to speak only to customers while he was gone. I lay on my stomach beside the hole and heard the door close below. I waited another moment, then peered down into the shop.

From my upside-down view, the shop seemed hazy and the oil and heat in the air made me dizzy. But Pierre looked stronger and sweeter than ever, hammering away to forge an iron tool. "Pierre," I whispered.

He didn't hear me over his pounding.

"Pierre!"

He started, nearly dropping his tools. He poked at the coals, stifling the flame, and looked all around the room. "Red?"

"Over here."

His eyes lit up when he found me. "Red! How are you? I haven't seen you for a week. I thought you might have … well …"

"I'm all right. I need your help. What do you know about Duke Laurent's masquerade ball?"

Pierre blinked. "Well, everyone's thrilled about it. Can you believe the Queen is coming? That's quite a visit for *La Rue Sauvage*! If it all goes well, the Duke might even be restored to power. Think of that!"

"I have," I said, sharing none of his enthusiasm. I pulled my head back up and tucked my legs into a crouching position. Then I dropped to a rung of the ladder and jumped down from there to stand before Pierre. He seemed impressed by my rapid descent. "Duke Laurent is behind the wolf attacks. He's one of them."

His face turned white. "Then … wait. Then if he's invited the Queen here …"

"He's going to kill her, along with everyone else attending the ball. I need to get inside without being seen. Can you help me?"

He narrowed his eyes, thinking. He shook his head. "Red, you're talking about sneaking into *Chateau de Laurent*. With the Queen visiting him. He'll have guards stationed at every entrance, and she'll bring her own entourage. To get into that party, one would have to be a girl."

"That leaves me out, then," I said.

His eyes widened and he struggled to find his voice. "That's … That's not what I meant, Red. I just meant … well, they're inviting dozens of women from the village." His face twisted with distaste. "From what I hear, they're picking all the most beautiful ones."

I looked away from him. "Again, that leaves me out."

"Red. I just meant that as ... as sort of a joke. I mean, *I* couldn't get in myself, with all those guards. But a girl in the village can just put on a fancy dress and walk straight in the front door. We'll need to be more discreet. There's got to be some way to sneak inside. I just need to think."

I sighed. I hoped for an immediate answer. If we didn't stop Laurent tonight, he would soon claim the throne. As King, nothing could stop him from preying on innocent children and families throughout the country. "I had better go before your father returns. But I'll be back later." I touched his shoulder.

He covered my hand with his. "I'll think of something, Red. Just be careful."

"More careful than you've been," Monsieur Leóne bellowed as he seized my other wrist. We were so preoccupied with our plans, we never heard him enter over the noise of the fire. He tugged me away from Pierre and toward the door, his cheeks puffing with rage, his grip like a vise. "Didn't I tell you not to admit her? Can't I trust my own son to protect our home?"

"She's no threat, Papa."

"No threat?" he demanded. "She makes war against these beasts and they come in greater force. If she would leave them be, we might escape their notice. But she brings them right to our front doorstep!"

My cheeks burned. "They'll come to your door someday, Monsieur Leóne, whether you provoke them or not. I want to stop them beforehand."

"Then stop them, if you think you can. But leave our family out of it! It's nothing to do with us."

He dragged me to the door so fast that I half-stumbled across the floorboards. He maintained his rough pace and hurled me out onto the lawn. A few men and women stopped, seeing me tumble off the front stoop, but did nothing. I rolled onto my knees and stared up at Monsieur Leóne's accusing finger.

"If I see you near me or my son again, I'll summon the police," he warned.

I glanced at the faces of those passing by. One couple frowned at Monsieur Leóne with disapproval, but neither of them stepped forward to help me up. A few others looked down their noses at me, as if sharing his contempt. Perhaps they also considered me a strange and dangerous girl, bringing trouble to their homes and their children. Behind Monsieur Leóne, Pierre looked on, helpless to interfere further.

    I stood slowly, brushed off the knees of my trousers, and turned to leave. I gave a shrill whistle for Crimson. A few women gasped and clutched at their throats as he bounded from his hiding place in the forest. I climbed up onto his back and kicked at his sides, returning in the direction from which we had come.

46.

From the cover of bushes and fir trees, I watched Celia Verdante stroll along the broad dirt path leading out of the village. Her well-coiffed friend, Marie Beauchamp, smiled beside her. Accompanying them both was Jean Paul Brocard, the Lycanthru whose barn I destroyed, charming them as they hung on his every word.

To get into that party, one would have to be a girl. A girl in the village can just put on a fancy dress and walk straight in the front door ...

I had about five hours left before Duke Laurent's royal ball would begin. Before he would lure nearly every villager to their deaths, along with the Queen, as he and his men transformed into ravenous wolves. I had no chance of passing myself off as a beautiful maiden from the village, or of forging a royal invitation. But if I could follow one of them, I might find another way in.

"I simply couldn't wait until tonight to see you," Brocard said. His voice rose and fell like low music. "I know I'm being impetuous, but I hope you'll forgive me if I ask to escort you home? I hear these streets can be dangerous."

Celia smiled and dropped her gaze as though blushing. Marie Beauchamp tittered at Brocard's compliments. "Oh, I can certainly forgive a slight indiscretion, Monsieur Brocard," Celia said. She spoke in the same fluid motion as her dress, drifting gracefully along the smooth path. "When it comes from such a distinguished gentleman."

Brocard bowed. "You honor me, Mademoiselle."

She curtsied in response.

"As do you," Brocard said, bowing again to Marie, who also curtsied. "I would never forgive myself if anything happened to you lovely young ladies, and I was not there to assist."

My heart felt hollow. Brocard was making another of those sick jokes the Lycanthru loved to make. He meant to kill them both at Celia's own home.

I found myself moving faster, sidestepping between trees and bushes to keep up, my crossbow raised. Crimson followed from about twenty yards back, just close enough to keep me in view. A twig snapped beneath his hoof. Brocard turned sharply toward the sound as I whirled to press my back against a thick oak.

"What is it?" I heard Marie ask.

Celia's own voice rose with concern. "Did you see something? Was it one of those wolves?"

Silence.

Dead silence.

"… No. Probably just a rabbit or some other animal. Come along."

They resumed their pace. I kept my back to the trunk, releasing a heavy breath. I peered carefully around it to make sure they moved along. Once they were further down the path, I glanced back at Crimson, whose head drooped slightly. I waited another moment, then hurried on as quietly as I could.

They soon came to Celia's country house, which sprawled over her estate lawn like a miniature fortress. Shingled rooftops covered tuffeau stone walls, while brightly colored roses and peonies adorned the lawn and the cobbled areas beneath the curtained windows. Circular stones formed a path to an ornate frame surrounding double doors.

Brocard had stolen glances up and down Celia's slim figure during the entire walk to her home. Now he stood at the edge of the stone pathway, clearly agitated. He wiped his forehead with his handkerchief as the girls turned back from Celia's porch.

"Are you coming no further?" Celia asked in a playful tone.

Brocard bowed politely, then straightened and spread his hands wide. "I could not impose on your discretion by entering your home uninvited."

Celia exchanged a wily glance with Marie. "Then, Monsieur, I'll have to invite you. Please. Come in."

Clever, Brocard. If only I could steal inside the front door so easily.

But no one else was about. And Celia's parents must be away, for her to invite a gentleman caller inside without even mentioning them. I doubted her father would approve.

Once the door shut behind them, I scrambled across the lawn. I slowed my pace at the house, to creep onto their stoop. I peered through the corner of the front window, feeling wholly perverse. I had no interest in Celia and Marie's immoral escapades, but I couldn't be discreet if I meant to save them.

I saw their hazy figures through the lace curtains of the parlor window. Celia extended her hand, inviting Brocard to sit with them. She fanned herself as they spoke, smiling and laughing. A minute later, Brocard leaned forward and said something that seized both girls' attention. Celia fanned herself more slowly as he drew something from his waistcoat pocket.

The fanning stopped. Celia and Marie edged back on the sofa as Brocard leaned toward them. Celia started shaking her head. Brocard stood abruptly to his feet.

The fan dropped.

Before I could blink, he leaped across the room and seized Marie. He tugged her to her feet as I stepped back and prepared to fire through the window. He turned with Marie and her body blocked my shot. I hurried to yank the front door open, then darted into the foyer. I entered just in time to hear Marie's neck snap, her body falling limp in Brocard's single-handed grip. He let her slump to the floor like a marionette with broken strings while Celia sprang to her feet and screamed.

"Brocard!" I shouted. I grit my teeth, trying to ignore the body lying at his feet.

He jerked toward me with feral eyes, then leaped backward and tugged Celia in front of him. He crouched low and held her close. "Stay back, Rider. I'll swallow her whole."

He held the nape of her neck with one hand, pinning her arms with the other. Tears streamed from her eyes.

I steadied my grip. "You can't eat her until you become a wolf," I reminded him. "And if you eat your shield, what stops me from shooting you? I think it's a poor plan."

Brocard hesitated a moment. Clearly, strategy was not his greatest strength. "I can still break her into pieces."

"Again. Broken shield, bolt in your head. Not wise."

Brocard reconsidered, wrinkling his brow.

I pressed my advantage. "I'll offer you a chance. Let her go and you can leave with your life."

Brocard hesitated as Celia's chest stopped heaving. She glared at me, her face a silent plea, while Brocard debated his options.

"I don't trust you!" he growled. Celia's eyes bulged as his hand moved around to seize her chin.

As he gazed at her, I fired into his right temple. He fell away from Celia with a grunt and collapsed to the floor as she shrieked.

My shoulders relaxed. "I know how you feel."

Brocard twitched a moment, then lay limp beside Marie's corpse. Celia's hands flew to her cheeks, then pulled at her hair as she shook her head.

I looked behind me, hoping no servants were close enough to hear her screams. "Celia, calm down. He's gone now."

She kept screaming and crying and shaking her head.

"I need you to be still. Celia, stop!"

She waved me off.

"Celia. Stop screaming. Celia!" I slapped her. She covered her cheek as she fell backward onto the sofa.

"You hit me," she sniffled.

"I know. Now calm down."

She said nothing, but gave a weak nod.

I knew Celia would consider me a brute, but she left me little choice. I moved back to the foyer and glanced outside. None of her servants were moving about. I shut the door and locked it, then returned to the parlor. "Celia. I'm very sorry about Marie, but I need to know what happened. What did Brocard say to you?"

She sniffed again, collecting herself. "He said he meant to wait ... until tonight. But he said he couldn't wait any longer."

"For what?"

"I don't know. I don't know!"

I resisted the urge to slap her again. "Celia, calm down. It's all right," I said in a soothing tone. "What did he want from you?"

"He wanted us to drink ... some potion. He said it would make us his."

I looked at the flask Brocard had dropped. The same one that all the Lycanthru carried, containing their Lycanum potion. But if it transformed them into their wolf form ...

"He wanted you," I muttered aloud. "He invited you to the masquerade ball, didn't he?"

Celia nodded, her eyes glassy.

"He wanted you both to drink it?"

"Yes."

I knelt before the flask. It was still corked. I picked it up and shook it. It was full. The Lycanthru only drank a little of it to transform themselves, so Brocard had plenty to share with Celia and Marie, and any other woman that struck his fancy.

They wanted brides.

As Jacquard said, they have cravings, like anyone else, and the means to satisfy them. They were about to lay claim to all of France, and they planned to secure brides for themselves. Brocard chose Celia, but he killed Marie to show what would happen if she refused to join him. This was why they invited all the young maidens to the ball, luring them with the promise to meet royalty. The Lycanthru would have their pick of the finest women of *La Rue Sauvage*. And anyone who refused them would die.

I glanced at Marie's body. A pretty young girl, so full of life only moments ago. Now dead on the floor with her dreams of tonight's ball, the first of many Lycanthru victims.

An insane thought struck me. The idea was ludicrous, but I had run out of time. The ball would start in a few hours. "Was Marie invited to the ball as well?"

"Yes," Celia sobbed. "He ... Monsieur Brocard ... made arrangements for her to accompany a friend of his, Monsieur Cézanne."

"Did you meet him, this Monsieur Cézanne?"

She shook her head. "Neither of us did. Only Monsieur Brocard."

I stood over her. "I need your help.

She lifted her tear-streaked face and regarded me with horror and outrage. "My ... Mine? What possible assistance could you need from me? I've nothing to do with you or, or any of your nonsense."

I clenched my jaw. "Except that I just saved your life."

She swallowed hard. "Very well, yes. You've saved me and I'm most grateful. Now ... Now be on your way."

I took a step toward her, my patience thinning. "I need your help. And I'm not leaving."

She half-laughed. "You honestly expect me to help you in your filthy escapades? I've nothing to do with you. You dress like a man and fire weapons at people, tramping through dirt and blood and every other vile thing. You. You're an insult to womanhood."

I held my tongue. Her words rang true. I had given up being a girl – even being a human – the night I put on this hood.

Her face suddenly softened. She shook her head. "But ... you're the only one who can stop these beasts." She began to weep again, losing all control. "I know I owe you my life. I do. But I cannot help you. What could I do? I'm nothing like you. How could I possibly help?"

I swallowed and straightened, shoving my wounded emotions aside. "I'm well aware of your limitations. But you can do everything I need you to do tonight."

She wrinkled her brow, perplexed. "What do you wish me to do?"

I felt a wave of relief. "That which you do best."

47.

I dragged the bodies of Marie and Brocard to the Verdantes' woodshed and covered them with a thick wool blanket. Celia understood that I meant no disrespect. A proper funeral for Marie would have to wait until after tonight's ball. It was difficult enough to enlist Celia's help. I could not expect her parents to also ignore two corpses in their parlor until morning. Thankfully, the servants had been allowed to retire early for the day, in celebration of the Queen's visit, so there were no witnesses.

The sun started to sink toward the horizon. It was about four o'clock, and Laurent's masquerade would start at eight. We might have enough time to prepare, but I had no way of knowing how long it would take. I had to depend on Celia to help me stop Laurent and rescue the Queen. Relying on anyone other than Pierre was difficult enough, but relying on Celia Verdante? I tried not to think about it.

I found Crimson and led him to Celia's rear stable, where she promised I would find plenty of oats. As he nuzzled in her feed bag, I recalled a mass in which Father Vestille preached about how the Scriptures say a good man is even kind to his animals. Perhaps Celia was not entirely selfish, after all.

Back in the house, she had already set to work, laying out the gown she had selected for Marie to wear. She sat at her spinning wheel and spread it over her lap. But as I entered, I saw her pause to stare at the golden dress and she started to cry again. I prepared to march into the room and make her collect herself. But then she seized up, biting her lip and making her spine rigid. She closed her eyes, sucked in a deep breath and released it. Then she opened her eyes and continued spreading out the dress. I watched her from the foyer, surprised. Not so selfish and not so weak as I presumed.

I entered. "So. Can you do it?"

She took another breath, forcing herself to focus. "Yes. I can. Though I don't know if –." She met my eyes. Stared at my marred face. "Well, we'll just do the best we can. All right?"

I nodded, saying nothing more.

I stood on a pedestal in the center of Celia's parlor like a mindless toy doll, while she pinched and poked and prodded me with pins. None of it intentional, but all of it exasperating as I waited for her to finish. To perfect my disguise.

I had not been so impatient since I persuaded Papa to take me hunting. Never felt so helpless since the Lycanthru tied me between the pillars of their barn. It was already time for all the village shops to close for the day.

"There, now," she said at last. It had been over an hour. "That part is perfect."

Perfect, I echoed in my mind. I stared down at myself in the golden gown, the one intended for Marie. It fit snugly, a little too snug in some places. Though I knew the dress was meant to fit this way. The sort of fancy dress I could never wear myself, to be worn at the sort of party to which I could never be invited. I couldn't help marveling at the irony. I was sixteen years old and I was attending a royal ball.

To kill some large wolves.

"And this will be easy to take off, when I need to move?"

She nodded. "I slit it in sections. I'll show you where to tug to break the threads." She stood back to cock her head at the gown. She seemed satisfied, at last. "Now for the hair and the ... the face."

I stiffened. I held out my satin-gloved hand and let Celia guide me down from the pedestal. Like I was a glass figurine that might break at the slightest misstep. She led me to a chair in front of a three-paneled mirror. I felt like royalty.

Royalty that received a triple-scar across her face from some bloody battle.

My eyes were lined with dark circles. My hair was muddy. And my face ...

What was I thinking? This would never work.

"Now I'm just going to add some powder and rouge and blend them in slowly, to see if –."

"I don't care how you do it, so long as it's done."

She nodded and set to work without another word.

An hour later, I struggled to keep from clenching my fists, from tapping my foot madly on Celia's polished wood floor. It was already dinnertime for the rest of the village. We had two hours left.

Celia had thoroughly cleaned and brushed my hair, like I was a prize stallion. I reminded myself that Crimson had been waiting all this time in her stable, probably just as anxious to get moving. At least he could rest and eat, while I had to stand and sit in place for Celia like a marionette.

My hair only came down to my shoulders. Hardly long enough to be curled and styled like Celia's, or that of any other beautiful girl attending the ball. But Celia offered me several wigs to choose from. I had glanced at each of the five and decided on the red one.

She continued the impossible task of hiding my scars with all her creams and lotions and powders. I sat in front of her, helpless to contribute, as she stood inches away from my face, examining every feature. I kept expecting her to twist her lips in disgust or shudder at her close inspection of me. Instead, she studied me like a sculptor trying to shape a masterpiece. She applied rouge to my lips, painted color over my eyes, and smeared her strange concoction of powder and mud over my indelible scars. Finally, she straightened. "Helena," she gasped. "You're …"

I frowned. I should have known it would be impossible.

She took me by the shoulders and gently turned me about to face the three-paneled mirror.

"… you're beautiful."

She was right. Above my gaping mouth, my eyes were large and full of wonder. My cheeks were soft and delicate, my lips ruddy and full, but shaded so that they did not appear deformed. The combination of dark and light powders around my nose produced the same effect, making it look slender and normal. My blonde hair fell straight about my face. Not as coiffed as the red-haired wig I would don, but still pretty.

I had no scars.

I shuddered as if I had entered a bizarre dream. I felt my cheek, to make certain the face was my own. For the first time in my life, I truly was beautiful.

I choked back my emotions. This was the life my mother wanted for me. To dress up in a beautiful gown and go to parties. To be sought after by eager boys, any of whom would be honored to escort me on his arm. To the ball, for a ride in the country, down the aisle of a church. To start a family, build a home, plan a future for myself and those I love. To be happy.

A life I could never know.

I stood abruptly. "Thank you. This will do."

She pressed my shoulders down, pushing me back into the seat. "You still need the wig."

"Oh. Yes. Of course." I sat again to stare at the angelic visage in the mirror. At my pure, unblemished face. A face Pierre could admire and stroke and even kiss without shame. I stiffened to keep from crying. It was only for tonight, nothing more. Tomorrow I would return to my normal appearance.

If I survived tonight.

Celia pulled back loose strands of my hair and fastened them with a slim band. She pressed the thick wig down, tugging it tight. It stood nearly a foot above my forehead, like a soldier's towering helmet and nearly as heavy. But once she secured it into place, it looked magnificent. With this elaborate hairstyle, voluminous gown and diamond jewelry gracing my wrists and neck, I could have passed for a princess, even without a mask. A princess who looked nothing like Helena Basque.

I smiled. Even Father Vestille wouldn't recognize me now.

MY MASK

48.

It took several attempts to convince Crimson to come with me and Celia, as the sky darkened and grew cold. He tugged back on the reins, refusing to take a single step toward me. Toward the strange redheaded royal princess.

It almost made me laugh, giving me greater confidence in my disguise. Of course, I only needed to fool Laurent and his men at the masquerade ball. But that shouldn't be difficult if not even Crimson recognized me.

I finally stopped tugging and spoke softly to him. I stroked his neck and continued talking until he recognized my voice, my touch. He looked at me three more times, as if trying to understand what I had done to myself. Then he nuzzled his neck against me, letting me pet him and hug him. Though I wasn't sure he liked the change.

In the remaining daylight, with torches lighting up the towering spires and high windows, *Chateau de Laurent* looked like a castle from a children's fairy tale. A place I could only dream of visiting, let alone being invited to attend a royal ball.

Of course, we weren't here for the scenery. And I wasn't actually invited.

We stepped down from Celia's private carriage onto the smooth stone path, accepting the aiding hands of Laurent's servants as we raised our embroidered masks to our eyes. We strolled together to the front gates, as I concentrated on balancing the weight of my gown on my narrow-heeled shoes. How could everyone be so shocked that I would wear boots but expect me to tiptoe across a dance floor in these contraptions?

I let Celia lead us to the iron gates, where two men stood guard with muskets. Celia's silver-haired porter followed behind us, carrying her large bag. A man in formal attire greeted us and asked for our names and invitations, which Celia produced. "I am Celia Verdante, the only daughter of Jean-Pierre Verdante, who oversees all textile manufacture in *La Rue Sauvage*. And this is Marie —."

She swallowed, her gloved hand still extended toward me. "Marie Beauchamp," Celia introduced, a slight catch in her throat. "Daughter of Philippe Beauchamp, winery producer. My dearest friend."

She strained to produce a stony smile, and I returned a weak one to the greeter. I felt sorry for Celia's loss, wishing her scarlet mask could hide her trembling lip, not just her eyes. But we couldn't afford to show any grief. Not now.

The man surveyed each invitation. Satisfied, he knit his brows together at me. "Duke Laurent bids you welcome. But where are your suitors?"

I stared back at him with my phony smile, wishing he would focus on Celia alone. Social etiquette and finery was her arena, not mine. She broke in to get his attention.

"They were unfortunately detained, but they offered to meet us inside," she said. Her face fell and she clutched her throat with wide eyes. "Oh, I *do* hope that won't pose a problem for Monsieur Laurent."

He stared at me a moment longer, unsure. Then he bowed to Celia and smiled. "Of course not, Mademoiselle. Please. Come this way."

He spread his arm toward the gates as two men opened them from behind. Celia curtsied to the greeter and thanked him. I followed suit, as best I knew how, and headed in with her, followed by Celia's porter. A guard stopped him.

"Oh, he is accompanying me," Celia explained.

The guard squinted at the porter's innocent, unmasked face and the large bag he held. A bag that held my boots and weapons. "That is quite a large bag, Monsieur."

"We're bringing a few surprises to the party," I said.

The guard eyed me sharply, and I realized this was the wrong thing to say. He turned back to the porter. "Open it, if you please."

The porter dutifully set the bag on the ground. Then he opened it wide for the greeter and castle guards to see. Inside, a display of diamond necklaces and earrings winked up at them from a blanket of black velvet.

Celia beamed. "I thought the Queen might wish to see some of my family's jewels. I would not want her to imagine we are all paupers here."

The guard continued to study the jewelry. Finally, he pointed to the porter. "Very well. Seal it up. You may accompany them inside."

The porter closed the bag, with my boots and weapons hidden beneath Celia's jewelry, and we went in.

49.

A round glass chandelier and several raised lanterns lit the dance floor of the *Chateau de Laurent* ballroom. It was surrounded by tables and high-backed chairs, filled with laughter and soft music and masked smiling faces. The miniature string orchestra played from a raised platform, set beside a bubbling fountain with a marble statue of a lion battling a wolf. Rich smells of exotic fruits, meats, cheeses, wines and chocolates issued from long tables graced by cream-colored linen. Tall etched windows and an array of circular skylights looked out on the field of stars overhead.

And on the rising full moon that would transform the Lycanthru into ravenous wolves.

"Marie Beauchamp?"

I turned to see a man in a silver mask smiling at me and offering his hand. I glanced at Celia.

"Yes, precisely," she said. "You must be Monsieur Cézanne."

He gave a deferential bow, the perfect gentleman.

Celia curtsied. "I'm so glad you were able to find us in this sea of masked faces."

Cézanne grinned, looking devious with half of his face covered. "I must confess. I asked the greeters to alert me when you and your friend arrived."

She leaned sideways with a coy smile. "Well, aren't you strategic?" She turned to me, and seemed to falter again with her masterful pretense. "Marie Beauchamp, may I present your escort that … that Monsieur Brocard arranged for us. Monsieur Francois Cézanne."

I frowned at his name. My stomach turned at the thought of a masked Lycanthru sharing the same name as the heroic woodcutter they murdered. "How do you do, Monsieur Cézanne?" I said, making a half-curtsy.

He took hold of my hand. I couldn't afford to arouse suspicion by pulling away. I let him take my fingers in his. Let him lift my hand to his filthy lips and kiss it, trying not to cringe over the fact he could bite it off at full moon.

"Please," he said. "You may call me Francois."

I calmed my raging nerves and smiled in a way that I hoped would seem polite. "Oh, Monsieur, I could never call you 'Francois'." Celia gave me a warning glance and I corrected myself. "Not until we have gotten to know one another much better, of course. Which surely will not occur until the very end of the evening."

Cézanne glanced at Celia, uncertain, then back at me. I smiled again to appear friendly. He half-laughed and bowed his head again. "Of course, Mademoiselle. I look forward to that." He turned back to Celia. "Where is Jean Paul?"

I saw her quiver before she lifted her chin with an engaging smile. "Monsieur Brocard apologized, but said he had some urgent business to tend to. He promised to join us later."

Cézanne gave her a puzzled look. "I wonder what could be more urgent. This party is rather important."

She maintained her winning smile. "I'm afraid he didn't tell us. But he assured me he would not leave me without a dance partner."

I seized the opportunity to escape from Cézanne. "Perhaps you can fill in for Monsieur Brocard until he arrives. I am certain I can manage."

Monsieur Cézanne hesitated for only a moment, while Celia threw me a frightened glare. Then he smiled at the prospect of enjoying her company instead of mine. "Well, if you insist, Mademoiselle …"

I touched Celia's hand to reassure her. "I won't be far. Don't worry. I doubt that anything much will happen before the Queen arrives."

"Very true," Cézanne said, offering Celia his arm.

Celia smiled into his eyes and took his arm. Then she cast a wicked look back at me as he led her away. I couldn't help feeling amused. Cézanne didn't seem dangerous, being far more self-controlled than Brocard had been. And Celia's charms should keep him at bay while I scouted around.

I surveyed the grand ballroom to find her porter. I avoided the eyes of other men who tipped their glasses to me as they caught my eye, most of them Lycanthru that I recognized from the barn. I finally spotted Celia's porter on the far wall, waiting patiently and inconspicuously with my heavy bag of weapons. He started moving sideways to keep close to Celia as she danced with Cézanne.

I spotted Gerard Touraine, also dressed as a server, standing behind a broad table filled with wine glasses along the opposite wall. It seemed that Laurent had secured the best local help to serve his guests, someone the villagers would know and trust. And perhaps someone that Laurent wanted to seize control of tonight, to secure his influence. All of *La Rue Sauvage* seemed to be here, most of them masked, with no idea what danger they were in.

I squinted at the server setting up glasses at the other end of the long table. I could have sworn he looked just like Pierre. If he was here when the Lycanthru attacked …

I started toward him quickly, graciously curtseying and making excuses to men who tried to engage me in conversation. I felt like a complete fool, but probably came across as merely a rude and distracted girl. It didn't matter. I only wanted to warn Pierre off, if that was actually him.

A young man intercepted me. "Excuse me, Mademoiselle."

I accidentally lowered my mask as I turned to see a server holding a bottle of champagne.

It was Jacque Denue.

50.

Jacque Denue stared straight at me and my golden gown, just inches from my powdered face. I gasped and prepared to punch him before he could alert the Lycanthru that I had infiltrated Duke Laurent's masquerade ball.

He stared at me in an odd way. Not threatened or alarmed, but perplexed. "Sorry, Mademoiselle. Didn't mean to frighten you."

I blinked at him. He didn't recognize me at all. I lifted the golden mask and smiled graciously through it, mimicking Celia's syrupy manner. "Why, that's perfectly all right, Monsieur. I suppose I'm just so excited to be here, my nerves are on edge. Do forgive me."

He gave me the same odd stare, then a curt nod. "Who's that man with Celia Verdante?"

I glanced back at Celia, who laughed from across the room at something Cézanne was saying. "Why, that's Monsieur Cézanne. He's my escort this evening."

Jacque lifted his chin and sighed, sounding relieved. "So where's her escort? … May I ask?"

I almost laughed. Jacque Denue struggled with polite manners as much as I did. "Oh, Monsieur Brocard was detained. He should arrive later this evening."

Jacque stared coldly across the room as if I was not even there. Then he glanced about the room. "This might not be the safest place for her to be tonight. You might wish to take her home."

He didn't seem to know what the Lycanthru planned, only that the ball was swarming with them. "Oh, don't be silly, Monsieur. This is the event of the season. Perhaps the event of our lives, with the Queen coming to visit."

He ignored me and kept watching Celia. In a way that seemed hostile but worried. My heart swelled. In his brutish way, Jacque Denue was in love with her. "Still, if you are concerned, I would be most grateful if you would keep an eye on her," I said. "I want to mingle with the other guests, and I would feel much better knowing a … a good man like you is watching over her. To see that she comes to no harm."

He glared back at me. I had said too much and given myself away.

But he gave a curt nod. "I would be honored to, Mademoiselle."

With that, he moved across the room. I walked on toward the table where Pierre stood. I glanced back to see Jacque standing near Cézanne and Celia, observing them as he served drinks to other couples. I had found the most unlikely ally. At least, so long as I maintained this disguise.

Pierre looked up from his table with a smile.

"May I offer you some champagne, Mademoiselle?" he asked.

I smiled. He had no idea who I was. Now that I was here, I felt less concern for his safety and more relief to have his company. Even if he didn't know me. "Why, that would be lovely and divine, Monsieur."

He smiled and turned over a finely etched wine glass. I glanced down the table at Touraine, who was close enough to hear my sugary voice. He barely glanced up at me. I smiled back at him, amazed that he didn't recognize me, either.

I returned to Pierre. "What's your name?" I asked in my sweetest, most simple-minded tone.

His brow wrinkled as he struggled to uncork the bottle. "Uh ... my name is Pierre Leóne, Mademoiselle."

I removed the mask. "Why, I'm Marie Beauchamp, Pierre. And I'm ever so pleased to meet a handsome boy like you."

The cork popped loudly as it burst open. "Uh ... thank you, Mademoiselle." The foam hissed and clung to his fingers. He tried to fling it off, avoiding my eyes. Even without the mask, he still didn't know me.

"As it happens, Pierre, my escort is a little preoccupied with my friend, Celia Verdante, and might be so for some time. Would you care to be my escort for the evening?"

He poured the champagne slowly, casting a nervous glance at me. "I, uh, I don't think that would be appropriate, Mademoiselle."

"Oh, don't you worry about that, Pierre. I can *make* it appropriate."

"Mademoiselle, I, uh ..."

He stared into my eyes. Into my new face.

"Yes, my Pierre?"

"Mademoiselle. You're very pretty. But ... I'm actually here to meet someone myself."

I lifted my hands up as if I were a gift to be unwrapped. "And you've just met her. Aren't you the luckiest thing?"

"No, I ... someone else."

I glanced about. "Well, where is this mysterious young woman?"

"She couldn't be here. But I'm here on her behalf, and I'll likely see her tomorrow." He shrugged to himself. "Depending on how things work out tonight."

I narrowed my eyes at him. He meant to try to stop the Lycanthru's attack. "Pierre, you can't –!"

He squinted at me. "What's wrong, Mademoiselle?"

I glanced back at Touraine, now talking with two other couples that had approached the table. "Pierre, it's me."

He kept staring. "It's *you*, Mademoiselle?"

I leaned closer. "It's *me*. It's *Red.*"

The champagne bottle dropped to the table and thankfully landed upright. "Red?" He glanced about, meeting the stares of Touraine and a few guests who heard the bottle thud onto the tablecloth. "What happened to your face?"

I wasn't sure whether to be offended. "What's wrong with it?"

"Nothing. I guess. But what happened to it?"

I frowned. "Celia fixed it. I mean, she used some powder to cover over it." I spread my hands out to display my sunny gown. "Do you like it?"

He looked me over, still appearing confused. "Yeah, I guess. But you don't look like yourself at all."

"Is that bad?"

"Well ... I mean ..."

"It doesn't matter. What are you doing here?"

He leaned across the table and whispered in a harsh tone as a masked couple passed near us. "I asked around about the party and found out Duke Laurent needed a few extra hands to serve guests. He's lost some of his servants over the last couple of months. So I made arrangements to get hired on."

In the center of the ballroom, Denue still hovered around Cézanne as he danced with Celia. She continued to charm her temporary escort, smiling up at him through her scarlet mask. "I just ran into Jacque Denue," I told Pierre. "He's serving here, too."

"I know. He's the one who helped me get the job. He didn't seem to care whether I was here or not."

No, I thought. *He only cares whether or not Celia is here.* "But what on earth do you plan to do? You said you'd alert me if you found a way in."

"You never came back. I checked back at the shop a couple of times, but I had to get over here for instructions."

I glanced over my shoulder as another laughing couple strolled behind me. "I found my own way in."

"Yeah, I see that." He looked me over again, seeming unimpressed.

"You don't approve?"

"I don't know. You just don't look like yourself."

"You're not really planning to battle all the Lycanthru yourself, are you?"

"No, now that you're here."

I leaned closer and whispered harshly at him. "Pierre, how exactly do you intend to fight them? Did you bring your own crossbow?"

He smiled and bent toward me. "Something better. I've been fashioning it all week. It's a collapsible blowgun. I brought a bag of silver shavings and dust that I can shoot through it."

I blinked. "Pierre, that is … absolutely amazing."

His cheeks reddened. "Thanks." Then he frowned. "When this is all over, you're going to change back, right? You're not going to keep dressing like that?"

I cocked my head at him, still wondering if I should be offended. "You don't think I'm pretty?"

He half-scowled. "Sure, but … you were already pretty. I want to see you the way you are." He looked high above my head. "Without that giant wig."

I put my hand to his cheek. "Thank you, Pierre. You're very sweet."

"… all right."

"Just promise me you'll watch yourself. Don't fight unless you have to."

He took my hand in his. "I have to."

I swallowed. I wanted to refuse him. To tell him this wasn't his fight. To tell him all the things that he and everyone else kept telling me. But I couldn't. I just prayed I wasn't sacrificing Pierre by letting him follow his heart.

"Father Vestille. So pleased you could make it tonight."

I turned and raised my mask again at the voice of Leopold Laurent, wearing a gold mask like mine and surrounded by three other Lycanthru, as he shook hands with Father Vestille.

51.

"Thank you," Father Vestille answered nervously, greeting Duke Laurent. He wore no mask, but had dressed in his usual priestly robes, which made him stand out strangely among all the masked guests in *Chateau de Laurent*'s opulent ballroom. "I was … surprised to receive your invitation this afternoon."

"Please forgive my oversight," Laurent said with enthusiasm. "I know we have had our differences in the past, but I was quite distressed to hear that your invitation had not gone out. After all, the entire province is here tonight. We can't have the Queen visit our fair community without the blessing of our local priest, can we?" The three Lycanthru flanking Laurent chuckled in their usual cruel manner.

"Father Vestille!"

They all turned toward me and Pierre.

"… Yes, Mademoiselle?" he asked.

I raised my mask, then smiled and stepped forward. "Why, I had no idea you would be here this evening. Isn't this lovely?"

Father Vestille narrowed his eyes, confused, as Duke Laurent and his men watched us. "Have we met, Mademoiselle?"

I offered my hand. "No, but I've been *dying* to meet you. I'm Marie Beauchamp."

He stared at me. "Ah, yes. I think we have met. I didn't recognize you."

I swallowed. Had he actually seen through my disguise? If he recognized me, then Laurent might recognize me, too.

Then I realized he meant the real Marie Beauchamp I was impersonating. "Well, I've grown a bit since then," I said pleasantly.

Father Vestille waved his hand to introduce Laurent. "Have you met the Duke?"

I stared into Laurent's inviting eyes. "Why, no," I said stupidly. "Is this him?"

Father Vestille gaped at me. "Uh ... yes. May I present the Duke of *La Rue Sauvage*. Your Grace, this is Marie Beauchamp."

Duke Laurent bowed, and I curtsied. If I had my crossbow or a silver-gilded sheath at hand, I could have ended the attacks right then. But that would only result in my arrest and might not stop the rest of the Lycanthru. They could still attack the Queen, tonight or at some other opportunity while I sat in a prison cell waiting to be hung. I had to wait patiently and hope my disguise fooled Laurent.

He towered over me, his face beaming behind his devilish mask. "Welcome to the party, my dear. I believe I know your parents."

I maintained my smile but felt my chest heave once as I seethed inside. Had he already seen through my disguise? Was he making another of his sadistic jokes?

"I believe they operate most of the wineries in the south, don't they?"

I breathed a little easier beneath my made-up face. "Why, yes, that's right."

"They've done rather well for themselves."

"Why, thank you, Monsieur. But I must say, we've never been invited to see the castle ballroom before. And the Queen! Why, I'm just so excited I can hardly stand myself."

Laurent blinked. "Well ... I'm glad to hear that, Mademoiselle. Had I known that your parents had such a lovely daughter, I would have extended the invitation sooner."

He held out his hand for mine. I hesitated, then smiled and held it up for him to kiss. The touch of his lips sent a tremor through my spine. "Oh, my," I said. "You're too kind."

Laurent glanced about the room. "Who are you here with this evening, Mademoiselle?"

"Oh, I'm here with Monsieur Cézanne," I said, pointing across the room. "He's over there entertaining my friend, Celia. I should probably get back to him soon, but I'm sure they're having a lovely time, just talking away about nothing. Well, it was a delight to meet you, Monsieur Duke, and thank you ever so much for inviting me."

"The pleasure is all mine, my dear, believe me."

"Oh, I do. Father, would you be kind enough to escort me to the refreshment table?"

Father Vestille looked perplexed, but graciously agreed. "Of course, Mademoiselle. I would be honored. Please excuse me, Monsieur."

Laurent bowed in response, looking somewhat relieved to be free of him, but eyed me with a mixture of admiration and distaste. I imagine he wanted me to stay with him a while longer, to have a charming young girl with a sugary voice to gawk at. But the longer I stayed, the more chances there were for Laurent or his men to recognize me. I had to get Father Vestille away from them, and use him to shield me from any further advances from the Lycanthru wandering about the ballroom. Not even a Lycanthru would be brash enough to cut in on a priest.

Something else unsettled me about Father Vestille's sudden invitation to the party. It reminded me of the banquet that Duke Laurent held to honor Francois, only to get him drunk and murder him later. Laurent had surely invited Father Vestille to the ball to devour him.

"You could have spoken to the Duke a little longer if you wished, Mademoiselle," Father Vestille said. "I presumed that was the reason you wished to greet me."

"No, actually, you're the one I wanted to see."

He blinked at me. "Me? How can I help you, Mademoiselle?"

I smiled at a gentleman passing by, then ignored him and focused on Father Vestille, leading him away. The man frowned and continued past us. "I wanted your advice. You see, I'm thinking of becoming a nun."

He paused in his steps. "I see. Well …" He cleared his throat. "That is a most worthy aspiration, Mademoiselle. But, ah, you realize it is a deep commitment to a life of prayer and service. It would require many sacrifices. You would not be able to attend many parties like this one."

"Oh, I'm sure I'll still get invitations from the right gentlemen. After all, you're here, aren't you?"

He frowned. "Yes. But not in the same capacity as you."

I giggled stupidly. "No, I suppose not." We reached the long table, where Pierre eyed us both stiffly. "Hello again, Pierre. Have you met my friend, Father Vestille?"

Pierre took my cue slowly. "Uh, yes. I've known Father Vestille my whole life."

"Oh. Then it would be silly for me to introduce you." I turned to Father Vestille. "Would you care for a drink?"

"Eh, no, thank you, Mademoiselle. I don't normally drink, apart from the sacraments."

"Oh, that's unfortunate. Do nuns have that same problem?"

A horn sounded from the outer courtyard, forcing the room to quiet its conversation as the music stopped. A messenger looked out the front entryway and received some unseen signal, then nodded to Laurent.

Duke Laurent returned the nod, then stood on a high platform and raised his hands. "Dear ladies and gentlemen of *La Rue Sauvage*! Her Majesty, the Queen, has arrived. Please prepare to give her our most gracious welcome on this auspicious occasion! I promise you all …" He smiled his devilish smile. "… the next few moments will be etched in your memories for as long as you live!"

My nerves raged. He planned to attack the Queen the moment she entered. I glanced around the room. Celia was talking with a few men and Jacque Denue still lingered near her. But I couldn't spot her silver-haired porter anywhere. "Oh!" I squealed with delight. "Excuse me, Father, but I must go!"

"Of course," he said with a small sigh. "I understand when I have been outranked."

I giggled again. "Aren't you sweet?" I curtsied like an idiot and turned toward the main entryway. Then I stopped and leaned toward Pierre. "I may need your assistance, Monsieur," I whispered. "Can you find Celia Verdante's porter? He has my bag." I spotted an open doorway leading to a side corridor. "Bring it to me over there."

He saw where I was pointing and nodded. He set the bottle and glasses down on the table and was off. I lifted my tresses and hurried to the exit as the orchestra blared to usher in the Queen.

Father Vestille watched me go, looking perplexed as I rushed beyond the main entrance, where the Queen's messengers were announcing her. But he seemed ready to dismiss my behavior as that of a flighty and foolish girl.

I ran out to the corridor. It held nothing of interest but a row of closed doors. I tried a couple and found them locked. I needed a private area to change. But with all eyes on the Queen, this passage might do just fine.

Pierre arrived with my bag and handed it to me. He glanced back at the ballroom as the musical fanfare ended and the Duke issued his welcome to the Queen. "Be careful, Red."

"I always am. Quick, get back to the table and don't do anything foolish."

He puzzled over my words as if he couldn't grasp my meaning. Then he returned to the ballroom without a word. And, I realized, without agreeing to my instructions. But I had no time to argue with him.

The crowd murmured with excitement as the Queen settled in among them. I set the bag on the floor and squatted to open it, shoving aside the top blanket of jewelry. Beneath it lay both of my crossbows, my boots and my weapons. I hurried to put on a glove.

A heavy hand fell on my shoulder. I gasped and whirled, hiding my gloved hand behind my back as I raised my mask.

Cézanne smiled down from behind his silver mask, looking cocky and hungry. "You're not attempting to leave, are you, Mademoiselle?"

I smiled and backed away. He moved toward me, a little too close. I took a step farther, but he kept closing in until my back met the corridor wall. I could barely see past him as Duke Laurent raised his empty glass for a toast. He removed a flask from his waistcoat, containing the sulfurous yellow Lycanum. He popped the cork and filled his glass with it.

Cézanne pressed his hand against the wall and leaned into me. "The Queen has just arrived," he said. "This party is about to get most interesting."

I smiled into his leering face, feeling suffocated. "More than you know, Monsieur."

I flicked out the blade from my glove and drove it up into his stomach. He gasped and bent forward in shock. His lips twisted into a cockeyed grin. As though he meant to frighten me with the fact that my knife could not harm him.

Then his face fell as he felt its effect.

"The blade is silver, Monsieur," I explained.

He glared at me with sudden horror as he sank to his knees. "You," he rasped. His hands reached for my throat like claws. His fingers slipped off as he fell to my heels.

I steeled myself against any feelings of pity and pushed him aside. He fell hard to the floor while everyone kept their attention on Laurent.

"... because she thought I was trying to conspire against the King," Laurent announced to the crowd, smiling and turning to each one. I pushed Cézanne's body aside and stepped away from the corridor entrance to escape his sight. "And she was right. Simonet assisted me and others in a failed attempt to poison the King, so that I could seize the throne."

The ballroom fell dead silent.

Only the Queen spoke, her voice firm and cold. "This is *not* good news, Monsieur."

"Oh, I assure you, Your Majesty," Laurent replied, unperturbed. "... I have *far worse.*"

He threw back his head, sucking down the Lycanum.

Laurent's charade was over.

So was mine.

MY HEROES

52.

I spotted other Lycanthru among the crowd, draining their own glasses of bubbling Lycanum. The broad skylights of *Chateau de Laurent* bathed the entire ballroom with moonlight. They would transform into wolves within seconds.

I cast off the redheaded wig and tugged hard at the catch on my gown's waistline. I pried the shimmering dress apart, breaking the series of slender threads that held it together. It split in half, opening like a golden theatre curtain, and fell off me to lie beside Cézanne's corpse. I turned the voluminous gown over to find the hooks Celia had sewn to the inside. The hooks held my tunic, trousers and cloak, which had been wound around the gown's interior. When it came to sewing, Celia was as ingenious as Pierre.

A woman started to sputter and scream from the ballroom. She must have seen the warping face of a Lycanthru as he started to change. I stepped into my trousers quickly, peering around the corner of the wall. The Queen's guards had stepped forward to defend her, but stood in shock at Duke Laurent.

The ugly transformation had started. Before everyone's eyes, the hair on Laurent's skin turned gray while his nose and jaw extended. Pointed ears grew atop his head as fangs protruded from his grinning mouth. He ripped away shreds of his uniform and stood before everyone as the enormous gray wolf, while women screamed and men backed away.

Only to find themselves surrounded by more monsters, beneath skylights that produced the same hideous results. Everyone shuffled about in a panic, searching for some escape. The musicians raised their instruments like weapons in a desperate defense. Women retreated from their once-handsome escorts and searched for a human man to protect them. Men scanned the room for an exit or a weapon, or something to tell them this was not a living nightmare.

I threw on my tunic and secured the cloak about my neck. I needed them to see me in full garb. The Lycanthru wouldn't fear an attack from Marie Beauchamp, even if she held a crossbow.

Someone fired a musket, and everyone paused. Then a wolf growled and slashed, presumably at the screaming soldier who tried to kill it.

I leaped into the room as everyone reeled with horror. Laurent had already grabbed the Queen by her wrist. He stood on his hind legs, looming over her. "Welcome to the party, Your Highness."

I aimed my crossbow at his skull while the Queen shrieked. "Laurent!"

He gaped at me in utter shock. "Impossible."

I fired.

He ducked aside. My bolt hit a Lycanthru a few paces behind him. The man gasped and grabbed at the bolt, then fell backward into the fountain, sending a wash of water across the floor. Only twenty-four wolves left.

Laurent rose with a wild glare, baring his fangs. He seized the Queen's shoulders and held her in front of him. "I don't know how you got in here, Helena, but you won't be leaving. At least, not in one piece."

"What did you say?" I asked, circling for a better angle. "It's hard to hear you while you're hiding behind the Queen's skirts."

He angled with the Queen to keep her between us. I held my position. No one dared move. We were all helpless to act and desperate to escape this nightmarish battle. Unless someone made a move soon, one of the Lycanthru could get reckless.

I scanned the room. Powerful as they were, the Lycanthru's eyes bulged as wide as those of the helpless guests. "I'll only kill the ones who interfere," I said. "Walk away now and you'll survive the night."

"She's alone!" Laurent shouted. "We can destroy her!"

"Try it," I answered. "Whoever wants to die first, step forward."

I waited while they considered. If they didn't withdraw, if they attacked in force, I would kill the first nine with the crossbow. I would have to finish off the others with my blades, if I could.

A single footstep broke the silence. Laurent's royal advisor, Simonet, stepped away from the crowd, still fully dressed. He had not drunk his Lycanum. He kept himself in full view of everyone as he slowly crossed the ballroom.

"Simonet!" Laurent growled, clutching the Queen closer. "What are you doing?"

Simonet regarded Laurent, then looked down at his doublet's lapel. He lifted his hand and tore off his royal insignia.

Laurent gaped at him. "Simonet! Come back!"

Simonet turned to meet his wolf-eyes. "It will not be today, Your Grace," he said.

"Simonet, stop! If you desert us, we'll hunt you down! You won't last another night!"

Simonet ignored him and stepped cautiously toward me, keeping his hands in sight. I kept a watchful eye on all sides, expecting him to distract me while the others attacked. But he continued toward the entrance. From a safe distance, he met my eyes and gave me a respectful nod. Then he passed by me and strolled out the front door.

"Simonet! *Simonet!*"

Two other wolves, one brown, one black, exchanged glances, then hurried out after Simonet. Including Laurent, that left only twenty-one Lycanthru.

"Come back, you cowards!" Laurent growled.

I crept forward, the crossbow raised, as Laurent took a side step toward the front exit. I moved to block him as the crowd parted, backing against the walls. "The only way you leave is if you release the Queen. Step away from her and I won't shoot."

"Forget the Queen, Laurent!" one wolf snarled. "We'll have another chance."

"We'll *never* have another chance!" Laurent barked.

"We can't rule if we're dead!" growled another man.

"She's the only one standing between us and the throne!" Laurent barked.

"Wrong!" someone shouted.

It was Pierre. He stood at the far end of the room with the other guests. His silver blowgun was extended and raised to his lips.

I wanted to cry out, tell him to stay back. But there was no stopping him.

"Let Her Majesty go. Now!" he ordered Laurent.

Everyone stared at Pierre. A wolf standing near him scoffed. "What can you do with that toy, Son?"

"Blow you away," Pierre said. He blew through the pipe, spraying silver dust at the wolf's huge face.

The wolf coughed, gave a short laugh. Then his eyes bulged and he fell to the floor.

As the wolf fell, another Lycanthru snarled and sprang forward. He backhanded Pierre, sending him sprawling to the floor.

"No!" I cried.

Pierre fell onto his blowgun and did not rise. I fired straight at the wolf that struck him. My bolt sank into his belly and he fell on his snout.

Nineteen left.

I gaped at Pierre, lying there motionless. I pried my eyes away and whirled back to Laurent.

He was gone. The Queen stood alone, looking about herself with a confused expression.

I scanned the crowd, the fountain, the pillars, the orchestra platform. Laurent had disappeared.

"Go, Your Highness!" I shouted. I swept my crossbow at the rest of the Lycanthru scattered around the room. They took the warning and stayed back.

The Queen came to her senses and summoned her guards. "To the coaches!"

The soldiers hurried to surround her and hustle her out the door, their weapons raised. She glanced back at me with astonished eyes as they rushed her to safety.

Now to clear the room before the Lycanthru grew impatient.

I searched for Laurent among the wolves, as the guests crowded together against the surrounding walls. "Everyone! Go home! Lock your doors and shutters. I'll clean up here."

The party guests leaped away from the wolves, shoving against one another in a mad frenzy.

"Not you!" growled a large wolf to my left.

The beast grabbed Celia and dragged her back as she screamed. In the rush of the crowd, I couldn't get a clear shot.

"Leave her alone!" a young man cried.

I thought it was Pierre, already up and fighting again. But as the people flew past, I spotted Jacque Denue, tugging against the massive paw that held Celia's hair. The wolf released her and turned on Jacque in a rage. He slashed Jacque's chest, tearing it open and spraying blood across the rear table.

I shuddered and fired straight into the monster's neck. He groaned and felt at the bolt, looking confused. Then he slumped to the ballroom floor.

The villagers streamed past me, bottlenecking at the front doors. I scanned the ballroom, accounting for each wolf. I counted ten, fourteen, seventeen of them positioned around the edges, near the straggling guests. Still no sign of Laurent.

I finally spotted him, stepping out from behind a long table. He stood on his hind legs with a gloating smile. Screams mounted behind me.

"Helena, watch out!" Father Vestille called from the far wall.

I whirled. A large black wolf broke through the escaping crowd and rushed at me. I lifted my crossbow but he knocked it aside. It flew across the room and skittered across the floor toward the feet of the remaining villagers.

The wolf snarled in my face with rage, its blue-gray eyes shining.

Sharrad.

He was the black wolf that fled the ballroom earlier. Only to return and catch me off guard.

My heart beat madly as I took a few steps back. Sharrad continued to advance, growling with vengeance. I flicked my wrists back, producing the silver-edged blades.

Sharrad's eyes widened. He lunged and seized my wrists before I could slash at him.

"So *that's* how you escaped," Laurent said, a few feet behind me. "You won't have that advantage this time, Helena. Bring her here."

"Gladly," Sharrad said.

I tried to jerk my hands free. Kicked uselessly at his side. He gave a guttural laugh, my childhood nightmare coming to life. He had stripped me of my weapons. Nothing could stop him from dragging my heels across the marble floor toward Laurent.

53.

I kicked at Sharrad's side again. He growled down at me through his fangs, more vicious than before, and kicked my thigh with one hind leg. I grunted at the blow. The remaining party guests stood helpless against the far wall beyond the fountain, the other wolves standing guard over them. I glanced over my shoulder as Sharrad dragged me to Duke Laurent.

Laurent smiled in triumph through his fangs as Sharrad deposited me at his feet. I glanced back at Pierre, still lying motionless on the floor. Behind him, Father Vestille and Gerard Touraine awaited their fate with the other guests. At least the Queen had escaped the ballroom with her soldiers.

Laurent turned to Sharrad. "Take care of her. We'll dispose of the Queen."

"I've been longing to, Lord Laurent," he replied. He twisted my arms up behind my back, stopping just short of breaking them off. I grunted at the screaming pain.

Laurent gripped my cheeks. "Don't damage her too much. When we return, we'll make her suffer publicly in the center of the village."

I struggled and prayed for some escape. The Lord couldn't let this happen, not after I came so close to stopping them. They couldn't destroy everyone in *La Rue Sauvage*. They couldn't kill the Queen and seize control of France!

"Wash off this paint," Laurent ordered Sharrad. "I want everyone to recognize Helena when she begs for her life."

"My pleasure." Sharrad tugged me toward the bubbling fountain.

"You!" Laurent called to an auburn wolf. "Watch our other guests. The rest of you, come with me!"

I heard them howling and loping out the entrance and the front gates. Sharrad dragged me to the fountain in long strides. Once there, he locked his sable paw around my wrists and forced my knees to the marble floor. "The party's over, princess. Time to show your real face."

He peeled back my hood, then grabbed the back of my neck and forced my head into the fountain. I barely gasped for breath before he plunged me into the underwater vacuum. I twisted my face away from the fountain's stone floor and prayed he wouldn't scrape my cheeks across it. A dizzy rush of water surrounded me as I pushed away from it, trying to rise as his enormous paw held me under.

He yanked me up. Water flew from my hair and neck as I sputtered. He tugged me against his chest, his fur brushing my cheek. "Not long enough. You still look pretty." He gave a husky laugh. "Let's try again."

He bent to wrap his arm around my thighs. Then he hoisted me over his shoulder and turned me upside-down. I shook my head in protest as he held me over the fountain.

He wouldn't wait for Laurent, any more than Jacquard did. Sharrad meant to finish what his brother started when he scarred my face. To humiliate and torture me right here, until he killed me.

I stared down at the rippling water like it was an open grave. I sucked in air as he shoved me back under.

He rested the top of my head on the fountain floor. I planted my palms there and twisted from side to side, as much as his monstrous grip would allow. My hands scrambled for something to use for a weapon or leverage, anywhere along the smooth surface. I bucked beneath the water, bobbing my head left and right, as the bubbles danced around me.

I couldn't hold out much longer.

He released my legs and I tumbled sideways into the water. I didn't wait to figure out what new torture he meant to inflict on me. I sprang up and sucked in the ballroom air, still stale from the lingering odor of Lycanum.

Sharrad gaped at me and shuddered. I rose to my knees, drenched, as water flooded over the sides of the fountain.

The shine left Sharrad's blue-gray eyes as his shoulders sagged. He dropped to his knees and fell face-first to the marble floor. Beyond him, the auburn wolf lay dead beside the guests he had guarded. One man held my crossbow in his fists.

It was Father Vestille.

I shook my head to fling away water and focus my eyes. I crawled out of the fountain, careful not to slip. Father Vestille still aimed the crossbow in our direction. He didn't move. "Father Vestille. You ... You ..."

"I have just killed a man. Yes."

I frowned. "It was a wolf."

"No. It was a man. But if I had not killed him, he would have killed you. I will always choose you." He swallowed hard. "Even if it means I can no longer be a priest."

The others fell silent. I stared at him in shock. He had given up everything he loved for me. "Father –."

Touraine broke in, stepping forward to address the crowd. "You all decide what you want. As for me, I'll have no other priest in this community." He met Father Vestille's eyes. "And you'll see me on Sunday." The others murmured agreement.

I turned from them and hurried to Pierre, still lying on the floor as water spread across it. I listened to his steady breathing, thankful he was all right.

Touraine stepped forward. "What do you need from us?"

I turned and stared at the waiting crowd. I wished I knew how to use their help, now that it was offered. But I had nothing for them to do. "Go find all the silver you can. Anything you have. Candlesticks, jewelry, knives, tools. Silver will kill them." I looked back down at Pierre and stroked his head. "Find what you can and protect your homes. I'm going after the Queen."

Touraine knelt beside me, putting a hand on my shoulder. "I'll take care of him."

I swallowed, withdrawing my hand. Pierre would be all right. So would the others. I had to go.

I caught Father Vestille's eye and pointed to the auburn wolf. "Can you pull the bolt out of that one for me?" He nodded and turned. I hurried to Sharrad's body, stepped on his furry back, and pried the other bolt out. I wiped the blood on my trousers, feeling utterly filthy.

"God be with you," Father Vestille said, tossing me the crossbow and the spare bolt. He made the sign of the cross over me. "Go save the Queen."

54.

I ran to the door, my boots slipping on the ballroom floor. I found firmer footing once I hit the ground outside of *Chateau de Laurent*. I squinted through the darkness at the line of coaches beyond the iron gate. I spotted Celia's and ran to it. Crimson stamped his feet, anxious. He surely hated being hitched to the carriage while the wolves escaped. I freed him and climbed onto his back. He snorted as I kicked at his flanks.

We charged down the path leading away from *Chateau de Laurent* and veered into the cool pine forest, well-lit by the full moon. The Queen's coach would have to follow the winding path, but the wolves could rush straight through the woods and the rolling hills beyond. I found two of them racing ahead of us. The night wind riffled my cloak as I urged Crimson after the snarling silhouettes.

I had no time to grab the other weapons from my bag at *Chateau de Laurent*. With the single-shot crossbow, I could fire with one hand. The repeating crossbow required both. I only had seconds to learn how to shoot it at full gallop.

I nearly hugged Crimson's neck, the reins in my left hand, the crossbow in my right. We drove straight up behind the wolves. I aimed at the dark gray one on my right and moved the crossbow's lever to grasp it in my left hand. I gripped it tight and thrust the entire crossbow forward, to force the lever back while I steadied myself. I struck the wolf's side and it howled. It tumbled over, dead, and Crimson leaped over it.

I shot a wolf while riding. Finally.

The dark brown wolf glanced back, wide-eyed and panting. I took the crossbow in my left hand and leaned toward him. I fumbled with it to shoot before he could dodge. I managed to switch hands on the reins, but my awkward shot struck a tree above his head. He quickened his pace. I charged after him, bouncing and jostling as I struggled to aim.

I tugged on the reins to slow Crimson down, letting the wolf flee farther ahead. I switched the crossbow back to my right hand, which was far easier to manage. I aimed and fired, dropping him with one shot.

I needed to shoot from my right side. I had to make it work, for the remaining fourteen Lycanthru.

We emerged onto a clearing to view the rolling hills that led away from the village. We bounded over them, following alongside the path, where dust clouds still rose from the coach's flight. I spotted the Queen's distant carriage escaping at a frantic pace. The wolves scrambled after her, about a half-mile behind.

We descended fast, my cloak flapping in the wind as we crested the next hill. One wolf glanced back to see me pursuing them. I ignored it and focused on our route. At the rate they were gaining, they would reach the Queen in a few minutes. Well before she reached the bridge leading out of *La Rue Sauvage*.

I leaned sideways to draw three fresh bolts from my hanging saddle pouch. Leaning against Crimson, I carefully dropped them into the top slot of the crossbow, loading them one by one. I hoped the bloody bolts from the ballroom would not slow the mechanism.

We continued charging ahead, over one hill and the next, catching brief glimpses of the carriage. As we ascended the next hill, five wolves raced toward us. Laurent must have sent them back to dispose of me, at any cost.

We descended the foothill to meet them, like armies charging into battle. They spread out to surround me.

I swallowed. I could only fire at the ones on my right.

55.

I pulled back on Crimson's reins to halt him. I whirled from one wolf to the other, wondering which of the five to focus on first. My crossbow held all ten bolts, but these wolves surrounded me, covering every angle of the grassy foothill. Laurent must have ordered these Lycanthru to sacrifice themselves while he continued after the Queen, which made them even more dangerous.

Especially since I could only fire from my right side.

They curved around from the left and right, some trying to circle behind me. In a few seconds, they would strike from every side.

I tugged Crimson's reins to the left as they closed in. "Turn! Turn!" I shouted. I lay against his flank, the reins in my left hand, the crossbow in my right, as he spun in a circle. I jerked the crossbow forward as I gripped the lever, firing again and again. I shot down one, then another, then a third, as they came at me, snarling. The eyes of the last two bulged as we whirled toward them.

Crimson made a second rotation before he finally stopped. The circle of dead wolves littered the grass around us.

My heart pounded in my chest, but I couldn't help feeling impressed by the maneuver. Though we had no time to congratulate ourselves. I kicked Crimson's flanks and we rushed on.

Nine wolves left. I bent to retrieve another round of bolts from the pouch, then leaned against Crimson as I dropped each one in, until I had fully reloaded.

We galloped over the hill and the whole world of *La Rue Sauvage* opened up. The full moon bathed undulating hills on all sides, and the cliff where they ended on the far left, where Papa and Monsieur Leóne helped us save our lost lamb. Beyond the cliff lay the distant plateau, stretching wide over the chasm like a sleeping crocodile, just before the bridge that led out of the province. Halfway down the winding path, the Queen's coach rolled along, kicking up a trail of dust as the remaining wolves swarmed after it like dark rats. I could never reach her before they did. I had no way to close the distance. Unless …

The tunnel. I searched and spotted the mouth of the cave at the bottom of the foothill. Three of the wolves had the same idea and scrambled toward the opening. I hesitated, trembling at the memory of the black wolf with blue-gray eyes that I last encountered there.

I stiffened and shoved my childish fears aside. I was only nine years old then. And Sharrad was dead.

I drove Crimson toward it.

The three wolves disappeared into the black mouth just before I reached it. We thundered in, Crimson's hooves echoing and skidding within the dark chamber. He clomped down the stairwell of logs within, descending faster than he had ever galloped. One wolf turned back, its yellow eyes helping me pinpoint it and shoot it down. We galloped past its body and raced down the passage at frightening speed.

I could barely see, but moonlight issued from the opposite end of the tunnel, outlining the silhouettes of the two wolves loping ahead of us. Near the bottom, my eyes adjusted to distinguish their sharp ears, rising and falling as they rushed toward the far end. Laying against Crimson, I took steady aim and fired at the one on the right. I dropped him and drove Crimson to jump over his carcass as the passage leveled out.

I shot the last one as he exited the tunnel and charged past him. Out in the whistling night air, I heard the stampeding hooves of the Queen's horses. I saw the whipping tails of the wolves pursuing it, not far ahead. We had gained ground, but not enough.

Then I remembered the path I had discovered, sloping down and around the left side of the mountain. The one Papa warned me away from. If Crimson could push himself a little longer …

We galloped toward the left side and found the path. We hurried down it, close to the edge. Crimson's skidding hooves kicked dirt over the side to tumble a few hundred feet down the mountain. I focused on the narrow path hugging the cliff as the wolves' snarls faded above us, leaving only the whistling wind and Crimson's steady gallop.

The path leveled out and curved upward. Crimson pushed hard, pounding up the steady grade as the wind ruffled his mane. Until we heard the rushing hoof beats of the horses above us, tugging the Queen's carriage.

We raced up the path. Her Majesty's coach burst into view, its driver leaning forward, halfway out of his seat. He glared at me in fright as I charged alongside the coach, then returned his attention to the path.

"Wha –? Stop her!" Laurent growled from behind.

I raised my arm to block the dust and glanced back, spotting three of the wolves. Over my left shoulder, I found the other three. Racing in front of them, I could do nothing but escort the coach safely out of the province. We had less than two miles to reach the bridge. I only needed to keep the Lycanthru from crossing it.

Two wolves snarled and rushed forward on my right. I shot one down. The other one dodged before resuming the chase.

"Kill the Queen!" Laurent growled behind us. "Drive her off the cliff!"

The dark brown wolf at my right surged ahead. On my left, the other wolves slowed to circle around. I pulled back on Crimson's reins, then shot down a black wolf as he passed. The others got through, with the coach between us. They snarled and snapped at the horses, forcing them to veer off the path toward the distant cliff.

I charged around the right side of the coach. Laurent, the dark gray wolf, led the other three. I shot down the two in the rear, then dodged their bodies as we struck bumpy terrain. Only one more wolf to kill and then Laurent. I aimed at the dark brown wolf in back.

The coach struck a bump and nearly spilled over on its side. I jerked the crossbow up, firing into the air to avoid striking the carriage wheels. The driver had enough to contend with, without having a crossbow bolt stuck between the rear spokes.

I noticed the driver stretching over the edge of his platform. I squinted at his dangerous position and realized he must have lost hold of the reins. The Queen was in greater peril than I thought.

They were less than a mile from the cliff. Even if I stopped the last two wolves, the coach would sail straight over the edge.

56.

I slowed, pulling away from the last two wolves as they barked and snapped at the team of horses. I drove Crimson around the other side of the coach, pushing him harder, faster. He pounded through the tall grass as the Queen's carriage tumbled toward the distant cliff. "Come on, boy! Go! Go!"

We gained on the coach and passed its compartment door. I resisted the urge to look in and see how the Queen fared, but urged Crimson ahead. "Come on!"

We passed the driver, frantic to retrieve his reins as they danced behind the horses like teasing black snakes. I ran Crimson alongside the team, thundering toward the lead horses. I slid the crossbow strap over my shoulder and pulled my feet from the stirrups. I half-knelt atop the saddle, steadying myself as I measured the rhythm of the other horses.

I pushed off with my boot and leaped onto a lead horse, landing on my belly. I clutched at its saddle, my foot fishing for the stirrup below. It slapped my heel a couple of times, flapping like the driver's reins in our mad rush toward death.

I gave up on the stirrup and gripped the saddle horn. I swung my legs around and dropped onto the horse's rear with a jolt.

The cliff's edge came into clear view. The expanse of night stars and distant mountains spread before us. I had less than a minute to turn the coach.

I pulled myself forward into the saddle. I looked down at the hitch that connected the four horses. The center bar was barely wide enough for one boot.

I swung my leg over the saddle to the inside. I paced my jump as the horses galloped on. I dropped onto the center bar, bending my knees and landing sideways. My feet hung off the edge of the bar, angled slightly. From my awkward position, with my left hip turned toward the cliff, I clung to the saddles of both lead horses.

We came near the edge, the winds whipping louder and cooler beneath the moon and stars.

I bent to seize the horses' reins and tugged them, steering the team away from the wolves, away from the edge. We circled wide, heading back toward the bridge. I spotted Crimson, still following close behind.

"Crimson, go!" I shouted.

Seeing our direction, Crimson raced ahead of the other horses to the bridge. I prayed thanks to God as the Queen's team hurried to follow his lead.

I studied the slim, bouncing bar beneath my feet. With my hands on the saddles, I carefully turned myself around, keeping a loose hold on the reins. I edged my way past the horses, step by step, bringing the reins with me. The driver offered his hand as I neared the coach. I handed him the reins and accepted his firm grip to climb up. "Thank you," I said.

"Thank *you*, Mademoiselle!"

"Don't stop until you're well out of the province," I said as I crept onto the roof.

His voice rose in alarm. "Where are you going?"

"To help you do it." I crawled to the back of the carriage. Laurent and the other wolf followed, the cliff's edge trailing away behind them. I knelt on the bouncing carriage and slid the crossbow off of my shoulder.

They kept after us, undaunted. As I hoped.

I took careful aim at the dark brown wolf. The carriage bounced, throwing off my shot. I set the crossbow down and planted my hands on the roof, steadying myself as we continued over rough patches. The brown wolf picked up its pace. I gathered up my weapon and fired, dropping him on the spot. I checked over my shoulder. We were almost to the bridge.

I had one bolt left for Laurent.

He weaved back and forth as I tried to train my crossbow on him. But he didn't slow his pace. We both knew he wouldn't risk losing the Queen.

The coach lurched upward as I fired. My body lifted into the air as the crossbow left my hands, the carriage rushing beneath me. Dark clouds rolled past the winking stars and moon as I rose to meet them. I dropped to the rough earth, bounced and rolled, unable to stop.

My body left the ground again. I was falling off the cliff!

57.

I landed hard on a dirt ledge and started to roll. Another second and I would plummet through the night air, past the rest of the black cliff.

The back of my head scraped through thick brush. I twisted and lunged for it, clinging to a scraggly branch. My feet dangled over empty air.

The Queen's coach rumbled across the bridge overhead. They were safe.

The wind tickled my neck as my toes searched for any sort of foothold. Passing clouds obscured the moon, pitching the mountain into blackness.

I kept one hand on the branch and felt for the grappling hook. I found it and slid the catch to release its prongs. I let out some rope and glanced up above for something to snag.

The night was thick as tar. I couldn't even see the outline of the mountain.

I swung the hook back and forth like a pendulum. I hurled it straight up, releasing plenty of rope and hoping it would sink into something firm. A tree stump. A rock. Even a patch of solid ground to support me for the few seconds I needed to climb back to the ledge.

I felt it hook something as the rope dangled. Perhaps part of the same tree root higher up. I tugged hard on the line. It held fast.

I heaved a sigh of relief and started winding the rope around my wrist. I climbed up, edging around the tree root, ready to rest on the ledge before ascending the rest of the cliff.

I suddenly felt myself rising. I squinted up into the darkness as clouds shifted to reveal the rope tugging me higher. Crimson must have grabbed hold of it to hoist me up fast. I smiled as my muscles relaxed.

At the top of the cliff, the moonlight spread to reveal the pointed gray ears of Laurent, grinning as his paws tugged me closer. I gasped and tried to free my glove from the bindings. He seized my wrists and hoisted me up to his face.

His breath was hot and stale. "You've saved the kingdom, Helena. Now reap your reward."

I kicked at him in vain and managed to flick out one gloveblade. He tugged the gloves straight off of my hands and flung them to the dirt.

His claws sliced through the rope and he hurled me across the foothill. I landed in a heap on the cool grass. Laurent stood upright at the cliff's edge, a massive monster with shining claws spread for revenge. On the distant path behind me, Crimson lay still.

"No!"

"He's only sleeping, Helena. I didn't want to kill him without making you watch."

Moonlight bathed the hills and the distant horizon, where the Queen's coach disappeared around the mountain. She had been saved, along with all of France. Now I would die for it.

My crossbow lay only a few yards away.

I held Laurent's gaze for a moment, considering. Then I dove and rolled for it. I snatched up the crossbow and rose to face him.

He paused. Then he dropped to all fours and crept forward. "No, I don't think so, Helena," he said in a low growl. "Not after you took so long to aim at me before. Not after you hesitated just now to retrieve your weapon. I don't believe you have a single bolt left. Do you?"

I took careful aim as he edged closer.

"If you did, you would have shot me by now. Wouldn't you?"

I trained the crossbow on him, letting him draw closer.

As if I had a bolt to fire.

"But you don't."

I shuddered as he stepped right up to me, calling my bluff. He stood on his hind legs and loomed over me.

He yanked the useless crossbow from my hands and flung it away. He backhanded me with a stinging blow and my feet left the ground. I spun and landed hard on my shoulder, rolling onto my stomach.

He circled around to leer at me with his open fangs. "Where are you going *now,* little girl?"

58.

Laurent dropped back on all fours and continued to circle, like a shark waiting to strike. The moon highlighted his muscular wolf-limbs, his glowing yellow eyes, his hungry fangs.

He left me nowhere to go and no way to defend myself, stripped of my glove-blades and crossbow. If I ran fast enough, perhaps I could hurl myself off the cliff before he swallowed me whole.

"Red!"

We turned to see Pierre, charging toward us on Diamond in a flurry of dust. My heart swelled, but he could only reach us in time to avenge my death.

A silver baton flashed in Pierre's fist as he flicked it out, to extend twice its length. "It's loaded!" he cried, tugging Diamond to a halt as he flung the silver rod.

It spun, sparkling through the night air, and I realized he was tossing me his new invention, the collapsible blowgun.

I lunged for it and flipped it over, bringing its small end to my mouth. Laurent snarled and leaped at me. I whirled and blew through the pipe. A spray of silver filings and dust filled the air, sparkling like stars as Laurent threw himself into them. His yellow eyes bulged as the silver cloud penetrated his skin like a thousand tiny knives. He lurched and twisted in mid-air before his contorted body fell to the ground. Dead.

I stared at the gray carcass in silence. Waiting for it to rise again. Watching for another attack.

None came.

It was over.

Pierre trotted up closer and jumped down from Diamond. I stood slowly to meet him, my brave young knight.

I strode toward him quickly, the boy I had pushed away time after time. The boy I wouldn't allow myself to care about.

"I care for you," I confessed as I grabbed hold of his jaws and kissed him.

My passion startled him as much as it surprised me. "Red!" he gasped as he pulled away. He glanced about to make certain no one had seen us. As if anyone had followed us all this way in the dead of night.

I stood there, refusing to pull my hands from his face. I couldn't, now that I had finally taken hold of him. "I'm sorry. I know I shouldn't have kissed you. I just ... I just couldn't help it." He stared at me, dumbfounded. I swallowed, embarrassed by my sudden loss of control. "I'm sorry. I'm too wild for you, aren't I?"

He relaxed and smiled with a look of understanding. "Well, *La Rue Sauvage* is a wild place," he said. "I can adapt."

He leaned toward me and kissed me, long and tender, as his strong arms cradled my shoulders. I let him carry me into his passion, into this beautiful dream for several seconds before I finally broke away.

"There are more of them," I said in alarm.

He looked quizzically at me. "Well, I would hope those weren't our last ones."

I blinked and almost laughed as I realized he was talking about kissing me again. "No, not ... that. Two more of the Lycanthru. Simonet and the other one who left the ball. They're still out there. I have to go after them."

He didn't release me. "They can't do any more harm tonight. They were only after the Queen and they've lost her. Everyone else is preparing to defend themselves. You can stop them tomorrow."

He leaned in to kiss me again. I let him. It suddenly felt natural and right and perfect. As if we were always meant to be together. As if we had never been apart.

"You love me," I said, half-choking with relief as he held me close. I shut my eyes, barely able to believe it. "You *love* me."

"Forever," he said, peeling back my hood and nestling my hair.

Pierre was right. We later found the remaining wolves and destroyed them, removing their plague from our province. My nightmares eventually passed, as they did for the rest of *La Rue Sauvage*.

I still search for heroes. But now I find them.

Whether I find them in my overprotective father, who taught me to be strong and prepared for trouble. Or in my elegant mother, who taught me I could be beautiful, in spite of my scars, and even because of them. Or my enchanting Suzette, who taught me how to love life.

In a brave neighbor like Francois Revelier, who taught me to stand up and take action to protect those in need. And in the service of Gerard Touraine, who risked his life and reputation to help me however he could.

In less noble actions, like Jacque Denue's final attempt to protect a woman he loved. Or Celia Verdante's willingness to help a girl she despised, to stop the monsters that threatened her village.

In the patient prayers of a priest like Father Vestille, who continued to protect and guide me, even when he disagreed with my actions. And in the loyalty and courage of Pierre Leóne, who always stood by me and believed in me, and loved me in spite of my scars.

In a God that remains unseen, but not silent or inactive.

And the hero I find in myself.

I hope you have enjoyed this story. If you would like to see more stories like this one, please provide your feedback on this book at your favorite retailer.

THE
RED RIDER
WILL RETURN!

Please enjoy the following sneak preview of the next Red Rider novel,

RED RIDER REVOLUTION

Thank you for your support!

Randall Allen Dunn

RED RIDER REVOLUTION

by

Randall Allen Dunn

MY VICTORY

1.

The laughter and shouts in *La Maison de Touraine* abruptly died, as if someone had sucked the wind from each man's lungs. At the bar counter, the tavern's owner, Gerard Touraine, paused in the middle of polishing a mug. He gaped, like everyone else, at the oak double doors that stood open, ushering in a chill night wind.

Siegfried Simonet stood there, flanked by four other rough-looking men. His belly had grown since the last time anyone saw him, though his face remained gaunt as a ghost. He stared back at the men, surveying each horrified face as they fidgeted in their seats to shrink away from him. Finally, Simonet stepped fully into the room, letting his friends shut the doors. He moved, almost glided, to the center of the room and turned slowly, addressing everyone in a calm voice.

"You may all leave," he said.

There was a moment's hesitation. Then everyone stood and moved out the front door as quickly as Simonet's men would allow them.

The entire room cleared within a minute, leaving Simonet and his band alone with Touraine.

One man locked the front doors.

Simonet strode toward him. "Gerard Touraine. No doubt this visit comes as a surprise."

Touraine polished his mug slowly. He cleared his throat with a slight stutter. "Y-You were the Duke's advisor, weren't you? Haven't seen you since --."

"Since the royal ball, two months ago," Simonet finished. He patted his protruding belly. "I've been preoccupied since then."

He stepped closer to the counter. Touraine stiffened and lifted his chin.

"You've ... had business elsewhere?"

"My business remains here, regardless of the other places I travel to conduct it. I've been preoccupied with the events of the past year, leading up to that night at the masquerade ball." He fixed his gaze. "You were serving there."

It was not a question. Simonet had a keen sense for details.

"Yes." Touraine cleared his throat again. "Yes, the Duke asked me to serve, since the people know me well."

"And you know them. You probably know something about every common man, woman and child in *La Rue Sauvage*." He sat at a stool and leaned across the counter. "Even Helena Basque."

Touraine quivered. He licked his lips, recovering. "Eh – of course. 'Course I do. Helena Basque, the, uh – the girl who lost her family."

Simonet nodded with a slight smile. "They were killed by wolves. – If you recall."

Touraine wiped his forehead. "Yes. Yes, I heard that. Her parents and her sister, right?"

Simonet lifted his chin, as if waiting for more. He folded his hands with a look of waning tolerance. His bulky companions spread out around the room, two of them approaching opposite ends of the counter. "You surely remember how she reacted."

"Yes," Touraine confessed. "She, ah – she told everyone that, uh – they weren't really wolves. She told people they were some sort of monsters."

Simonet studied him quietly. He leaned forward again, his fingers still interlaced. "She told *you.*"

Touraine took a step back, looking alarmed and confused. "Me? What makes you think --?"

"I've thought about it a great deal, Monsieur," Simonet said. "It occurred to me that for a sixteen-year old like Mademoiselle Basque to learn about those so-called 'monsters' and find them, she would have needed information. Someone to go to for town gossip. Someone whose information she could rely on, on a regular basis." He offered a grim smile. "Someone like you, Monsieur."

Sweat trickled from Touraine's forehead. He made no move to wipe it away. "Monsieur Simonet. I don't know what – what your business is with Duke Laurent or these wolves, and I don't want to. But I've had no dealings with Helena Basque except to give her some water here at the counter a couple of times."

"You were also there at the royal ball, Monsieur Touraine. You saw me there."

"Yes, well – I never saw you as a wolf. I have no reason to believe you're one of them."

"One of *who,* Monsieur?"

Touraine paled. His mouth hung open, his lip quivering.

"The word you're searching for, Monsieur Touraine, is 'Lycanthru'. That's the name of our order. Those of us who can transform ourselves into wolves."

"Monsieur, I don't need to know anything about this."

Simonet rose, planted both palms on the counter and leaned across it. "You already know, Monsieur."

The men flanking Touraine moved behind the counter. They each took a step toward him.

"But you have not had firsthand knowledge, apart from the Duke's party," Simonet continued casually. "To experience for yourself what others described."

The other four men reached inside their waistcoats. Each one produced a thin flask and uncorked it, releasing a sulfurous odor into the air. They gulped down their serums and grinned at Touraine.

"Until tonight," Simonet finished.

The man by the window set his flask aside and stood with his arms apart to greet the moonlight shining down on his face. Then his face changed, his grinning lips widening, his ears extending toward the top of his head. His nose and chin grew, stretching over his chest to form a canine snout. His fingers sharpened into claws that tore away his clothes, shredding them until he stood naked. Dark brown hair bristled from his jaws as he fell to his knees and a furry animal tail sprouted behind him. He lowered his head as pointed ears appeared on top of it. Then he raised his yellow eyes and stood on his hind legs as an enormous brown wolf. He whirled at Touraine, grinning like a demon.

"You see?" Simonet said, as Touraine tried to gather his breath. "You will now tell us where to find Helena Basque and tend to her. It is your choice whether to tell me in a calm voice or between screams."

Touraine shook his head. His feet shuffled backward on the wooden floor. "Monsieur, you're – you're mistaken. I – I haven't been talking to Helena Basque. About anything."

"In fact, Monsieur, you have told her everything. Every piece of information you gathered to help her in her little war against us." He grinned at Touraine. "How else could she have known where to find us?"

I had seen enough. I stepped into the room from the entryway behind the counter, my red cloak wafting from my shoulders.

"Perhaps I'm smarter than you think," I said.

Simonet and his men turned to gape at the scar-faced, red-hooded girl they had been searching for, as I aimed my repeating crossbow in their direction.

ADVENTURE TAKES FLIGHT

Missionary flier Jack Benjamin braves crocodile-infested streams, savage warriors, and diabolical deathtraps to rescue his danger-prone fiancée, Amanda, from Imperial German forces. With his modified Avro 504 biplane and his Maasai warrior friend, Mayani, he races to protect the mysterious Solomon Ring, hidden within a secret chamber of Mount Kilimanjaro and rumored to bestow King Solomon's wisdom on anyone who wears it. Can he arrive in time to save Amanda and stop the Germans from using the Solomon Ring to conquer all of Africa?

She was grateful to get into Gameland. Now she's desperate to get back out.

Amy Raven insists she's innocent. She never saw the steroids until her coach found them in Amy's locker. Expelled and friendless, she takes a dead end job at Grater Gameland, an abandoned theme park that's preparing to make a comeback.

But Gunther Grater's not interested in re-opening his father's park. He only wants to use it to trap Amy for himself. And he's enlisted nine other gamers to compete in a deadly hunt to track her down.

Given a pair of night vision goggles and a hunting knife, Amy finds herself fighting an onslaught of predators, each with their own deranged plans for her. To survive, she must outwit, outmaneuver, and outrun each one of them. But how can she escape when even the rides are rigged against her?

The only way out is through.

"Upon reading *Making Fiction Funny: How to Create Story Humor*, I was blown away by the author's detailed knowledge of not only how to recognize comedy, but also how to construct it within a story. Whether you're a comedy writer or not, do yourself a favor and buy this book!"
   Dave Burns, Founder of The Ottawa Writers' Guild, and Author of *A Million Little Gods: The Clearwater Chronicles*

If you've struggled as a writer to create humorous scenes, *struggle no more!*

In this easy-to-follow guide, you'll learn how story humor actually works and how to create it yourself! Storytelling examples from popular films show you how to get both smiles and laughs, from comedic characters and situations as well as satire.

You'll learn how to formulate the funny, making your stories more fun, make your characters more endearing, and make your writing more marketable to editors and agents. Learn the techniques for making readers fall in love with your stories and characters so much that they'll keep coming back for more!

MAKING FICTION FUNNY!
HOW TO CREATE STORY HUMOR
by
RANDALL ALLEN DUNN